the forever girl

the forever girl series
sophia's journey

REBECCA HAMILTON

IMMORTAL INK
PUBLISHING

THE FOREVER GIRL

A Novel by Rebecca Hamilton

www.theforevergirl.com

The Forever Girl Series | Volume One

Copyright © 2012 by Rebecca Hamilton

All rights reserved.

ISBN: 978-0-9850818-2-9

Third Edition

A NOTE FROM THE AUTHOR

Sophia's journey is representative of one fictional Wiccan, not all real life Wiccans. No character's actions are intended to represent any religious group or sect. This novel is for entertainment purposes only and not intended as social commentary. I do not subscribe to or condemn any belief system.

DEDICATIONS

For my husband, David: It took three laptops, countless hours, and all your patience, but we're here, and you're mostly still in one piece.

For my business and writing partner, Rudy: May we forever evade unfollowing, email-blocking, pineapples, and all other phobias.

And, most importantly, for my children: I love you for who you are and who you've made me. Thank you for being my heart and inspiration.

THE FOREVER GIRL BY REBECCA HAMILTON

{one}

MY MOM DIED DURING AN EXORCISM on my eighteenth birthday. On that same day, an ever-present static moved into my head like a squatter I couldn't evict.

Ever since, I *thought* getting rid of the noise would be my best shot at survival—like all I needed was silence, even if only within myself, to feel at home again.

I was wrong.

I crossed the black-and-white tiled floor to the jukebox, hoping Pink Floyd's 'Wish You Were Here' would drown out the wasping in my mind.

Instead, Mrs. Franklin's high-pitched, singsong voice cut into my thoughts. "So-phiii-aaa!"

Bound by my waitressly duty, I gripped the sides of the jukebox and turned my head toward her. "Yes?"

She smoothed invisible wrinkles from her paisley, ankle-length dress. "Check, please. I'd prefer to leave before any secular music touches my ears."

She actually touched her ears as she said this, and it took all I had to suppress a groan.

I walked to the register, printed her check, and headed over to the red vinyl booth where she sat. "Anything else, Mrs. Franklin?"

"I was hoping you'd reconsidered my offer on your house."

Of course I hadn't. Why would I sell my inheritance unless I would make enough to leave this rotten town?

"I'm not interes—"

She grabbed my arm, and I forced my glare from her whitening knuckles to her scowling face. I considered pulling free, but if we caused a scene, I would be the one to go down. The customer's always right, after all.

She leaned closer and lowered her voice. "Your mother would have wanted it that way," she said sweetly.

I stared back, uncertain what to say. But I didn't need to say anything. She gave me a long, condemning glare, then released my arm, gathered her purse, and hurried to the checkout counter.

I get it, I thought at the back of her head. *You think it's my fault my mom died during the exorcism.*

Why not? Everyone else did. After all, it'd been my touch that killed her. At least they weren't blaming me for my father's murder, but that was likely because I was only six at the time.

On my way back to the kitchen, one of the two boys sitting at table four flagged me down to request a milkshake. I tried focusing on the order as I ran the blender, but I couldn't tell where the sounds in my head ended and the sounds of the real world began.

"*I heard she's a witch*," the older boy whispered loudly.

His friend grinned. "She's blonder than your sister, even . . . and probably twice as dumb."

Right. Sophia Parsons, town idiot. Pale, blonde, and brown-eyed. As bland as oatmeal, yet somehow I was the rumor mill's hot sauce.

I wanted to dump the boy's shake over his greasy little head, but instead, I recalled the Wiccan Rede that had so long guided me: *An it harm none, do what ye will.*

Too bad my Colorado State University education was proving fruitless. Apparently, no one wanted to hire a twenty-two-year-old fresh out of college to teach history.

The greasy-haired boy nodded toward the diner's front door. "Let's get out of here. She's giving me the creeps."

Though they left, the itchy feeling of their judgments did not. I blew a stray hair from my eyes and gazed past the booths, out the window to the Rocky Mountains on the horizon. Belle Meadow was thirty minutes from Denver but ages from the modern day. This town was a trap, a collection of crazies. Including myself. If Colorado was the heart of the southwest, Belle Meadow was a clogged artery.

The ding of the diner's front door opening brought me back to reality: burnt grease and coffee on the air, along with my duty to serve whoever strolled in. It just so happened that 'whoever' was Sheriff Locumb. He entered the diner with a purposeful gait, scanning the room before heading my way.

"Hey, Sheriff." I righted an upside-down coffee mug and began to pour. "Anything besides the usual?"

His mustache twitched. He brushed some crumbs from where his stomach bulged against his brown police uniform and lifted his gaze. "Miss Sophia Parsons?"

I stopped pouring mid-cup. *Hello? I serve your coffee every day.* "Yeah?"

Jack came up beside me, drying his hands on a towel. "Hey, Sheriff. What's going on?"

Locumb cleared his throat. "I'm, uh, afraid I need to ask Miss Parsons to come with me."

Jack and I stared at each other and then back at the sheriff.

"Is this a joke?" I asked.

I didn't really think he was joking. Sheriff Locumb wasn't the joking kind. Everyone in the diner watched. Even the jukebox went silent.

Jack leaned closer to the sheriff, lowering his voice. "What's this about, Jerry?"

Locumb sniffed. "Can't discuss it. We just need to ask Sophia some questions."

My heartbeat picked up. Sheriff Locumb could be a nice guy . . . *in a diner*. But I didn't want to be on the other end of his questioning. Not again. Not ever.

Trying to appear calm, I removed my apron and gently placed it on the counter.

"Okay," I said. "Let me get my stuff."

After promising Jack I would make up my shift over the weekend, I headed to my Jeep and pulled up behind Sheriff Locumb's cruiser.

I spent the drive to the sheriff's office in a cold sweat. No handcuffs, no reading of my rights. At least this time I wasn't under arrest. He was even allowing me to follow him to the station.

That whole thing with Mr. Petrenko—that was long over with, right? I'd only *found* his body.

I hadn't killed the man. No matter what anyone thought.

☪

SHERIFF LOCUMB AND I sat in a small room with a table and two chairs and a cheap light embedded into the suspended ceiling overhead. I wiped my palms on my pants, but the sweat kept coming.

He pulled up a picture on his cell phone. "Look familiar?"

Maybe he should've gotten an eight-by-twelve print. What was the picture of? Wood? A reddish-orange figure eight and a cross? I frowned and shook my head. "*Should* this look familiar?"

"Someone spray-painted this on the abandoned grain elevator," he said coolly. "Why don't you tell me what you know?"

"What I know about spray-paint?"

"Look." He leveled his gaze at me. "Mrs. Franklin said one of the women in her congregation—well, her daughter got sick. They think you had something to do with it."

"Mrs. Franklin thinks I have something to do with everything."

"Well?" he asked.

"Well, what? I didn't get anyone sick."

He puffed his cheeks and blew out a breath. "I'm not saying you got anyone sick, Sophia. They think you hexed their child by spray-painting this satanic symbol."

"You think I *hexed* someone? You're kidding."

Belle Meadow might be a small town, but surely it wasn't so dull that they needed to call me down to the station for *this*.

"You're here because Mrs. Franklin suggested you might be the one who vandalized the abandoned grain elevator, not because you 'cursed' someone."

"And?" I asked.

"Well, did you?"

"I'm Wiccan."

He stared blankly. "What's that have to do with the case?"

"Wiccans don't *believe* in Satan."

"Listen, lady. I don't care what you believe in. Why don't you just tell me where you were when the offense took place?"

"Which was when?"

"May tenth."

"At Colorado State, taking my senior year finals." Something a few minutes of research would have told him without dragging me down here. Besides, how did Mrs. Franklin know the date? Did she take daily drives around town with her calendar and journal, looking for signs of demonic worship?

Sheriff Locumb leaned back in his chair, slapping his hands against his knees before standing. "I'm sure you wouldn't mind waiting here while I check with the school?"

I gestured toward the door. "Go ahead."

I would like to say I enjoyed the silence while he was gone, but the constant hushing in my brain made that impossible.

Sheriff Locumb returned with a cup of coffee and an apology. I didn't drink the coffee, but I did ask him about the sick kid, and he told me it'd just been a case of chicken pox. Not a demonic plague or anything like that.

After squaring everything away, I returned outside to my Jeep and gripped the steering wheel. I couldn't deal with Mrs. Franklin's crazy accusations *and* the damn hissing. Something had to give.

Taking three deep breaths, I pushed the hissing as far into the back of my skull as possible. I wasn't about to go back to work. Someone was bound to interrupt my relaxation efforts with a request for a drink refill or a complaint that their jalapeno loaf was too spicy or their ginger-lime chicken wasn't chickeny enough.

As I drove home, I concentrated on the road—on one mailbox after another, on the way tree branches laced overhead, even on the glare of traffic lights, counting the seconds until they turned green. Anything to distract me from the noise.

My Jeep shushed along the pavement, but the roll of the road didn't do me any good. The quieter the world around me, the louder the buzzing in my brain. Coping was no longer a viable option.

At the last major cross street before my neighborhood, the noise in my head roared. I slammed my palm against the steering wheel, gritting my teeth.

Enough was enough. I flicked my turn signal in the other direction and veered onto the highway before my courage fled. It was time to turn away from caution and toward Sparrow's Grotto. Toward something that might silence the hissing forever.

G

THE FORTY-MINUTE DRIVE to Cripple Creek, home of Sparrow's Grotto, was worth spending the bit of cash I made at the diner. A Wiccan shop would not fare well in Belle Meadow, but thankfully the surrounding towns had pulled themselves into modern America.

I shrugged off my seatbelt and grabbed my list from the glove compartment before stepping out of my Jeep. A wad of fingerprinted gum blocked the parking meter slot. No way was I hunting down another space. I dug the gum out with the blade of my car key and forced a quarter past the sticky residue.

There. Twenty minutes for me.

I stared at the shop I'd first set foot in when I was sixteen—the place that always provided answers. Doctors hadn't been able to help with the noise. Tinnitus, they'd said, as if this were only a ringing in my ears.

Tinnitus, my ass.

But I'd gone to them first because magic was something I turned to only when necessary. After today, I was convinced this was one of those times.

I shoved my thoughts aside and headed into Sparrow's Grotto, where coyote figurines prowled the shelves, patchouli and sandalwood infused the air, and notes of Celtic music relaxed my nerves. The wall opposite the checkout counter was stacked with books, and the center aisles were filled with herbs, oils, candles, chalk and salts, small dishes, and other ritual implements. Athames, bolines, and other sharp objects were kept locked in the back.

Paloma, the shop owner and my long-time mentor, burst through a beaded curtain, her out-swung arms breaking the image of bamboo shoots. Her long hair, brown as coconut husks, tangled in her large, gold hoop earrings.

"Oi, Sophia!" she said. "It's been far too long!"

"You're telling me. How've you been?"

Following a quick bout of chitchat, she reviewed my list, her gaze only interrupted for a moment as she wiped a stray hair from the sun-weathered skin of her forehead. "What sort of ritual do you have in mind?"

"Something for positive energy." Less demanding than a ritual for silence; I never felt right making demands while using magic.

"Ah," she said, tapping a finger against her lips. "I'll see what I can do."

She disappeared behind her beaded curtain while I admired a few antiques on a shelf near the counter. A small violin charm made me smile. I set the charm beside the cash register. It would be a perfect addition to the bracelet Grandfather Dunne had given me shortly before he died. He'd even removed several links so it wouldn't slip from my wrist.

Paloma returned with four plum-colored herbal pouches strung shut with thin black cords. "I hope you don't mind, but we're out of agrimony. I've substituted with eyebright."

"I thought agrimony was best for banishing negative energy?"

"The eyebright will bring balance. My mother used this for a similar ritual in Belém when I was young. In Brazil, we grew agrimony in our garden. The sweet apricot scent is lovely."

I bit my lip. Eyebright was not part of the plan, and I hadn't come all this way for air freshener. Mental clarity might help, but it generally wasn't suggested to rush into a ritual. That included changing details at the last minute. One herb could change everything, and I didn't have time to redo all my research.

But I needed the noise gone—yesterday.

"Have I ever steered you wrong?" she pressed.

She had a point.

"One more thing," she said, retrieving a large book from under her counter and handing it to me. "A gift. For you."

The leather binding displayed a labyrinth of leafy spirals and branches of laurel. A handwritten cover page read *Maltorim Records, Volume XXVI, Salem Witches*.

"Are you sure?" I asked. Gifts always made me feel as though I needed to do something nice in return, and I could never figure out what. "It looks . . . valuable?"

"You mean it looks old? That's why I'm giving it to you."

"You're giving it to me because it's old?"

She waved me off. "You know what I mean. You study those ancient texts and all, don't you?"

"Paleography," I said, surprised she remembered the special interest I'd had in college. If the book was handwritten, I'd certainly enjoy analyzing the text.

"I've no use for it," she continued. "In some people's hands, that book would end up as a gag gift and eventually a door stop in some old man's house with too many cats and too many back copies of newspapers, not to mention that one woman who used to come here to buy books just to burn them."

"You mean Mrs. Franklin?" I asked, only half-joking.

"I'm rambling again, aren't I?" She let out a brief sigh and gestured toward the book. "Consider it an early birthday present."

Early was an understatement. The start of September was a far cry from December 21st.

"Thank you, really." I pulled some crumpled bills and a few Tic-Tac-sized balls of lint from my pocket.

Paloma tapped several keys on her register. "A discount, since I didn't have the agrimony," she said. "Now how about a cup of tea before you get going?"

We chatted in the back room, the light aroma of green tea hidden beneath the scent of hot ceramic. I smiled at the mismatched crockery stacked high in Paloma's pale blue, doorless cabinets and her eclectic selection of orphaned dining room furniture. For the first time all day, I could almost relax. Almost—if only the hissing in my head would stop blotting out my thoughts.

Paloma wanted to hear more about the ritual, but every time I opened my mouth, I told her about something else instead. I just couldn't bring myself to tell her about my curse—yes, a curse. The incessant hissing was too dreadful to think of as anything else.

After we caught up, she saw me to the door and made me promise to call if I needed anything.

"Anything at all," she pressed, closing the door behind me.

I wasn't halfway down the walk before I told myself I'd misread the concern in her voice.

{two}

INKY SHADOWS from the oak tree in my front yard cloaked the soothingly dark windows of my colonial-style house from the eyes of prying neighbors. I went inside. The bedroom at the end of the hall had been Grandfather Dunne's before he passed away, willing my mom the house along with his scrolled walnut furniture. Now this family home was mine, without a family to share it with.

This place, however, was not a reflection of me. I certainly wouldn't have put sea-foam green carpeting in all the bedrooms. Here, I was merely a placeholder, occupying free space, keeping the house in the same tidy condition my ancestors before me had left it in . . . except for the closets and drawers. Those were mine for the taking. I had a lovely habit of cramming my disorderliness out of sight.

My down comforter called me to sleep, and my small carriage shelf-clock urged the same, but there was something I needed to do first.

I set the supplies from Paloma's shop on the dresser and tucked the book she'd given me in a drawer, unsure when I'd have time to tackle such an immense read. I retrieved my Book of Shadows and an altar candle from beneath some clutter in the next drawer down and unfastened the hatch on the casement windows to swing them out like shutters.

A stone-topped altar sat flush against my windowsill, and I kneeled down to place a white candle on the altar pentacle's spirit point. This wasn't what Mrs. Franklin and her cronies liked to think of my Wiccan practices. Judging by the way they acted, one would think I performed naked rituals in front of the local elementary school or spent my evenings sacrificing animals. Goats, perhaps.

But that wasn't true. I practiced indoors, fully-clothed, using only an open window to connect with nature. Not a single animal sacrifice, either. I hadn't even been able to evict the raccoon family that spent last winter in my attic.

After reading through the ritual, I adorned the remaining pentacle points with four wooden dishes filled with the herbs from Paloma's shop, then chanted the Wiccan Rede:

"Be true in love, this you must do, unless your love is false to you. With these words, the Rede fulfill: An it harm none, do what ye will."

Then I lit the altar candle. The flame cast a pale flickering glow over the pentacle. Outside, moonlight filtered through the trees, throwing patchwork shadows on the rain-soaked grass below.

I sprinkled chalk dust on the sea-foam green carpet to create my physical circle, then called forth the Guardians to watch over my rites and cast my circle in the spiritual realm as well.

Tonight would be the perfect night—a waxing moon, the fresh fall of rain.

Come what may.

I lifted the sage from the pentacle and blew across the dish's surface to conjure wisdom. The sage flittered like snowflakes to the ground outside. Tipping the next dish outside my first floor window, I listened as cloudy fluid dribbled into the bushes, sure to evaporate in the early autumn warmth, garnering truth.

Where was that balance Paloma had promised? So far, the white noise in my mind had only amplified. A cool breeze drifted in, and I lifted my hair away from my neck and shoulders to help me relax.

I crushed marigold petals between my fingertips until they stained my skin, releasing an almost chemical scent, and envisioned a fire burning away all negative energy. I leaned out my window and tossed the marigold to the sky. The petals swirled and rained from above, scattering into my hair, back onto the altar, and across my front lawn.

I inhaled deeply, listening to the breeze in the trees and the chirr of crickets below. It was as though I could hear the sound of night— the sound of the very moon looming above and the sound of the bruise-like shadows beneath the bushes.

The right edge of my vision darkened. A streetlamp on the other side of the street had winked out. A man stood beside the iron post, staring. The overlapping spread of light from the flanking streetlamps revealed the muted gloss of black shoes with red outsoles and the frayed hem of denim, but otherwise, the shadows obscured his features, leaving him silhouetted against the Jackson family's prized hydrangeas.

My heart flip-flopped, and I narrowed my eyes, a silent dare for him to keep standing there. He stepped further into the shadows. When he didn't reappear beneath the next streetlamp, I squinted into the darkness. He couldn't have just disappeared.

Forget it. I needed to center my thoughts on bringing in positive energy. Getting distracted during a ritual was dangerous.

I settled back into the room. Light spilled from my window to illuminate teardrops of water on the blades of grass below, and I sprinkled the myrrh resin, watching it plummet downward to carry the request for transformation.

As the first speck hit the ground, the offering bowls toppled, clattering against the altar. The remaining herbs stormed through my room. My altar candle extinguished.

I fumbled around, frantically grabbing at the dishes, unsure what was happening. The bottle of liquid eyebright tipped, its contents staining the altar to a darker shade of gray. Flecks of myrrh resin stung my eyes. I blinked, but the gritty substance blurred my vision.

What the—

Strong currents pressed through my window with unnatural intensity. The lights flickered. Through the chaos, I saw someone in the street again. A glimpse of a girl standing across the street. No. Four girls.

Just as quickly as they appeared, they were gone.

Maybe it'd just been a strange reflection in the dark windows of my neighbor's house, but that thought didn't stop the howling wind from swirling around me, assaulting my senses and stirring panic in my chest.

The bedroom stilled, but my heart did not. Leaning against my dresser, I took in the mess scattered across the bedroom.

A swarm of voices rushed into my mind. I spun around and glanced back out the window, but the streets were empty.

The whirring and rattling in my brain—that was gone. Instead, the haunting white noise passed in spurts, punctuated by voices, as though I was rapidly switching from one radio station to the next, never settling on one clear signal.

I shook my head to clear my thoughts and focused instead on the rustling breeze of early autumn and the cool scent of earth and leaves. I would clean the mess in the morning.

After closing my circle, I climbed into bed, listening as the sounds of evening ticked on. Televisions blaring. Babies crying. I lay awake until all of that faded, until all that remained was the hush of curtains whispering against my bedroom walls.

That . . . and the sound of my curse, pecking away at my senses with static-like crackles. Just as I started to drift off, I heard someone talking. I jolted upright. Voices echoed through my window, but it felt as though they were echoing through my mind, saturating my brain with strange vibrations and overlapped whispers.

I pulled my curtain aside. Four figures in brown hooded cloaks strolled down the street. The limited outdoor light revealed little of their features, but their eyes glowed in smoky purples and eerie greens.

The face of one of the cloaked figures contorted into something wolfish before quickly transforming back. My heart thumped, and the air in the room thickened until it felt solid in my lungs.

The figures glided down the road, their formation choir-like, their rhythm without sync. Shapes bobbing into the distance until all I could see were the backs of their hoods. As they turned the corner onto the main road, their unintelligible mutterings faded from my mind.

What *was* that?

But the longer I stood staring at the empty street, the more I questioned what I'd really seen. What if my problem wasn't that I was losing my mind . . . but that I already had?

☪

THE NEXT MORNING I sat at my kitchen table with a blend of white tea flavored with wild cherry bark and blackberries. I nibbled at an English muffin as I picked my way through the classifieds. Nearly every job for teaching history required experience. How was I supposed to get experience if no one would hire me without already having some.

I had to consider the real reason no one wanted to hire me. Death followed me everywhere I went. My dad when I was six, my mom when I was eighteen, and Mr. Petrenko two years before that. Even the cops considered me a suspect for Mr. Petrenko's murder.

Mrs. Franklin, one of the first to arrive on the scene behind the flashing lights of police cruisers, hadn't been quiet in her implications. What she—and everyone—wanted to know was why my clothes were saturated with his blood and why I hadn't called the police.

I didn't know who called them. I couldn't tell anyone I watched him die—watched him die, but hadn't seen who'd killed him. No one would believe that. I just said I found him that way.

No one believed me, but there was no evidence to say otherwise. When my mother died at my touch two years later, the rumors began.

It had started innocently enough. When I was fifteen, Mom and I moved from Keota to Belle Meadow. Shortly after, Mrs. Franklin showed up in our lives, inviting Mom to her 'church' with a promise of a cure for her Bipolar Disorder.

Truth was, I'd lost my mother a couple years before the exorcism. I lost her when she stopped taking her Lithium—medicine was the witchcraft of man, Mrs. Franklin said. After that, life took a drastic turn for the worse. Dishes careening through the kitchen. Fists pounding the floor.

The exorcism was supposed to fix it all. But I'd had enough. I'd wanted my mom back—the woman she was before Mrs. Franklin showed up. I stormed into the church/basement and grabbed my mom's arm, intending to pull her from her seat and drag her home. I wasn't sure what I would do after that, but I never had the chance to figure it out. Mom died the instant I touched her.

Many nights after that, Mrs. Franklin and her congregation would gather outside my house, clasp each other's hands, and try to pray the Wicca out of me. They believed it was my pagan faith that brought a plague of death to our town, though she never considered that Mr. Petrenko had died before my beliefs began.

Mand. Br. Shhh. -kened. Shhh.

I put a hand on my forehead and pushed my breakfast aside. The voices in my head demanded my attention. Before I did anything else, I needed to silence the overlapping whispers rattling through my brain. If they didn't shut up, I would go certifiably insane.

If I wasn't already.

☪

THERE WAS ONLY ONE PERSON I could go to without turning to the doctors who had failed me before: Great Grandpa Parsons, my great-grandfather on my father's side. A man I'd never met.

Only one problem: he was dead, leaving me with nothing more than records and mementos. He'd spent years researching the human mind to find answers about his mother, Abigail. The family called her schizophrenic, but Great Grandpa Parsons insisted her affliction was more complicated.

The thought propelled me from the couch to the fraying nylon cord hanging from the attic loft hatch in the hall. Inside, light spilled through the rusted blades of a stilled fan that blocked the porthole window, exposing unfinished beams and cardboard boxes.

Grandpa Parsons' old chest rested between two dust-covered lamps near the window. I would have rummaged through these things sooner had the curse presented itself as a whispering from the onset. Instead, I'd spent years chalking the noise up to some kind of post-traumatic stress caused by my mother's death. I'd wanted it gone, yes, but not nearly as badly as I *needed* to get rid of the voices that replaced it.

The voices in my head rushed by, one thought indistinguishable from the next. I tried a few deep breaths.

Please, GO AWAY.

My stomach churned as I struggled to find a quiet place. After several minutes, the overlapping voices finally faded.

I sat and traced my finger over one of the trunk's tarnished metal buckles. Then, hands trembling, I unfastened the cracked leather straps and lifted the lid. Buried at the bottom of the chest, beneath old sepia pictures and plastic-sheathed Spiderman comics, awaited a promising book: *Voices—Into the Minds of the Disturbed.*

My fingertips scanned the words as I read, releasing the book's essence into the air. Having studied old texts, I knew this scent— vanilla, anisole, and sweet almond—wafted from the pages because the paper was fabricated from ground wood. I inhaled with a smile. Books often made better company than people.

My smile faded as I pored over the words for nearly an hour, my posture wilting more with each page I turned. None of the afflictions outlined in the text sounded anything like what I was experiencing.

Big surprise.

I probably needed to look into something current. I snapped the book shut and placed the book back into the trunk. But before I closed the lid, I noticed the corner of a handwritten, yellowed slice of paper with quill pen calligraphy sticking out from between the pages of another book. I gently lifted the document and found a photocopy tucked behind the original.

This wasn't how old documents should be stored. I slipped one of the old comics from a plastic sheath and eased the brittle paper inside. The plastic cover wouldn't do for the long-term, either; I would find an acid-free folder to store it in later. I set the original document aside and rested back against the chest to read the photocopy.

On this 28th day of February in the year of 1692

I, John Thornhart, Magistrate, being of the Jury last week at Salem Court, upon the trial of Elizabeth Parsons, am desired by some of her relations, due to the disappearance of the body after hanging, to supply reason why the Jury found her Guilty of witchcraft after her plea of Not Guilty. I do hereby give reason as follows:

Standing to consider the case, I must determine her words as evidence against her, for her attempt to put her Sense upon the Courtroom. Anne Bishop affirmed to the Court that her sister, Sarah Bishop, had been afflicted by Elizabeth, myself being of witness to this affliction as the words of Sarah Bishop on that day were found to me as principal evidence against Elizabeth Parsons.

Within these pages are the words of the Court, as spake by the condemned and those present at the time of conviction.

My heart knocked against my chest. I searched the trunk for the remaining pages. Nothing. I could almost imagine what it must have been like for my ancestor to be an outcast in her own town. The trial, the conviction, the hanging. Then what? She certainly didn't rest in peace, not if her body went missing.

I'd read legends of entire families cursed over such things, and now I wondered . . . was that what the whispering voices were? A *hereditary* curse? A new energy coursed through my body. There had to be more information somewhere. If this curse ran in my family, then finding out what *really* happened to Elizabeth's body might be my only hope of silencing the unintelligible whispers.

{three}

I TUGGED on a pair of Eskimo boots, piled my long hair into a messy bun, and tucked the book Paloma had given me into an organic wool tote. I wasn't sure of the book's credibility, but it couldn't hurt to give it a read. I wasn't sure how much I could trust Internet sources, either. Besides, I couldn't afford a computer on my salary, and I couldn't exactly borrow Ivory's computer or use the computer at work for this kind of research—not unless I wanted to explain what I was looking up and why.

On my way out the door, a kid on a skateboard rushed the sidewalk, scaring the Inca doves from my lawn. The rapid flutter of wings whipped against the air, startling me, but I shook away my nerves and hopped in my Jeep.

Sunlight beat the sides of buildings to cast a shallow shade, but despite the bright sun, the weather was much cooler than I'd expected. Since Paloma's book was only intended as backup to more legitimate resources, I stopped by the library and checked out the only two books they had on the witch trials.

Miriam Jennings, the librarian, was all-too-eager to help. It was a fellow outcast thing. In high school, she'd been the one Mrs. Franklin's church shunned. Apparently, they wanted to save lesbians from burning in hell, too. After all, Wiccans weren't the only ones who needed such godly help.

I didn't profess to be a theology guru, but I was certain of one thing: if hell existed, no one as sweet as Miriam Jennings would be sent there. While she scanned my books for checkout, I offered her a small smile and asked her how her partner was doing. The entire exchange renewed my sense of hope. I didn't need to let people like Mrs. Franklin get under my skin.

Outside the library, an elderly woman gave me a sideways glance, her gaze shifting over the top of her aviator-style glasses to my skirt and boots. I shrugged. Today it was my clothes. Tomorrow, they would think my hair was the wrong shade of blonde, or that I was too short and read too much.

Once back on the road, I turned onto Midland Avenue, heading toward the edge of town—toward my favorite forest trail, where I could connect with nature while I read. The road narrowed near City Hall and curved to the left. The area used to be a graveyard, but when they decided to build a street there, they dug up all the coffins and moved them to the new cemetery, which, even if not uncommon, was still weird.

As I passed by City Market, the darkness of memories I'd rather not remember rolled in. The streetlight turned red, and the whispering curse throttled through my mind. For once, I wished the whispers were loud enough to distract me from my thoughts.

To tourists, the market was merely a place to stop in and purchase a few items for their hotel fridge. Belle Meadow, mountain resort town! They didn't care about the town's history in coal mining, and they certainly hadn't heard about the murder, or how Mrs. Petrenko, now a widow, sold the building to City Market. The windows had been replaced with new treatments, the parking lot repaved, and the inside freshly painted and retiled. But the shell of the building remained, a constant reminder.

For months after the murder, I'd visited Mrs. Petrenko twice a week. She taught me to garden, taught me to identify the different herbs and their natural properties. She inspired me to look at what connected nature with humanity, which ultimately led me to my Wiccan faith, though I was certain that hadn't been her intentions.

Mrs. Anatoly Petrenko was perhaps one of the sweetest women I'd ever met. And her pelmenis, hands-down, made for the best Russian cuisine I'd ever tasted. A few times, she told me I was the daughter she'd never had. She and Mr. Petrenko had come here to start their own business, and their hardships had gotten in the way of starting a family. For all these reasons and more, I eventually stopped visiting.

I didn't deserve her kindness.

A car honked behind me—the light had finally turned green. I hit the gas and took off toward the hiking trails.

According to local legend, a girl had once been killed in the forest on this side of town. Eaten alive by cannibals. Bite marks all over her body—not quite human, not quite animal. The local teenage rite of passage was to spend a night in these woods, to face the ghost of the girl or the demonic forest-beings who had slaughtered her.

Of course, it was all a fallacy. We just sat beneath the forest canopy drinking cheap liquor. By adulthood, our fears eased. The poor girl had likely been mauled by a mountain lion.

I parked my Jeep and hiked to a small clearing. I sat on the ground and leaned back against one of the aspens. Cracks in the bark carved a road map to the rusted leaves above, and the sun leered through the tree's skeletal branches.

I took my books from my bag and laid them out in front of me, inhaling their camphoric, oily smell. I cherry-picked relevant notes from the two library books, trying to find record of my ancestor.

When the library books bared no mention, I opened the book from Paloma. The preface spoke of the more than two hundred people accused of witchcraft. At first, only the homeless and the elderly had been damned. All because Reverend Parris' daughters had a few temper tantrums. Or maybe it'd been the weather causing ergot of rye, which led to alkaloid poisoning. The result? Screaming, seizures, and trance-like states.

Soon after the early accusations, witchcraft became a weapon against those with enviable plots of land, those too old to be unwed, and those who were simply misunderstood. Twenty innocent people were executed. More died awaiting trial.

A footnote on the page read: 'Only one true witch was executed during these times. She remains unlisted in traditional history.'

One 'true' witch? Who had decided that woman was really a witch, and on what basis?

At the same time, my mind began entertaining ideas. Elizabeth Parsons' execution had taken place shortly before the Salem witch trials, and all I had to go on was the court document I'd found in my attic. Maybe traditional history books didn't list her because her body had disappeared. What if she'd been the one assumed true witch? Or was I nuts to consider any of this?

I flipped idly through the pages, stopping at one with markings scrawled along the margins: 'LC 47' and, beneath that, a partial address: *793 Basker St.*

The home of the previous book owner? If so, they might know more about the book.

A voice interrupted my thoughts: *Can't you do anything right?*

I clutched my bag and glanced around. It'd been clear. Distinct. Not tangled with the mess of voices usually in my head. But, as quickly as it'd come, it was gone, sinking back into the pits of my mind.

Something wet struck my lip. Clouds gathered above, threatening rain as dusk closed in, the moon already visible. Absorbed in the book, I hadn't noticed daylight slinking away.

A family of raccoons darted across the clearing, straw-like grass crunching beneath their paws. As they ticked across the field, my gaze followed them until a soft breeze picked up and muffled voices crept from the shadows.

I scanned the glade. Nothing. "Anyone there?"

The evening wind changed direction, carrying a moist chill and the stink of death.

I tossed my books into my bag and hurried down the path. As I stepped over a fallen tree, the thicket of silvery peeling aspen trees clustered together and obstructed the remaining light. The darkness sent tingles up my spine, just like in my childhood.

I will not panic. I am not afraid of the dark.

If I told myself enough times, maybe I'd believe it.

Tugging at my jacket sleeves, I waited for my eyes to adjust, then plowed through the underbrush and made my way over the knobby roots of the forest path. A squirrel scampered in front of me and perched on a cluster of burgeoning mushrooms.

I jumped back. Squirrels aren't nocturnal, and there was something wrong with this one. Its eyes were lucent and the color of green apples. I'd never seen eyes like those—not in people or animals. I leaned forward to get a closer look, but it bolted into the brush.

A saccharine odor weighted the air. A dead raccoon, its body twisted and bloodied, slumped against a tree. Newly dead, too, if the blood still smelled sweet and only a little rusty. Beyond the raccoon was a pile of several more discarded animals, torn apart, blood matting their fur.

Unable to catch my breath, I stepped back. Something crunched beneath my boot. *Don't look.* But I couldn't stop myself. I'd stepped on a raccoon's head. Its tail twitched by my foot. Nearly getting sick, I covered my mouth.

What would cause this? A mountain lion? How had it gotten so many animals all in one place?

Okay, Sophia, don't panic. Don't be like that idiot girl who ran and got herself killed by some wild animal.

I tried to remember what to do. Back away and keep eye contact. Keep eye contact with what? And I wasn't supposed to turn my back to the mountain lion. I *could* throw rocks or sticks to scare it away, but now that I thought about it, that made no sense. How could I pick up rocks and sticks if bending over would make it easier for the mountain lion to lunge for my neck?

I scanned the spaces between the trees, looking for any sign of life.

What if it wasn't a mountain lion?

Footsteps fell behind me. I glanced over my shoulder. A dark figure, running away from me, turned back, and I glimpsed a man's face before his shape bled into the shadows between the trees.

I ran for the main trail. My foot caught on a tree root, and I shot forward, my bag tumbling from my shoulder to the ground. Wet soil dampened my palms and knees.

Two feet away, several more dead animals were piled beside a tree. I looked down to my palms, realizing the soil was not wet from rain or water but from blood. As I tried to back away, something pulled at my scalp. My curls had tangled in a branch.

Shaking, I wiped my hands on my skirt and carefully untangled my hair. I climbed to my feet and looked at my hands. The darkness and my trembling made it impossible to see straight, but my stomach lurched when I spotted the cut bleeding on my palm, near my wrist.

Please don't tell me any animal blood got in there.

I bolted the rest of the way down the forest path, slowing to glance back as I neared the trail's entrance. A dark shape moved between the trees. *What the heck is—*

I stumbled into something.

It moved.

I shrieked and jumped back, my hand fanned over my chest as I sucked in a large gulp of air. "Shit, you scared me."

Ivory, my friend from college—not the boogieman—stood in front of me. She grabbed my shoulders and held me at arm's length. No wonder I hadn't seen her. She was dressed in a black sweater and dress pants, with a black cable-knit beanie pulled low over her ears.

Sleek bluish-black hair brushed her shoulders as she leaned to look past me into the woods. She shifted back, crystal blue eyes on mine. "Are you okay, Sophia? Why were you running?"

"Is everyone hell-bent on sneaking up on me?" I snapped.

Her eyebrows knitted together and the moon cast a pale glow on her milky skin. "What's gotten into you?"

"Nothing." I dug through my bag for my car keys. I thought she mumbled something else, but when I glanced back, her lips weren't moving. *Stupid, crazy, unintelligible voices.* "What are you doing here, Ivory?"

She pointed to my Jeep. "I passed by on the way to Lauren's and saw you parked."

"Lauren's home from Cali?"

She vacationed there every August to attend the Nihonmachi Street Fair in San Francisco and Nisei Week in Los Angeles.

"You'd know that if you answered your phone," Ivory said. "No one can get a hold of you."

"I left it at home."

Part of me wished I'd gone with Lauren this summer. The year before, she'd taken me to see the pageants—the ones she refused to participate in because some people there didn't think '*haafus*' should enter.

It wasn't the first time Lauren was shunned for her heritage. Lauren's dad, after learning his parents weren't thrilled he had married and impregnated an Irish woman, stopped speaking Japanese, changed his daughter's name from Yumi to Lauren, and, as she grew older, forbade her from studying the Japanese language.

Now, with her parents gone, Lauren was eager to connect with the culture of her ancestors . . . while I stayed behind waiting tables.

Ivory grabbed my wrist, drawing my attention back to her. "You're bleeding. And your skirt is covered in blood."

"I fell." I snatched my hand away and rubbed where her fingers had pressed. "Why are you going to Lauren's anyway?"

"For the love of the Goddess, Sophia. She might not be the illest person on the planet, but it's not like I hate her." She was laying heavy into her Boston-talk. Sometimes I wondered if she did that purely for my amusement, or if she'd just lived there too long to shake the slang.

Ivory was still staring at my wrist, and I gave her a pointed look. "I *fell*, Ivory."

"Yeah." She frowned and took a step back. "You all set? Lauren's expecting us."

Great. Now she thinks I'm suicidal or something. "I can't go," I said. "I have work early tomorrow."

"You're a mess, Sophia. You need to . . . you know, be a normal twenty-two-year-old. Have fun and stop stressing."

Just being in her presence was rapidly calming my nerves. My reaction in the woods had been a huge overreaction. Dead animals in the woods—really not *that* uncommon. Not even worth mentioning, especially not to Ivory, who would just laugh at my paranoia.

"I'm taking you out next weekend," she said when I didn't respond.

"I don't know if I can. I might have work." Truth was, the idea of going out in the city frightened me a little. At twenty-two, it seemed I had little more experience with life than I'd had as a teen.

"You're going," she said, matter-of-fact. "You can't use your studies to get out of it like you did in college, and you know Jack will leave you off the schedule if you ask. Besides, it'll be wicked cool. I'll take you to that club I told you about."

It was almost amusing listening to her, because only Ivory could say all that with about as much excitement as someone reading the Gettysburg Address.

"You can meet Adrian," she said, perhaps picking up that I needed further convincing.

"The guy with the books?" I asked.

"I'm talking drinks and dancing and your mind is on books." She shook her head, her expression somewhere between amazement and

25

pity. "Yes, the guy with the books."

Ivory had shown me some of Adrian's Wiccan spellcasting books before, and they were definitely more legit than anything I'd found in stores. Maybe he would even have something that went more in-depth on the Salem witch trials. I could look into those first, *before* I worried about intruding on the lives of whoever lived at 793 Basker Street.

"Fine, I'll go," I said.

With that, Ivory took off in her little red Honda, and I headed back over to my Jeep. I fumbled around the glove compartment for some napkins to dab the blood away from my wrist. My stomach lurched at the bright red on the napkin, and every time I closed my eyes, images of dead animals played behind my eyelids. With my company gone, anxiety crept back in, and my hands got jittery again.

I started the engine and switched on the heater, hoping the heat would somehow calm my nerves. The scent of warmth filled the car long before the chill subsided, but my shaking remained.

There was a flash of green and what appeared to be an owl perched on a nearby fence. When the owl turned its head, goose bumps rushed over my skin. That owl did *not* have the same eyes as the squirrel I saw earlier.

It just didn't.

Before I could speculate further, the owl flew off, its image becoming nothing more than a lingering memory.

For a long time, I sat staring at the roots of an old oak that had broken through the earth. I spotted a toppled bird nest, and, a few feet ahead, close enough to the road to be illuminated by the streetlamps, a small bird twitched its wing.

Damn it. I couldn't leave it there.

After scanning the area until I was certain no monsters were going to pop out at me, I slipped on the winter gloves I kept in my glove compartment, crept over, and gently scooped the bird into my palms. It weighed next to nothing, but it wasn't too young to be saved. And it was a cardinal, no less, which was odd, seeing how cardinals weren't common in these parts.

I hurried back to my Jeep, set the bird on my passenger-side seat, and eased the door closed, though I wasn't so gentle about getting my own ass back in the car. I might have been crazy paranoid, acting like my six-year-old afraid-of-the-dark self, but I was *not* about to spend one second more than necessary out there alone.

Once in my car, I headed for the nearby animal clinic. I'd be able to sleep better if the bird still had hope.

☪

MY EVENINGS AFTER THAT were filled with nightmarish sleep: dreams of my ancestor, Elizabeth, and her hanging; dreams of people in town learning of the whispered voices in my head and condemning me next. Sometimes I woke in a cold sweat, chiding myself for letting my subconscious affect me so deeply.

One of these nightmares woke me early on the morning I was meant to go with Ivory to the club. I headed to the kitchen, not realizing the nightmare had been more premonition than subconscious freak-out.

I leaned against the wall beside the birdcage Paloma had given me on loan. It was a charming little thing, the feeders and iron bed painted sage and the wooden top embellished with rose and cream porcelain flowers. The vet who'd set the bird's wing with green tape said my cardinal should be able to fly again within six weeks.

Not that I was thinking of him as mine.

"I know you won't be here long," I said to the bird, "but perhaps you need a name."

The bird tilted his head and chattered softly.

I crouched to meet his gaze. "How about Red?"

He pinned his eyes on me and made a *whoit, whoit, whoit* sound.

"Red it is."

So maybe I'd never been very original when it came to naming animals. Bob the bobcat, for example, was my 'backyard pet' when I was seven.

I took a small bag of peaches from the fridge and arranged them with vanilla beans and cinnamon sticks in a large metal bowl. The centerpiece filled the room with a spicy-sweet aroma, like freshly baked peach pie.

Things were looking up. Ivory was going to introduce me to someone who might help me find out more about Elizabeth Parsons.

But as anxious as I was to find answers, I would have called and cancelled if I'd known how the night would end.

{four}

IVORY PICKED ME UP at eight. Trees rustled outside the car window as she navigated the wind-raked road. I wished I was home, curled up in bed, but Ivory insisted tonight would be fun. Stress-free. A chance to pick up some books that might solve the problems she didn't know I had.

A blur of crimson and gold leaves and the occasional blip of yellow highway paint raced outside the passenger window. If only I could shed the haunting visions of dead animals and the layers of voices blotting out my enjoyment of the autumn scenery.

The sun disappeared behind a wall of trees, and I pushed away the lurid images, leaning forward to read a green and white road sign: DENVER 30 MILES.

"Where is this place?" I asked Ivory.

"You'll see." She hooked onto an exit ramp for Castle Rock then turned onto a side road miles before the city. This wasn't the Castle Rock I was familiar with; this place was some run-down, off-the-map kind of place. "We're almost there."

Several blocks later, she turned down a narrow, garbage-strewn road. The street was a dead end, with a beat-up building backing up to a wooded area. A rickety billboard towered without anything to advertise. Ivory pulled into the lot and parked beside cars I hadn't noticed from the road.

Soft whispers throttled through my mind. A chill prickled at my arms and goose bumps ran all the way up to my scalp, a tingle burning the back of my neck and along my ears. Taking a deep breath, I fought to push the voices away.

"Guess I'm overdressed?" I asked, motioning to my silk dress.

"You look good all decked out. Black suits you."

She climbed out of the car and tugged the bottom of her charcoal gray sweater as she walked to my side, while I slicked on some iced-pink-champagne lip-gloss. When I stepped onto the sandy asphalt, my foot slid, but Ivory caught me by the arm.

"Sorry," I mumbled, regaining my balance.

High heels—especially of the strappy variety—were not my forte, but Ivory had insisted the Eskimo boots stay parked in my closet tonight.

"I think you have the wrong address." I waved a hand, indicating the lone warehouse and long-abandoned gas station on the other side of the parking lot.

"This is Club Flesh." Amusement laced her voice. "You'll love it, trust me."

I would have loved anything indoors at this point. The air was far too cold for late September. I nodded toward a steel door lit by a lone, broken streetlamp. "We going in?"

Ivory grinned. "That door's just for show."

Turned out the real entrance was the storm cellar doors on the side of the building closest to the forest. Ivory pressed a brick jutting out from the wall, and the storm doors opened. Faint notes of music, seductive and enchanting, carried on the air. I peeked in, only able to make out the first few concrete steps descending into the subterranean depths.

Talk about an underground club. The design must have cost a fortune yet seemed like a lawsuit waiting to happen.

Ivory led me down the dark stairway. My nerves kicked up, but once the light source ahead revealed the last few steps, my heart rate slowed. When we reached the landing, the doors clanged shut, and I jumped.

"Door sensors," Ivory said offhandedly. She sauntered through the dimly lit stone passage, heels clicking in an even, upbeat staccato.

The eerie dance music grew louder as we walked toward a distant, crimson door. An imposing figure emerged from the darkness, powerful arms folded across his chest and black hair slicked back from the high slope of his forehead.

Ivory's hand slipped from mine as she bounced up on her toes to plant a kiss on his cheek. "Hey, Theron, busy night?"

"You vouchin' for that one?" He nodded toward me.

"Sure am. Now, don't give me a hard time. Let us through."

Theron spoke in a low, unintelligible rumble, but he must have said, 'Go on in,' because he opened the door and stepped aside.

Ivory patted his shoulder. "Lighten up, will ya?"

Once inside, Ivory leaned close, her voice overpowering the thundering music. "Pretty neat, right?

'Neat' might not have been the word I would use for the wine-colored walls, stone flooring, and black tables. Gloomy, maybe, if a place can be gloomy and classy at the same time.

I smiled. "It's . . . nice. Yeah."

Ivory pulled me past the bar and around the crowded dance floor to snag us a booth in the back corner of the club. A buxom waitress, bulging from her black patent-leather skirt and a red corset, came to take our order. Her springy blonde curls bounced even after she stopped, and her cheeks were bright from too much rouge.

"I'll take one of the house's reds." Ivory snapped the menu shut and handed it back.

I reviewed the list, trying to decide.

The waitress used her whole body to roll her eyes. Good thing, too, because I wouldn't have noticed her annoyance otherwise.

"Are you going to order, or what?" she asked.

Ivory pointed to a selection on my menu. "You'd love their Bordeaux. It's fabulous."

"Okay, the Bordeaux it is."

Eye-Roll Barbie snapped her order pad closed and stomped off. She returned impossibly fast and slammed our drinks—wine served in tall beer glasses—on the table.

"Sixteen-forty." She held her hand out and tapped her foot until Ivory forked over the cash.

Once she took off, I turned back to Ivory. "So where's the ever-elusive Adrian?"

"Books, Sophia? Really?" Ivory frowned. "He's the DJ. We'll catch up with him after hours. For now, we drink!"

Great.

For the next hour, we chatted while tossing back drink after drink. I wished I could tell her about the voices, but my gut told me to wait, to test the waters first before revealing something that would most certainly make me sound crazy.

☪

IVORY CONVINCED me to join her on the dance floor. The dark music quickened my pulse and one song blended into the next: smooth, enchanting, hypnotic.

A gathering of voices, somehow clearer than the music, swelled around me, reminding me of the real reason I'd agreed to come along. If I didn't take a break, I'd burn out before I got a chance to talk to Adrian about his books. I hollered to Ivory that I would meet her at the table.

On my way, I passed a group of women piled into one side of a booth, crowding a decent-enough man. Two other men sat across from them. The lady-killer captured my gaze, and a cool sensation, followed by warmth, tingled my brain. For the first time in weeks, my mind grew quiet. But, instead of the calm I expected, the silence was unsettling.

He leaned across the table to one of his male friends. After they exchanged words, the friend rose and approached me.

"His name is Marcus," the friend of the woman-collector said, leaning in close and speaking over the music. He was shorter than me and smelled of beer and disinfectant. "He's visiting from Damascus. Would you like to join him?"

No thanks. "I'm sorry, I was just—" I glanced around for an excuse, but found nothing. "You'll have to excuse me."

Dazed, I hurried back to my table, plopped into my seat, and scanned the crowd for Ivory.

But Ivory was not who caught my attention first.

A young man by the bar, clad in dark-washed jeans, took a final sip of his wine and slipped a tip for the bartender under his glass. His fitted black shirt showed the confident set of his shoulders, the contour of his chest, and his trim waist. The way he dressed, the way he carried himself . . . he looked both entirely in control and completely reckless at the same time, standing out in the sea of people as though the crowd had parted around him, though that wasn't the case.

The case was, he was sexy as hell.

And I hated him for it.

When his gaze captured mine, he offered the briefest of smiles. A curious swooping pulled at my stomach, and I quickly glanced away. When I dared to peek again, he'd seated himself at a nearby table beneath the golden glow of one of the wall sconces. I dreaded the idea he might catch me staring, but I couldn't stop myself. His toasted-almond hair fell forward to shroud his eyes, and flickers of blue—or was it green?—peeked through the disheveled strands.

The whole thing felt strange, as though I'd seen him before, seen him from this same distance.

It was then, with his body turned away from the table and one foot resting on the opposite knee, that I realized how I knew him. His shoes—dull, black shoes with a red outsole—gave him away. He was the mystery man who'd been outside my window the night of my positive energy ritual.

I should've marched over to him and told him off, but what was I supposed to say—'How dare you walk down a public street and look at a woman throwing flower petals out her window?'

His eyes flickered to mine as though my staring had drawn his attention. There was an intensity in his expression, something dark as his gaze slid over my body, assessing me, and I started surveying the room in hopes he'd think our eye contact had been accidental.

No one looked at me like that, let alone someone so absurdly handsome.

I peered at him from under my eyelashes, but I couldn't tell if he was still looking at me until too late. Until I'd already been caught checking him out.

He turned away, but it wasn't shyness that averted his gaze. The strong lines of his jaw were softened by his uplifted cheeks and the curl of lips. He smirked, shaking his head.

Realization set in: He was laughing at me.

Heat rushed to my face, leaving me thankful for the club's dim lighting, dark enough to hide the blush that surely reddened my cheeks.

Staring at my drink would be a safe bet. Drinks don't stare back. I plucked nervously at the hem of my dress, wondering what the hell had come over me. I didn't have time for this. I needed to find Adrian.

"Dance with me," came a husky but gentle voice.

I looked up, and my heartbeat stuttered. It was *him*. How hadn't I noticed him take the seat across from me?

The way he stared—his crisp, teal eyes pinning me—sent a current of warmth through my body, pulling the fear under and away. Even in the low lighting of the club, the stark contrast of blue and green in his eyes was evident, like the oceans off the coast of Greece.

Determined to appear unruffled, I tipped my drink against my lips and drew in a sip of my Bordeaux. The earthy wine provided a momentary relief to my rattled nerves.

"Do I know you?" I asked.

A half-smile rumpled the perfect symmetry of his face. He was even more gorgeous up close—fiercely beautiful, from chiseled cheekbones to strong, shaded jaw and attractive Roman nose. "Clearly you recognized me, no?"

"That doesn't mean we've met," I countered.

He knew he looked good, he knew I thought so, and now he was mocking me. *Great.*

"You're funny when you're angry," he said.

"Glad you're amused. Keep it up, and I should be able to keep you laughing all night."

"All night?" The tumble of his hair obscured the sudden arch of his eyebrow.

I wanted to stay mad, but it was a lost cause. Annoyance had always been my defense against attraction, but his looks and candor were crippling. "You haven't answered my question."

He tilted his head to one side and scratched the nape of his neck. A grayish-pink scar lined the inside of his forearm, and I dropped my gaze, as though I'd somehow intruded into his life, though it was more like the other way around.

"Well?" I asked.

"I thought you wanted something. You were staring."

"No I wasn't," I replied too quickly.

He crossed his arms, slouching back, and challenged me with a grin. "No?"

My pulse quickened and my breathing went shallow and I wished I would just disappear. This time, I wasn't going to respond. He kept his gaze steady against mine, his dark, tangled lashes framing his eyes. Lauren would've recommended some special eyelash comb. Thinking of Lauren might help distract me from this gorgeous specimen sitting before me.

The roof of my mouth felt like the shell of a walnut. I wanted to swallow and lick my lips to relieve the dryness, but his staring made me hyper-conscious. His gaze dipped, and I felt a rush in my chest.

Was he checking me out? Was he aware of my erratic breathing or the rapidly beating pulse in my neck?

His gaze continued down.

To his watch.

Not checking me out.

When he lifted his eyes to mine again, my insides filled with a chaotic energy. Attraction or warning, I didn't know, but I couldn't break away. The men in Belle Meadow had no interest in me, but this guy—he didn't know me. He hadn't heard the rumors, hadn't heard about my mastery of the dark arts or how I sometimes painted demonic symbols on abandoned grain elevators.

The longer I went without speaking, the more uncertain I became that I'd find my voice again.

I crossed my arms. "So you're stalking me, or what?"

He chuckled. "Pretty full of yourself, are you? Do all pretty girls think every man in a public place must be stalking them?"

What? "I'm not—" Grrr. I refused to defend myself to his moronic accusations. Even if he had called me pretty. "It's one thing you saw me through my bedroom window, but are you telling me you just so happened to show up here, too?"

"I must be pretty special to have followed you here but arrived first." He reached into his pocket and slid a wrist bracelet across the table. The fine marker-script on the side of the band displayed today's date beneath the club's logo. "Happy hour discount—starts at eight here. You'd have gotten one if you'd arrived before nine. Now, then, perhaps I might inquire if *you* are stalking *me*?"

"Well—"

"Well what?" he asked smugly. "Believe me, darlin', I'd prefer you weren't here. It doesn't bode well of your sensibilities."

"My sensibilities?"

He smirked. "Tell me why you were watching me, and I will help you get out of whatever you've gotten yourself into."

"What's that supposed to mean?"

Now he scowled. "Don't test my patience. I'm offering you an out."

What was his problem? "I have no idea—"

"Fine," he said. The angry lines in his expression relaxed, but his posture remained slightly stiffer than it'd been minutes ago. "We'll go with that for now."

"If you would tell me what you're talking about—"

"If you've truly only come here for the drinks, I recommend you find another place next time."

"That won't be necessary. I don't go out much."

"I can tell."

Okay, so maybe I was being a little edgy. Ivory shouldn't have let the hermit out to play. "Point taken."

He rested his forearms on the table and leaned forward. "Was that a yes or a no to dancing?"

I shook my head, but my smile said 'yes'. Not to mention Marcus was still staring—and in the least intriguing way. He gave me the creeps. If I was dancing with someone else, that might get the weirdo's attention off me. I spotted Ivory dancing with another girl, perhaps a friend she'd met here before, and figured one dance without her wouldn't hurt.

The man across from me stood and offered his hand. My palm warmed as I accepted, but when I rose to join him, my balance shifted. I wobbled, nearly falling right back into my seat.

He hooked his arm around my waist, supporting me against his body, his breath soft on my ear. "Careful there."

At his sudden embrace, a small shock flashed through my body. After a moment, my vision steadied. With his biceps behind my back and his forearm against my side, I felt somehow smaller and safer at the same time. I tilted my face up, catching his gaze. The candlelight from the table danced inside his irises. He cocked one eyebrow slightly, his amused expression also somehow gentle.

The moment rapidly becoming too intimate, I tensed. I needed to put some distance between us, to ignore the unwanted fluttering in my stomach. I stepped back. The air in the room lacked the warmth and comfort of his body.

"I'm okay," I said, which could've been true, depending on what one's definition of 'okay' was.

We wedged into a small opening in the crowd near the speakers. The burning scent of hot electrical wires replaced the fruity aroma of liquored drinks. He tilted his head down toward me as he stepped tentatively closer, then he rested his hands firmly on my hips, his arms bent at the elbow, relaxed.

I was decidedly not so relaxed.

I peered up at him, unsure what he expected. I'd never danced with a guy before.

Awkwardly, I placed my hands on the front of his shoulders, steadying myself as I swayed with him. A shiver flashed down my spine at the firmness of his body. How could he be so solid and still so graceful? His hands easily covered my hipbones, his fingertips pressing just behind my sides, into the muscles of my back. In that moment, I felt another kind of vulnerability.

He leaned forward and pressed his lips to my ear. "You all right?"

I nodded, stepping closer and sliding my hands around to the back of his shoulders. I buried my face against his chest, safe from his imploring gaze. He smelled like vanilla and musk and sandalwood, and I tried to commit the intoxicating scent to memory.

What the hell was I doing? I hesitated backward, away from him, but he easily guided me right back, and I had to stifle a gasp as an unexpected shudder ran through my body. The heat radiating from his flesh burned through my dress, the warmth igniting in my stomach and snaking outward in an involuntary arousal.

"My friend is probably looking for me," I said unconvincingly.

"Ivory?" he asked.

"You know her?"

"Well enough to know she'll wait."

There went my iron-clad excuse for getting away from the moment without revealing what an idiot I was.

The seduction of the music wound around us, sinking into my skin and pressing us closer. Each bass note reverberated along my spine, playing over every nerve in my body, and every time his hand grazed a new place on my skin, my want for control melted away, replaced by a desire to return his touch. He trailed his finger across my collarbone, over my shoulder, down my arm.

Soon, the music muffled beneath a cottony sensation in my head. His hands slid up my waist, over my ribs, his thumbs barely grazing the sides of my breasts. My breath caught in my throat, and I smiled nervously.

His jeans rubbed against the bottom of my dress and my bare legs, and the heat there spread over my thighs. This was more than I could handle.

"My name's Sophia," I said. It was a little late for introductions, but I wanted to shift the conversation and move as far away from the arousal as possible. "Yours?"

"Charles," he whispered. His voice sounded clear, as though the music in the room had faded to make room for him to speak. He cleared his throat and dipped his gaze to mine. "I saw you in the woods the other night."

I swallowed around the lump in my throat. "And through my bedroom window."

"Yes," he replied.

"So you *were* stalking me."

"I was unaware the woods belonged to you alone," he said against my ear, his hands moving to the small of my back. "Is there anywhere else I shouldn't already be when you get there, in the event you might continue with your accusations?"

"Jack's Diner," I said, fighting to hold onto the conversation instead of the arousal. "I work there, so you might want to stay away unless I invite you."

"Then invite me."

I bit my lip. Of course I wouldn't have shared that gem of information with him if I didn't want to see him again, but I hated that he realized this.

"Sure," I said quietly, hoping he wouldn't hear me over the music as easily as I could hear him.

"That night in the window . . . you looked so . . . strange."

Was that supposed to be a compliment?

I started to pull back, but it only brought our faces closer together—so close our lips nearly touched.

"And in the woods?" I asked carefully. "Did I look strange there, too?"

"No," he said, his voice cold now. "I hadn't expected to see anyone else out there. I stayed only long enough to make sure you were all right."

"*Why?*" I asked, like it was a bad thing.

"Why not?" He closed his eyes, tensing his jaw. "Do you always assume the worst of people? Or is it *yourself* you think so poorly of? Perhaps you might consider life is complicated enough without you helping things along."

Damn him. Yes, I could be immature and even a little insecure sometimes. Okay, a lot of times.

His eyes flashed on mine, and he stepped away, his expression shifting to something apologetic and regretful. "You should go, Sophia."

{five}

"GO?" I ASKED.

"That's what I said," Charles replied.

His sudden mood swing left me bewildered. I searched his eyes for answers, but there were none.

"If you don't want to dance anymore—"

"I didn't say that," he snapped. "I just said you should go. Now, please, get out of here."

"I don't under—"

His eyes flashed with the anger of a storm. "Leave!" he shouted. "Go. Home. Forget about this place. Back out of any agreements you have before it's too late."

He started off, but then backed up two steps, turned around, and grabbed my arm.

The cursed whispers invaded my thoughts all at once, scattering like marbles down a staircase, making it impossible to think . . . impossible to make out what they were saying. Just the shhhing and the fragments again—a word here and there . . . *dangerous* . . . *too late*. The rest of the words overlapped and tripped up my own thoughts. I couldn't push the voices away—only press them into the background.

A pulsing sensation tapped against my mind, followed by a compelling voice: *Come here, little mouse.*

I stepped back, but Charles slipped his hand to my elbow and shouldered his way through the crowd, ushering me past my table. He snatched my purse and thrust it toward my chest. The room spun as I staggered beside him.

"What's going on?"

He didn't answer, and I didn't get a chance to tug my arm free until after we were already outside, standing beside the forest with the club's storm doors clanging shut behind us.

I glared at him. "What the hell are you doing? I'm not leaving without my friend. You can't just tell me when to leave."

He spun toward me and placed his hands on my shoulders. "Sophia, listen. Whatever brought you here, I won't judge you, but now—"

The club doors flew open again, and his grip tightened. A couple rushed out, stumbling for the parking lot in a cloud of drunken laughter. Lipstick smeared the woman's flashing white teeth.

"Sophia," Charles said, his voice gentle now.

"What?"

His eyes steadied on mine. "You've associated yourself with the wrong people."

"*Obviously*," I said, thinking mostly of him.

"We should get you out of here. Ivory will catch up."

"Get out of here *why*?" I asked, unable to keep the edge from my voice.

His hold loosened. "You don't know what you are involved in. I will pay you double just to leave."

A fog settled over my mind. I blinked rapidly, bringing his face back into focus. My thoughts were muddy. "Huh?"

"Do you understand me?" he asked. His voice was far away, ominous.

"I'm drunk, not stupid." I didn't feel drunk though. I felt . . . confused.

His jaw tensed. "Why did you come here?"

"*Me*?" I raised my eyebrows. "You're asking why *I'm* here?"

The doors opened again, and this time one of the guys from the lady-collector's table stepped outside. He smoothed his dark, thick, shoulder-length hair away from his face and grinned with pale lips.

"Charles. Good and well to see you," he said, but he was looking at me, not Charles. The man clasped his hands in front of him and leaned forward with a slight nod. "Marcus would love her company."

Charles clenched his jaw, and a quiet growl reverberated in his throat. "I don't think that's a good idea, Cody."

"Marcus won't be very happy if she declines," Cody said in a playfully warning voice. He turned to me, smiled, and hooked his arm out. "Care to join us?"

It didn't sound like a request.

"No thank you," I said, inching closer to Charles. "I'm only here to spend time with my friends."

"Marcus is your friend." His smile twitched on one side. "But if you are certain?"

The more he pushed the issue, the more certain I became.

Charles pulled me back a step. "We'll be in shortly. Tell Marcus to order us a few drinks."

Like hell.

I opened my mouth to speak, but Charles gave me a measured glare. He offered the man a tight-lipped smile. "He'd want you to deliver that message, wouldn't he?"

Cody studied Charles for a long moment before disappearing inside.

"We need to go." Charles' voice sounded more demanding now. "You're putting us both in danger."

"We were just dancing," I said. "And Ivory—"

"She'll meet us."

"No." I shifted away. I'd read things like this in the paper; it never ended well.

"You're in no place to argue. Unless you *want* to visit Marcus' table," he said, as though it were an accusation. His eyes narrowed. "Perhaps you do not understand the extent of what you've gotten yourself into."

Another seductive whisper prodded at my mind: *Come back inside.*

Was that the same voice I'd heard earlier? It was more demanding now.

"You need to come with me," Charles said. "*Now.*"

If I had to choose between an unknown voice and the man standing before me, my choice was clear.

The air reeked of pine and rotted wood. I squinted into the forest's darkness. A spider web created a lacy barrier between two claw-marked trees, remnants of an afternoon shower beading along the silk strands and glittering in the moonlight. A glowing fog shifted over the forest floor.

Charles grasped my hand and plowed forward. My arm stretched until my feet finally got the message to move, and I stumbled after. In a miserable attempt to keep my balance, I reached with my free hand for every tree I passed. Tree bark chafed my fingers, but the cold and confusion numbed the pain.

"Move," he said over his shoulder.

I pointed to the strappy black heels. "You try walking in these. And for what? I don't even know why I'm following you!"

My cell phone chimed in my purse. A new text message from Ivory.

Meet you two soon. Go to the Shell station.

One of my heels sunk into mud, and thanks to the firm grip Charles kept on my hand and the way he continued onward without consideration, I nearly fell over while trying to pull free.

"Where's your car?" I asked.

"Not in the parking lot."

Boy, that was helpful. "I asked where it is, not where it isn't."

He huffed sharply. "I don't park in the lot. Sometimes they block people in. Now would you please—"

"Block people in? Why the hell would they do that? Is Ivory going to get stuck?"

He stopped, and I bumped into him. "They'll be searching for *you*, not her. She'll be fine." He rubbed his forehead. "Can we hold off on the questions? We need to find the main road."

"Don't have to be so snappy," I said. If anyone had the right to be annoyed, it was me. His words sunk in. "Wait. They're searching for me?"

He kicked some forest underbrush out of our path. "Don't play stupid. I don't even know why I'm helping you."

"Don't get shitty with me. You're the one who asked me to dance and then shoved me out the club two minutes later."

He growled under his breath. "Walk faster and keep quiet."

Maybe I should've gone back. I didn't need help from some nut-job who thought he was doing me a favor. "Why are we going through the woods?"

He lowered his voice. "Listen."

Branches cracked somewhere behind us. Adrenaline flushed the alcohol from my system. I felt as though a veil had been lifted from my eyes and cotton extracted from my ears.

My breathing quickened, and Charles jolted forward. "Run."

His urgency propelled me, but I couldn't keep his pace. I wasn't even sure why we were running, though I feared stopping to find out. One of my heels snapped, and a few steps later, the strap on the other heel popped.

As I continued forward, my shoes tumbled off, and the ground scraped the soles of my feet. Small pebbles and dried pine needles entrenched inside the small wounds, and pain shot up my legs. Branches whipped against my shoulders and stomach. I inhaled one sharp breath of icy air after another, my chest aching with cold.

The path abruptly ended. A tangle of brush and entwined trees blocked our way.

"I thought you came in this way?"

"Thought this path would be faster," he replied between efforts to rip the branches away.

I pulled him from the natural barrier. "Follow me."

"We can't run toward them, Sophia."

"We can't wait for them to corner us, either." Whoever *they* were.

I gave him a final, measured look, then turned and ran. Hair clung to my face and neck. My legs burned nearly as much as my lungs.

Another trail, paved with mud and dead leaves, veered off our current path, and we followed the curve into a more densely wooded area. Footsteps thudded behind us, louder with each step.

At first, my heart pounded more from fear than exertion, but soon my whole body ached. Fear could propel me no further.

I leaned forward with hands on knees, sucking in huge gulps of air. "Have . . . to . . . stop."

My heart was nearly bursting in my chest. Moonlight pierced through the forest canopy, revealing gashes and lacerations staunched with mud. My stomach lurched, and I blocked my mouth with the back of my wrist.

"Please, Sophia, we must continue."

"I can't."

Charles bounced on his toes, looking in every direction. "Stay here. I'll be right back."

I took a couple steps toward where he had retreated into darkness. "Hey!" I hissed. "Where are you going?"

The noise of pursuit ripped through the forest. Trees blocked my vision. I leaned back against a tree until the bark dug into my flesh. I pressed my lips together so no sound would escape.

Why had I followed him? *Stupid, stupid, stupid.*

A twig snapped somewhere behind me. Footsteps shuffled closer. Maybe my pursuer couldn't see me. I held my breath, fighting to stay silent, but I trembled, and my dress rustled against the tree.

"You're far too pretty to hide." My pursuer had a deep, masculine voice. A familiar voice.

Shit.

A short ways forward, trees parted to another path. I ran for it and squeezed through. The hem of my dress caught on something. I was stuck.

My pursuer stood on the other side of the natural barrier, his eyes aglow and his gaze fixed on me. Over a foot taller than me and three times my size in muscle mass, there was no way for him to squeeze through.

He pulled on one of the trees, and it uprooted slightly. What the—who the hell was strong enough for that?

One look at his face gave me my answer.

Cody.

As I yanked my dress, he reached through and grabbed at the black silk hem.

"There you are," he said.

I shook my head, trying to free my dress from his firm grasp as he pulled me closer. My feet shuffled in an effort not to get too close, but another hard tug from him made me tumble forward. My forearms shot out to protect myself from being pulled back through space between the trees.

When he reached through with his other hand, I saw my chance to reach down and give my dress another hard yank. The fabric ripped, leaving behind the swatch he firmly clutched in his hand.

I backed away and turned to run. A protruding root tripped me. I crashed into another tree but remained upright. My feet throbbed with each step, stinging as more rocks and debris shredded my skin.

Cody stepped out from behind a tree in the path ahead. I screamed, stopping so fast that I nearly fell forward.

He took a few calculated steps, but I didn't let his slow advance stop me from scanning for a way out. A guttural vibration rumbled in his chest as he stalked ever closer. I couldn't make out his features beyond his shadowy eyes and twisted smile.

I stumbled back, and my arm scraped against a tree as I sunk to the ground. Blood trickled between my knuckles.

He flashed his teeth. His eyes were completely black, and two of his top teeth extended with a sharp snap. He ran his tongue across one of them, and I nearly choked as I gasped.

Frantic, I tried to see the ground through the fog, but it was useless. My hands fumbled until I grabbed a heavy branch. He lunged. I jumped to my feet and swung. He stopped the blow mid-swing and caught my wrist with his other hand. My wrist crushed in his grasp, and I cried out sharply as the bone cracked. Shattered. Shards stabbed like needles beneath my flesh, the pain darkening my vision.

He released me, and I collapsed. I couldn't hold back the scream or the flood of tears. I shook violently and vomited. Wiped my mouth with the back of my uninjured wrist. My throat burned. Bitter, acidic fluid coated my tongue and teeth.

"Don't do this." The words choked out. "I won't say anything . . . just let me go."

An unnatural smile curled the corners of his mouth. He hovered over my crumpled form. "Doubt it, Blondie."

A shuddering pain worked into my lungs. Then, suddenly, the man's already pale flesh became translucent, all remnants of color draining from his face. A large bird—an eagle?—swooped down, and my attacker jumped back.

I hobbled to my feet and stared as the bird's beak tore into his face. Something thudded at my feet. A burning scent stung my nostrils, and I nearly vomited again.

Without waiting to find out what was going on, I ran a straight line in no particular direction. The forest had to break eventually. I stumbled twice. On the second fall, I avoided landing on my wrist, but my head smacked into a rock. As I struggled with one arm to get up again, I fought off another wave of nausea. The forest was spinning. Which way had I been running?

I staggered forward. I couldn't think. Couldn't stop shaking and crying. Couldn't breathe.

Light swept between the trees.

Headlights.

I bolted. Footsteps pounded behind me again. So close to where the forest walls broke. I pushed myself harder, but someone grabbed me tight around my arms and stomach. The excruciating pain in my wrist intensified, and I thrashed to break free.

"Shhh. You are safe." The soft voice was masculine and deep.

An unexpected sense of security swept over me. My desire to escape drifted, replaced by a warming tingle in my mind and a soothing voice like a whisper: *Relax.*

I couldn't escape the odd sense of peace that seemed to press into my skin and seep into my mind from the outside. Peace that was not my own.

The man lifted me. "Please do not draw any further attention."

My breathing slowed. Sleepiness overpowered my senses. I blinked, fighting the drowse, taking in the man whose arms I lay limply across. Smooth, dark skin and kind, dark eyes.

Another figure walked up behind him and placed a hand on his shoulder, face still shrouded by the shadows.

My eyelids drooped. Closed. My mind screamed, but my voice failed. The world tilted as the man laid me down, the persistent rumble of an engine beneath me. I struggled for wakefulness, but soon failed.

{six}

SOMETHING WET on my scalp. A droplet trickling into my ear.

I struggled with the weight of my eyelids. Through the fog, a figure with shoulder-length black hair dipped a rag in a nearby dish of water, then dabbed it near my temple. I blinked until my vision cleared.

"Ivory?" I rasped.

"Yeah, sweetie, it's me."

Across the room, an old dresser with shallow incising and grooved panels held a television airing an episode of some crime-investigation saga. As I eased my head to one side, pain pulsed through my body. Black lace curtains framed a bay window beside a red-oak bookshelf, full of familiar books. *The Scarlet Letter*, *Don Quixote*, and *Oedipus the King*.

Ivory's bedroom? I didn't remember falling asleep here.

I didn't remember falling asleep at all.

Outside the window, the dark, cloudless sky and the breeze in the trees made the night air appear thin and cold, but the air in the room was almost too hot.

From the corner of my vision, I saw someone standing in the middle of the road, but when I looked over, they were gone.

Great. I'm hallucinating.

The door creaked open. Charles stepped in, his stone-washed, button-up jeans hugging his thighs and his black short-sleeve shirt tight against his chest. My gaze trailed up, taking in the soft glow of his bronzed skin and the way his toasted-almond hair fell in perfectly careless tousles to obstruct his enchanting teal eyes.

But as his gaze met mine, the events of the previous night rushed back—the attack, my pain. All *his* fault. Thankfully the pain wasn't as bad as I would've expected for a broken wrist and a crack to the head.

Before I could speak, a man with dark skin and neatly-formed dreadlocks followed him into the room, dressed in black dress pants and a deep red shirt with a plum sheen. His hands clasped tightly in front of him and his suit jacket lay neatly folded over one arm.

He'd saved me.

The unfamiliar man clenched his jaw, hanging back by the door, balling his right hand into a fist and relaxing it over and again. Maybe he was angry with Charles. I wouldn't blame him.

Pain pulled into my lungs as I breathed. "What happened?"

Ivory helped me sip a glass of water. "You've been in and out for a few hours. I hope you aren't too groggy from the pain killers."

"I'm sure that hit to my head didn't help."

Ivory gave me a worried smile.

I tried to sit up, but pain shot through my arm. I crumpled back to the bed and raised my wrist. It was swollen to twice the normal size and twisted at an odd angle.

I should've freaked out, but I'd never been one to panic when I should. Yes, a stubbed toe was like world war three for me, and maybe I was a little scared of the dark, but put me in the center of tragedy and I could be eerily calm.

Or maybe some part of my brain just shuts down when things are too much for me to handle.

"Charles left me," I whispered.

Ivory nodded. "He went for help."

A cold sensation pushed on my mind, followed by another warm tingle, and my thoughts returned to the same unnatural stillness I'd felt in the car and at Club Flesh. Something was happening with my curse. Some kind of shift. Whatever it was, I was certain last night was to blame.

"What's going on? I should be in the hospital."

Ivory edged away. "I'll have the men leave," she said gently. She grabbed Charles' arm and pulled him toward the door. "You're freaking her out."

"She doesn't seem freaked out to me," Charles said coolly.

Ivory flicked her gaze toward the ceiling. "Well, I know her, and she's freaked out, okay? Just take a hike. I told you I'd take care of this."

"A few minutes is all I ask." He lowered his voice. "Adrian's the best person to help."

Without waiting for Ivory's response, Charles squeezed around the bed and settled into the window seat beside me. "I have some questions for you. Are you well enough to speak?"

I scowled. "What do you think?" I turned toward Ivory, interrupting her and the other man's whispered conversation. "What about you, Ivory? Obviously you're okay."

"I'm fine."

"Some guy tried to kill me."

She walked over and slid onto the edge of the bed. "You had an unfortunate night."

Charles scoffed. "Unfortunate? You shouldn't have brought her there."

"Oh, like you weren't having the time of your life with her."

"Only because I was trying to figure out who she was working for."

Who I was working for?

"Shut it, Charles," Ivory snapped.

I held back a growl. "Is anyone going to tell me what's going on?"

Ivory and Charles exchanged a glance, then they both looked at me expectantly.

"What?" Did they think *I* was going to tell *them* what happened?

Charles tilted his head back and covered his face with his hands. "You sound genuinely unaware of what you've gotten yourself into, and I have given you the benefit of the doubt. But you must have been up to something if you garnered Marcus' interest."

"Are you freaking kidding?" I looked to Ivory, but her crystal-blue eyes just stared back without expression.

"Were you following me?" Charles asked.

Ivory lifted her hand. "I told him you weren't."

Charles glared at her before returning his attention to me. "Answer the question."

"I thought *you* were following *me*, remember?"

His chest puffed out, and he scowled. "Why would someone be following you? Is there something you're not telling us?"

"Why don't you tell me why someone would be following *you*."

"When we were dancing, you had guilt written all over your face."

I'd felt guilty all right, but not because I was following him. "I wouldn't have even been there if Ivory hadn't invited me. I don't see why I'm defending myself to you. You're the one who left me stranded in the woods."

"How do you know Marcus?" Charles pressed. "Did he hire you? I can't help you if you aren't completely honest with me."

"Why are you interrogating me? I'm the one who was attacked!"

"Nothing," he said, which wasn't at all a response to my question. He shook his head, the scowl slowly slipping from his features. "She's telling the truth," he said to Ivory. "She doesn't know anything."

"I told you," Ivory said.

"Can someone tell *me*?" I asked.

Ivory frowned. "It's just . . . things like that don't usually happen there."

"Well, I fucking hope not."

I could've strangled her. How could she be so cavalier? My world was crashing down, and I was stuck here in this stupid bed, no one giving me a direct answer, while some man I didn't know stood to the side of the room, watching the whole thing as though he was about to self-combust.

I slanted my gaze back toward Ivory. "How do you know Charles?"

"We met at the club a while back," Ivory said. "It's always been safe for humans."

"Safe for *humans*? As opposed to . . . ?"

Charles stood. "Take her to the hospital and keep an eye on her."

"No," Ivory said, giving him a hard stare. "You don't get to make a bigger mess of things and then walk out as if nothing happened."

"Not my problem."

"*I'll make it your problem.*"

Charles glowered, but her words stopped him in his tracks. "Did you not say you were taking care of this? If you care about your friend, you'll leave it alone. It's bad enough she got Marcus' attention. Did you know she was . . . ?"

Ivory shook her head. "How could I?"

Just before a scream of irritation nearly burst out of me, the man in the corner interrupted our conversation.

"Tell her," he said, his voice calm, even.

Charles and Ivory turned to him, their expressions blank.

"Tell her," he repeated. "If they know of her, it's better she knows of them."

Charles reseated himself by the window, but Ivory paced away. She approached the other man, who leaned against a wall by her dresser. When she reached his side, she put a hand on his shoulder and gave me a pleading look. "Sometimes people are not what they seem."

"Go on . . . ," I said. I tried to shift my weight on the bed, but the pain in my wrist shuddered through me. I rested back, closing my eyes. "Whatever it is, please, just tell me already."

"Club Flesh is a supernatural establishment."

Okay. Maybe I would've preferred being eased into things after all. At least my 'too-shocking-to-induce-panic' gene was kicking in.

"So why did you take me?" I asked.

"It's always been welcoming to humans."

"And of course I'm the exception."

"I didn't know, Sophia," Ivory said. "You never told me."

"Never told you *what?*"

She chewed on her bottom lip. "Some humans can see differences like yours. For example, Charles can see you for what you are, while the rest of us are limited to what is immediately visible. Such as the Cruor."

"What the hell are you talking about?"

The man by the door pushed away from the wall and approached. When he reached my side, he tossed his crisp dreadlocks over his shoulder.

"I'm sorry our introduction couldn't occur under better circumstances." His voice was deep—formal in tone. He did not offer his hand in introduction. His body seemed tenser now than it had from across the room. "I am Adrian."

"*You're* Adrian?"

"Yes," he said, "and I am one of which she speaks."

"What does that mean?"

"Please understand," he said smoothly. "We are not all bad. The actions of the Cruor who attacked you do not speak well of our kind."

"Wait—what?"

Adrian paced over to the dresser to switch the television off. As he fumbled with a small radio, tuning to a classical music station, a gold ring on his right hand glinted in the lamplight. There was a large scripted 'A' at the ring's face.

Adrian frowned. "You are familiar with the Cruor, yes?"

"The what?"

"Earth elementals, as they were originally known."

I turned to Ivory. "You believe this?"

She swallowed and gave a slight nod.

I shook my head. "Quit playing."

"I sense you are not a believer," Adrian said.

"A believer in 'elementals'? Seriously?"

"No one believed in the cobra until someone was bitten." He closed his eyes for a moment. "Marcus works for the Maltorim, our elemental council. No doubt he was here on council duty. They're always on the lookout for the dual-breeds as well as anyone who might be of value, and Marcus is one of their leading men. He is one of the oldest Cruor—an earthborn."

"Earthborn?" Who were they trying to protect with these lies? Maybe Adrian wouldn't be the best person to borrow books from—not if this was the kind of nonsense he was pushing.

"Earthborns were the first chosen as Earth elementals. A darkness had overtaken the human race, and without positive energy for the Universe to feed on, it was beginning to die. At the time, people were being buried alive, mistaken for dead, and the Universe saw this as an opportunity."

"People being buried alive? Happened a lot in the thirteenth century, right?"

"And the centuries before." Adrian's nostrils flared. "The Universe resurrected those who didn't survive the live burials. They were chosen to protect humans at night. Guardians, or, if you will, Earth elementals. With their ability to sense the pull of the moon, they knew to rise when it loomed high and to flee from dawn."

"So you're a vampire? That's what you're getting at? And the guy who attacked me . . . he's a vampire, too?" Something was up. Yeah, the guy last night had fangs, but anyone could purchase a pair online.

"The Cruor are the reality from which legends of vampires arose."

"You're full of shit."

"You may believe that if you wish," Adrian said, "but I assure you the Cruor are real, and this is as true as I am standing before you."

I opened my mouth to speak, but Adrian's sharp gaze trampled the idea. What was I supposed to say to that? I couldn't argue with his presence. If he wanted to be a 'vampire' or 'Cruor' or whatever, who was I to argue?

"These guardians cherished immortality with greed, concerned only to prolong their own semblance of life. They lusted for the blood of their prey, for to drink the blood of another is to steal the life source and maintain immortality."

I recoiled deeper into the bed but refused to give in to the panic rising in my chest. "You're trying to tell me some kind of monster was trying to eat me?"

"You make our kind sound so . . . carnal."

"Aren't you?"

He pushed his lip out in an expression more indicative of a shrug. "I will admit it is not easy. Right now, my natural instinct would be to pierce the main artery in your neck and feed. I'm not going to do that, however, because I am civil and have already eaten today. Not a human, mind you, but it did take off the edge."

These people were more whacked out than Mrs. Franklin's cult. "If that eagle hadn't come along, then what? Cody was going to turn me into a fruit bat?"

"Those bitten are reborn as Cruor. Newborns. The change was intended to purify evil in the humans, to help those humans harness their desires to kill. They were supposed to join their makers to comb the earth and hunt other impure humans."

"Wouldn't your Universe-people just kill the bad humans?"

"The Universe can only create. It cannot destroy."

"What does that have to do with me? You make it sound as though the Cruor are here to protect. Are you trying to say he mistook me for a criminal?"

"No." Adrian returned his gaze to mine. "You don't seem to understand. The Cruor were not supposed to turn on the pure. There must have been some error in their creation . . . some lingering darkness. The result was elementals who cared about only one thing— eternal life. This means stealing lifeblood from others, whether they bind themselves to their prey's soul or kill them."

"So the Universe—which is, for all intents and purposes, like GOD—screwed up the humans, then made some elementals and screwed them up, too?"

"Perhaps," Adrian said. "No one can say for sure where the original darkness came from, but, since then, laws have been set. The Cruor are no longer permitted to attack a human unless the human becomes a threat. Such as those who learn of our true nature."

"You said Club Flesh has always been safe for humans."

"It's a great place to make . . . connections. Exchanges, if you will."

"I don't even want to know," I said, trying not to think about what Ivory or Charles could possibly get out of that place, or what they were doing to get it.

Ivory must have read the disgust on my face. "Money," she said. "In exchange for blood, information, services . . . ."

"And you?" I asked, imploring her with my gaze.

"Accounting."

"Accounting for elementals?" I shook my head. "Accounting? Really?"

51

Adrian nodded, touching his hand to his cheek. "Our world is not so different than your own, yes?" he asked. "Things do not always work as intended. Some may simply claim a human is a threat, even if they are not. Most, however, would prefer not to draw the Maltorim's attention to their actions. They'd rather find another way to get what they want from humans. Marcus, being one of few remaining earthborns, is strong and set in his ways. He'd surely be excused, as he's a member of the Maltorim himself, but he's not known to act on his desires without prompt."

At least we were getting somewhere. Cody attacked me for a reason. "So what was the prompt?"

"You have something. Or rather, you're missing something."

"Like what?"

Adrian shrugged. "You tell us."

"If you don't know what it is, how do you know I don't have it?"

"Some people can tell. Charles being one of them."

"Oh, yeah?" I didn't try to hide my disbelief.

"Anyone can have a supernatural gift. Immortal, Mortal . . . it matters not," he said. "While Charles may not be able to see *why* you drew Marcus' attention, he can see *how* you did."

"How is that, then?"

"Your aura."

Charles could read auras? If that were true, he would've known I wasn't guilty of following him. That's what auras were for, right? Reading emotions, intentions, that sort of thing. Surely I didn't glow some vicious shade of evil. That'd be reserved for someone like Marcus or Cody.

"What about my aura?" I asked finally.

Adrian smiled. "You don't have one."

{seven}

IF THIS AURA THING were true, perhaps that was how Charles earned his pay with the club. Did Ivory issue him a check for his services, or were such payments made in cash?

I still wasn't sure I was buying it. Why did they expect me to know I didn't have one? "Are you telling me nothing bad would have happened if I had an aura?"

"Mock the situation all you like," Adrian said, "but I am trying to help you. Would you prefer I leave?"

I couldn't bring myself to tell him to stay, but I didn't tell him to leave, either. "In theory, then, is it bad I don't have an aura?"

Adrian's jaw tensed. "This is not a *theory*, Miss Sophia. And no, it's not bad to be without one. It's merely rare and not well understood, which would be reason enough for Marcus to seek you out."

"Then why didn't any other Cruor approach me?"

"Because Cruor can't see auras. One of his party, however, might have been able to. It is likely you were pointed out for that reason."

"Charles was also able."

Charles cleared his throat. "If you're implying—"

"I'm not implying anything."

"Some people think it's not possible to read them," Charles said.

I tilted my head toward Ivory, suddenly hating her stupid room and her stupid bed that my injuries left me prisoner to. The whole idea of Cruor was bizarre, but Ivory wasn't one to play pranks.

"The aura-thing would explain why they would come after me," I said, turning to Charles, "but it doesn't explain why you thought someone was following *you*. Or why you thought that person was me."

"First you're talking to someone from Marcus' table, then you're staring at me. What would you have thought?"

"So you decided to save me from the people you thought I was helping follow you?"

"I thought you might be playing stupid," he went on, "but once I noticed how he was looking at you, I realized you were in trouble."

"Let me express my eternal gratitude that you found it in your heart to save the enemy. Or, rather, abandon her in the woods with her attacker. That was *so* helpful."

"Just because you make lasting judgments doesn't mean we all do. I gave you the benefit of the doubt as no one deserves to fall victim to the ways of the Maltorim."

"How very noble of you," I said. Sarcasm was my way of masking the gratitude beneath the surface that threatened to deflate my pride.

Charles cocked an eyebrow. "Anything else you'd like to complain about, princess?"

I huffed, turning to Ivory. "What about you?" I asked. "You knew the dangers, and you took me to Club Flesh anyway."

"She shouldn't have," Charles said from beside me. As if he should talk. He hung around those monsters, too.

"Thanks for that, Charles," Ivory said, "but we've been going how long without incident? It should've been safe for Sophia. How was I supposed to know Marcus was visiting? Or that she didn't have an aura? Maybe if you'd told me—"

"Maybe if I could *reach* you, I would have said something," Charles replied through his teeth. "Instead, you don't come around for months, and when you do, *she's* with you."

Say it like I'm a disease, why don't you.

I was shaking from anger. Anger at myself for my attraction to Charles and anger at Ivory for being so reckless.

Shit. If I was getting mad, that meant I believed them.

Ivory sat in the upholstered chair beside the bed. "You must know I wouldn't have taken you if I'd known this would happen?"

She rubbed the sides of her pants in a repetitive, inexact pattern, her eyes trembling with regret. She hesitated as she curled a strand of hair behind my ear.

"Adrian needs to get going soon," she said, "but before he does, he will help with your wounds."

"Is he a doctor?"

"This is going to sound worse than it is." She grimaced. When I said nothing, her words rushed out in one breath. "You need to drink his blood. It will—"

"What? Why would I do that?" I shook my head, which only made me wince in pain. "You're all insane. *This whole situation is insane.*"

"Cruor blood accelerates healing."

"You're seriously going along with this shit? What the hell, Ivory?"

Charles put a hand on my shoulder. "You'll have to trust us."

A familiar calm pushed into my mind. Pain swayed my thoughts, but I grasped to my last shreds of logic. Drink someone's blood? It didn't sound sanitary or sane.

"Besides," Ivory said, "you can't go home in your condition. What if someone stops by?"

I sat up as much as my body allowed. "So, I guess this won't turn me into one of these Cruor things? Most people would freak out about that, too, just so you know."

"Adrian won't bite you. He's very controlled."

While Ivory might be willing to trust him with *her* life, I didn't exactly share her sentiments. I barely knew him. But even though I wished to fight the offer, something stronger and unnatural urged me to accept. Emotions out of my control smothered my desires, and before I could stop them, the traitorous words tumbled from my lips.

"Just tell me what to do so we can get this over with." Part of me fought against what I was saying, but I was on autopilot, a dial turned to someone else's settings.

"Relax." Adrian crossed the room, and Ivory stood to allow him her spot next to the bed. He pulled back his cascade of neatly woven dreadlocks, revealing striking eyes so dark they were almost black.

His fangs extended, and he lifted his wrist to his mouth. Visions from the night before flashed through my thoughts. I took a deep, shuddering breath as Adrian's teeth crunched into his flesh. Blood seeped out, and, as his wrist inched closer, I turned away.

He cradled my head with his other hand. "Try thinking of something else."

My stomach churned—*I can't be doing this*—but the cooling sensation in my mind strengthened. I wanted to fight the warmth that followed, but my body melted into a calm, as if I was being carried along by a slow-moving river. The panic fled, but my thoughts remained. *Don't do this.* I opened my mouth to protest.

Adrian thrust his wrist against my mouth. "Drink."

Cold, thick fluid gushed into my mouth. I pushed feebly on his arm, trying not to swallow, but I had to choke down some of the blood in order to breathe. The whispers and hissing in my mind faded, as though suffocating in a glass coffin, until finally they vanished. Until I only *felt* them, like a pulse, present but silent.

A small surge of strength awakened in me, and with it came the desire to drink. Adrian's blood was sweeter than I expected—like blackberries, but also like dirt—and the pain dispersed enough for me to take hold of his arm.

"Easy, girl," Adrian said, but the sensation urged me to continue. "Enough!"

Charles jumped to his feet. He leaned toward Adrian, as though ready to pounce. "Adrian!"

Adrian jerked his wrist from my mouth. The puncture wounds on his wrist closed in mere seconds. I blinked, the simple action like the snap of a camera aperture.

This can't be happening.

"Sorry." My voice floated on the air with a strange, smooth lilt.

"No apologies necessary." Adrian's tone softened. He backed up to the other side of the room. "It hurts giving blood to a human."

Human. My thoughts rattled around the word. How could there be anything else?

The blood left a salty, metallic coating on my tongue, and my stomach bubbled. "I can't believe—"

"You are in no place to avoid this reality," Adrian said.

Ivory dropped her gaze.

"What's wrong?" I asked.

"Adrian had to . . . use his influence. You wouldn't have cooperated otherwise."

"His influence?"

"Influence is what nearly got you killed in the first place." Adrian interlocked his fingers and stretched his arms up. Each knuckle cracked and every joint popped, the volume of the movement strangely loud and distinct in my ears. "Marcus had you before you even left the club. How you resisted is a mystery in itself. You are lucky whomever he sent after you wasn't stronger. It is a testament to your own strength that you fought as much as you did."

The aching in my wrist ebbed, and I crossed my arms with a surprising ease. "You're suggesting mind control?"

"The Cruor—especially those who've transcended many centuries—can push into the human mind and control emotions or plant thoughts. They can also track humans, either by scent or by sensing their location through a sensitivity to heat that acts as thermo-receptor."

"Thermo-receptor?"

"A thermo-receptor is—"

"I know what it is. It just sounds like a load of crap. If they are stronger than humans, and apparently see heat waves through trees"— I flicked my gaze upward—"why would they need influence?"

"If the victim is awake when captured, the influence will keep them in a state of calm, controlled by the Cruor until the bite releases its venom and mutates the human's blood. It can also be used to lure their prey. Without influence, the process is exceedingly more difficult, as some humans are not as easy to track. Same can be said of animals."

I sat upright and explored my wrist from every angle. Bruising remained, but nothing more. I looked at Adrian, a glimmer of trust rushing through my veins. Fear and disgust, however, would not be so easily kept at bay.

"This is all pretty fucked up. Killing other people to live?" The words were leaving my mouth, and the questions were being answered, but none of it felt real. Could I deny what I'd seen with my own eyes?

"You confuse opinion with truth. Many of us control our impulse for blood. We are more in danger from your kind than you are from ours. What do you think humans would do if they knew of elementals?"

"Apparently bring their friends to your underground clubs." I shot Ivory a glance, but immediately regretted doing so when I saw the pure remorse weighing on her features.

"I understand you are afraid," Adrian said, "but we must ensure no one else learns of your exposure to the Cruor. Your life would be in danger."

I flexed my wrist. The pain was all but gone, along with the swelling. Everything came into sharp focus. "I thought you said there was no real danger in knowing?"

"It is true the more recent laws protect your kind from ours," Adrian said, "but the laws commanding they not kill humans are meant to protect *them,* no one else. Anyone who learns their secret may be turned or killed. Especially if they are of interest or threat."

"What's the point? Even if they said something, no one would believe them."

"Under no circumstance are you to say anything. It's bad enough you've drawn attention to yourself—you wouldn't want anything to happen to your friends or family." Adrian's hand cupped the doorknob, gripping it so tightly his fingernails somehow dug into the tarnished metal. "As for a 'point'? There is none. It is only an excuse."

I turned to Ivory. "How is my life in danger, but not yours? You've known longer than I have."

"Marcus has shown an interest in you."

"Maybe I can borrow your aura," I mumbled. "I don't understand, Ivory. Why would you hang around people who can control your mind or kill you on impulse?"

"Please," Ivory said, her voice pleading. "You cannot judge an entire race of elementals on a few bad of their kind. These are the people who have been there for me since . . . since . . . "

Tears welled in her eyes, and I swallowed. Her lover had been murdered. That was why she'd moved to Colorado. Now she was flirting with danger, unless, like she said, not all Cruor were bad. Adrian *had* saved me and healed my wounds. Even if he still looked like he wanted to eat me, he was clearly nothing like Marcus and Marcus' companions.

Of all people, I should've known not to get all judgmental, but life had a funny way of showing me what a hypocrite I was on a regular basis.

Either way, I didn't need acceptance so badly as to befriend the Cruor. Not that they came across very friendly to begin with.

Adrian released a heavy sigh. "Marcus has strong ties with the Maltorim. It's best if none of you return to Club Flesh."

Don't need to tell me twice.

Ivory nodded. "You can't repeat any of this to anyone—not even Lauren."

The whole, 'with great knowledge comes great responsibility' crap. Except the last thing I wanted was more responsibility.

Charles pressed his hands onto his knees and stood. "Adrian and I ought to get going."

"Not so fast," I said, and not entirely because I wanted to stare at his gorgeous face a little longer. "I have a lot of questions to ask *you*."

"I would rather you didn't," Charles replied.

I raised my eyebrows. "You don't think I deserve at least that much?"

Without a word of response, he bowed to kiss my hand, his lips smooth and warm against my skin. The mauve of his lips, hinting at tones of cognac, only made his eyes seem all the more deep teal. I couldn't break my gaze from his face. Those lips were perfect—full, soft . . . kissable. But sexy lips wouldn't excuse him from leaving me to be attacked. He could have taken me with him when he went for help.

Now here he was, moving about so calmly, so confidently, as though he'd done nothing wrong. That alone rendered my attraction to him irrelevant.

Ivory glared in his direction, and he gave a small dip of his head. "Goodbye for now, Sophia."

"Bye," I whispered, too stunned by the severity of his gaze to press him any further. I turned to Adrian. "Thanks for . . . well, thank you."

Adrian saluted us. "Take care, Miss Sophia. Miss Ivory."

As Charles passed Ivory on the way out the door, he grabbed her arm. "She deserves to know."

Ivory pulled free and narrowed her eyes. "I'll tell her everything," she said. "Anything to keep her safe."

{eight}

MORNING ARRIVED within an hour of the men's departure. The sun glinted through the bedroom window, magnifying heat on my face. I rolled away.

"You look much better," Ivory said from the bedside. "Would anything else help?"

I circled my wrist before pushing myself to my feet. "A shower?" *And about a hundred more questions answered.*

Did my aura—or lack thereof—have something to do with my curse? Or was I just a vessel for all things horrid and unexplainable?

"Follow me." Ivory led me down the hall, the carpet in her old home worn but comforting. "I dropped by your house while you slept and picked up a few things. Hope you don't mind."

"That's why I gave you the spare key."

Actually, when I'd given her the key, it wasn't so she could pick up clothes for me if I lost my purse while being attacked by vampire-like creatures in the woods behind a supernatural club.

Ivory retrieved two towels from the hall closet. "These are wicked soft."

The towels blurred somewhere beyond the sudden vision clouding my gaze. A dead bear. Then . . . darkness. Fur pressed to my nose, my forehead. Well, not mine, but whoever owned the vision.

The vision tilted back, panning across the carcass to the top of someone's head of dark hair and their hunched shoulders, their face buried against the blood-matted fur. Blood smeared over dark-skinned hands, and a familiar ring with a large scripted 'A' I'd seen only hours before hugged a finger on one hand.

Adrian.

The images faded, and Ivory's towels filled my sight. Egyptian cotton, cinnamon red, according to the tag. I would have called the color *rust*. I opened my mouth to say something about the vision, but since I didn't know whether it might be related to my curse, it was probably best to keep quiet.

Ivory opened the bathroom door. "It's not much," she said, flipping on the bathroom light. "Shampoo, conditioner, soap—all that stuff is in a shower caddy. Holler if you need anything."

She shut the door, and I jumped at the volume of the click. I set the towels on top of the bag of clothing she'd left on the toilet seat lid. A pale yellow decorative towel hung over a bar on the wall, lace trim fluttering around the hem, and the flames of lit candles on the vanity flickered in the vanilla-scented draft.

The bathroom light created a sudden pulsing pain in the front of my head. Once in the shower, hot water pelted against my skin, and the body wash surrounded me with the scent of wisteria petals, fresh melon, and cherry blossoms, layered over base notes of coconut and vanilla.

My senses were in overdrive, and the silence in my mind felt unnatural, almost uncomfortable. A pulsing but painless throb. It wasn't truly peace. The noise had merely been locked away in a soundproof room where it pounded its fists on the walls, trying to burst out again.

Had Adrian's blood silenced the noise? Could his blood also cause me to see flashes of his memories?

How was I supposed to make sense of the last twenty-four hours? That Ivory had kept this from me for so long created a distance between us, yet knowing the same secret also brought us closer together. Who was I to judge? I had secrets, too.

After I rinsed the shampoo from my hair, I stepped out, wrapped myself in a towel, and turned the faucet off. Just then, another image flashed into my mind. This one was faster. A mausoleum in a cemetery. Adrian's hand lifting to wipe a tear, his gold ring swiping against his eyelashes. The images vanished.

Shaking, I huffed and fumbled for my clothes. My hips ached as I pulled on my khaki skirt, and I looked down to examine the cause. Four tiny bruises stacked above each hip.

Oh.

A soft gasp escaped my lips as realization set in: the tiny, barely-there bruises must have been from the dig of Charles' fingers as we danced. Had his grip been that strong? How hadn't I noticed?

Thinking of his hands there again sent a shiver blazing down my spine, and I had to force myself to push away the betraying sensation.

I pulled on the sky-blue cashmere sweater Lauren had given me last Christmas and tugged on my chocolate Eskimo boots. Maybe I could get some answers from Ivory without being too direct.

Back in her room, Ivory was folding down the top of her comforter, which looked like burnt wood against her bone-white sheets. The room smelled of clean linen and the soap I'd used, but strangely, the room carried another scent. One I recognized to be Ivory, though I'd never noticed the scent before. Kind of like watermelon candy and something heavier. Loneliness? Could a person smell lonely?

My head was probably playing tricks on me due to knowledge of her past. She'd never told me the details, but one night in my college dorm room, she shared with me that her lover had been murdered. I saw her in a new light after that. A light I couldn't share with Lauren, even though it might help her understand why Ivory was a little rough around the edges.

I flopped onto Ivory's bed and stared at the henna design on the ceiling. "Where'd you find that body wash?"

She leaned against the bed. "The dollar store." She laughed. "It's nothing special. The Cruor blood is assaulting your senses. Usually that side-effect fades within a few hours."

"You've drank it before?"

"Once or twice." She patted the comforter. "Come sit. I'll brush your hair."

I sat up and hugged one of her throw pillows to my stomach, and she sat close behind with her legs tucked under her.

I clicked my tongue, quickly replaying Charles' parting exchange with her. "What were you going to tell me . . . you know, when you told Charles you'd tell me everything?"

She grabbed a hairbrush from the side table drawer. "You'll need to know a few things," she said. "About fighting the Cruor."

"I don't plan on running into them again."

"Did you plan on running into them the first time?" She pulled the brush's soft bristles through my hair and then leaned over one of my shoulders. "Staking, decapitation, and burning. That should cover it. Pretty self-explanatory."

"Forgive me if I don't share your enthusiasm. I'm still trying to come to terms with how this is real, yet people don't know."

Ivory parted my hair with her fingernail and brushed the ends on one side, flattening my curls. "You remember Mr. Petrenko?"

My heart stuttered at hearing his name spoken aloud. Spoken outside my own thoughts. "Mr.—Mr. Petrenko?"

"Yeah. Read about him in the news when I was in high school. I think the whole country heard. Surely you know all about it. You lived here when it happened. It was the media-mystery of the century! Who's dead body is found surrounded by so much of their own blood, without a single wound on their body? People *still* talk about his murder."

Some people still thought about it, too. Thought about how he'd been standing outside with a cigarette burning down between his fingers, smoke billowing from his mouth as though he were breathing into the cold, while they snuck into his store to fill a large paper bag with food.

I'd known stealing was illegal. I wanted to feed the runaway girl I'd met down by the tracks. Get her help. I couldn't have stolen from Mother's cupboard or asked even asked her for the money. I feared Mother might try to 'help' that girl in all the wrong ways. Mother might not consider the girl's situation. The abuse. The girl's stepfather, and the things he'd done. But none of those things excused my actions.

As I'd been sneaking out the back near the dumpsters, Mr. Petrenko saw me. He hollered and started after me, but then he was bleeding, and thoughts were tumbling in my mind—*You have to die, you have to die, you have to die*—and I told myself those couldn't be my thoughts, but then he was dead on the ground and it was only me in that parking lot.

I don't know what happened. I just know I didn't kill him.

I couldn't have.

I swallowed and forced myself to speak. "Murdered in front of his own store. I doubt anyone will forget."

"People don't notice the Cruor because they don't believe in them. They've never seen them, or, if they have, they know to keep their mouths shut." She started to brush the other side of my hair. "You'd be wise to do the same."

"Are you saying a Cruor killed Mr. Petrenko?"

"As good a guess as any."

"Why didn't he have any wounds?" I asked, though I knew that wasn't true. He'd had them, at least when I'd seen him die. They were just gone by the time the cops arrived.

"Alls I know is, Adrian's blood healed you. His own wrist healed in mere moments. You saw, right? Well, they can also seal smaller wounds with their saliva. Small wounds . . . like punctures to the main artery in the neck."

"How can you be sure? It could have been—" Been what? A human? Me? I'd been there, and I hadn't seen him killed by any Cruor. I hadn't seen what killed him, or who. I'd just seen him alive one second and dead the next.

"Can't say for sure." She smoothed long strands of hair away from my face. The brush scraped through my shirt and snagged on my bra strap. I winced, and Ivory eased up. "But isn't it strange?"

I guess she hadn't heard I'd been there when it happened. I'd never talked to her about it. Heck, she didn't even know about how my mom died. Ivory was a private person, and maybe that was why she never asked many questions.

Across the room, a beaded lamp with fringe the color of paprika dimmed. One of the tassels swayed, as though a breeze had passed through. Pinpricks of cold spotted up my arm and neck, but when I blinked again, the tassel had stilled. I forced myself back to conversation, making an effort to keep my tone light.

I couldn't talk about Mr. Petrenko anymore, but silence would make my discomfort too obvious. Thankfully I wasn't lacking in the things-to-say department.

"Does Charles always stalk people?" I asked.

"Charles? Stalk people?" Ivory let out a bark of laughter. She combed her fingers through my hair a few times, springing my curls back to life. "Why would you even ask?"

"I saw him outside my window one night. Then again at the woods."

"I found you by the woods, too. Do you think *I'm* stalking you?"

Okay, so I was a paranoid, self-absorbed idiot. But I was *also* cautious.

"Ivory, do you believe one person's life can be closely tied to another's?"

"I do." She stopped brushing, and I turned to face her. She was frowning. "This about Charles?"

"I'm not sure. But for a stranger, he's been popping up in my life a lot. And at the strangest times."

"You like him?"

"After last night . . . " I shrugged, trying to hide the hurt that confusion and uncertainty were pressing into my chest. "I still don't know why he left me. I could have gone with him to get help."

Ivory sighed, shifting her gaze out the window. "You'll have to ask him, then."

I turned around, and Ivory resumed brushing in silence. We shared a secret now. If the Cruor trusted her with their secrets, then I could trust her with mine. I could tell her about the voices.

"About the whole Cruor-thing." My hands were shaking, but I held them tight in my lap, doing little more than causing my shoulders to tremble instead.

"I said I'm sorry. You need to understand why I didn't tell you. And don't just *say* you do, because you need to keep it a secret for the same reasons."

"I do understand. There's something I've been keeping from you, too."

"There . . . is?" She nearly stumbled over the two words, her voice smaller than usual.

The Cruor's existence defied explanation, just like my curse. Ivory might be the only one who would understand. The only one who might accept me even knowing about the voices. "Remember the positive energy ritual I told you about? A few weeks back?"

She nodded.

"Well, ever since, I've been hearing these voices—"

The hairbrush paused. Ivory's voice came out clipped and quiet. "What kind of voices?"

I shouldn't have said anything. Obviously feeding on blood was fine. Seeing auras was acceptable. But no matter what 'world' you lived in, hearing voices meant you were crazy.

"Nothing," I said, closing my eyes against the hurt. "Anyway, they're gone now. Probably just stress or something."

"Maybe." She dropped the brush on the bed. "We should get you home."

☪

ON THE RIDE HOME, we passed yards of grass covered in frost. A finger unable to move less than three hours ago flicked the car lock back and forth with ease. How powerful was Cruor blood? Could it cure cancer?

"Will you be there for Samhain?" I asked, blurting the first thing that came to mind. Blurting anything, really, that might break the silence between us. Though the Sabbat was still nearly two months away, it was present in my mind as the best chance to speak directly with my ancestor's spirit. I hadn't given up on that, even if the voices were on vacation.

"Sure." Ivory's eyes didn't break from the road.

"Ivory—"

"I said I will. Okay?" She pulled in front of my house. Her hands gripped the steering wheel, eyes straight ahead.

With Ivory not bothering to look at me, I felt as though she'd already driven away. "You gonna tell me what's wrong?"

"What's the point?"

"Ivory, it's not like you weren't keeping something from me, too."

Her eyes watered, and her jaw tensed. "I knew someone who heard voices." Her face swung toward me, her expression full of a hate and anger I couldn't place and couldn't bring myself to ask her about. The raw emotion made me flinch.

"I—I'm sorry." I swallowed, but my mouth and throat only became drier. "Are they okay now?"

"They're dead. So what do you think?"

I didn't know what else to say. "I guess I'd . . . better get going. See you soon?"

"Yeah, see you."

As soon as I stepped out of her car, she tore off down the road. I was an idiot. No matter how close I was to anyone, no matter what secrets they shared with me, I'd be foolish to think they'd accept my problems.

My breath formed clouds in the air. It'd gotten cold so fast. Too cold for mid-September. This would be one of Colorado's early winters. And, with the way things were going, one of the loneliest.

Pushing my emotions away, I faced my house. Another flash of Adrian's life played before my eyes: a dual grave arrangement. The image cut off before revealing the names on the headstones. Something in my head *popped,* and a pressure on my mind released.

Please let that be the end of that.

As I opened the front door and hung my coat in the closet, Red chirped, bringing a smile to my face but somehow making me sadder at the same time. I headed to the kitchen, where my yellow, pink, and purple lupines wilted in their vase on the windowsill from too much sun and not enough water. It felt like weeks had passed since I'd been home, but it hadn't even been twenty-four hours.

"I haven't forgotten you," I said to my little cardinal. "You need fresh water."

After refilling Red's tray, I headed to my bedroom. All the thoughts and feelings I'd been avoiding charged at me. How many people knew about the Cruor? How many people had died at their hands?

I plopped down on my bed and stared at the ceiling. Dust piled like dark clouds on the blades of the motionless fan above, but instead of grabbing some cleaner and a rag, I just stared, wondering at the intensity of the stale odor the dust created in my room.

Being Wiccan, I believed in the energy of the earth, of the gods and goddesses . . . but vampire-like creatures? It wasn't as though being Wiccan was synonymous with believing in things such as UFOs or thinking Elvis was still alive. Having faith in one thing didn't mean I had to have faith in *everything.*

Yet, what choice did I have? Today I'd learned vampires *were* real. There was no erasing that—no ignoring what Adrian had proven to me only hours earlier.

With a sudden burst of energy, I darted across my room to grab my Book of Shadows. I gripped it tightly, staring at the brown leather and the black, scripted letters and the pentacle's imprint on the front cover. I flipped through to a blank page, took my black ink pen, and, trying to stop my hands from shaking, transcribed all I'd learned onto the parchment.

Cruor: Also known as 'Earth elementals'. Vampire-like creatures sent by the 'Universe' to protect humans. Something went wrong. They live by feeding on human blood and have mind-control powers. Their blood heals injury and disease. Can be killed by staking, decapitation, or exposure to sunlight.

Influence: What Cruor call their mind-control powers.

The Maltorim: The elemental council.

I shut my book, closed my eyes, and took a deep breath. Great. I knew more about their world than most people, but still had no answers about my ancestor.

Though the noise was gone from my mind, the empty space where it'd once been thrummed against my skull. I couldn't give up on my ancestor. I would have to look into the book's previous owners of the book Paloma gifted me. I'd run a search on the address after sleeping away the sickness roiling in my stomach over everything I'd learned.

When I finally drifted to sleep, the nightmares returned: Elizabeth's court document tumbling in a cold breeze through the dirt roads of a Puritan settlement. A noose cutting into her neck. My ancestor kicking her legs and digging her nails against the rope, looking around for someone—anyone—but the town was quiet. Then people started gathering, shuffling with empty eyes and sluggish steps.

They'd come to watch her die.

They smiled, and moonlight glinted off their fangs.

Elizabeth's thoughts whispered on the breeze: *Don't tell a soul, Sophia. Don't tell anyone of our curse.*

But the warning had come too late.

{nine}

I AWOKE to dawn's russet sky—a shepherd's warning, some said.

I shook away the eerie fog of sleep by refreshing myself with a dose of reality: people's hands were bound during hanging. My nightmare wasn't real, or even reasonable for that matter.

Yesterday, though, was *not* just a bad dream.

Green electric numbers glared at me from the alarm clock on my dresser: 6:17 am. I glared back. I'd slept straight through the day and night.

Once out of bed, I stared into my open closet. Dress pants or jeans? Jack wouldn't care if I wore jeans to work. Some of the girls never wore uniform pants.

Since when did I care?

I settled for a boho casual look: an earthy brown, cream, and green-toned mandala print top with small touches of peacock-blue and a gathered keyhole neckline. I'd never worn it before. Not wanting to hunt down the scissors, I took the tags off with my teeth. I paired the shirt with medium-wash blue jeans tucked into my Eskimo boots.

The full-length mirror mounted to the back of my bedroom door revealed no visible traces of the attack. I grabbed a hair tie off the doorknob. With the elastic in my mouth and my hands pulling my hair back, I changed my mind. Maybe I should leave my hair down. For me. Not at all because I was hoping to run into anyone. Especially not Charles.

I bustled into the kitchen and made myself a quick breakfast of toast and orange marmalade with a glass of milk.

Red chirped from the corner of the kitchen. After I changed his food and water, I slung my workbag over my shoulder and started out the door for Jack's, but when I spotted the note taped to the inside of my front door, I froze, hand hesitating on the doorknob.

My gaze dropped to the signature first. The note was signed, *Yours Truly, Marcus.*

Heart slamming against my chest, my eyes shot up to the words above.

> *So lovely to meet you, Sophia. Such a shame about*
> *your parents, your father especially. Do not let*
> *curiosity blind you as it did him. I do hope our paths*
> *cross again one day soon.*

I yanked the note from the door, shredded it with my hands, and threw it in the trash. My heart pounded in my ears as I ran, shaking, to my Jeep. What the hell was that creep doing in my house? How did he know where I lived? How did he know about my dad, or perhaps more importantly *what* did he know about him?

What if he'd done something to me while I'd been sleeping? I swallowed, then pressed my hands against my neck and slid them over my arms. I'd feel different. I'd know, somehow. I would have to know.

I needed a way to protect myself. Ivory's suggestions were useless if the Cruor could break into my home without my knowing. I sped to the diner, flipping open my cell as I drove.

Come on, Ivory . . . pick up. Come on, come on.

After two rings, the call shot over to voice mail. Great. She wasn't taking my calls. I hung up, my hands still shaking. I considered calling out of work, but I had nowhere else to go—not with these problems, not if Ivory was avoiding me. At the very least, I would surround myself with people until I could get in touch with someone who might help.

☪

MAIN STREET was one of the few streets in my town with parking slots in front of the shops. I usually sat in my Jeep for a few minutes before going into work, staring at the bold lettering of Jack's light-up sign. At night, the sign read, 'Jak's Dine', thanks to the dead bulbs Jack never replaced. Today I would tell Jack I couldn't work night shift for a while. He wouldn't mind. He almost never put me on the night shift anyway.

When I arrived, Charles was parked nearby, leaning against a blue Toyota Prius. Earth-friendly, at least. I'd give him that. His eyes seemed more alert today, his dark tousled hair slightly less erratic. The sun and shadows on his face sharpened the lines of his jaw and nose, and his heather-grey, short-sleeve shirt revealed the contours of the muscles in his arms.

Flutters started in my stomach, and a strange sensation rushed into my lungs. I shouldn't be happy to see him. I certainly wasn't surprised. Just nervous, in that breathless, pulse-drumming kind of way. The kind of way that probably indicated something other than a dash of hope he might help me deal with Marcus.

I raised my chin and straightened my shoulders, as if that alone would make me seem confident. I needed to push this attraction away. Far, far away. The last thing I needed was another person to hide my secrets from, especially someone who had abandoned me when I was in danger. I needed to focus solely on getting some helpful information.

I hopped out of my Jeep and locked the doors. Turning toward the restaurant, I found Charles standing only a breath away, his scent of vanilla, musk, and sandalwood immediately hitting me at my core. My heart thrummed. I stepped back, hoping to put more distance between us, but my back was met swiftly with my car door. He exhaled, warm air caressing my cheek and sending shivers over my body.

"Could you . . . give me a minute?" *Or at least some space.* I stepped around him before turning back to face him again—this time with my back to the diner, so I couldn't get trapped. "Aren't you cold?"

"No."

Huh. "So . . . you came to my work . . . ."

"You said I'd find you here, remember?"

"Yep. I'm here. This is where I work, so I come here sometimes. For work." *Shut up, Sophia.*

He tossed a half-sneer toward my Jeep. "That thing yours?"

"Is that a problem?"

"I'm sure the ozone is none-too-thrilled." He scrutinized me, and his lips softened into a secretive smile. "You're all dressed up. Special occasion?"

"None that I know of." I would never achieve a normal heart rate in his company. Surely he wasn't implying I'd gotten dressed up for his benefit, even if it were true.

He lifted his finger to my lips, and heat rushed to my cheeks.

What the hell was he doing?

His eyes searched mine, his gaze so unrelenting I had to remind myself to breathe. The heat spread to my ears, my insides trembled, and the fresh pull of oxygen did nothing to cure the lightheaded feeling. I hoped none of this was visible, as I could think of only one thing worse than being attracted to Charles, and that was him knowing it.

As he grazed my lip with his finger, a minty scent filled the air between us, and his thoughtful expression turned into a chuckle.

"Toothpaste," he said.

Mortifying.

At least now I wouldn't walk around all day with toothpaste crusted to my face. Though that might have been better than *him* mentioning it. Not that I cared what he thought, because I was definitely telling myself I didn't.

I started to walk away, but his voice stopped me.

"I didn't wish to come here."

I spun toward him, hands clenched. "Of course not."

"I mean no offense," he said, in the same way everyone did before saying something offensive. "I'm certain you're a very nice girl, but I've come only to give the explanation I promised. I am a man of my word."

A very nice girl. "What makes you think—"

"Don't bother," he said, giving me a cutting look. "I can offer you nothing more than this. If you're not interested, that is fine. Perhaps even better for us both."

"I'm interested," I said. "But now's not a good time."

He looked to the sky and squinted, the sun highlighting his bright eyes and dark lashes, then his gaze dropped to mine. "You've experienced something most people never will."

"Lucky me."

He grinned. "Did you just roll your eyes?"

"Did I?" Heat gathered in my cheeks.

A light breeze lifted the gentle curls that nearly tumbled into his eyes. Damn him for looking good.

"You appear to have recovered well from last night's events," he said.

As if I needed the reminder. "Look, I have a lot on my mind. Marcus was in my house last night and—"

Charles stepped forward suddenly, and I leaned away from his advance.

"Marcus was in your house?" he asked. All his carelessness fell away in that moment, and, in its place, I simply saw a man. A very *concerned* man. "Did he—did anything happen?"

"He left a note. Said he hopes we meet again, or something."

Charles' shoulders visibly relaxed. "He wants you on your terms. Perhaps he had nothing to do with Cody coming after you. Do you have to work today?"

"Yes." I didn't really, but I desperately needed to be busy. Needed something to ground me in my *own* world, however crappy my world might have been. Plus there was that whole bill collectors wanting to get paid thing.

"Well, he won't come here. We'll figure something out before nightfall."

"So now you want to help me? I thought you just wanted to give me some answers and be done with me."

Charles' jaw tensed. "Is that what you'd prefer?"

"No, but—"

"I don't wish to be 'done with you'."

I raised an eyebrow. "Back to Marcus," I said, my words jolting the tender look from his eyes. "Would he send someone else? Since apparently humans like to help these people out?"

"If he'd wanted, he would have taken you last night."

"Comforting."

Charles scowled. "Regardless, most humans don't help in *that* way," he said, slipping back into his know-it-all tone. "He wouldn't hire a human to do something he could take care of himself."

"I'm not something to be 'taken care of'," I said sharply.

With a low chuckle, he stepped closer. "That's debatable," he said. "Try to stay in one piece until I return. I'll meet you for coffee after your shift."

Attempting not to sound enthused, I offered a non-committal, "Okay."

"What time?" he asked.

"Shift's over at four."

"Perfect." He smiled. "It's a date."

"It's not a date," I said. "It's coffee."

I turned and headed into the diner. Coffee. And, more importantly, *answers*.

Not a date.

☪

THE BREAKFAST CROWD THINNED. This would be the only lull in my day—my one chance to catch a breather and spend some time by myself. My eleven AM 'lunch' break.

As I started for the backroom computer to see if anything came up on the Internet for that Basker Street address, a voice called across the diner.

"Hey! Sophia!" I'd recognize that voice anywhere. Lauren. Exactly what I needed right now: a human exclamation point.

I turned around. She was sitting at table six, one of her Japanese street wear magazines open in front of her. She'd started reading those when she began studying Japanese, hoping one day she would know enough to fly across the Pacific and confront the relatives that had shunned her as a child.

I hadn't seen her in forever. So long, in fact, that her black hair had grown from a short pixie cut to fall in layers of satin around her shoulders. Hot pink headphones draped over her neck, flattening her silky strands. California hadn't changed her olive complexion, and she apparently still had an affinity for mascara and lip-gloss.

At any other time, seeing her would have lightened my mood, but right now, her timing sucked. Just last night, I'd officially been shoved from one world into the next. A world she was not a part of.

I headed over to the booth, and she wrapped me in a tight hug, holding a Styrofoam cup behind my back. She pushed back to hold me at arm's length. "I cannot *believe* you didn't call me when I got to town!"

"Are you kidding? I've called four times and left a message last week." I sat, and Lauren reseated herself across from me.

"You could've stopped by," she said. "You made time for Ivory, which I expect you to tell me all about." Her bottom lip, full and creased down the middle, stuck out in a fake pout. "Who was that cute guy you were talking to this morning?"

Inwardly, I groaned, but for Lauren's sake, I let out some uneasy laughter. "You saw him?"

"On my way to pay the water bill." She sipped her soda directly from the cup, the tip of the straw already chewed shut. "So, is he as gorgeous up close as he is from across the street?"

"I didn't see him from across the street, so it's impossible to compare."

"You know, it wouldn't be the end of the world to say you saw a cute guy."

I tried to look super busy with the napkin holder. "I sort of know him."

"What? How?" She set down her drink and gave me her best 'serious' look. "What kind of *sort of knowing* are we talking about here?"

"Not *that* kind." I might have rolled my eyes, since I apparently did that sometimes. "We met at the club, through Ivory."

"I knew I should have tagged along! Ivory said you were going, but I don't like to stick my chin where it isn't welcome."

I managed a smile. "Stick your nose."

"That's what they say. So, is that what this is all about?" she asked, reaching out and touching my curls. "I almost didn't recognize you with your hair down." Her chocolate brown eyes shifted from one side of my face to the other, and she held up her hand before I could reply. "It is, isn't it? It's this mystery guy you're dying to tell me about. Oh my God! That's why you've been MIA!"

"Charles is not why I've been 'MIA'."

"Charles?" Lauren asked. "Now there's a sexy name! Well, out with it. You have to give me the spoon!"

The scoop. I slipped around to the other side of the booth. "Let me get my lunch first."

I hated keeping secrets from Lauren, but I didn't have much choice.

Jack swooped by the table with Lauren's previously-ordered salad. He stood at the end of the table, pencil tucked behind one ear. I never understood why he carried a pencil around, since he never wrote down anyone's orders. "You ordering, Sophia?"

"I'll get it," I said. The diner was short-staffed enough, with Jack having to tend the tables while I took my lunch.

"Do I need to redefine 'break' for you?" Jack winked.

Not being hungry, I opted for a strawberry milkshake and thanked him before he hurried back to the kitchen.

Lauren leaned closer. "Sooo? Are you going to spill the rice about your big, mysterious night out?"

"I hate to disappoint you, but there isn't much to tell." *Other than that whole 'almost killed by a Cruor' thing.*

"Well, which club did you go to?" Lauren kept her eyes on me as Jack breezed by the table, dropping off my milkshake.

I smiled my thanks to him and returned my attention to Lauren. "Which club?" I repeated. I cleared my throat. "Oh, some club in Denver. Hush, or something."

"Hush?" she asked, shaking pepper onto her salad. "I can't believe *you* went to Hush."

"Well, believe it, because I did."

Actually, I'd never been to Hush. I felt terrible about all this lying I'd been doing lately. I couldn't even blame my parents, because Mother had never lied on purpose.

Delusions don't count.

Growing up, Mother always encouraged me to tell the truth. *The truth will set you free*, she said, and she'd reinforced the idea by letting me off the hook for anything I did wrong, so long as I was honest about it.

But I still grew up to be a liar, even if I hated doing it. Whenever possible, I opted for evasion instead.

"You okay?" Lauren asked, concern-lines creasing her brow. "You look a little green."

I was starting to *feel* a little green. "I'm fine."

"So, this guy—er, Charles? You met him there?" As she spoke, she waved her fork around dangerously. "He doesn't look like the type that frequents Hush."

"Yep, he was there, I was there . . . we were both there."

"And?" Lauren crunched on a piece of iceberg lettuce and smiled. "Give me the details."

"We chatted for a bit, then I went back to Ivory's house."

"That's no fun." She impaled a cherry tomato. The salad was under attack. Or maybe I felt under attack from Lauren's barrage of questions. "When are you going to see him again?"

"Honestly, Lauren—it's nothing. We're just meeting for coffee. We aren't even friends."

"Then why are you two meeting for coffee?" she teased. "I should go with you. Make sure things don't get too serious."

Pins and needles tingled my fingers. I'd been gripping my milkshake the entire time without realizing, numbing my hand with pressure and cold. I sipped my drink and pushed the glass away—far away, to the land of ketchup and mustard bottles.

"I'll manage. Jack will still be around. I'll call you afterward."

Lauren must have sensed my discomfort, because she immediately dropped the subject and began talking about henna hair dye and organic nail polish.

I was glad for a friend who knew me well, but there was still something about me that neither of us knew:

I was a horrible judge of character.

{ten}

WITH SOME TIME LEFT before I planned to meet Charles, I ran a search for Basker Street on the break room computer—one of Jack's few modern-day indulgences.

Nothing at all.

Not one street by that name anywhere in the world. Not even some place in Indonesia or France or anything. Growling, I closed my search and stuffed my red work shirt and apron into my workbag, showing off the mandala print top I wore underneath.

When I returned to the main dining area, I spotted Charles seated in booth seven. The only other customers were paying their checks at the register.

Finally. Time for answers.

Charles stood and swept his arm toward the table. "Please, sit."

I obliged, cramming my bag and coat into the corner of the seat.

He slid back into the booth. "Ivory said she told you everything."

Good—right to the point. "She didn't say why you left me, but she told me more than enough."

He raised his eyebrows. "You don't seem surprised."

"I'm trying not to think about it," I said. "Why didn't you say you knew her?"

"I wasn't concerned with her while dancing with you." His gaze lifted, grazing over my body to settle on my face, and my stomach fluttered in response. He grinned. "You're blushing."

Thanks for pointing that out.

I picked a menu from behind the napkin holder and pretended to read, trying to ignore the increased warmth in my cheeks. "Hungry?"

"Sorry," he said, looking down to his own menu. "I wasn't trying to embarrass you. I thought if you were aware, you could stop."

"Stop blushing?"

"Stop thinking about me that way."

That was a bit straightforward. It wasn't like I *wanted* to be attracted to him. "Did you already order?"

"I was waiting for you." He turned to the hot beverages and side dish selections. "If I'm wrong, please, tell me otherwise."

So much for changing the subject. "I recall the attraction was mutual," I said with all the confidence I could muster. Which wasn't much.

He smirked, lifting his eyes to mine, and a shiver trembled down my spine, straight through to my toes. "That is not why I'm here," he said. "I'm here to ensure you receive whatever answers you need to get on with your life."

One of the new waitresses, Tina, walked up. She was dark-haired and all hips with a flat tummy. Everyone at the diner—customers and employees alike—loved her. She served two tall glasses of iced water with two straws. "Know what you want?"

She wasn't really asking *us*. Just him. Charles nodded toward me. "Ladies, first."

Tina's shoulders sagged as she turned to face me. "Well?"

Unable to think, I ordered coffee, then I started folding the straw for my water into a tiny plastic accordion—anything to get her questioning gaze off me. *I know! I don't drink coffee!* Everyone who worked at the diner for more than five minutes knew that. I was starting to think Jack had made it part of the training. *Over here, you'll find the silverware. And, if you look to the left, you'll see Sophia. She doesn't drink coffee.*

"I thought you don't—" she began.

"Coffee," I said firmly, glaring at her. No wonder people in town thought I was crazy.

With a shake of her head, she turned to Charles, who ordered his coffee in a tone of voice much lighter than the one he used with me.

When Tina was out of earshot, I lifted my gaze to Charles.

"About the other night . . . "

Charles plunked his straw into his water. "The less I tell you, the better."

Better for who? "You left me."

He placed one of his hands over both of mine. I'm sure he meant it to be calming, like trying to relax a child on the verge of a tantrum, but instead his touch sent tingles up my arms.

"I didn't leave," he said.

Tina returned, and Charles released my hands. She poured two fresh cups of coffee and set a dish of creamers between us. I tapped my foot under the table. *Hurry up!*

"Let me know if you need anything else." She waited expectantly, staring at Charles, who busied himself stirring his coffee.

"That's all," I said. "Thanks."

She continued staring at Charles, smiling. "Are you sure?"

He looked up. "We're fine, thank you."

She frowned and headed back to the kitchen.

At least I wasn't the only one hopelessly attracted to him.

Charles cleared his throat. "Sophia," he whispered. "Stop staring at that poor girl."

"Tina?" How was she a 'poor girl'?

"Why are you staring at her?"

"I wasn't. *She* was staring at *you*." I immediately regretted my catty remark.

Teal eyes, dark beneath the shadow of his tangled eyelashes, centered on me. A smile crept onto his face. "You're jealous."

"I'm not. I just . . . noticed."

"She doesn't hold a candle to you, if that makes you feel better."

I was *so* not talking to him about this. "This isn't why we're here."

"Of course it isn't." Something in his tone suggested he was mocking me.

He wrapped his hands around the ceramic mug and rubbed his thumb across its smooth surface. My gaze drifted to his forearm, to the way his muscles flexed each time he moved, but I forced my attention back to his face.

I needed to stay focused. "You were going to tell me about why you abandoned me in the woods."

"I didn't," he said. "I changed."

"You *changed?*" I lowered my voice to a harsh whisper. "What? Your clothes? *That's* your excuse? You better be joking."

"I'm an elemental." He spoke quietly enough. Even if anyone else had been in the diner, they wouldn't have heard.

Or had a clue what he was talking about.

I blinked and pulled back. "You're one of the *Cruor?*"

"I didn't say that," he snapped, but then his expression softened. "I'm a water elemental. Some refer to us as the Strigoi."

Earth elementals, water elementals . . . there had to be others, but the more I learned, the more I thought I'd be better off not knowing. I recalled the mythology books I'd read in high school, but I didn't remember them referring to the Strigoi as elementals.

"You turn into an owl and prey on infants?" I asked. "Their internal organs or whatever?"

Same thing, right?

"Sometimes we turn into owls, though it's the *Stryx* who transform into owls exclusively," he said. "Unfortunately, the Strigoi have somehow been tied in with the *Stryx* legends."

"So you prey on infants or not?"

"No. Not infants."

"Then what?"

"Animals."

"Infant animals?"

His gaze hardened. "Is this what you want to know?"

No. I *wanted* to know what happened to my ancestor and how to cure the whispering curse. Instead, I'd been thrown into a world of elementals.

I added several creamers to my mug until the coffee thinned and clouded. I swirled my spoon in the mug. Click. Clank. Swirl. Click. Clank. Swirl. *I'm not sitting in this booth I've wiped a hundred times, listening to a strange man tell me he can morph into an animal.*

I found my voice. "What else?"

Charles leaned back and gave the edge of the table a tap of his fingers. "What do you mean . . . *what else?*"

"I mean, what else exists? Santa Claus, the Easter bunny?"

He smiled from behind his mug and took another sip. "You're taking this better than I expected."

"I get that a lot. My 'time to panic' meter has always been out of whack." I stared into his eyes, but his gaze never wavered. "This doesn't explain why you left."

"I thought I could return in time, but when I got back, you were gone." He looked out the diner window and frowned. "You've asked enough questions now. It's not safe to know these things."

"It's not safe for me to not know, either," I said. The last moments of the attack whisked through my mind. "The . . . eagle?"

"If I had chased him off in time, we wouldn't be in this predicament."

"But a *bird?*"

"In our animal form, our attacks are more potent to their kind."

"So what took so long?" I asked.

"Shifting can take a while. Then I had to find you again." His jaw tightened. "You didn't stay where I left you."

"Forgive me for wanting to stay alive."

He nodded solemnly. "Everything happened quite quickly."

As my trembling hand stirred my coffee, I stared at the milky swirls. "I don't know what to say."

My logical mind didn't want to accept the revelation, but I would worry about making sense of everything later. Charles took the final sip of his coffee, then he reached across the table to still my hand. The clanking stopped. I lifted my gaze to meet his, and my nerves settled.

"I'm not going to say anything," I promised. *Not that anyone would believe me anyway.*

"I wouldn't have told you if I thought you would."

"So you trust me?" I asked. "Why? I don't trust you." I bit my lip, immediately regretting my blurted sentiments.

His grin slipped, and he shook his head. "You're a good person. You deserved to know."

"You don't know what kind of person I am." Why was I arguing? It's not like I wanted to convince him I was horrible.

"Sophia," he said, leveling his gaze at me. "This is part of who I am. As a Strigoi, I can read auras. You will not leave me quickly fooled."

"I don't *have* an aura, *re-mem-ber*?"

Charles raised his eyebrows at my immature over-enunciation. "All elementals have their gifts," he said. "The Strigoi's ability to read auras was intended to detect and hunt the corrupt Cruor. It's said those who don't have an aura come from a pure soul."

Seriously? I was a liar and a thief. How was that 'pure'? "If that's the case, then why did you think I was following you?"

"You could have been under Marcus' influence. Or starting down a bad path. I gave you the benefit of the doubt."

"So your kind hunts the corrupt Cruor. Does this mean you can get rid of Marcus?"

"We're *intended* to hunt them. We're not mindless robots. We haven't all become hunters."

"Can you get rid of him or not?"

"I understand your concerns, but no, I cannot 'get rid of him'. While it was inexcusable for him to break into your house, I have no authority to intervene. As it stands, the Cruor can't afford to draw any attention to themselves with menial tampering in humans' lives, and if I went after him, it would only make things worse for us both."

"I can't risk it," I said. "I need to do something. What can I do?"

"I suppose you will stay with me." He sighed wearily.

Gee, don't sound too enthused.

"I have a spare room," he continued, "and my location is safe. I would be right down the hall if you needed me."

"I can't," I said, partly because I barely knew him and partly because he obviously didn't want me to stay with him. "Are there any other options?"

His sharp gaze cut through me. "It wasn't a suggestion, Sophia. Unless you wish to further expose yourself to the unsavory of my kind, you will stay with me."

The idea crashed into me. My come-what-may attitude was being tested, but I refused to let Charles witness any weakness in me. "I can take care of myself."

"I will escort you to my home and gather your things," he said. "Now, why don't we get out of here? You've been here all day."

Just like that? He wanted to move on with the afternoon, as though he hadn't just tried to make my decisions for me? As though my whole world hadn't changed over the course of our conversation?

Things *had* changed. Like a flash flood in the canyons. It started as a thunderstorm, but the water rushed down from the high plains, quickly turning a three-foot creek into rampaging water. That was where I stood now. Right in the path of the oncoming torrent.

"By all means, don't make haste for my benefit," he said.

Fresh air *would* be better than dwelling on supernatural creatures. "Sure. Let's go."

While I slipped into my coat, Charles paid our bill. I left a couple dollars under my mug before meeting him over by the door. He placed his hand at the small of my back as he held the door open and ushered me outside, and my whole body warmed at his touch. The mixed signals—his as well as my own—were driving me crazy.

As soon as we were outside, his hand dropped away, and he rubbed his hands together against the cold afternoon air. Cars whooshed past, and, in an alley across the street, a garbage truck hoisted a dumpster.

We walked down a side street. Wind slapped my cheeks with scents of rusted metal and Cantonese takeout. Snow crunched beneath our feet, and the late September sunlight reflected so bright off the white sheet it made the day appear warmer than it was.

I glanced down the road, to the forest obstructing the mountains on the horizon.

"What were you doing in the Belle Meadow woods that night?" I asked.

"A couple of weeks ago?"

"Was there some other night?"

He focused on the middle distance as we walked. "I'm there a lot of nights. Hunting."

I dug my hands into my coat pockets. "Hunting?"

"You saw when you were leaving."

I shuddered, thinking of the lifeless animals strewn across the forest path. I slowed my steps. "You need blood? Like the Cruor?"

"Cruor can never eat human food. While the Strigoi can, we still need blood to survive."

My hands, hidden inside my coat pockets, trembled. Outwardly, I maintained my calm. "Gross."

"Without blood, we can't read auras to tell good from evil." He reached over and grazed the scar I'd gotten the night I found the animals in the woods.

"It's a necessity," he said, dropping his hand away again.

Something about the way his fingertips grazed my wrist sent a pulsing heat through my body, and before I realized what I'd done, I'd slipped my hand from my pocket. Part of me feared getting involved with him on any level, but another part of me craved the connection.

The back of my wrist brushed his, and he gently grasped my hand. We walked in silence for a moment, his hand loosely wrapped around mine. I could feel my hand slowly slipping away, and, when it did, he made no effort to take it again.

Tentatively, I grazed his knuckle with my pinky, and he smirked as he slipped his hand around mine once more.

"Don't get attached." He whispered the words so quietly, I didn't know if the words were meant for me or for himself.

"You okay?" I asked.

"Yes," he said, his voice more rigid than usual. "I just don't want you to expect anything from me."

Wow. Talk about blunt. I took my hand back. More than anything, I wanted to disappear. I told myself his words had only hurt my pride, but it was more than that.

"I don't expect anything from you," I said defensively.

"Good."

I wasn't sure why I cared, but I did. Why did he keep leading me on if he didn't want anything to do with me? "I better get going."

"We can go to my place now if you like. Perhaps you need some rest."

I glowered at him. "I don't need any rest, and I don't need your help."

Observing me like one might observe the clouds to determine if it might rain, he let out a sigh. "I hurt your feelings."

"No," I lied.

He frowned. "Hurting your feelings is exactly what I'm trying *not* to do."

Sure had me fooled. I shrugged one shoulder.

His eyes searched mine. "You can't trust your feelings right now. There's still a lot you don't know, about me or my world."

"So tell me."

"Look," he said gently, "I will make sure you're safe, but I can offer no more. I can't risk telling you everything."

"Forget it," I said, starting to walk away. "I don't need a babysitter."

He stepped behind me and closed his hands firmly over my hips. I froze, and his voice deepened to a low vibration in my ear. "Stop being childish, Sophia. There is no room for that in your life any longer."

My breath caught in my chest.

"Do not ask me any more questions about my world. I am not your enemy. We will leave for my home now."

"I don't need your help," I said again, fiercely angry now.

Who was he to tell me what to do, let alone *demand* I obey his every word? I threw his hands from my hips and stormed off, too infuriated to accept whatever protection he might be able to offer.

☪

IVORY HAD ALREADY TOLD ME what I needed to do if I encountered a Cruor. Staking, decapitation, and burning. I picked up everything I could need at the local hardware store and hurried home before darkness settled over Belle Meadow.

But once night fell, I sat up in bed with my knees tucked to my chest, too on edge to fall asleep. With all my worries tumbling through my mind, sleep didn't come until long after the moon stitched itself into the sky.

{eleven}

A SOFT TAPPING jarred me awake. I held my breath. Silence. I rolled over, and the noise sounded again—louder this time. My window? I rubbed my eyes and checked the clock on my dresser.

2:17 am.

As I stretched across my bed to pull the curtain aside, the glass pane rattled from the force of another knock. I flinched, and the edge of the drapes slipped from my grasp. Probably a branch from the overgrown bushes out front. Shaking my head, I peeked again.

A shadow filled the window frame. I opened my mouth to scream, but clamped it shut when I recognized Charles. I shot out of bed and opened the casement windows.

"What the hell are you doing here?"

"Nice to see you, too."

"Might have been if I wasn't sleeping."

His gaze touched over my body then back up to my face, and my heart thundered in my chest at the idea he was seeing me this way, dressed in nothing but a white tank top and sleep shorts. My face was surely all puffy, and my long blonde curls probably resembled something of Medusa's offspring.

I crossed my arms. "Are you spying on me?"

"You're not so interesting that I came to watch you sleep, darlin'," he said, leaning his hands on the windowsill. He dipped his face to meet my gaze. "I only came to check on you. Now admit it—you're glad I'm here."

I wasn't about to admit anything.

"It's two in the morning," I said, hoping to illuminate the oddity of him standing outside my room in the pitch black of night.

Charles arched an eyebrow. "Aren't you going to invite me in?"

"No."

I turned to find something to slip over my tank top, thinking I would meet him outside, but immediately spun back around. The last thing my already tattered reputation needed was my neighbors spotting a man outside my window at this hour.

"Just hurry and climb in before anyone sees you."

He obliged, closing the windows behind him, while I grabbed my organic terrycloth robe from the hook behind my door and slipped it on.

"Most people knock on doors," I said, turning around as I tied the belt of my robe tight around my waist.

"I tried. No one answered."

"Because I was sleeping. You know, that thing most people do at two in the morning?"

He didn't seem amused. He was too busy standing around with the poise of a male model, dressed in a tidy black shirt and fitted jeans that suggested no one had woken *him* unexpectedly.

In the dark, his strong jaw, deeply-colored teal eyes, and wide shoulders carried the same seductive heaviness as the night we'd danced at the club, and, in that moment, I craved him from my very core. Craved his hands on my hips, his body pressed to mine . . . I pushed the attraction away.

He reached up with one hand and touched my hair.

"I like it better down," he murmured, his hand lingering on my hair, grazing where my collarbone peeked out from my robe.

He brushed my cheekbone with his fingertips to move a loose tendril of hair away from my face. His touch rivaled my better judgment, and I wasn't entirely sure who would win out in the end. The moment was too intimate.

I stepped back. "Why should I care what you like?"

"I deserve that," he said, the expression on his face dissolving.

I nodded, though the small movement might not have been perceptible to him. "So what is so important that couldn't wait till tomorrow?"

"Your life."

"Pretty melodramatic, don't you think?"

"I apologize for being so overbearing earlier. I shouldn't have shown my concern in that way."

Yeah, he had been pretty damn bossy, but being concerned for another person wasn't exactly the *worst* trait a person could have.

I mumbled a silent, "It's okay."

He frowned. "Though I will not force you to do anything you do not wish to do, I can't stand here and do nothing."

"Sure you can. No one made you my keeper."

After awarding me a long scowl, he took a deep breath and gentled his voice. "Sophia, will you please come stay with me so that I may ensure your safety?"

"No."

He ticked his head back, his irritation breaking through into his expression once more. "I really don't wish to fight with you—"

"Then don't."

"I only desired to offer protection. I'll leave you alone now, since I'm clearly not welcome here."

At the thought of him leaving, my stomach sank, and I frowned. "No . . . ," I said. "Please stay."

He reached out and took my hand. "I know I've been . . . contrary with you."

"Hot and cold," I said. "Mostly cold."

"You have to understand that I go to Club Flesh to get *away* from the human world. I liked you from afar, liked you safe in the world that doesn't know about my own. I never would have approached you if things hadn't played out as they have."

"But they did."

"They did," he repeated. "And now I hope it's all right with you if I stick around, if only to look out for you until this all blows over."

"I don't object," I said quietly, even though I knew I should.

"Then you will come stay with me."

As much as my pride screamed for me to say no again, my desire to be able to sleep without fear of who might come for me in the night was stronger. I'd be better off with Charles around, staying at a place Marcus didn't know about and hopefully couldn't find.

"Only until a more suitable arrangement can be made," I finally agreed.

His gaze searched mine. I wasn't sure what he expected to find in my expression, but I was content to stand there with him, despite the rattling of my heart and the flip-flopping in my stomach.

My gaze slid down, taking him in, contemplating how he might look without a shirt on. Definitely there would be stomach muscles involved.

"You all right, Sophia?" he asked.

I shot my gaze back to his. "Of course. What were you saying?"

He leaned closer and whispered, "*Nothing,*" his gaze now trailing the length of my body.

Charles cleared his throat and traced his finger over the edge of my altar behind him. "You don't look Wiccan," he said.

I tried not to smile. Charles wasn't the first person to say that. For some reason, people thought Wiccans had to be 'Goth' or 'Emo' or something. Like we're bound to some law that doesn't allow us to have pet bunnies or paint our toenails pink or smell like something other than patchouli.

Some people believed something bad must have happened to drive us away from more acceptable religions. As though any other religion can inspire a person, can be something you feel is right, except for Paganism. Paganism, they thought, only happened out of desperation or as some sort of childhood fad.

Then there was the idea that we had nothing to identify with other than being Wiccan, as if our brain was on a constant ticker all day, *wicca wicca wicca.* What a shocker, we actually thought about other things, too.

So, maybe Charles touched a nerve. A little.

I raised my eyebrows. "What *does* a Wiccan look like?"

He shrugged. "You, I guess." He glanced around my room. "Not much of a basketball player, then?"

"Huh?" I followed his gaze. He was staring at the corner of my room, by the door. *Oh no.* A pair of lacy-black, boy-short underwear lay crumpled in a ball on the floor in front of the hamper.

"You missed."

Thinking I would be breaking some kind of unspoken rule to touch my underwear with him in the room, I shoved him into the hallway and asked him if he wanted some tea. I pulled the door shut, and before he could respond, my robe caught between the doorframe and the door, and I tripped over my feet and crashed into him, knocking him back against the wall.

He laughed.

Worse: he didn't stop laughing. He looked down at me, his arms wrapped around me from catching my fall, his shoulders shaking from laughter. My heartbeat ratcheted up at the press of his hard stomach against my breasts.

Finally, he stopped. "You're blushing again," he said, his voice low in my ear.

I started to pull back, but he gathered me closer, pressed his face to my hair, and breathed against my scalp. "You smell like honey and amber."

"My shampoo?"

"No," he said assuredly. "You're missing the human smell entirely."

This coming from the man who sometimes took the form of an animal?

The idea was just too much. I stepped away, the moment a reminder of why we couldn't be together. This time, he didn't pull me back.

"If you need blood, that means you're immortal, right? Like the Cruor?"

His hands slid to either side of my shoulders, and he held me away from him. "I've been alive for over three centuries," he said. "Does that bother you?"

"Not any more than anything else." I considered him for a moment. He didn't seem any older than me. "So you're immortal?"

"Not exactly."

"Then what?"

Charles dropped his hands to his sides. "You are the nosiest woman I've ever encountered."

"You didn't answer," I said pointedly, leading him down the hall to the living room.

"We can age if we stop shifting," he said.

"Then why don't you?"

"Me?" His voice faltered. "I stick around for my family."

"Parents? Siblings?"

"Parents."

"What about work?" I asked. "You can't keep one employer for three hundred years."

We stopped at the end of the hall, at the entrance to the living room, and Charles' gaze panned the room.

"I have enough money without working."

"I hate people who don't have to work." Crap. Did I have to say that out loud? "That doesn't mean anything. I . . . well, I don't mean you."

Usually, I had no problem biting my tongue. With him, I apparently didn't know when to shut up.

He leaned against the arm of the sofa, ankles crossed, not at all trying to hide his laughter.

"Glad you find me amusing." I turned on the television and handed him the remote. "I didn't catch if you wanted tea."

"Because you fell," he said, still chuckling.

"Want some tea or not?"

He nodded.

While the kettle brought water to a boil, I gripped the lip of the kitchen counter so hard the trim dug into my palms. What was I going to do with him? A man. In my house. In the middle of the night.

He's just a man. A strange, ancient man—but still a man.

After I prepared some loose tea in an infuser of a small ceramic pot, I arranged a tray with sugar, cream, and two teacups. I brought out the tray and placed it on the coffee table before taking a seat beside him.

"Please, help yourself."

He prepared his tea—three sugar cubes to my one, and no cream, like me. Not that I was keeping track.

"Is it okay?" I asked.

He took a sip, then set the tea aside. "I have a feeling you don't like coffee."

Somehow, my hyperactive nerves had overshadowed my distaste for the terrible stuff, but I wasn't about to tell him that. "Maybe next time you'll ask me out for tea."

I shouldn't entertain the thought of getting involved with him, but I couldn't deny the increasing attraction between us, either. After tea, Charles helped me pack up my most important belongings. We would wait until morning to relocate.

We watched television for a bit, but I wasn't taking in anything other than the glow and mumble of the screen and the warmth of Charles' body. As the minutes passed, our bodies inched closer together. His arm rested around my shoulders, and I leaned slightly into him. He pressed his lips against my forehead, and I inhaled the clean scent of his skin and the fabric softener used to wash his shirt.

I was getting myself into trouble. Nothing could become of us— not if he lived forever. I would grow old. I *wanted* to. And immortality? How could life have meaning without death?

Charles caressed my arm with his thumb. "I was worried you'd be frightened of my nature."

"The turning into an animal thing. I don't find that scary. Weird, maybe. But not scary." *Not that part, anyway.*

"Hey, watch it. We can be scary when we want."

"You want me to be scared, or not?"

He laughed. "Not."

"I don't know," I said, smiling. "Maybe I better be careful."

He returned my smile with a grin. "One never can tell. I might be dangerous to your good sense."

The eye contact lingered long enough for me to realize how comfortable I'd become. *Too* comfortable. Having him here felt natural. Like we were *supposed* to be together. I needed to shift gears and remind myself why that wasn't true.

"Earlier today you were talking about 'the Universe'. What's that mean?"

"We don't know who, or what, the Universe is. Our council communicates with them."

Huh. So the Universe was a *them*.

"What's it like?" I asked.

His eyebrows pulled lower over his eyes. "What's what like?"

"Shifting."

"It hurts," he said emphatically. "Your bones grow or shrink or rearrange. Your skin stretches or snaps smaller. Every muscle explodes and every bone breaks and resets."

"That'd be interesting to see."

He chuckled. "I just told you how painful it is."

"Right." I pressed my foot nervously against the base of the coffee table. "Sorry."

"It's fine." He nudged me away and stood. "I'll show you."

"What?" I leaned forward, my muscles tense. Now that it wasn't hypothetical, I wasn't sure I wanted to see.

I shoved my teacup aside, spilling a warm splash of tea onto my pajama shorts in the process. My eyes never left him as I blotted my pants with a napkin. "Really, you don't have to."

He shrugged. "If I trust you enough to tell you what I am, what's the problem in *showing* you? It's nice to—" He cut himself short.

"Nice to what?"

"Trust someone," he said softly.

There was a pause where neither of us spoke, then Charles cleared his throat and rubbed his hands, as though he were trying to wash himself of his confession.

A bead of sweat pearled at the nape of my hairline and trickled a slow path down my neck. "I didn't expect you to show me now."

"Won't hurt less if I show you later." He winked and backed away several paces.

"Wait!" I lifted my hands to stop him. "Just—never mind."

"I'll be okay," he said. He took off his shirt. "Watch."

I was watching all right. Or maybe staring. His body was firm, lean. Not too muscular—not in a way that implied he obsessed over going to the gym—but defined and strong. Equally as strong was the heat spreading from my stomach down to my thighs and up to my breasts. I sat back, holding my breath.

His body trembled. Pain etched into his face as his figure blurred. My heart thundered in my ears. I wanted to tell him to stop, but the words remained trapped. Wild vibrations coursed through him.

Then, I heard it.

Several loud pops sounded over a deep growl. He hunched over as his skin forced his body smaller. His spine protruded against a thin layer of flesh. At the sound of bones crushing, I dug my nails into the couch cushion.

His face deformed. Hair pierced through his flesh as his form shrunk. I almost gasped in horror, but bit it back, my teeth digging into my bottom lip hard enough to draw blood. At any moment, the tea I'd drunk might surge from my stomach.

The end of the transformation came suddenly, leaving a pile of clothes on the living room floor. A bushy-tailed squirrel pounced out of the pants and scampered over.

This was the man I was planning to move in with?

Perched on his hind legs, he tilted his head and chittered. I cupped my hands together and lowered them to the floor. He padded into them, and my hands shook as I brought his face to mine.

Charles was in there, somewhere. His eyes had changed, too—no longer teal but an eerie shade of green, like the squirrel I'd seen in the woods and the eerie, smoky eyes I'd seen outside my window after the ritual.

"Your eyes," I said, lost in a sense of wonder and dread. "You were the squirrel in the woods."

He placed his tiny paws together and nodded. Surprisingly, having witnessed his change firsthand made me feel less freaked out. If I was scared of anything, it was *for* him, not *of* him—scared of the pain he had to endure with every shift. And if I cared about that, I had to admit I cared about him. Somehow, some way, he was working his way into my heart.

I released him and watched as he returned to his human form, the process seeming quicker in reverse. He stood naked before me. Hastily, I dropped my gaze, but the image might as well have been burned into my retinas.

Out of the corner of my eye, I could see him smirking as he redressed, but I didn't dare allow my peripheral to take in anything more than the expression on his face. Even after he dressed, my heart thudded over the memory of him without clothes.

He sunk onto the couch beside me, his brow heavy above his eyes. "You sounded afraid."

"Your eyes—" I shook my head. "I would swear I've seen them before, and not just in that squirrel."

"Happens to all elementals at night."

"My attacker didn't have eyes like that," I said.

"He wouldn't if he was hungry. The eyes only glow when the elemental has lifeblood in their system."

"Why a squirrel?"

"It's one of the easier ones"—he swept loose hair from his eyes—"and it doesn't rip my clothes."

"That was—I mean—" I paused to gather my thoughts. "An owl outside the woods had the same strange eyes. You?"

"I had to follow you to make sure no one else had. I wasn't the only one hunting those grounds."

This man was not good for me. My life might not have been normal before he showed up, but at least it'd made sense.

I was shaking just thinking about what would have happened without him. Charles cradled me against him. He probably meant for it to be comforting—and, at first, it was. But when I peeked up at him, and our gazes locked, all I felt was lust. I saw the shift in his eyes, too. The shift from wanting to protect me to simply . . . wanting me.

He released me and cleared his throat. "This—Well, you and me . . . You know it's not a good idea."

"Then what is it you want?" I asked.

"You," he said, his expression unreadable and his voice heavy and full of . . . full of what? Sadness? Regret? "To understand you. To know that you're safe. To not have to avoid the only person I can be myself around."

He swept the back of his finger down my cheek and nuzzled his nose against mine, eliciting from me a shaky breath. Maybe this was okay—giving into the physical—so long as I kept my heart out of things. So long as we didn't commit to anything.

The urge to kiss him surged through me, but he pulled away. The missed opportunity left me a little sad, but I sighed quietly in relief.

Ancient man, Sophia. Remember that. How long can it last?

"And you?" he asked. "What do you want?"

"I can't answer that," I said.

I knew exactly what I wanted. It just wasn't what I *should*.

When Charles excused himself to make a phone call, I added a few more notes to my Book of Shadows.

Strigoi: 'Water elementals', also known as Shape-shifters, sent by the 'Universe' to hunt evil Cruor. They feed on blood to see auras, which help them determine who to hunt. Not all Strigoi become hunters. Strigoi are only immortal if they keep shifting.

Charles wasn't going to stop shifting.

☪

WE SPENT THE REST of the night and early morning talking. Charles wanted to hear about my life, which meant telling him about all the people who had died and left me behind. He seemed concerned when I told him about my parents, but, more importantly, he *didn't* look at me like I was some kind of freak.

I asked him about the side-effects of Cruor blood, and he said sometimes a bond would form and the human might be able to 'sense' the Cruor whose blood they had drank.

Those types of side-effects would fade within a couple of days, as they had with me. But I didn't tell Charles I'd been able to do more than just 'sense' Adrian. My Grandpa Parsons had always told me to never offer up anything I didn't have to. While others gave their sage wisdom of 'the only stupid questions are the ones that go unasked,' it was his advice that resonated more: 'Only ask questions you can't resolve yourself.'

Without more answers, I didn't know which questions were safe to ask.

Charles told me about his life, too. About his early urges for blood and his struggle to temper his supernatural energy. He'd never dated a human before—had always been certain they would run the second they learned about his true nature.

Was I any different?

Our chemistry aside, a mortal woman couldn't have a future with an immortal man, though my reservations were no match for my impulse to live in the moment or my need to learn more about his world. The supernatural perhaps offered the only explanation for my ancestor's missing body and my family's curse, but I *couldn't* turn to Charles about those things. Not because he'd told me not to ask any more questions, but because I'd made that mistake when I'd confided in Ivory, and I wouldn't make it again.

I'd have to find the answers I wanted on my own. The question was, how was I going to do that under his watchful eye? Moving in with him might bring me some protection, but I wasn't sure how much that protection could outweigh the looming complications.

{twelve}

SIX WEEKS HAD PASSED since I'd moved in with Charles. Six tortuous weeks of struggling between my physical desire for him and my mental determination not to get involved. I admit to deriving some pleasure in that he didn't seem to be having an easy time with it either.

His demeanor around me had relaxed a great deal, but there were still times the tension between us was so palpable I feared I would toss caution to the wind. But anytime I thought something was building between us, a week would go by before I would see him again. In that way, living with Charles was fairly similar to living alone.

I had to admit, his house—which was once Belle Meadow's old library—had some advantages over my own. For one, when my house was ransacked two days after I moved out, Charles' house was not. Secondly, a moat of daffodils surrounded his lot. But this wasn't an advantage because of my love for landscaping—which didn't exist. Charles explained that narcissus, while only mildly poisonous for humans and animals to ingest, was outright debilitating to Cruor even to the touch.

After Charles explained the purpose to me, I'd immediately jotted down what I'd learned in my Book of Shadows, cross-referencing the new knowledge under both Daffodil and Cruor.

> *Daffodil was discovered as a Cruor repellent incidentally, back when flowers were put on graves to cover the stench of death. When bodies in some graves began to go missing, it wasn't long before humans noticed the dead buried beneath the daffodils always remained. At first, the humans believed the daffodils were warning off bad spirits. But once news broke forth of grave-robbers, humans began to think the effect had been only a coincidence. In reality, the daffodils had prevented the Cruor from rising. During that time, however, the Cruor discovered a way to turn humans, and the necessity of Cruor being earthborn came to an end.*

Between this information and Charles' declaration that I would be safe so long as I traveled in groups, especially at night, I realized I didn't have many options. I couldn't move in with Lauren; she would freak if I overpowered her home with daffodils because of her whole 'floral scents give me a headache' thing.

I wasn't exactly stuck where I was with Charles, but I couldn't think of better solution, and I wasn't sure I still wanted to. Our location was safe. All I had to do was leave the house during daylight and return before nightfall. The daffodil did the rest.

I wish that would have been enough forever.

[?]

OCTOBER 31ˢᵀ marked the beginning of the darker half of the year. Red's bandage had come off the week before, and I thought he'd be ready to fly home. Wherever that was.

I took him from his cage and lowered him to the ground. "Here's your chance. Get on with your little bird life. Just be sure to build yourself a nest and stay there at night."

Red walked across the cold ground, stared out at the muted clearing, then hopped back to the perch in his cage.

I crouched to peek inside. "Don't you want to be free?"

After several failed attempts, I let out a sigh and headed back to my Jeep with Red still in tow.

With the fading of daylight, the voices returned. Slowly at first, pulsing into my own thoughts in place of the thudding silence, but then more rapidly, rushing by with renewed intensity. Unintelligible. Tangled. I didn't know if it'd be better to understand them, or if that would only make me feel crazier.

This year, Samhain would be especially important. On this sabbat, the spirits of ancestors visit their descendants—to help them and advise them—and I needed all the advice I could get. This would be my last hope of getting answers on my own.

My friends would be joining me in Charles' backyard to perform our ritual. Well, *my* ritual, mostly. Lauren wasn't Wiccan—she was only joining the ceremony to support me in my beliefs, just as I often celebrated Christian holidays with her. And Ivory said she didn't want to do a ritual for her ancestors but would come along for my sake.

We met at dusk. I draped an orange cloth over a stone I'd chosen as an outdoor altar and perched pictures of Grandpa Dunne, Grandpa Parsons, and Dad, along with Elizabeth Parsons' court document, in a semicircle around the altar's pentagram. I never included my mom in these things. Even with her gone, I wanted to honor her distaste for my beliefs.

As I performed the rites, I kept my thoughts to myself, wanting the support of my friends but not wanting them to know what I needed support for. Start to finish, the ritual took nearly an hour and was entirely uneventful. Maybe the answers would come later. I stubbed out the mint, apple, and nutmeg incense sticks, then shared cakes and a bottle of sparkling wine with my friends.

Lauren suggested we spend the evening making grave-rubbings, and Ivory said she knew just the place. I wasn't sure. I hadn't been out after dark since I'd gone to Club Flesh with Ivory . . . not even to buy milk or bread.

After I closed the circle, I stepped aside to call Charles, who was out for the evening. "Ivory and Lauren want to go do grave-rubbings."

"That one of your Wiccan things?"

"No," I said, incredulous he was even asking. "Grave-rubbings. You lay a piece of paper on the grave, then rub it lightly with lumberman's chalk. It gives an 'imprint' of the grave. Didn't you ever do coin-rubbings in school? It's like that."

"I didn't go to school," he said, "but it sounds fun."

"It does?" I walked farther from my friends, lowering my voice. "I mean at night. They want to go now."

"You won't have to worry at the cemetery. Cruor don't go there. Besides, you should be fine in a group."

An icy breeze crossed the yard, biting at my nose and cheeks. I pulled my coat tighter to ward off the chill. "No Cruor in the cemetery? You're sure?"

"None in *that* cemetery," he said. "The only Cruor residing in a cemetery are the Maltorim in Damascus. The Queen, Callista, says it keeps other Cruor away. Cemeteries are where the original Earth elementals came from and the one place they don't want to return. Moreover, there's nothing there for them. They want living blood, not dead bodies."

"Okay, if you're sure." I waited for him to say something else—anything—but he didn't. "I better get going. Meet you later."

We said our goodbyes, and I snapped my phone shut.

Ivory cleared the black taper and white pillar candles from the altar. She hadn't said much since arriving.

"How've you been?" I asked lightly, coiling the black cord that had marked our circle.

"Dealing with family issues." She turned away, abruptly dropping the conversation.

Ouch. I knew she was still upset with me, but I couldn't

understand why and didn't want to start an argument over it. Instead, I helped Lauren clear away the plate of fruit, vegetables, and bread from the top center of the altar, then packed the black votive candle along with the cauldron into my box of supplies.

As I cleared the ashes of dead twigs, each having been named for things that needed to end—for myself, for others, and for the earth— Lauren crouched beside a stone statue in the yard and pulled a camera from her bag. She snapped a picture of herself and the marble lion. After a few more clicks, she checked the camera screen.

"Cool that Charles bought the old library." She shoved her phone back in her bag and turned to me. "Cocoa?"

"Please," I said.

She headed inside. I packed away the boline we'd used to cut our ritual apple. The crosswise slice had created a pentagram at the core, honoring the five elements—earth, air, water, fire, and spirit. I also put away the half-slice of apple we'd eaten from during the ritual, but the other half-slice I wrapped in a piece of cheesecloth to bury later—an offering to feed the souls of nearby spirits.

Ivory stood at the edge of the yard, staring off into space. I should've gone to her; instead, I folded the altar cloth away and carried the box to the back steps. She followed me inside, dragging her wine-colored nails along the wood-paneled walls as she peeked into every room. Old offices were now bedrooms, and the single-stall bathroom had been fully renovated.

"What did Charles do to this place?" she asked.

"He couldn't live here the way it was."

Lauren called from the kitchen: "Everything's new!"

Ivory pointed down the hall. "I'll wait in the parlor."

I offered Lauren a hand in the kitchen. She nodded toward the mugs.

"So, are you calling him your boyfriend yet? You're keeping things at his house."

Lauren didn't know I was actually *living* here. It was easier that way. "We haven't exactly pulled out the label-maker." I opened the cocoa packets and dumped them in the mugs. "Spoon?"

"I'm going say he's your boyfriend." Lauren poured the hot water over the cocoa mix, snatched a spoon from the dish rack, and leaned over me to stir. "I don't see how he could be anything but."

I moved the mugs to a tray. What made someone a 'boyfriend'? I'd been avoiding any attachment to Charles. He would live forever, and I would not.

I carried the cocoa tray into the living room and pressed a steaming mug into Ivory's hands before lifting my own. "Are you joining us for the grave-rubbings?"

Ivory's gaze flickered upward, the flash of an eye roll I'd seen her give Lauren hundreds of times but never me. "Why wouldn't I?" She set her hot cocoa aside. "We'll visit the cemetery near my house."

Back when our town had moved graves from the old cemetery, a few families insisted that their loved ones' coffins not be moved to the new cemetery. In one newspaper interview, an elder of the town said the dead should never be separated from their 'first soil'.

As a result, the town set up about fifty graves, all from the same three families, in a small cemetery at the end of Litton Avenue. They'd had to move not only the coffins, but the soil that had covered those graves as well. Moving the soil for *all* the graves would have been too much of a hassle. That was how our town ended up with two cemeteries. One much smaller than the old one, and one much larger.

A wide grin splashed onto Lauren's face. "I heard that cemetery is haunted."

Ivory spat out a laugh. "You're the one who started the rumor!"

I wasn't sure about that, but I didn't say anything. Neither did Lauren.

Before we left the house, I made Charles a turkey and cucumber sandwich and left it in the fridge to hold him over until dinner. He'd once told me he liked to eat a human meal after hunting, because it reminded him that there was more to him than his need for blood. I'd been making those meals for him ever since. Maybe it didn't feel safe to speak my affections, but I hoped he knew I cared.

Probably more than I should.

☪

LITTON AVENUE was clear of trick-or-treaters, but the night offered the scents and sights of Halloween through the open car windows— the smell of gutted pumpkins heated from the inside by small candles that flickered through triangular eyes. Stitched mouths with sinister toothy grins were carved into the flesh of jack-o-lanterns, and the aroma of pumpkin pies and roasted pumpkin seeds carried on the crisp night air.

About two thirds of the way down the street, Lauren's headlights reflected off something in an alley. A half-destroyed sign: Basker Street. Could it be the same Basker Street scribbled in the book Paloma gave me? I'd never noticed the sign before, but that wasn't the first time I'd had that experience. Many times I would swear I'd never seen something, only to start seeing it everywhere I went.

Coming back tomorrow was always an option, but we were

already here, and the voices had only been growing in intensity. As the Cruor blood faded from my system, a permanent solution became more and more important—and the truth surrounding my ancestor's death was the only stone I'd left unturned.

"Stop the car!"

Lauren jerked her 1978 orange Ford Pinto to a halt. I jumped out and popped my head back inside the passenger window. "I want to check an address. Be right back."

"Wait!" Lauren scrambled after. "I want to come, too."

"Hey!" Ivory stepped out and yelled after us. "Where are you going?"

"Come with us," I called, halfway to the alley. I waited for Ivory to catch up while Lauren plowed ahead.

We caught up with Lauren. I expected consuming darkness, but light slanted in from streetlamps to reveal shoe-printed gum and stains of oil on the concrete. Doors with padlocks on the outside and broken windows repaired with plastic bags and duct tape lined the alley.

Toward the end, dirty bricks framed a plain wooden door. The numbers seven and nine hung above the knocker. I could see the outline of another number; there were dirty spots around the edges, and the rest of the door was sun bleached, leaving the shade of a number three.

793 Basker Street.

"This is it." I traced my fingers over the numbers. "This is the address from my book."

Ivory stepped closer. "What book?"

I put my finger to my lips, trying to hear the muffled voices behind the closed door and boarded windows, but the whispers clattering in my mind prevented me from focusing on what the people inside were saying.

I frowned. Now what? Knock on the door? When I turned back to offer my friends some kind of explanation for why we'd come here, a shadow shifted behind Lauren. I screamed. She screamed in response, and Ivory laughed.

"Damn it, Charles! Don't sneak up on me."

He grabbed my arm and pulled me away from the door. "What are you doing here?" he asked, his voice dark, maybe even a little angry. "You said you were going to the cemetery."

"I saw this address in a book." I tilted my head. "What are *you* doing here?"

"Taking you and your friends to dinner." His offer didn't sound friendly.

"How did you find us?" Did he see the car parked on the side of the road? Why was he on Litton Avenue?

"We're leaving," he said. "Now."

I grasped Lauren's hand and started to follow Charles. Ivory stayed a few steps behind, and Lauren kept flashing narrow glances my way.

"What's *his* problem?" she asked.

"I have no—"

Several strangers jumped from somewhere above, landing almost silently to block our exit. To my left, several more stood on a fire exit, all dressed in familiar brown cloaks. They peeled back their hoods, some male and some female. Each had the same unnatural pallor, the same glistening fangs.

And they weren't dressed for Halloween.

They must have been Cruor. Judging by Charles' earlier reaction, he knew this too—and had known since before they showed up. So much for the idea I'd be safe traveling in a group.

There were at least a dozen Cruor. Most stood as if frozen by pain, hands balled in tight fists, teeth pressed firmly together. A few leaned toward us, some inched closer. None looked like the type I wanted to invite over for tea.

I backed away, heart speeding. Charles turned to me, jaw clenched. Lauren moved aside, pressing her back against the building's brick wall—even *she* sensed something was off. Ivory took a protective stance in front of her, but I was too stressed to be surprised.

I glanced over my shoulder. More Cruor crowded the other end of the alley. There must have been three dozen or more in total. I stepped closer to Charles, and he wrapped his arm around me.

A petite, dark-haired woman stepped out of the gathering. She circled us, seemingly more at ease than her companions, then stopped by Charles and rose on her toes to put her lips close to his ear.

"Hello, *Charlie*." She drew out each word and emphasized his name with a giddy lilt. She ran her fingernails slowly down the back of his neck. "Who are your friends? We've never met *them* before."

Charles recoiled from her touch.

A tall Cruor-man with cropped blond hair glided over. Ivory pulled Lauren farther behind her.

"They don't know anything," Ivory said.

He tilted his head, and his lips pulled back. The expression was too unnatural to call a smile. "I could enlighten them."

He peeked around Ivory and waved at Lauren.

"Back the fuck off," Ivory warned.

Lauren glanced to me, but I had nothing to offer. This was one of those times where I was too scared to freak out. Whatever part of the brain reacts to such events just shut right down. Just like it always did when a situation was too much for me to handle.

Lauren clutched Ivory's hand, her eyes wide, her stance wooden. Her olive complexion paled, and the skin above her cheekbones and around her lips turned ashen. Clearly her freak-out meter wasn't broken like mine.

The dark-haired Cruor circled behind me. She placed her hands on my arms. My skin crawled, and I shrank closer to Charles. Her hair grazed my neck as she leaned over my shoulder.

Charles pushed her away, holding her at arm's length, and glared at her.

She giggled. "She's cute. Is she your new girlfriend, *Charlie*?"

Each time she said his name in her singsong way, anger overtook my fear. I locked my gaze on him. "Do you know her?"

Her irritating grin stretched into something plain sickening. "Of course he *knows* us, honey. Or hasn't he told you?"

{thirteen}

THE DARK-HAIRED Cruor-woman looked at Charles and laughed. "This is rich. You should drop by more often."

His fists clenched—one at his side, the other at the base of my spine. "Back off, Thalia."

She giggled. A tangle of eggplant-black curls tumbled down her back as she sauntered in front of him and snaked her arms around his neck. "Oh, don't be like that. You used to be fun."

She walked her fingers up the side of his arm and clicked her teeth. "Don't you remember? Oh, but these last few months—where have you been? I've been so lonely."

The pout on her face filtered into her voice. I wanted to smack her. My hearing blotted and my stomach churned. The stress frenzied the voices in my mind worse than ever, but soon a warm push at my mind calmed them away. The Cruor were trying to influence me. I pushed back. *Not this time*.

"Cut the crap, Thalia," Charles said, a warning cloud settling across his features. "I know what you're trying to do."

"I'm just playing, *Charlie*." She cinched her gaze on my friends and me. Violet rimmed her large pupils—two large voids illuminated with an eerie glow. At least she wasn't hungry, not with such a bright glow to her eyes. "How did you meet these . . . *girls* . . . anyway?"

Charles' energy was palpable; a barely controlled anger coiled in his body as Thalia spoke. He shoved her away and grabbed my hand. "We're leaving."

"Not so fast!" She snapped her fingers, and two stocky Cruor emerged from the crowd. They blocked Charles' path. A willowy, red-haired woman appeared at their side, her smile unnatural.

Thalia scowled. "Check them, Circe."

Circe's large green eyes widened. "Yes," she hissed. She flitted between my friends and me, grasping locks of hair and inhaling deeply. Her nostrils flared at Ivory's scent, but she passed her over. She reached me and nuzzled a long strand of my hair. As I leaned away, she smiled and stroked my head. "Such a life, this one!"

"Enough, Circe. Thank you."

Once Circe disappeared into the crowd, Thalia smiled at Charles. "That one"—she bit her thumbnail and indicated me with her pinky— "would be valuable."

A vein pulsed in Charles' neck and a soft hum vibrated through his body. Why didn't he just shift?

"Surely you aren't attached?" she asked, dropping her hand away from her mouth.

"You are outside your rights, Thalia."

"Temper, temper." She sighed, the sound sickening coming from her. "But, my sweet Charlie, we've missed you. And what of Adonis and Blake? Have you forgotten who your *real* friends are?"

"These women know nothing. Do not cross me." His voice sounded rougher, more gravelly.

"Cross you? Oh Charlie, I'd never cross you." She patted his chest and winked. "You've already *been* crossed."

A young, scrawny Cruor pushed his way through the crowd. He bowed toward Thalia. "I'm sure Charles can handle this . . . misunderstanding. He's been around longer than both of us put together." He arched his eyebrows.

Thalia stepped back, cocked her head to one side, and tapped a finger against her cheek. "Fine. We have their scents." To Charles, she added, "Pray you handle this well."

She turned up her nose and spun on her heel, then threw her hand to the air as she stormed off. The Cruor scattered, some following her into the house while others disappeared into the shadows.

The young Cruor remained. "You owe me."

"Thanks, Adonis. Could you . . . ?" He nodded towards Lauren, who trembled behind Ivory. "Escort them to their car first. We'll meet you there."

"You got it," Adonis said. "But be careful, man. Thalia's been into some things lately . . . And Blake—"

"Blake doesn't concern me."

Adonis lifted his hands. "Just keep an eye out, that's all."

"I always do."

I looked back as we walked away. "What about Ivory and Lauren?" My voice shook uncontrollably, and I realized how much my body was shaking. I felt cold and sick, as though I would never sleep again.

"Adonis can erase and change human memories. We'll circle back and meet them at the car. Lauren's memory of tonight's events will not be the same. You'll have to convince her to go to the diner instead of the cemetery."

"But Ivory—"

"Adonis knows her. She'll help."

We walked in silence. Maybe if I waited long enough, my heart would slow and breathing would come easier. When no peace came, I turned to Charles.

"What were you doing here? Why didn't Adonis want to erase *my* memory?"

He stopped walking. "We need to talk."

"That thing . . . *Thalia* . . . knew you."

"I stayed with them for a while," he said, dropping his voice so low I barely heard. Even the Cruor, with their enhanced senses, wouldn't be able to hear him now—not at this ever-growing distance Charles had placed between us and them. "I used to hunt with them."

"Stayed with them?" I rubbed my palms against my thighs, wiping the cold sweat on my jeans. "Why would you do that?"

He stuck his hands deep in his pockets and his shoulders hunched forward. "I haven't been completely honest with you."

"Such as . . . ?" My heart sank, dreading the untold news.

"There's more you need to know, things I hoped I wouldn't have to tell you."

I nodded for him to continue.

"Some of the Strigoi hunters didn't only hunt the inhumane Cruor. They turned dark, hunting all Earth elementals, good and bad alike. The Universe tried dealing with this by creating air elementals—the Ankou."

"There are others?" I pressed the heels of my hands into my eyes. *Of course* there were others. "I'm not sure I want to know any more."

"You need to hear the rest to understand what I need to tell you."

"Those were Earth elementals."

Charles gently squeezed my hand, regret etching into the lines around his eyes. "The Ankou were sent as grim reapers of the evil Strigoi and also to collect the spirits of elemental who have met a final death. With their magic, however, came the ability for elementals to crossbreed. The blending of bloodlines caused discoveries to increase. Humans attacked the elementals out of fear. Many innocents died.

"As a result, the Maltorim banned the mixing of bloodlines to protect the elemental species as a whole, as well as many innocent humans. The Ankou were enslaved to perform purifying procedures, using their gift of advanced supernatural medicine to get rid of one or other of the bloodlines in each dual-breed. But the results were unreliable, and so the Maltorim decreed death to all of the dual-

105

natured."

"I still don't see what that has to do with the Cruor back there or how you know them."

"The Maltorim will kill all dual breeds and anyone who associates with them." Charles gave me a long look. "To answer your question, Sophia, Adonis doesn't want to erase your memories because he believes *I* will."

"You? But—"

"Those Cruor . . . they think I'm a pure Cruor, too. If Thalia learns any different, she'll have me and my family killed."

I shook my head. "They can't do that."

"They can, Sophia. They do so all the time."

"How do you pretend to be Cruor? Can't they tell? I don't understand." I closed my eyes and shook my head. "Please don't tell me—"

"I didn't choose this."

Shit. Charles was dual-natured? "But I've seen you, every day. I mean every *day* . . . in the sun."

"Being Strigoi—being born instead of turned—changes things. I shift slower, but can tolerate sunlight. I'm not as strong as the Cruor, but I'm faster."

"But the daffodil oil. You never had a problem coming into my house."

"This is the very reason the Maltorim sees dual-breeds as a threat to the supernatural race. Despite our strengths being less potent, so are our weaknesses less severe. Our tolerances to such things—sunlight, silver, daffodil oil—are remarkable. It's a bit draining and makes us feel . . . off . . . but we can still function."

"Does Adrian know?" I asked quietly.

Charles' Adam's Apple bobbed. "Ivory and Adrian are the only ones who know I'm dual-natured. And obviously my parents. Now you, too."

"You should have told me."

He swept a lock of hair from my face, his hand warm against my chilled skin. "I didn't want to scare you. Or put you in any further danger."

"Who you are means more to me than what you are," I said, knowing I was in no place to point the finger. I had my secrets, too.

His eyes burned into mine. He caressed my cheek with the back of his fingers and slid his hand down my arm to my hand. Goose bumps rushed over my skin and my heart quickened as our faces inched closer together, his breath feathering against my cheek. All those times before we'd been this close I hadn't been sure what I wanted to happen, but now I had no doubts.

He lifted a hand and trailed his thumb over my bottom lip. His gaze lowered to my mouth and then he tilted his forehead against mine, locked his eyes on mine, and lowered his voice. "Sometimes I wonder what it'd be like to kiss you."

In the limited light, through the shadows frozen between our faces, I could make out the lines of his face and the brightness of his eyes. I wished he *would* kiss me. Wished to drum up the nerve and kiss him myself.

Charles closed his eyes and bent his head closer to mine. My eyes closed, too, and the world was silence and we existed in the darkness behind our eyelids. A breeze slipped between us, and, for a moment, I thought possibly his lips had brushed mine.

He pulled away, eyes full of regret. "I may never be able to give you what you want. It's better for you if I don't . . . if I—. Sophia, even if I wanted to grow old with you, I could not."

"It's okay," I whispered, but I wasn't sure what 'okay' meant. The one hope I'd had of a future between us being possible had just been torn away.

"Can you understand why I didn't tell you?" he asked. "If they knew I was the Strigoi who had helped you at Club Flesh, they'd realize I wasn't pure. That would have ended badly for us both."

I cringed at the word 'pure'. Now I understood why he'd feared being followed when we'd met at the club. Did he live his whole life this way, always questioning the intentions of anyone who crossed his path? Always wondering if someone was 'onto' him?

"I would never say anything," I told him, giving him a long look to impart the sincerity of my promise.

"You might not have to."

"What do you mean?"

He looked into the distance. "How did you say you found this place?"

"A book my mentor gave me had the address. And some code: LC 47."

"Local Coterie 47," he said, returning his gaze to mine. "Every Cruor coterie has a number. What book was it?"

"Maltorim records for the Salem witch trials."

"Sounds like one of Adrian's books."

One of Adrian's books? It made sense, I guess. Perhaps Ivory had borrowed it and accidentally left it at Sparrow's Grotto. Paloma probably thought it had shown up out of nowhere.

"So what are we going to do about the Maltorim?" I asked.

Charles frowned. "They must be aware something's up. That a Strigoi saved you and now you're with me. If they put it all together . . . " He shook his head. "We can't risk drawing more attention to ourselves. Marcus' interest in you was bad enough. Now he's finally back in Damascus, and you've got Thalia's attention instead."

"Do we need to leave?" Was anywhere safe?

"No one would make a move without being sure. I don't think they're even considering it, not yet, and they have no knowledge of where I live. If needed, though, my parents have a place in the Japanese mountains where we could stay—one of the few locations left in which the Maltorim has no real presence. We would just have to be careful we weren't followed there."

"This dual-breed thing is the real reason you don't age?" I asked, suddenly uncertain of everything I'd learned up until this point.

"Even if I stop shifting, I'm still part Cruor. Only pure Strigoi can age."

I didn't care if he was part Cruor, but if we could turn him into a pure Strigoi, then there was hope of a future for us. Us, together. Though I wasn't looking for any major commitment, I needed to know if it was *possible*. I needed to know how much to protect my heart.

"What about the procedure?" I asked. "The one the Ankou once used."

"I said I'd be *able* to age," Charles said darkly. "I didn't say I would."

At his sudden change of tone, I pulled back, trying to keep my face a mask of indifference.

After a long moment, he added, "I have my family, understand? And the Ankou might turn me over to the Maltorim." He closed his eyes and breathed in through his nose. "I can't think about this right now, Sophia. I'm sorry."

I gave him a solemn. "You mentioned the Ankou as a third elemental race," I said. "There are more?"

He nodded. "The Chibold, once, but not so much now."

"Fire elementals?" I asked.

"They were sprites that materialized as small human children, though some aged into their late teens. They needed host families to survive, but as adoption became more of a bureaucratic process—and these weren't real children—the host families became fewer and further between. The Chibold also had a reputation for causing trouble, thus not many supernatural families being willing to take them in."

"What happened to them?"

"They died off, as happens if they go longer than a century without a host family. They were around during the War, back when the Maltorim first declared the dual-natureds be killed. The Chibold caused a lot of destruction with their fires and telekinetic powers."

Wouldn't that throw the Universe's balance completely out of whack? Missing an entire element? Then again, they'd thought it was a good idea to only introduce one at the start. As crazy as I was, I had no place making judgments about 'balance' or the Universe's decisions.

The Maltorim, on the other hand, was another story entirely.

We walked the rest of the way around the block in silence, stopping when Lauren's car came back into view. Adonis was still with Lauren and Ivory, but no other Cruor were anywhere to be seen. Judging by the glazed sheen to Lauren's eyes, she was still under his influence. We stayed far enough away to talk privately, so long as we kept our voices low.

"I'm still worried about Thalia," I said. "She said they have our *scent* now. Whatever that means."

"Thalia has the attention span of a gnat. She'll find something else to occupy her time by the end of the night. You'd have been better off never coming to her attention to begin with, but she's not going to hunt you down."

I raised an eyebrow.

"You're not that important, darlin'," he said, smirking.

Though his light candor broke the tension surrounding my concerns, Thalia still struck me as someone far too passionate to let things go.

I shuddered, remembering the other Cruor—the crazed redhead. "What about Circe?"

"Circe is a marionette controlled by its puppet master. She's not going to do anything unless Thalia tells her. Those two are always together."

"Thalia might not want to kill you," I said, "but there's no reason she wouldn't come after me."

"Thalia isn't as dangerous as she likes to believe. She's too busy sucking up to the Maltorim to break any laws."

"Still, maybe it would help if I learned more about your world," I said, hoping I could use this opportunity to get answers about my ancestor without him learning about my family's curse.

"Such as?" he asked.

"You said humans once killed some of your kind. That some who died truly were elementals."

Charles nodded.

"This is going to sound crazy"—I stole a glance at him—"but an ancestor of mine was killed during the Salem witch trials. Her court document was in my attic, but there's no mention of her in any public records. Could she have been an elemental? Like, say, a spirit elemental?"

"Oh." He sucked in a deep breath and nodded. "Wow." Another moment passed. "Well, she might have been a human who got dragged into things."

"Or not," I said.

"There were spirit elementals," Charles replied. "Witches. But they were an extremely small population."

"Witches?"

"Humans chosen by the Universe, imbued with unique powers that would have been too risky to give an immortal. They died with their human bodies. Their existence was short-lived. I don't know anything more than that."

"You're a huge help."

"If you'd let me finish . . . . I was going to say Adrian might know more. I'll call him tonight and arrange something."

Feeling a little more secure, I allowed myself the indulgence of asking him more about the Cruor lifestyle. It hadn't mattered before, but if it was part of who Charles was, I would need to understand everything.

He explained how their blood cravings worked—how he didn't struggle with them as much as a pure Cruor. He told me how most didn't live as well as they could afford out of fear they might draw attention to themselves. Those who integrated with society lived their lives through forged documents and false family trees; they kept their money spread throughout different banks and in Swiss accounts.

As for the Strigoi, their animal forms also put them at more risk, such as if they crossed the path of a hunter. A human would have no way of knowing they were more than an animal. The idea of it made me happier I didn't eat meat.

I asked Charles what happened if Strigoi *were* killed in their animal form, and he said . . . nothing. They just stayed in animal form; it was the Universe's way of protecting their secrets.

"Don't you worry about hurting your own kind during a hunt?" I asked.

Charles shook his head. "We know who we are. We would never accidentally confuse another Strigoi for a real animal. Their scent, their eyes . . . even the way it *feels* to be around them . . . it's too unique to mistake for anything else."

So this was 'life' as an immortal? Suddenly my own troubles didn't seem so bad.

☪

WHEN I ARRIVED BACK AT CHARLES' PLACE, I flopped down on my guest bed with my Book of Shadows to make some additions and updates.

Charles had confessed that pure Strigoi don't really need blood to survive; he only needed it because he was part Cruor, something he'd hidden from me as an attempt to protect me from the dangers of his world. Knowledge of their world was a gray area. Knowledge of a living dual-breed was a death-sentence.

I crossed out the Strigoi's need for blood from my Book of Shadows' entry, then added the rest of what I'd learned.

> *Strigoi are faster than Cruor. If they are in animal form when they die, they remain that way to protect their secret. They can sense others of their kind by scent and appearance.*
>
> *Cruor are stronger than Strigoi.*

I made new entries for the Ankou, Chibold, Witches, and dual-breeds as well.

> *Ankou: These air elementals are like grim reapers. They also have magic that can help elementals crossbreed <u>as well as magic that can purify a dual-breed into a pure bloodline.</u>*
>
> *Chibold: These fire elementals are sprites that materialize as small children. They need host families to survive; if they go longer than a century without a host family, they die. The Chibold have powers over fire as well as telekinetic abilities. They are believed to be extinct.*
>
> *Witches: Also known as spirit elementals, Witches were humans chosen by the Universe. Their powers were too potent to give to an immortal. They died*

with their human bodies.

Dual-breeds: Any elemental born of a pairing of two different elementals. Their strengths are less potent and their weaknesses less severe. The Maltorim sees them as a threat, and any discovered will be executed.

Mentally exhausted, I closed my Book of Shadows and tucked it away in my dresser drawer. Though my sleep was fitful, it came easily.

In my dreams, I saw Elizabeth again. She was standing in front of the gallows, inches away from me. She stared into my eyes, slowly lifted the Samhain ritual apple to her lips, and bit into its red flesh.

Inside, the fruit had rotted.

{fourteen}

THE NEXT MORNING, I sat at the kitchen table and gave Lauren a call. She picked up after the first ring, her voice easily filled with ten times more energy than I could ever muster.

"Amazing night last night," she said. "We need to go there again next year!"

Too bad the 'there' she was thinking of didn't exist—not in the way she remembered. "It was okay, I guess. I'm just calling to check on you."

"It was *okay*? Just *okay*? That was the best haunted house *ever*. Do you remember the address?"

"Drats, I don't," I lied. "Can't even remember the street name."

She sighed heavily, and my heart sank. To her, this was reality. Charles' friend, Adonis, had made sure of that. Though the Cruor's practice of stealing memories unnerved me, what bothered me most was their ability to place thoughts into someone's head and create memories of things that had never happened. And now I enabled their lies.

When I didn't say more, Lauren continued. "I just thought . . . well, that guy who walked us back to the car. Does Charles know him?"

"I don't think so," I lied.

"Too bad. I wouldn't mind *him* taking me out to dinner sometime."

That's what you think. "If I see him around, I'll be sure to tell him. So, really, you're okay?"

"Why wouldn't I be?"

"Nothing. Look, I gotta go. Work. Catch you later?"

"You bet," she said.

I should've been relieved she didn't remember anything, but I was too busy stressing over lying to my best friend.

☾

ALL THROUGH WORK, I couldn't stop thinking about Charles. What was life like for him? He harbored secrets for fear of judgment, something that should have brought us closer together but instead placed a whole world between us. He trusted me with the knowledge of his dual nature, while I would never be able to tell him of the whispering voices that occupied my mind.

I simply *could not* risk him responding the way Ivory had.

When my shift ended, I found him outside, sitting on the hood of my Jeep. He wore an olive-green, button-down shirt left open to a white tee. No jacket, of course. Charles never wore a jacket. Not even in sub-degree weather.

My heart sped, but I managed to keep my voice smooth. "I thought we were meeting later?"

He grinned, hopping down. "I wanted to see you in that sexy work uniform."

I pushed his shoulder in playful response, but he didn't budge. He chuckled, then eyed my Jeep and tapped a knuckle against the metal body. "Still driving this thing?"

"Spit it out. You think women shouldn't drive or something?"

He laughed. "Not at all. Though you realize your car isn't at all gas efficient, don't you? And the emissions—"

"I'm not getting rid of my Jeep, okay?"

"Would it be so terrible to trade it in for something a little more . . . eco-friendly? Some of us plan on being around for a while."

"Fantastic reminder. Thanks. In case you haven't noticed, your Prius doesn't handle the snow very well. That wouldn't happen to be the reason you left it home today, would it?"

"I like walking," he said, an easy smile playing at his lips.

"I'll remind you of that after our next snowstorm, when you're asking for a ride to buy groceries."

He stepped closer and swept a strand of hair away from my face. There was that heat again—a chemistry that spun between us and made me feel like a fly stuck in a web. A chemistry I needed to ignore.

"I have to go." I opened the door to get in my car, but then turned around, shaking my head. "I can't believe you came here just to give me a hard time about my Jeep."

His jaw clenched, and his fists balled at his sides. "I didn't."

"No?" I raised an eyebrow. "Then why?"

He closed the distance between us and placed his hands on my waist, stopping me from climbing in. Despite the early November chill, my skin suddenly warmed. His gaze dropped to my lips before he leaned in gently to close his mouth over my own.

I parted my lips to welcome the kiss, and he pressed closer, his tongue exploring my mouth, the kiss singing through my veins as I tried to deny the pulsing knot forming in my stomach. The kiss ended too soon.

"I really should get going. I still have to pick up groceries," I whispered, though my reasons for wanting to leave had changed completely. And it wasn't like I could get away from him. I was heading back to the house—his house. Hopefully the drive would cool me down.

"Let me give you a hand." He stepped between my legs, grabbed me by my hips, and lifted me into my seat. His arm was wrapped around the small of my back and his hips pressed against the inside of my thighs, his heat playing against my own.

Moments like these made me want to give in to my physical desires, even if I wasn't ready to turn over my heart.

Charles turned my palm up and kissed the inside of my wrist, and my skin tingled beneath his warm, velvety lips. Then he pulled away, the tips of his fangs dipping past his upper lip. I wondered how he'd hid them before—apparently Cruor's fangs often descended when they engaged in *any* carnal activity, though I'd never seen Charles this interested until recently. His fangs weren't so scary, though, not with the knowledge they belonged to a man who would cause me no harm.

"See you tonight," he said, taking another step back. He was scowling now, or maybe that was the only way for him to hide his fangs.

I cleared my throat. "Mmhmm. See you."

I settled into my seat and closed the door. After I started the engine, I glanced back up, but he was already gone.

☪

WHEN I ARRIVED 'home', the sky was drained and pale and the air easy to breathe and smelled like fresh snow. The front door swung open before I knocked, and Charles ushered me inside. Of course with his super speed, he'd managed to return home faster than I could drive there.

"Were you waiting by the door?" I teased as he helped me shrug off my coat.

"I heard you pull up." He hung my coat on a peg of the hall coat rack. "Adrian will be here soon. Should I put on some tea?"

"That'd be great."

He motioned toward a black leather sofa, complete with red silk pillows. It wasn't the sofa I'd seen there this morning. "Please, sit down."

"Ummm . . . what happened to the sofa?"

Charles laughed. "The other one was only temporary. I finally got around to ordering something new."

Once I seated myself, he headed for the kitchen. A young woman outside caught my attention. She was standing across the street in her nightdress, her hair dark and her gaze empty, her bare feet reddened by the snow blanketing the pavement. Her thin lips hinted at a frown, and she stared straight at me, unmoving.

My heart rate picked up, and I craned my head toward the kitchen. Charles was pouring the tea.

I looked out the window again, and I shivered. She stood in the middle of the road now, her gaze still cutting toward me as though she'd not moved at all. When I'd first looked, she'd been across the street, on the sidewalk. I was *sure* of it.

Moments later, Charles returned from the kitchen and pressed a steaming cup of tea into my hands.

"What is it?" he asked, following my gaze out the window to where the young woman still stood. She turned woodenly and walked away. "We could sit on the porch, if you prefer."

Couldn't he see her? I should have been freaked out that I was either seeing ghosts or hallucinating, but in the scheme of the last few months, the turn of events seemed almost mundane somehow. Or perhaps my numb-reaction-to-horrible-events gene was in overdrive.

I opened my mouth to say something but decided I'd better figure a few things out first. Last thing I needed was another repeat of the whole Ivory situation. She was *still* barely talking to me, and it wasn't for my lack of trying. If that was the general reaction to people 'hearing things', I wasn't sure I wanted to know the reaction to people 'seeing things'.

I forced a smile at Charles. "The living room is fine."

The teacup warmed my fingers as I sipped. "Honey?"

"Yes, Dear?"

"You've put honey in the tea, I mean." I smiled, shaking my head. "Tell me you've been waiting all day to use that line."

He grinned, flopping on the couch beside me, and wrapped his arm around my shoulders.

The streetlights outside flickered on, reflecting off the icicles hanging from the storm gutters on the houses across the way. The street was empty, and I sighed my relief, snuggling closer to Charles and relaxing against his warm body.

Mentally I struggled to block any emotions trying to surface. Sure, last night changed things between us. I knew we were 'together' now, in our own way, but I would age, and he would stay the same. We had no future, not unless he rid himself of his Cruor side so that we could age together. I wasn't ready to make a commitment under these circumstances.

His breath was hot against my neck, and a fluttering repeated in my stomach. He touched his lips to the hollow beneath my ear, then he buried his head against my shoulder.

"I want to be with you. To not resist the urges you create," he murmured against my neck, "but more than anything, I am compelled to protect you. Compelled beyond reason, perhaps, but I know I must. What happened earlier today, outside the diner . . . "

"I'm glad you kissed me," I said with sudden boldness.

He sighed, leaning back and closing his eyes. "I can't let you get hurt."

"I've made it this far," I said quietly. "Still in one piece, too."

His jaw tensed. "That's not the kind of hurt I mean."

I knew that. I knew he didn't want to hurt me physically *or* emotionally. And I was trying not to get attached. Really and truly.

Some things were beyond my control.

"This wouldn't be a problem if we could age together." I regretted the words almost as soon as I'd spoken them.

Charles scoffed. "Many would kill for immortality."

"All I meant—"

"Would you sacrifice *your* way of life for *me*? Or do you expect only the reverse?"

I didn't want to be selfish, but, when it came to this one thing, I had to be. As much as I wanted to explore the possibilities of getting more involved with him, I refused to allow myself to *commit* when we had something as huge as immortality standing between us. Maybe I wasn't capable of keeping strong against my desires, but I would fight to protect my heart.

The front door rattled as Adrian stepped inside and stomped snow from his tidy black dress shoes. "My apologies. Am I interrupting?"

I stood. "No. We were waiting for you."

I turned back to Charles, frowning.

He stood and kissed my forehead, then whispered low in my ear, "We'll figure things out. I promise."

He continued over to the front door and clapped his hand against Adrian's arm. "Good to see you. Come sit."

Adrian pulled a stack of books from a navy-blue messenger bag and stretched his arm to set them on the coffee table, keeping the furthest possible distance from me.

"These may help, though I must warn you, they contain some . . . non-traditional views. And," he said, taking some small USB-port-type thing from his pocket, "there's always the Internet."

"Ha!" I said, trying to contain my laughter. "*The Internet.*"

"Why do you say 'ha'?" His brow furrowed as though I'd suddenly grown a third arm. He slid the device across the coffee table toward me. "That is D-connect."

I examined the wireless card, studying the red encircled symbol of a snake on the side. "What is this?"

Adrian grinned. "Something we should not have in our possession. Queen Callista—and anyone else on the Maltorim—would impose some undesirable consequences for such an offense. The alterations I've made should ensure that doesn't come to pass."

Charles cleared his throat.

"I should say, actually, that Charles is the one responsible for the alterations. He placed an electronic leech on the card, thus erasing data as entered. Activity cannot be tracked."

Charles tapped his fingers against the coffee table. "It's not perfect."

"How does it work?" I asked.

"As an Internet card would, though the websites are different. Here," Adrian said, taking out a laptop and booting up. "I'll show you. What are we searching for?"

"Anything pertaining to a relative of mine, Elizabeth Parsons, or other spirit elementals."

"Ah," he said. "Witches."

He brought up an online supernatural database and left me to browse the selection, but nothing caught my eye. Charles took over, while I looked through the hard-copy books Adrian had brought.

I settled on *The History of Witches* and returned to my seat. A lot of work had gone into making this book: hand-sewn binding, pages creased with a polished piece of bone. Definitely one-of-a-kind.

The couch shifted as Charles settled beside me with the laptop. Adrian grabbed a book and sat in an adjacent recliner.

"The spirit elementals were chosen around the time the Salem witch trials began," Adrian said. "In effect, they ended up being called 'Witches', even though only one true elemental was hanged."

"That's what I'm looking for." I cracked open the book in my lap. "Information on that one witch. She's not listed in the traditional histories, right?"

"I'm not sure. Admittedly, I've never had any reason to look into this."

I skimmed the Table of Contents and flipped to the first section, marked 'Victims', which listed the names of all the people killed over the years for 'witchcraft'. The list contained two sections: Humans, Witches. If the section had only listed one name, it would've been sickening, but the way pages spilled on, name after name, was nothing short of horrifying.

All those innocent people.

I scrolled through the list of humans first, and, nearing where my ancestor's name might be, I held my breath. Did I want her to be human? What if she was—would it mean I'd never escape the whispering curse? Were the two things even related?

Elizabeth's name was not on the list. I scanned a second time, and my concerns doubled. What if she wasn't on either list?

The supernatural list was significantly shorter, the cause of death for those listed not being attributed to the trials but simply to having been killed during those times. I trailed my finger over the names. Halfway down the page, I found her: Elizabeth Parsons, 1674-1692. The only elemental hanged during the Salem witch trials. Others had died from typical deaths, such as old age, sickness, or murders unrelated to the trials.

She'd died at age eighteen . . . the same age I was when the hissing in my brain started.

I glanced from the page to Charles and Adrian, now buried in their own research, and decided to read a bit more before sharing what I'd found.

Nothing else caught my attention until I began reading about the Universal Necessity of Witches.

> *Humans had fallen to the practice of killing the elementals, believing them to be accursed, naming them as witches. The penalty of the claims resulted in the death of many innocent humans. And so, at the time of the Salem witch trials, coinciding with the dual-bred cleansing, the Universe chose the spirit elementals—witches.*
>
> *Their immortality was not tied to their nature, however, as was true of other elementals. Instead, their immortality existed in their magic, carried through their bloodlines. These were the most vulnerable of*

the elementals, but, so long as their powers were used for good, they could perform without limits. However, should they choose a darker path, their magic would draw harm to themselves.

Okay . . . so not what Charles had told me. Charles believed the magic of those elementals had died along with their human bodies.

The Maltorim continued to lead the genocide against the Universe's command, and the spirit elementals, being under attack themselves, did little to slow their efforts.

However, in time, the dual-breeds dwindled so low in number that the war subsided to quieter efforts. When the spirit elementals died, their magic was halved and passed on to their descendants. With each passing generation, the magic halved again, and after several centuries, the witches' powers tapered away to virtually nil.

Because the efforts had failed, and the witches were so often in danger of persecution, they never had the chance to use their powers. The Universe chose no further spirit elementals.

The section defining spirit elementals said they kept the same life expectancy as any other human, though rumor spread of witches who gained immortality through being turned by the Cruor. This weakened their powers, but left them with more tolerance to sunlight than their makers.

After the book's sixth chapter, I settled on the floor, lying on my stomach as I leafed through page after page. I skipped past the witch trials, covering the Middle Ages, Early Modern Europe, and the Modern Era. They'd taught us about all that in high school, and I'd studied even more extensively in college. The eighth chapter grabbed my attention: Spirit Elementals—The Genetic Legacy of Witches.

I read a few pages, then stood, finally having found something of use. Apparently, there was more to ancestral magic than the 'halving' rule.

I held the open book in the crook of my arm. "I got something."

Charles and Adrian set their books aside and focused on me.

"This Chapter on Genetic Legacy says the descendants of spirit elementals are at times granted their ancestor's magic on loan. It can manifest in a small burst of power or may develop over time, though most descendants are unaware of their potential."

Adrian gave me an empty look and tossed his dreadlocks over his shoulder. "What does it mean?"

"It means I might be able to borrow my ancestor's powers."

Adrian shook his head. "I mean, how does the information relate to *you*?"

"Oh, right." I brought the book over to Charles and Adrian, flipped to the front, and pointed to Elizabeth's name. "That ancestor of mine? Well, she was a spirit elemental. Which makes me—"

"The descendant of a witch," Charles finished. He leaned back into the sofa, interlocking his fingers behind his head. He stared at the ceiling and pressed his lips together. Finally, his gaze shifted back. "So you have the potential to acquire her abilities. What are they? How do you tap into them, and would you even want to?"

Did I want supernatural abilities? Not exactly. I just wanted to silence the voices in my head. But maybe learning more about my ancestor's powers would help me protect myself from the Cruor, should we ever cross paths again. It might even mean being able to protect Charles if he embarked on the journey to relinquish his Cruor side and grow old with me.

I held the book up. "Adrian—do you have more like this?"

"What do you have in mind, and do you truly suppose the information would make any difference?"

I didn't ruffle at the condescending edge to his voice. I sensed Adrian never took things like 'feelings' into account. He just wanted to find solutions and implement them.

After stacking the book on the coffee table pile, I walked to the window. Light from streetlamps glinted off the snow floating to the streets. The old man across the road, wearing a thick plaid coat, frigidly shoveled snow from his driveway. He paused a moment, staring over at me, but I didn't look away. *Everyone* stared at me.

I let out a deep breath. "Scrying would be a good start and can also be done with fire, which might be best since I'm a fire sign."

I kept my back to them, hoping to conceal any evidence on my face that I was hiding something. Yes, I wanted to protect myself. But I *also* wanted to end my family's curse. "And might you have anything on the effects of magic on the mind?"

Those words having been spoken, I turned to face them. No one flinched. My request had been vague enough. Then again, what were the chances Adrian would bring me a book about hearing voices?

Adrian nodded. "I will check my collection and drop anything relevant off here."

"Wonderful." I smiled over at him. "Where do you get these books anyway?"

"The library."

I lifted another book from the table and fanned the pages. "I would have noticed something like this at the library."

"Different library, Miss Sophia," he said in his usual refined articulation, a bit of friendliness hidden beneath his stuffy conventions.

"So this library just gave you these books?" I asked, smirking.

"I worked there for a time. When they sought to have some books destroyed, I offered my services." He grinned mischievously. "I, of course, did nothing of the sort. I realized the Maltorim only sought to hide the truth behind their efforts to eliminate the dual-natured, thus I hid the books instead."

I hated this mysterious Maltorim and that there wasn't something more we could do to stop them. But while I might never save all the dual-breeds, I might be able to harness enough magic to protect Charles and myself.

"Please, bring more books if you can."

"I will," Adrian promised.

As I watched him leave, the young woman I'd seen in the street earlier reappeared outside the window, this time standing in Charles' yard. The breeze swayed the leaves in the trees behind her, but her hair and nightgown were unmoving. The more she closed in with her gaze fixed on me, the more I hoped answers would quickly come.

{fifteen}

ON THE MORNING OF YULE, I woke with a strong sense of purpose. I'd spent the last couple of weeks reviewing some books Adrian had dropped off. I hadn't found out anything more about my heritage or curse, but I *had* found out how to help Charles become a pure Strigoi.

I set a tray of chocolate chip pumpkin spice cookies on a rack in the kitchen to cool. Outside, the melted snow had caked dead leaves to the yard and sidewalk. The surrounding houses showed no trace of the season, overstuffed black trash bags stacked high along the roadside, each yard an immaculate carbon copy of the last.

Charles and I had been dating for over three months now, and while I wasn't seeking a commitment—not now, anyway—I wanted to know if a future between us was even *possible*. Now I knew it was, but that was entirely up to him.

I headed down the hall to his room and pushed open his bedroom door. His blue plaid comforter covered him from head to ankles, only his feet peeking out to hang over the edge of the bed.

I sat beside him and pulled the comforter away from his face. "Charles!"

He jolted upright. "Huh? What?" His gaze darted around until his attention settled on me. Confusion slipped from his features and a crooked grin worked into place. He pulled me onto the bed and propped himself on one elbow.

I giggled and poked his chest. "You overslept. I ate breakfast without you."

"Oops," he said, walking his fingers up my belly, between my breasts. "I was out late. Hunting."

"You at least have to get up to open your gift."

Charles shoved his blanket away and tossed his legs over the side of the bed. His feet thudded against the hardwood as he stood. My gaze drifted downward, his flannel pajama pants slipping lower on his hips to reveal the upper crest of his butt. I bit back a smile.

He glanced over his shoulder, tugging up his pants, and kissed my cheek before stepping into the master bathroom—another one of his renovations.

I flopped back against his pillow. It still smelled like him—like vanilla and sandalwood and musk. I couldn't deny my attraction to him, which seemed to be taking over more with each passing day, but we'd never made it beyond what Lauren called the 'heavy petting' stage.

Truth was, that was already a lot further than I'd gone with any man before. But so what if I was a late bloomer? Not everyone started dating in high school. At least that was what I'd always told myself.

Besides, I wasn't sure it was right to be intimate with Charles when I couldn't be completely honest with him. Would he still want to be with me if I *did* tell him everything? Ever since I'd told Ivory, she rarely answered my calls, and we'd been friends for years.

Maybe first, before worrying about sharing my secrets, it would be best to find out if a future between us was even possible, though he wouldn't like what needed to be done to make that happen.

Charles emerged shirtless from the bathroom, the muscles in his stomach stacked down to where his jeans rested at his hips. My heart thumped against my lungs, and I hopped to my feet. I wanted to run my hands over the muscles of his shoulders and press my cheek against his bare chest, but I remained firmly planted where I stood.

He smirked as he pulled a black and grey striped sweater over his head, and I sighed as all that beauty was hidden from view.

"Just going to run a comb through my hair," he said.

"To sit in the living room?" I grabbed his hand and tugged him closer, snaking my arms around his waist. "You look good with bed-head. Reminds me of the night we met."

He planted a gentle kiss on my lips, then grabbed my hand and led me out to the living room. We sat on the floor beside our potted pine tree decorated with candy canes and pinecones and a popcorn garland. I insisted he open his gift first. He peeked into the silver gift bag, removed the pocket watch, and smiled at the inscription.

"'It's not what you look at that matters, it's what you see'," he read.

"Henry David Thoreau."

"This is perfect, Sophia." He smiled, then reached behind him and handed me a box wrapped in recycled paper. "Now your turn."

I ripped a small area of the wrapping, and a gold foil box peaked out. "What is it?" I asked.

"Open it."

I tore the rest of the paper away and lifted the lid to the box. Cushioned inside was a spiral bracelet, threaded with iridescent glass balls of gold and garnet and plum, accented with tiny pearls and crystals.

The air rushed from my lungs in a sigh. "Oh. Charles, it's . . . amazing."

I was relieved to find the bracelet fit perfectly. Only Grandfather Dunne had ever known to buy me bracelets small enough not to slip off.

I lied back and stared up at pinecones in our tree. Charles was perfect for me in every way but one: he was immortal. I would age, and he would not. How weird would that eventually become?

How could I make sense of all this—of my feelings for him and the reality that a future together was unreasonable?

Charles propped himself on his elbow beside me. "Something's wrong."

I rolled to my side, resting my head in the palm of my hand. My legs stretched out, though my feet didn't reach far past his knees. I was looking at our feet only because I feared what I might find if I looked in his eyes—not just in his expression, but in my heart as well.

Could I be with him even with his immortality and my own secrets standing between us?

"Look at me," he said in a firm-but-gentle tone. I lifted my gaze, and his eyes burned with a familiar intensity that heated me from my core. "I know you are worried about what will become of us, but you need to trust things will work out."

"How can you be sure?"

"Because," he said. "Because I have never allowed myself to get involved before, but with you I am unable to deny the connection. Things *have to* work out." He tucked a loose curling strand of hair behind my ear. "You're my life now, Sophia. That will remain so. Always."

"Am I?" I whispered. I grazed his forearm with my fingertips. His skin was warm, smooth, and buzzing with energy. Touching him . . . it was how I imagined it would be to touch light. Not the heat, but the very essence.

"I've stopped protecting my heart from you," he said. "I've stopped fighting the way I feel, stopped fighting the natural draw I feel toward you. Now you need to do the same."

My throat tightened, and I squeezed my eyes shut, wanting to disappear from the moment.

"Stop fighting it," he murmured. "You can't treat everyone in your life the same. You can't treat us all as though we've hurt you."

I shook my head slowly, opening my eyes. "I don't."

He grinned, lifting my hand and grazing his lips over my knuckles. "Don't you?"

Shit. He was right. "It's not that easy," I said, finally. "It's not even about that."

"Everything has to make sense with you." Charles' voice edged on frustration. "It all has to add up, to be perfect, neat, in your control. You make your decisions based on fears of how others might judge you. How can you live like that?"

I eased my hand away from his grasp and sat up. "Wow," I said, unable to contain my defensive tone. "Don't hold back for my sake."

He sat up and grasped my hand again. "I wouldn't want you to hold back for mine."

"I'm not holding back," I lied.

"Do you think, after three centuries, I can't read a person? Auras or not?"

As much as I hated the way he challenged me, it was also the very reason I knew he was my perfect match. He inspired me toward growth. Now I worried what I was about to say would ruin the one thing he appreciated about me: that I'd accepted him for who he was when the rest of his world, and probably my own as well, would not.

"Fine. You want me to tell you what's bothering me?"

"Yes," he said. "That's exactly what I want."

I searched his face. Should I tell him what Adrian's books had said? How would he react to the idea of sacrificing his Cruor side? His immortality, at the very least, would remain so long as he continued to shift. I wasn't asking for a commitment, only the promise of possibility.

He caressed his thumb across my bottom lip and along my jaw. "Thinking again?"

I inhaled deeply, repressing a sigh. "I read something in one of Adrian's books about your . . . you know . . . problem?"

I hated calling it a problem. Being a dual-breed wouldn't have really been a problem if the Maltorim hadn't made it one. But his immortality—admittedly, that *did* bother me.

His easy smile slipped. "Is this in regards to the Ankou?"

I straightened, trying to contain the fluttering in my stomach. "I know you're skeptical," I said, "but this sounds promising."

"They do have a special form of magic—especially where transformations are concerned—but they aren't going to help unless something's in it for them." His hand dropped back to his side. He was all discussion now; clearly, this wasn't what he expected me to bring up.

"It's worth a try," I said quietly. "I have a feeling this might work."

"First tell me what the book said."

I spun the beads on the bracelet he'd given me. He wasn't going to like my answer.

"We kill the part we want gone?" I said, my uncertainty strong enough to turn my statement into a question. "They performed the same procedure at the start of the genocide, but the recent success rates have been nearly flawless."

"Genocide?" Charles repeated. "*Nearly* flawless?"

"The Maltorim killing people who aren't 'pure'."

"Not exactly a genocide. Go back to what you were saying: I have to die first? What kind of theory is that?"

"How is it not like genocide?"

"They didn't kill off all of one kind. Only those who were dual-natured."

"The dual-natured *are* a kind of people." Sadness tugged at my heart. He'd grown up in a world where his mixed nature wasn't accepted, and this had become his 'truth'. "I'll stop looking into this if you aren't interested."

His expression sagged. "I don't trust the Ankou. They might do a lot of good, some of them, but they aren't any better than any other supernatural race. There's a good chance they'll turn us in to the Maltorim, and the Maltorim gave up their efforts for purification long ago. If they find out about my nature, I'm dead. My family's dead. *You're* dead. That's all there is to it, Sophia."

"The Ankou have been helping save other dual-natureds from being killed," I persisted.

"Even if this were true—and we have no way to know for certain—you must understand my position. I'm trapped between worlds. You are mortal, and my parents are not. I refuse to let go of either of you. There has to be another way."

"*What* other way?" I asked.

He exhaled quietly, setting his gaze on mine. "Please try to understand what it's like for me. There is no in-between. There will never be any sense of death coming. It's not something that will creep up on me as the years pass. When I die, it will be at the hands of someone else—someone who knows how to kill my kind. It's not as though I asked for this life. I wouldn't wish immortality on my worst enemy."

He spoke with such conviction that chills pricked my arms.

"It doesn't have to be like that," I said.

"I've lived to see a lot of people die," he said solemnly, "and I have to spend eternity carrying those losses. If I lose my parents, I would be alone in my grief forever. I would be giving them the same if they lost me. You must understand: immortality is not an escape from death. It's an accumulation of loss. I risk too much by exposing myself on some whim my Cruor side can be removed."

"I would never ask you to give up your parents," I said, hoping to impart my sincerity. "And I hope you know that if immortality weren't an issue, there's nothing I would change about you."

"I know, Sophia," he said warily. "I wish I had answers for you. For us."

"I just don't know how to be with you completely when there's no possibility of a future for us."

"Being the world's biggest pessimist isn't everything," he said. "Maybe if you show a little faith, things will work out."

"*How*?"

"Faith, Sophia. Life isn't always going to give you the answers to the questions you're asking. Sometimes you have to make do with the answers you get."

If only he knew that was exactly what I was doing. "Thanks, Yoda."

"Like it you do, when I tell you these things."

"You're hilarious. Really. But what are you going to do? Fetch my walker when I'm eighty?" As I spoke the last sentence, a bit of my deeper hurt jabbed into my voice, and I swallowed, hoping he hadn't noticed. "I'm just trying to be reasonable."

"That's your problem. Your head keeps getting in the way."

"What's that supposed to mean?"

"You're asking me to kill part of who I am, and yet you won't even open up to me. What is plaguing you, Sophia? You toss and turn all night, you're never fully there when I'm talking to you. *Something* is bothering you. I might be able to help if you would talk to me."

I opened my mouth, but no sound came out.

"Give and take, Sophia. It needs to go both ways."

I stared at my hands, wishing more than anything I could just disappear entirely.

"Let me tell you something, Miss Reasonable. We definitely can't be together if you're dead, and you might as well be signing a death wish if you plan to seek out the Ankou under these circumstances. They aren't called 'the elemental grim reapers' for no reason. If something happened to you, I wouldn't be able to forgive myself."

"All I wanted to know is if you would be willing to grow old with me, if things ever developed between us that way."

"What do you think all this is about?" he asked, spreading his hands. "This *is* about wanting to be with you. But it's also about what being with you means."

☾

THE NEXT DAY, Charles and I cuddled in the bedroom with our favorite movie—*Red Violin*. Charles rested back against his pillow, eyes closed. I couldn't see past his youthful face—couldn't see him as a man who'd lived through centuries.

"How much of your life can you remember?" I asked.

"Remember?" He opened his eyes, his expression soft and curious. "I don't. Everything blurs together, to the point most major life events carry about as much weight as tying shoelaces. But there's always a new adventure. Always something new."

"Like me?"

He pulled me on top of him, so that I straddled his hips. "You are more than an adventure, Sophia."

I crossed my arms behind his neck, and his heartbeat quickened against the inside of my forearms. He planted several soft kisses along my jaw, his fingers playing across my collarbone. Anticipation robbed me of my breath, and my heart leapt to my throat.

He tipped his forehead to mine, his face too close now to make out anything more than his teal eyes and dark, tangled lashes. My heart went wild in my chest. I quickly realized I was holding my breath, and it took a conscious effort to release it slowly.

"Charles?" I whispered, my lips brushing his as I spoke.

His mouth closed over mine, and I kissed him, tasting him with a hunger that belied my outward calm. He wound his hand in my hair, his lips pressed firmly on my own. A wave of heat traveled over my skin as desire pulsed through my body like wildfire on a hot Colorado day, consuming me the way those fires consumed whole stretches of forest.

Charles' warm hands untangled from my hair and slid down my back, his fingertips tracing small circles across my skin, just under my shirt. Swimming through the haze, I fought to control the swirl of emotions and relax away my doubts as his hands slowly moved up to caress my breasts through the lace of my bra. His thumbs grazed my nipples through the material, and my breath quickened.

"Sophia," he said softly, pulling away. "We should stop."

But when I kissed him again, he didn't resist. Our breathing shifted into deeper, heady breaths, the air surrounding us growing thicker and effused with passion. A growl rumbled in his chest as I slid my arms around him. I leaned back on the bed, pulling him on top of me, his body flush with mine, his mouth moving to my neck, dropping kisses across my chest, down to where the plunging neckline of my blouse came to a halt.

His body shifted between my knees, his interest pressing the inside of my thigh as his lips returned to mine and his hand caressed over my hips, up toward my navel. His fingers played along the waistline of my jeans, skimming the skin beneath the top of my underwear, and I sighed. He paused, kissed me once more gently, then flopped back on the bed to stare at the ceiling.

Moonlight shone through the window and gleamed off his fangs. My heart sped, but desire replaced my usual fear. I didn't care about his fangs. I only wanted to give in to the steady pool of warmth in my stomach.

I sat up and cupped my hands around his face, strands of his hair feathering against the pillow. "We can't stop every time."

He pointed toward the movie. "Look. Your favorite part."

"Your fangs bother you that much?" When he didn't answer, I straddled over him, blocking his view of the television. I leaned forward, my hair spilling over my shoulder onto the pillow beside him, and pressed a kiss against his neck and another along his jaw. I ran my hands over his shoulders and whispered in his ear, "They don't bother me."

Charles grabbed my wrists, and, in one swift movement, pinned me to the mattress. He didn't need his strength to hold me there—the suddenness of his actions were enough to leave me frozen. Heat radiated from his body, warming against my thighs, stomach, and breasts. His scent of vanilla and sandalwood and his close proximity sent my body into a state of arousal, and my nipples hardened beneath my bra. I peered up at him, unsure what to make of the situation. His body suggested passion, but his eyes were cold and hard.

"You are the most aggravating woman I've ever met," he said. The muscle in his jaw twitched. "You expect far more self-control from me than any man could have."

"I'm not asking for your self-control," I said firmly.

He released my wrists and climbed off me. "You're not ready for this."

"I am."

"You've never done it before," he said, sitting on the edge of the bed, looking to the wall across the room.

I swallowed past the tight lump in my throat. "You don't know that."

He turned, raising an eyebrow. "Tell me otherwise."

I couldn't bring myself to meet his gaze, and I pressed my lips together, for once unable to conjure a lie.

"That's what I thought," he said. "There may be many things I cannot give you, Sophia, but I can give you the time to learn yourself. To be certain—"

"I *am* certain."

"—of our future," he finished.

How could either of us be certain of *that*? "I'm not asking for any promises. I understand why you can't—won't—change, and I've decided to accept that."

"You decide a lot of things."

"What's that supposed to mean?"

"You allow your mind to silence your heart."

"*What do you want?*" I asked, both defeated and determined to figure him out. "You don't want to be with me, but you don't want me to leave. You don't want to grow old with me, but you don't want me to be with you so long as you're immortal. Tell me, what is it I'm missing here?"

"You should expect more."

"You don't want me to!"

"I *do* want you to. I may not be able to give you these things, but they are things you should want. They are things *I* want, too," he said, his voice tight and his words strained. "I don't want to hurt you."

"You can't. Your fangs . . . well, only a pure Cruor can turn a human, right?"

Charles climbed off the bed. "It's not about that." He walked over to the bedroom window before turning back, his face a marble effigy of contempt. "I'm sorry," he said, his voice with a raw edge. "We're going to get through this. But I don't know if I can promise you what you want."

He returned his gaze to whatever was outside the window, and I watched him in silence from the bed, wondering how the world looked through his eyes.

☾

LATER THAT NIGHT, the spirit lady watched me through the kitchen window while Charles cooked dinner. Her eyes were bleeding.

I never panicked when I saw her anymore. She was as constant as the rising sun—with me wherever I went for the past few months, her figure drawing ever nearer.

"It's not terrible I'm immortal," Charles said, glancing away from the grilled cheese he was making on the stove. "For you, I mean."

I froze. His sentiment came out of nowhere, and I wasn't sure how to respond.

"No?" I asked.

He stared stonily back. "I can protect you. If you understood the potential dangers—"

"I understand fine," I said. "And I can protect myself once I figure out how to tap into my ancestor's powers."

"You're still upset I won't seek out the Ankou," he said.

"You have your reasons," I said, even though he was right.

"The Ankou should be focused on why they are here," Charles said, engaging in the argument I was trying not to have on the surface. "It's beyond me how they find time to do these things when they are supposed to be moving the spirits of deceased immortals to the afterlife."

Moving spirits? *That's* what the Ankou did? The revelation panged through my chest, and lungs constricted. Suddenly I couldn't breathe.

Of all things, this revelation was the one that would shatter my resolve. It meant I wasn't safe from Charles' world, not if the spirit following me had anything to do with elementals.

Charles dropped the spatula for the grilled cheese and turned to hold me against his chest. "I didn't mean to upset you," he said.

I shook my head. "Charles, there is a spirit following me."

{sixteen}

"A SPIRIT IS FOLLOWING YOU?" he repeated, the lines across his brow deepening. "Why didn't you tell me sooner?"

I gave an insignificant shake of my head. "I didn't think it was a big deal."

He arched his eyebrows. Yeah, I sounded crazy.

"Look, where I come from, they exorcise people, so seeing things that other people can't isn't exactly something I want to broadcast. I didn't think it had anything to do with elementals."

"We still can't go to the Ankou," he said firmly.

"Why not?"

"First of all, the most helpful of them are in Brazil, and secondly, I don't think it's wise to approach them. There's no telling how they might respond."

Defeat settled heavily on my shoulders. "So there's nothing we can do?"

"Sophia, there is something you must always remember about my world. You cannot count on running or hiding forever. Whatever you do, fight. Always, always fight, until your dying breath. That is your only chance at survival."

"Until I *die*? Stop being so morbid!"

"You can't be passive about this. Morts don't follow people for the fun of it."

"Morts?"

"Mortuss Phasmatis. Spirits of elementals who have met their final death but are stuck between this world and the afterlife. The Universe tasked the Ankou with moving these spirits—either to new lives or to the afterlife—but if the spirits remain too long, they sometimes possess humans."

"Seriously? *Seriously*, Charles? Why the heck does it want me?"

"Likely because you don't have an aura. That makes your ability to resist possession stronger, but if they succeed, they can take you over completely—not only to use your body but to bind with your spirit as well."

"How can you be so calm about this? What am I supposed to do? Could it really possess me?"

Charles placed his hands on my shoulders. "Calm down. Let's talk about this. When did you first see it?"

"It's a her, and I first saw her when I woke up in Ivory's room after I was attacked at Club Flesh." My eyes widened with realization, and I covered my mouth. "Oh shit. She followed me here, didn't she?"

"How close is she now?"

I peered over the ridge of his shoulder, through the window of the kitchen door that led out to my backyard. The young woman with the dark hair now had her face pressed to the windowpanes.

I shuddered. Her face was pressed to the windowpanes, the blood from her eyes smeared across the glass. A shudder ripped through me and threatened to empty the contents of my stomach. I hadn't been so afraid of her before. Maybe ignorance really is bliss.

"She's right at the kitchen door, literally pressed against it," I said, my words leaving me breathlessly.

"I'll call Adrian," Charles said. "He'll advise us on what to do. In the meantime, stay away from the windows and don't look the mort in her eyes."

Thank my lucky stars that Charles knew how to keep calm when I did freak out, though I much preferred my usual state of numbness over such events.

The only room in the house with no windows was the bathroom. I settled down in there and had Charles bring me every magical references book I owned.

"Would smudging help?" I called out into the hallway.

Charles popped his head into the bathroom. "Smudging?"

"Burning pine needles and sage."

He looked at me like I'd grown a second head. "Why would that help?"

"We could use mint or salt," I offered next.

Charles just laughed. "I thought you went to school for history."

"I did."

"Think about it, Sophia."

Ah. Right. Mint and salt kills bacteria and germs. That would have helped keep people from getting sick, which would have made them less likely to hallucinate. That might help if I were sick, but not in dealing with actual Morts.

Adrian arrived shortly before midnight. "She'll need to do this under nightfall," he said to Charles. "If you try moving her to another location at night, you're more likely to draw attention from the Cruor than if you just attract the Ankou to come here."

"This is less than ideal," Charles replied. There was a weight to his voice that unnerved me. "This could risk our location entirely."

Adrian frowned in a way that seemed almost apologetic. I could marvel for hours at how that man's expressions could be so nuanced, how something as simple as a frown could evoke so many different things.

"There's no other way."

Charles raked his hand through his hair. "Then we better get started."

Their genius plan was to use me for bait for all the Morts in the area. Then call the Ankou to come exterminate the problem. My anxiety over the whole ordeal was mounting more and more by the second.

I kept mostly to the bathroom, but I did peek occasionally to see what was going on. The backdoor kept wrenching open and slamming shut, and I couldn't help but cave to my curiosity. The thought reminded me of what Marcus had said, that it was my dad's curiosity that got him killed.

Had he been somehow involved in this other world?

Adrian went outside ahead of us and set up a circle of wooden poles in the yard. He returned inside to retrieve a chair from the kitchen, which he placed in the center of his circle.

I leaned into Charles. "Why did he paint the poles blue?"

"It's lime, milk, and pigments that make a blue paint. It's supposed to look like water."

"Ghosts don't like water?"

Charles didn't answer me. Increasingly, the stress in the pit of my stomach could be more readily attributed to Charles' demeanor, rather than any knowledge that would lead me to feel afraid.

The spirit of the young woman wandered over to Adrian's structure, concern etched into her features. Her arms hung limp at her sides. Within moments, two more spirits joined her: a young boy with blond hair and, with him, a tall, thin woman with short, dark-red hair.

"There's more than one," I said nervously.

Charles wrapped his hand around mine and squeezed.

A few moments later, Adrian had attached wind chimes to each blue pole. He came inside and wordlessly ushered me out. I opened my mouth to ask what would happen next, but he whispered harshly, "Don't speak."

He seated me in the chair surrounded by the poles and started walking in circles around me, dragging a stick along the wind chimes. He was chanting something in a language I hadn't heard before. My heart rate picked up, and I couldn't decide if I was too afraid to close my eyes or too afraid to leave them open.

Then something blurred the spirits and they burst into black particles that flurried to our feet. Their remains coated the ground in ash that quickly dissolved to smoke and floated off on the breeze.

Was that it?

I started to stand up but Adrian shook his head at me as though the simple movement were a reprimand for my actions. I froze, then inched back into my seat. He handed me a chalice full of rose water and I took the hint to drink it.

"Now we wait," he said, and he walked inside, leaving me there. He and Charles watched me through window, unmoving. I wondered if my face revealed my fear as much as Charles' revealed his concern.

How had my life turned to *this*?

Perhaps I'd always had one foot in the supernatural world, but over the last few months, things had been shifting. Now here I was, being thrust further into the darkness, my fingernails gripping helplessly to hang onto these last threads of the world as I'd known it.

All I could think was how much I wanted to leave the supernatural world behind.

All of it.

C*

WHAT FELT LIKE AGES LATER, but what my watch revealed had only been one hour, my time sitting alone in the dark was over. Adrian came outside, grinning the full effect of his pride.

"They won't be bothering you again for quite some time. We will take you inside now and you will rest."

Once I was inside, lying down in the bedroom and completely unable to fall asleep, my heart still pounding in my chest, Adrian left. I was too frazzled to care that no one had explained to me what had just happened.

Charles came and sat on the edge of the bed. "You all right?"

"I think one of them killed my mom," I said.

"How so?"

I recapped for him how my mother had died. "Mrs. Franklin thought it was witchcraft, because right after my mom fell to the floor, there was smoke rising from her body. It was just like the smoke outside."

Charles' expression was grave. "It may have tried to take you instead."

"Oh no," I said certainly. "My mom wasn't really possessed. Mrs. Franklin just thought she was."

"Exorcisms are the best way to invite Morts into a home. She might not have been possessed when Mrs. Franklin brought her there, but it's possible something happened once they began their endeavors."

I swallowed around a lump in my throat. "Well, anyway, it doesn't matter because that was a long time ago."

"Sophia," Charles said in a way that made me want cry, simply by overwhelming me with his compassion.

"What's done is done. Can't change the past," I added as cheerfully as I could.

The smile on my face felt so unnatural I wasn't sure how to sustain it nor how to let it fall naturally from my face. I turned away instead.

{seventeen}

JANUARY CAME AND WENT. I would not be returning to work. Maybe I would eventually, but for now I needed to keep my distance. I spent all my newly freed-up time poring over books from Adrian, looking for more answers about my ancestor and how to tap into her gift. I needed to be able to protect myself. Charles couldn't be there to protect me all the time.

Adrian's books provided minimal support. The information on fire scrying—using fire to see visions—was useful, but the books addressing magic of the mind talked about telepathy and telekinesis and other things of little-to-no help.

Charles and I had been together for nearly six months, though the time felt more like a lifetime. I'd learned some important things from the experience.

One: I didn't want anything to do with Charles' world. Two: I wanted everything to do with him. And three: I couldn't have it both ways.

As though my current stresses weren't enough, the voices had amplified. I contemplated telling Charles. He'd need to know eventually; if not now, when? Was I ready to tell him these things, even at the risk of losing him?

Charles' footsteps sounded in the hall outside out bedroom door— footsteps I'd memorized and loved for their reliability. The kind that echoed with a dull, non-threatening thud. His approach replaced my stress with joy, and I bit back a smile.

Somewhere along the way, we'd ended up sleeping in the same bed. I couldn't think of any other man I would trust enough to do that with.

Charles placed a hand on each side of the doorjamb and leaned into the room. "I have a surprise for you."

I arched my eyebrows in reply and followed as he led me to the spare room—the room I'd stayed in when I first moved in here. It'd been locked up for over a month now.

He swung open the door and stepped back, allowing me to enter first. The entire wall to my left had shelves, wall-to-wall, ceiling-to-floor, packed with books. Beneath the window, candles scattered across the surface of a small desk. I smoothed a hand over the arm of a microfiber love seat near the door.

"Charles." I shook my head, smiling. "I can't believe you did this!"

A smile tipped the corners of his mouth. "Adrian and my mother donated books to your collection."

Charles stepped fully into the room. "Do you like it?"

"Like?" I asked, spinning back toward him. "Charles, I *love* it!" I wrapped my arms around him, locking my lips with his. He murmured against the kiss, and I pulled back. "What?"

"I forgot to tell you—my parents are stopping by tomorrow evening for dinner. They called right before you arrived. I hope you don't mind."

"Mind? Of course not. Should I make plans with Lauren?"

His eyebrows pulled together. "That's why I was telling you."

"To let me know not to be here?"

"No." He chuckled. "What are you talking about? They're looking forward to meeting you."

"Oh," I said. I sunk into the loveseat, and Charles sat beside me. "I've never met a boyfriend's parents before."

Actually, I'd never done anything more than date a guy for a few weeks here and there in high school, which had amounted to little more than hand-holding in the school hallways or kissing in the back corner booth at the local ice rink.

Charles wrapped his arm around me. "You have nothing to worry about."

But I did. I had a lot to worry about. I was going to meet Charles' parents—the people I would be stealing him from if he ever became a pure Strigoi and started aging with me.

Was it now, more than ever, important to tell Charles about the voices? Or was now the worst time to bring up my secrets? If I didn't say something soon, should I never say anything at all?

☾

I DECIDED TO TACKLE THE BASEMENT. It was huge and bare—the perfect place to hold rituals. The floor stretched out in an unwrinkled slab of concrete, only chipped in a few places along the walls.

Charles made a run to the hardware store to purchase some paint. When he returned, he set the two buckets on the bottom step. "You're cute when you're determined."

Cute. Not a word most women like to be called, but better than *crazy.*

Charles cut in the wall edges using the antique white paint, and I rolled out the rest. Within two hours, we'd completed the task, thanks to Charles' incredible speed.

We headed to the kitchen for a break, leaving the cellar doors open with a rotating fan circulating the air to dry the paint. Charles served peach cobbler and lemonade, but while the cobbler was warm and sweet, the room was cold and heavy with silence.

My basement project was a foolish attempt for distraction. Painting over the imperfections did me no good: waiting for the paint to dry forced me back to my thoughts—forced me to think about Charles' parents coming to visit and whether I needed to open up. There was one major problem with sharing secrets, though. Once the words left my mouth, I could never take them back.

Charles sipped at his lemonade in a way that seemed almost scripted. "Is something wrong?"

"No," I said, poking at a slice of peach on my plate.

No, just a bunch of frenzied whispering voices assaulting my brain. As usual.

Not only were they as non-distinct as ever, overlapping and running wild in my mind—*Sto. Are y. Bel. Didn't see th. Shhh.*—but now they were accompanied by dread and anger and other emotions that didn't line up with what I was supposed to feel.

When the paint finished drying, I returned to the basement and applied a stick-on decal to the wall—a brown tree with yellow and pear-green leaves and a bird cage hanging from an outstretched branch with an orange sparrow inside. In spite of all the brightness and openness of the room, I felt only like the caged bird. Trapped inside myself by the truth I refused to share.

Leaving the floor a deep, gray color, we moved the old upstairs couch—just a few shades too pale to be lemon—from under the basement stairs to the space along the wall where I'd applied the tree decal. I tossed a couple poppy red pillows on either side, and still I wasn't happy.

As if decorating were a substitute for addressing my emotions. But even this realization didn't stop me; it only made me hate myself more as I continued.

"Do you mind if I finish up alone?" I asked.

Charles placed a gentle kiss on my temple. "I'll start dinner," he said, and he left me in the drearily cheerful room.

In one corner of the basement, I set up two wooden chairs I'd painted daffodil yellow and a small table I'd painted avocado green. Beside the couch, I placed a cream-colored cabinet from my grandfather's house, the only family heirloom I had in my possession. Using the cabinet as a side table, I filled a clear vase with crystal beads and tucked in several silk flowers, creating an arrangement of candy pink gerberas, bright blue hydrangeas, and lime-colored daisies. I spritzed the flowers with a spray that lived up to its promise of crisp rain and traces of fresh mint.

I stepped back. The bright, airy room radiated a warmth I couldn't share. To say the room reflected me in any way would have been a lie. This room, this house, was merely a reflection of who I *wanted* to be. Not who I was.

I sank into the sofa, dissolving into tears. Guilt became a steady undercurrent to my emotions. Why was it so hard to tell him the truth? I'd told him about the spirit following me, and he'd been able to help with that. He hadn't thought I was crazy. Even if he couldn't help with this, there was no reason I shouldn't be able to open up with him about it.

I took a deep breath, pulling the air all the way down to the bottom of my lungs, then headed upstairs. Charles was in the bedroom, flipping through his music collection. When I stopped in the doorway, he snapped the binder of CDs shut.

Despite all effort to remain calm, my breathing was unsteady. "I need to tell you something."

His forehead creased. "Anything, Sophia."

"I have this thing," I said. The space from the bedroom door to the dresser where Charles stood extended a hopeless distance. "I hear things sometimes—thoughts that aren't my own."

Charles blinked but said nothing.

"It started as a hissing noise a few years ago but has gotten worse over the past six months." Even my voice was shaky. I tried to swallow, but my mouth was too dry. I needed to say this. If he didn't want to be with me because of this, then maybe we *shouldn't* be together. "I'm sorry. I've been one disaster after the next. I'm complicating your life. If you want me to leave, I would understand."

Charles crossed the room and grabbed me by the elbow. "You're nuts if you think I would want you to leave. This is what's been bothering you?"

I shrugged one shoulder, as though that would hide my hurt. "I was afraid to tell anyone. Everyone else I've ever opened up with has turned away."

"Sophia," he said, touching my cheek. "I'm not going to turn away from the only person I've ever trusted to accept me. Not for anything. You belong to me. If for a moment, then for eternity."

"Eternity?" I asked wearily.

"We're going to find a way," he promised. "This is one of many hurdles we will face, but we will overcome this—this and everything else standing in our way. Whatever it takes. We can fight for this, too."

"I know, I know. Whatever you do, fight," I droned. "But I've *been* fighting this for a while now. The voices aren't going anywhere."

"Perhaps they aren't supposed to. Remember, you're the descendant of a spirit elemental. If she was telepathic, you might be, too."

Charles didn't understand. I pressed my lips together and shook my head.

"Will you at least look into it?" he asked.

My breath rushed from my lungs. "I don't think—"

"Good idea. Don't think for a minute."

All this time I'd worried that opening up to him would cause problems, but it was the secrets that kept us apart. The more open he'd been with me, the stronger our bond became. I needed to start opening up to him, too.

I sat on the edge of the bed, and Charles knelt in front of me. The cardboard box he pulled from beneath the bed ripped a little as he tugged. He sifted through the contents until he found a large, unmarked book.

"This is one of my mother's old journals." He leafed through the pages, fingers running over the lettering and lips moving rapidly until they reached a page headed 'Telepathy'. "Do you try to tune out the voices or listen to them?"

"Block them," I said. "Sometimes I can't hear myself think because they're so loud and they're all clattering at once."

He set the book on top of the box. "Perhaps you try so hard to block the voices that you block your own thoughts in the process."

I spread my hands. "What am I supposed to do?"

Charles sat beside me on the bed, his hands resting in his lap. "My mother used to say, 'much confusion can be lifted with an open mind.' Try."

I curled my legs beneath me. "Try *what?*"

"To stop fighting. Stop pushing the voices away."

"If I focus, the voices get louder. Not clearer."

"Don't focus. *Open your mind.*"

Open my mind? How was I supposed to do that?

The closest I'd ever come to clarifying the voices was when I was relaxed, so I closed my eyes and slowed my breathing while Charles waited quietly. Several minutes passed. Just as my frustration threatened to take over, something sparked in my head.

. . . help in some way.

"Is that you?" I asked.

"Is what me?"

"The voice."

"No. Telepaths only hear their own kind." *But it might help.*

Now I was certain it was Charles' voice echoing in my mind. "Help with what?"

Charles stared at me for a long moment, as though considering, then gave a silent nod. "That's not telepathy."

"I know."

For a minute, hope fluttered in my stomach at the idea Charles might be able to help. But either way, at least I was no longer alone in this.

We spent the next thirty minutes testing my ability. Sometimes the thoughts of several elementals floated through my mind at once. At least I assumed they were elemental. Last I checked, humans weren't very concerned with their fangs or the pain of shifting or whether their wings would be visible in sunlight. If I pinpointed Charles' voice, the others fell away. I dropped the connection, and all the voices snapped back to a jumbled mess.

Charles pinched the bridge of his nose. "Other elementals wouldn't like this, you in their thoughts. Perhaps this is why you were so easy for Cruor to influence at first but are now capable of blocking their attempts. We need to tell my parents."

"Do we?" I asked. I didn't want to tell anyone more than necessary.

"If you want answers."

He stood and paced the room, not looking at me as he spoke. His fingers rested over his lips and his thumb rubbed the stubble on his cheek. My hands twisted in my lap, my stomach tightening each time he passed. Back and forth. His thoughts too rapid to focus on.

He lowered his hand to his side. "This might have something to do with your ancestry."

"I thought so, too. The voices left for a while after I drank Adrian's blood. Maybe that's a cure."

"You're talking about getting rid of them?"

143

I stared at him blankly. Of *course* that was what I was talking about. "Did you have a better idea?"

He turned to me, his expression deflated and uncertain. "You could use your ability as a warning system. A way to protect yourself." His gaze swept over my face, undoubtedly taking in the skepticism that had surely arrested my features. He frowned. "Before we talk about getting rid of them, let's at least see what my parents have to say."

{eighteen}

AT A QUARTER TO SEVEN, voices tingled my subconscious. I listened long enough to determine their source before stopping by the kitchen. "Five minutes."

Charles leaned against the stove. "They called?"

"I *heard* them. Something about you used to mash food in your hair as a baby," I teased.

"Very funny," he shot back.

I waited in the foyer until the doorbell rang. Charles walked up behind me, drying his hands on a dishtowel. He tucked the gingham square in his back pocket and placed a hand on my shoulder.

This was it. Meeting the parents.

I smoothed some non-existent wrinkles from my brown slacks and took a calming breath while Charles reached past me to open the door. I greeted each guest with a small nod. They weren't at all what I expected.

Mr. Liette didn't look much older than me. Mid-twenties, maybe? Same dark, toasted almond hair and deep teal eyes as his son, though Mr. Liette was pallid and sallow—not at all the same radiant glow of Charles and Mrs. Liette's skin—and his style of dress was far more formal than his son's, a red brocade vest peeking out from beneath his suit jacket.

Mrs. Liette looked younger than me, with hair all soft wisps and curls of auburn spiraling to her snow-dusted shoulders. Her cheekbones shimmered a pale lavender-pink and her eyes were bright emeralds, with facial features small and sharp, her hands tiny and fingers thin. She wore a lavender, empire-waist gown, the belt below her breasts braided with strands of cream-colored suede.

Charles cleared his throat, and I realized I'd been staring too long without speaking.

"Mr. Liette, Mrs. Liette," I said. "Such a pleasure to meet you." I offered my hand to Charles' mom, who accepted and placed her other hand on top, her skin smooth and warm.

"The pleasure is mine, dear. Please, call me Valeria." Valeria spoke in a warm voice that matched her smile. She turned to her husband. "This is Henry. We've heard wonderful things about you."

She released my hand, and I offered mine to Henry. His touch was icier than Adrian's had been, and I wondered if all Cruor were so cold or if Adrian and Henry were anomalies.

"Please, come in." I stepped aside and motioned toward the living room.

Charles wrapped his mom in a hug. They looked more like siblings than mother and son. She closed her eyes and held him in the embrace for a long moment before releasing him, then her hand lingered on his cheek as she focused on him with the gentle, loving gaze only a mother could impart.

"I'm so glad you two came," Charles said. "How was the trip?"

Henry, looking at Charles, tilted his head toward the door. Then he turned to Valeria and me. "Excuse us, please."

What was *that* about?

Valeria's smile never wavered. After the men stepped outside, Mr. Liette's thoughts echoed through my mind: . . . *if we didn't lose them at the edge of town.*

My heart quickened, but I gave Valeria a smile I hoped covered my concerns. "I'll put on some tea."

I walked to the kitchen and tapped my fingers on the granite counter while water heated in the kettle. I needed to stay busy, stay out of the Liettes' thoughts. I grabbed two carrots, an onion, a stalk of celery, and some white beans from the fridge.

Lost *who* at the edge of town?

"Let me give you a hand."

I jumped. When I turned, Valeria was standing in the doorway.

"You startled me," I said.

"Is everything all right, dear?"

"I think I'm just nervous."

"Don't be. Now, what're you putting together?"

"A quick soup. Or I'm trying to. Charles is better with the cooking."

"Scooch over." Valeria eased beside me and chopped the carrots into tiny disks. "Whatever you have in the oven smells delicious."

"Another one of Charles' creations," I said, immediately comfortable. "Hummingbird cake?"

The smile she offered didn't reach her eyes. "His sister's favorite. Fresh pineapple, bananas, cinnamon. Roasted pecans on top. I never would have guessed Charles would remember the recipe after all these years."

She went on about the cake, but I was stuck on something else: "Charles has a sister?"

"Oh, dear." Valeria stopped chopping. "Please, don't mind me." She went back to slicing, working a little slower. She slid the sliced carrots aside with the edge of the knife.

I debated responding, but by the time I worked up the nerve to speak, the moment had passed. We sliced the remaining vegetables in silence. Though I shouldn't have, I tried using my curse/gift to pry for more, but she'd pushed the sister from her mind. Two other children—young twins, one girl and one boy—lingered in the first sister's place.

The front door creaked and clicked shut, jolting me from her thoughts, and the men thudded their way to the kitchen. I felt as though I'd been caught stealing . . . a feeling I knew all too well and never wanted to relive. I needed to stay out of their heads.

"Smells good in here," Henry said.

Valeria smiled over her shoulder. "Oh, hush." To me, she said, "You do have blood on hand? Henry of course can't have soup or cake."

"Charles has some from his last hunt," I said.

I'd nearly forgotten pure earth elementals couldn't eat human food. When I was first getting to know Charles, he'd said he needed blood because he was Strigoi. In truth, he needed it because he was part Cruor. I gave Charles a long look as I swept the vegetables into my hand and plunked them into the soup pot.

Were there other things he wasn't telling me? He'd never mentioned a sister.

Pouring some animal blood into a glass, I tried to pretend the red liquid was something else. I thought of blood oranges, but that put me off from oranges more than comforted me over the idea of warming blood.

I carried everyone's drinks into the living room on a tea tray. As I handed Valeria a cup of tea, I glanced at Henry. He sipped his blood, and my stomach lurched. Charles never drank blood in my presence. The jug in the fridge was tolerable, but consumption was another matter.

Henry set aside his glass. "Relax and join us, Sophia."

Everyone was already sitting. I'd been staring. I hurriedly sat next to Charles on the couch. "So . . . how did you two meet?"

Another award-winning icebreaker.

Valeria plunged right into her story. She told me she was born to one of Queen Anne Boleyn's maids in 1531, and she and her mother

147

stayed with the royal family even after Anne's death, continuing under Queen Elizabeth the First's reign.

"My mother hadn't known my father was Strigoi," Valeria said, "but once I hit my teen years, I began shifting. We confronted my father, who explained what I was and what it would mean for me, but he refused to offer any support. He wouldn't even accept responsibility over my life, as it was frowned upon for someone of the court to mingle with servants.

"At first, I'd been unable to control when the shifts occurred. My mother feared someone at the court might learn and have me executed. She gave me what little money she had and sent me to the street, swiping tears from beneath her eyes and trying to keep her composure so that no one would read anything into the exchange taking place between us. Different times, back then."

The air in the room grew heavier. I curled up my legs and sipped my tea as Valeria shared the story of how she met Henry, her words painting the history between them like a movie in my mind.

· · ·

AS THE LAW OF 1547 said, after three days without a job, Valeria had to offer to work for any employer for any wages, even if only for food and drink. But no one would hire her; they all wanted strong men.

It was Henry's father who, after finding her begging at the market, finally took her to the local magistrate, where under law she was made a slave to their family for two years. She'd been in service to Henry's father for a year when he found a necklace she had kept hidden—the only keepsake of her mother, her only symbol of hope. He took the necklace from her as payment for the food and shelter he provided, and she dared not argue.

One night, Henry went out, and a week passed before his return. He knocked on Valeria's window and asked her to leave with him. "I've wanted you since the first time I laid eyes on you. Now I am certain we can have a life away from all this."

"If they catch me, I'll be branded to a life of slavery."

Henry shook his head. "I promise no one will hurt you. Come now."

She climbed out the window, and the two ran as far and as fast as they could—Valeria in such a state at the time that she hadn't even noticed Henry keeping up with her own unusual speed. They didn't stop running until they reached a small, windowless house with a thatched roof.

"You don't open that door," he told her.

He didn't say anything else to her for three days.

Every night, he set out to hunt and returned with a small animal. He shucked its skin in silence, cleaned its meat, and cooked for only Valeria to eat. Rain fell on the forth night. The roof sagged, and vermin and insects fell from it to the dirt floor below. Though the beds were made from straw and ridden with lice and fleas, neither attempted to bother Valeria or Henry. Even the rats stayed away.

Why had Henry left his comfortable life with his father for *this*?

That night, Henry arrived home from his hunt with a live rabbit. He sat across from Valeria and locked his gaze on hers. Her stomach clenched, and she leaned back. Henry's fangs descended, and he bit into the animal's flesh and drank.

Valeria gasped.

"I didn't ask for this," he said in a low, gruff voice.

She softened. "I know."

"And you?"

Valeria swallowed, looking down at her hands.

"I saw you," he said, "shortly after my father brought you to us. You were a bird, and then you were standing naked in the service quarters."

She bit her lip. "You didn't say anything."

"Would you prefer I had?"

Henry told Valeria how, coming home from a pub one night, he had been bitten and drained, left for dead. He sensed his maker out there somewhere, but could not find him. He found other Cruor and learned as much as possible before returning for her.

In the late 1600s, they learned of the new supernatural law—the law that the races were not to mix. But they were already pregnant with Charles and so were forced into hiding. Even today they stayed as far as possible from society—supernatural and otherwise—hoping that would provide Charles the opportunity to live without fear of persecution.

• • •

"WE WERE ON OUR OWN after that," Valeria said, "but I think that was the least alone we'd ever felt."

"I still don't understand how you carried a child," I said. "I thought the Cruor can't have children."

"They can't," Valeria said, "but as I am Strigoi, it is of no concern. So long as I didn't shift, my womb and the child could grow."

"Charles explained the Strigoi age if they don't shift, but this isn't true for him."

Valeria pressed her lips together. "Charles and—" Valeria covered her mouth and coughed quietly. "Charles aged like any normal child would . . . the way a Strigoi would. At nineteen, he gained the ability to shift. But even without shifting, he'd stopped aging. We realized then his Cruor heritage ran deeper than we'd thought, more than merely his need for blood. Charles will never age beyond nineteen."

Nineteen? He certainly looked older. Technically, he *was* older. I couldn't let the revelation rattle me. He was too old for me, he was too young for me . . . either way, all that mattered was the opportunity for us to age together.

"What if he *could* grow older?" I asked.

Valeria beamed. "Ah, yes! He asked us about this, and he has our blessing. Believe me, anything for love."

He'd talked to his parents about this? I couldn't contain the small bubble of hope that stirred within me.

"I think we've chatted enough," Charles cut in. His voice had a steely edge, and he didn't wait for a reaction before continuing. "Sophia is the descendant of a spirit elemental. We should focus our energies on discussing that instead."

The change of subject was so sudden that even I was shaken by his statement. Valeria's eyebrows arched, and Henry's face gave a flicker of expression—concern, perhaps?

"Is this true?" Valeria asked.

"Yes." I looked hesitantly to Charles. "I also hear people's thoughts. Like you and your husband."

"Well, that is something of a dilemma." She sipped her tea and then set her cup aside. "But only because you think it to be, Sophia."

"What do you mean?"

"Might you be able to tap into human thoughts as well?"

I bit my lip, considering. "I don't believe so."

"Clairaudience, then," she said. "Not as odd as you might think." She placed a hand over mine. "The thoughts of mortals and immortals are anchored in separate realms in order to protect elementals from mortal telepaths. However," she continued, "clairaudients like yourself can bridge over to access the thoughts of immortals. It's believed to be a common gift among witches and their descendants, since they are both supernatural as well as mortal."

"The voices left once before," I offered, "after Charles' friend gave me Cruor blood to heal some injuries."

"With his life source in your system, you were temporarily pulled from your own realm. Clairaudients cannot access thoughts in the realms they occupy, so you will not hear immortal thoughts when in the immortal realm." She stared into the middle distance, smiling softly. "I've met someone like you once before. In Nepal. Anytime she drank Cruor blood, though, she heard human thoughts until the immortal essence filtered from her system. Did you experience likewise?"

I shook my head. Part in answer to her question and part in shock to learn others like me existed. "I don't think so."

"Your gift will protect you more than it puts you at risk," Valeria said, "so long as you do not fear it."

☪

AFTER THE MORE SERIOUS MATTERS had been discussed, the Liettes engaged us with their light banter. Mrs. Liette asked a lot of questions, though nothing too personal or too hard to answer. She clung to every word spoken, listening intently, inhaling through her nose with a small smile, her chest rising at the intake of air, as if the very oxygen in the room made her happy. She was breezy, and the moments with her seemed to freeze time.

Mr. Liette, however, was the one who most shared my interests. It happened he was a firm believer in the possibility of the Ankou having a cure for the dual-natured. His wife and Charles shared a look over his ramblings, but I was enthralled as he sustained the possibilities with information that seemed to make sense of it all. I was most charmed when he brought up Nostradamus' predictions. He believed Nostradamus was an early messenger of the Universe, and any disproven theories were merely evidence that the future wasn't set in stone.

Charles huffed at his father's sentiments and implored him to talk about something else. "Anything else," he said. "Area 51. Elvis is still alive. Aliens. Just please"—he rubbed his hands down the sides of his face—"stop talking about Nostradamus!"

Mr. Liette chuckled and leaned closer to me. "He hates when I talk about this stuff."

I stole a glance at Charles and smiled. He was smiling back.

After dinner, dessert, and another round of tea/blood, the Liettes gathered their things and said their goodbyes before disappearing into the night.

As it was too early for bed, and Charles and I wanted a reprieve from the lingering energy in the living room, we headed to the basement.

Charles plopped onto the sofa, pulling me into his strong, comforting grasp. "They like you. I can tell."

151

"Yeah . . . ."

"Oh no." Charles frowned. "What now?"

"Your dad thinks someone followed them."

Charles scratched the back of his neck. "He mentioned that outside."

"Aren't you worried?"

He smirked. "My dad thinks everyone's out to get him."

Charles switched on a spare television set he'd brought down earlier in the day, and I tried to pay attention to the screen. Some show on the Discovery channel talked about human cloning.

We snuggled under a throw blanket, and Charles wove his fingers through my hair. During one of the commercials, he looked right at me, and my heart jumped with his heavy gaze. He swept his nose slowly across my jaw, bringing his lips to my neck and inhaling.

The glow of the television reflected off his fangs, but, this time, he didn't pull away. He cupped my face and gently kissed me, his fangs rubbing against my bottom lip. I shivered, partly from nervousness and partly from the desire building within me. He broke the kiss but didn't move his face away from mine.

"Are you afraid?" he whispered.

"No."

"You sure?"

My heart beat unsteadily, and I couldn't infuse my voice with any level of certainty. "Yes?"

His fingers grazed over my thighs, between them. He kissed my neck, then pressed his lips near the curve of my ear. "Ready now?"

I wanted to say yes. He knew my secrets, and I'd accepted we'd take the issue of our 'future' one day at a time. There was no reason to resist my intimate desires toward him. Finally, I managed to squeak out a quiet, "I think so."

He leaned back into the couch, chuckling. "Of course."

I sat up. "What? Did I say something wrong?"

Faint amusement replaced the fire in his eyes. "No," he said. "You were too busy thinking."

I frowned.

Charles wrapped his arm around me and pulled me close. "It's okay," he said. "It was a long day—let's relax."

I took his advice, but, inwardly, my frown remained. Hoping to get everything off my mind, I forced myself to focus on the television.

The airing had moved on from talk of human cloning to talk of curing hereditary abnormalities through stem cells, reminding me of the talk I'd had with Mrs. Liette about the rules of procreation in their world.

"I'm wondering—" I peeked up. "—about your sister?"

Charles dropped his head into his hands. "My mom brought her up?"

His voice was so tender that a knot formed in my throat.

"She started to," I said. "If you don't want to talk about it . . . "

"I don't mind—it happened a long time ago, during the war. Warriors from the Maltorim discovered Kate was a dual-breed through a friend she had trusted. They tortured her, trying to get her to reveal our parents, bringing her close to death several times then waiting for her to heal before starting again. She was only fifteen—not yet able to shift." His voice fell, hoarse now. "It's my fault they killed her."

"You aren't responsible."

His eyes remained on the floor. "I was there. It was during the war, and at the time, any one known as a Cruor was expected to fight. Fight or die. I did my best to show my allegiances without hurting anyone, but my sister acted more on her honor, and that's how they eventually discovered her true nature. She never revealed our relation, and I didn't say anything. I did nothing to stop them."

"They would have killed you both," I said, knowing it wouldn't be any consolation.

"If I'd done something—*anything*—at least she would have known I cared. When they abandoned her dead body, I snuck her home to my parents for a proper burial. I cannot describe to you the guilt, the grief—" He shook his head as his voice cracked. "I failed her."

"I'm sure she knew your love for her," I said gently.

He didn't respond, and I opted for a shift in conversation. "Your other siblings—they were okay?"

Charles' eyebrows pulled together. "My other siblings?"

"The twins."

"What twins?"

I searched his expression for answers, but the only emotion there was confusion. I spun the beads on my bracelet. "A misunderstanding, I guess."

Charles let out a heavy sigh. "I don't think my parents wanted to have more kids after what happened to my sister, and I certainly didn't want more siblings. I'd failed my sister. That can't be redeemed with new life."

"We can't bring her back," I said, "but you can do *something*. We can change things."

He scoffed, but the strain around his eyes revealed he was more hurt than annoyed.

"We'll fight back, somehow. The war against the dual-breeds can't go on forever."

"I shouldn't have dragged you into this." His expression softened, along with the edge in his voice. "If I could do it over again, I would have—"

"Done something different? Like with your sister?" I didn't need clairaudience to evaluate his thinking. He was afraid he might lose me to the darker side of his world, the same way he'd lost his sister.

"I'm not going anywhere," I said. "We'll think of something."

Something, yes, but what?

I didn't know.

{nineteen}

THE EVENING AFTER the Liettes' visit, I attempted to use my clairaudience to locate Thalia's coterie. I'd already tried twice, hoping to zone in on them and see if their thoughts would reveal anything useful, but both my attempts had been unsuccessful.

Charles said not to worry about his father's fear of being followed, but I wanted to make certain. If anyone would know anything, it would be Thalia and her coterie. Despite what Charles had said, I was certain Thalia wasn't harmless. He might know more about his world than me, but his intuition sucked.

Soon, however, I'd learn my own intuition was lacking as well.

I turned off my cell phone and the lights. A few lit candles, scattered around the room, released sweet walnut and vanilla into the air, and the red light of the setting sun burned through the basement windows. I sat on the floor in my chalk circle, straightened my posture, and took several deep breaths. I imagined vines growing from the earth, gently embracing me, leaving me connected and comfortable. I fell into the practiced rhythm of breathing until even the sound of my breath dissolved in my ears.

My world grew silent, but the voices blared. I centered my energy on the back of my mind, visualizing a map beside a tray of pushpins. As I descended deeper into my meditation, the tingling sensation in my mind intensified. I focused on the loudest whisper until the others fell away. A single voice remained; it would be Charles. I listened long enough to use his voice as a marker, just as I'd practiced late last night with him and Adrian. I dropped Charles to focus on the next closest voice.

Last time I tip Lucia on the best hunting grounds. I come back here, and what do I find? Nothing. Greedy little—

I tuned out and scanned for another voice, at what I guessed was about a mile further out than the last.

Why should I bother hiding? If anyone said they saw me, they'd get booked to the nearest mental institution.

Another failed attempt.

When I tried a third time, the pain of a young woman shifting for the first time filtered into my mind. The voices were one thing, but sharing the sensations was too much. I quickly tuned out and moved onto a voice that registered about three miles away.

The location was close to Basker Street. My heart sped as I listened.

The chick works at a blood bank for God's sake. Match made in heaven.

Not Thalia. I couldn't lock on her—or track her at all for that matter. Ditto for Circe. The rest of the supernatural world surrounding us was vacant of any thoughts regarding the Liettes.

I panned the area for an hour before calling it quits. Releasing a final slow breath, I concentrated on blocking the voices altogether. It wasn't foolproof. The voice of one elemental or another still occasionally punctured my own thoughts but, overall, I was getting a handle on my abilities.

The trance-working drained all my mental and emotional energy. As Paloma had taught me, I drank the water and ate the cookie I'd set nearby to replenish my energy.

Almost immediately after I flicked the lights on, Charles tapped the wall at the bottom of the basement stairs.

I yawned, though I'd been aiming for a smile. "You still haven't heard from your parents?"

"They don't usually call back right away. Come on. Let's get to bed."

We headed upstairs. Just as I shut the basement door behind me, a voice swirled through my thoughts.

Close.

Too close.

The next moment happened so fast, I didn't have a chance to fully process the thoughts of our invader. Where had they come from? I'd just been searching.

They lunged at Charles, and instinct threw me in front of him. Pain stabbed my shoulder. My gaze dropped to the stake, coated in dark fluid, that jutted from my body. A sharp gasp echoed—not just my own, but the attacker's as well.

Two shapes flashed around the room. Charles fighting another Cruor. As my vision faded, their preternatural movements blurred into meaningless colors. A heavy fog pushed over every synapse in my brain. The attacker's influence. I couldn't fight it—couldn't keep my eyes open.

I fell away, into the dark.

AN OPEN DOOR revealed a simple white bathroom and a hairbrush on the vanity. I was lying in our bed. Light streamed in through the small window to my left, marking the comforter with a long, pale rectangle.

A stringent antiseptic smell burned my nostrils, and I lifted a hand to touch the pain gnawing at my shoulder. My fingertips brushed a rough, damp material. Blood-stained gauze clung to my skin. Images from last night—was it last night?—replayed in my mind. Someone had invaded our home. Someone had tried to kill Charles, and might have succeeded if I hadn't gotten in the way.

Shit. What if it'd been Marcus? Why hadn't I heard anyone near the house? It'd been too dark to see anything more than Charles' shape beside me and a moving darkness in the shadows of the hall.

I parted my lips to speak, but my mouth was too dry to form words.

I licked my lips and tried again. "Charles?"

His name left me like a breath, but no sooner had I rasped those words than he appeared in the doorway and, another moment later, at the bedside.

"How are you feeling?" he asked. Through my groggy vision, the lashes framing his eyes looked darker, his eyes more arcane and intense.

"Not so great." I winced, pulling the shoulder of my nightgown back into place. "Is it okay?"

"Not as bad as it looks."

"My clairaudience didn't pick up anything." I shook my head. "I was listening, but—"

"Hey," Charles said softly, "don't think about that now. Your gift . . . it's still new."

"Where's the attacker?" I asked. Before he could answer, my clairaudience registered their life. Their thoughts sped too fast to tune into. I got a sense of anger, regret, and . . . love? I shot up in bed, alarm pulsing in my chest and throat. "They're still here?"

"Stay calm." He touched his palm to my face. "What you did last night—jumping in front of me—I would never have wanted you to do that. I'm glad you're okay."

Something wasn't right. We didn't have time for platitudes. I tried to break into his thoughts, but he blocked my attempts. I felt each beat of my heart, hard and distinct, slamming against my chest.

157

I put up one finger to silence him and tapped into my clairaudience. Pain muddled my ability. After a few tries, I barely managed to discern the attacker was female. Thalia? But I'd been searching for her all night. "Why is she still here?"

He gazed toward the hallway. A bruise yellowed his forehead, already fading, and pink scratch lines puffed beneath his left cheekbone. His injuries would be gone soon, leaving behind only the scars of his childhood.

"I didn't know what else to do," he whispered.

I hopped from bed. Pain shot from my shoulder to my elbow, but I forced myself forward, gritting my teeth as I stormed to the basement door.

Charles darted ahead, grabbing my uninjured arm as I reached for the door handle. "Wait, Sophia. Let's talk first."

"Move. Now."

He let go, and I opened the door and started down the stairs. When I saw my attacker, my heart thudded with a strange pressure, shock coursing through my body. My eyes were lying to me. This had to be some horrible mistake.

Ivory, now chained in our basement, couldn't have been our attacker.

She kept her gaze down, the fringe of her lashes casting shadows onto her cheeks. Blood splattered to the floor in front of her. More crusted beneath one ear and clotted her hair against her scalp. Chains weighed against the bubbling flesh of her wrists.

I turned toward Charles, dread sinking deeper into my stomach, my gaze pleading for him to correct my assumptions.

"I didn't know what else to do," he said, his voice full of apology.

Adrenaline wore off and pain took over, but this pain came more from the tightening around my heart than the wound on my shoulder. What was happening?

Ivory's hoarse, tear-smothered voice broke the silence. "Sophia?"

"No," I said sharply. I wasn't doing this. I couldn't talk to her.

I ran back upstairs to the kitchen, to the one place I sat every morning until the nightmares of my slumber disappeared. Recently, my nightmares had all been of my ancestor, the ghost of her dead body hanging from the gallows, but this nightmare was far worse.

This nightmare was real.

As my trembling hand drew a chair from the table, the chair legs rattled against the linoleum. Charles crossed the floor and filled a kettle with water.

I gazed at my hands, not really seeing them. "I *heard* her."

"Of course." His soft voice soothed the edge of my anxiety.

"But that would mean . . . she is . . . " The pain had been too severe for me to tap into my ability. I'd assumed our attacker had been Cruor, but that couldn't be the case. "What is she?"

"You already know," Charles said, pouring me a cup of chamomile tea. "She's an earth elemental."

"I sure as hell *didn't* know." My words sounded accusatory, and part of me wondered if they should. How could she be Cruor? I blew out a deep breath. "Why would I know that?"

"After that night at Club Flesh—" He set my tea on the table and stared out the window. I followed his gaze, but the yard was empty, the trees bare. "She didn't tell you?" He shook his head. "She said she would tell you everything. You *said* she told you everything."

"That wasn't what I meant," I said. "She told me about the Cruor. Not that she *was* one."

Had I been too absorbed in my relationship with Charles to notice what was going on around me? I thought back to all the conversations Charles and I had. None of them had been about her. All of our talks had been about the people I feared, not the people I trusted.

Charles turned toward me. "Haven't you ever 'heard' her before?"

I rubbed slow circles over my temples, trying to think. "I haven't seen her in months, since before I understood my ability." I shook my head. "Are you certain?"

Charles nodded.

"Then she's a dual-breed, like you."

"Not like me, no," he said. "She's protected herself from the sun through Ankou magic."

"Can they do that?"

He shrugged. "It appears so."

I stared at the rings of the wooden kitchen table, trying to make sense of everything. "Why didn't she tell me?"

"I trusted she had." Charles tucked his hands deep into his pockets and gave me a look that told me he had more to say, but didn't want to say it. And since he didn't seem sure he wanted to say it, I wasn't sure I wanted to hear.

"What about her aura?" I asked. "You would've noticed something off about her, right?"

"Aura-reading is more complicated than that."

"Is it?" I asked, eyes brimming with tears and heart overflowing with hurt and skepticism.

Charles swallowed. "You know things are different for me. I am not a pure Strigoi—I cannot use my abilities with the same strength. And I hardly have the training. Auras are complicated. Red might mean life-force, raw passion, or anger. Orange might mean sensuality or lacking reason. Green, healing or envy."

"She was all of those?"

"Mostly red, though always a bit muted. The Ankou magic may have affected her aura." His eyes searched mine. "Now do you understand?"

I pressed the heels of my palms into my eyes. I needed to rein in my emotions if I was going to make sense of all this.

"I'm sorry, Charles. I just don't get it. Why was she trying to attack you? What do we do now?" I stood to pace the kitchen but a dizzy spell hit and rooted me at a standstill. Ivory's name echoed in my thoughts, and I sunk back into the kitchen chair. "Can't you remove her memory of us—use influence or something?"

Charles knelt beside me and grabbed my shoulders. I knew he wanted me to look at him, both by reading the thoughts in his mind and also from the way his head dipped slightly to bring his face closer to mine.

I couldn't look.

"That can't be done to an earth elemental," he said.

"We need to think about this." I pushed him away. "*I* need to think about this."

My gaze lingered apologetically on his, then I headed for the place I always went when feeling my darkest: the bathroom.

I closed the door behind me and took a long look in the mirror. The woman staring back couldn't be me. She was a husk of her former self—a lost child or a silhouette of who she might have been. Sobs fought to break through my anger. I splashed cool water on my face and tried to steady my breathing. Leaning back against the wall, I slid to the bathroom floor.

Did Ivory think killing Charles would protect me from his world? If she would just forget about me, Charles and I could be together without worrying about her trying anything like this again. There had to be a way to make her forget.

Paloma came to mind. She'd said I could come to her with anything. 'Anything' included what? Certainly not blood-sucking creatures of the night. I hadn't even told her about the voices. Would it be wrong to subject her to the knowledge of this world, especially given how the Cruor dealt with people who found out about them?

Suddenly I was in the bedroom, phone in hand, the memory of walking there like a dream. My fingers dialed the numbers and the receiver rang in my ears. I willed myself to hang up, but my body would not comply.

Paloma's voice came over the line. "Sophia?"

Had I said it was me? "Yes," I managed.

"Sophia, is everything all right?"

"There's a problem," I said. "With Ivory."

I could almost hear her frown through the phone. "I was worried this might happen. I'll come straight over."

The line went dead.

{twenty}

THE CHILL OF WINTER leaked through the cracked bedroom window. The backyard fence rotted near the bottom, decaying from the moisture of dirtied snow, and a clammy chill crawled over my skin. Darkness would be a relief from what the day had revealed.

Something crinkled and shuffled outside the door. A clock ticked. All these things overpowered my senses, and yet they didn't really matter.

I was still sitting on the bed, phone in hand, when Charles brought Paloma into the room. She smelled like roses and fabric softener, not incense and hot ceramic. The hem of her long flowing skirt flickered against the burnt yellow light of the room. I felt drugged.

Charles returned the phone to its cradle and draped a blanket over my shoulders. I'd been shivering, but not from cold.

Paloma kneeled down and cradled my face in her hands. Her eyes looked more tired than usual, her usually vibrant skin faded and grayish. "Charles told me what happened."

"Ivory is a . . . she's a . . . "

"I know."

"You knew?" Everyone had known but me? Somewhere beneath my barriers, hurt and anger threatened to surface.

"It's my job to know." She lowered her hands to her lap, and for the first time ever, I noticed her fingernails. She'd always seemed so put together, so light and worry-free. But her fingernails were so horribly bitten—a lifetime of worry showing from the habit—that scabs formed where her nails had been chewed to the quick.

I pulled the blanket tighter around me, shielding the torn, bloodstained fabric at the shoulder of my waffle-knit sweater. "You run Sparrow's Grotto, in Cripple Creek. *That* is your job."

Paloma trapped her bottom lip with her teeth and cast Charles a pained, watery gaze.

Charles wrapped his arm around me. "Paloma called on her way over. She's a generational witch, like you. She works to make sure things like this don't happen."

Not very good at her job then, is she?

My friends weren't my friends. My mentor was more than a mentor. This wasn't the town I'd grown up in, and this house—this house that had once been a library—was nothing more than an empty shell, the walls with little purpose beyond hiding a truth I'd have rather not known.

For a moment, I thought of the world outside, going on without me—a world where elementals did not exist because people didn't know about them.

My brow tensed, and I turned toward Charles. "Paloma knew about me, too?"

He offered a weak shrug; of course he wouldn't know. I shouldn't have directed my question toward him with Paloma standing right there. Talk about rude. I gave her an apologetic look, imploring her with my gaze.

She sighed heavily. "I wasn't sure. Even if I had known, there would've been no way for me to tell you. A witch must come to the realization on her own. I did my best to guide you in that direction. Your recent ritual had been my first key intervention. The rest was up to you."

I suddenly understood why she'd given me the eyebright instead of agrimony. That one herb was likely the cause of my gift coming to the surface.

"Ivory is a witch, too?" I asked.

"She was intended as a spirit elemental," Paloma said, "which means she would've been pure when she was chosen. Something must have happened, maybe around the time she was turned. Many of her powers are obsolete now. But because she was one of the original witches chosen by the Universe, there was no discovery for her to make. She's always known. There was no place for me in her life to act as a mentor."

The room slowly came back into focus: Paloma, with her heavily beaded earrings; Charles, in his jeans and black t-shirt; me, clueless as ever.

"Okay," I said quietly. "I think I understand."

"Yes," Paloma said. "But now we must take action to protect you from her—" Her worried gaze flickered to mine. "—though I fear you won't like what needs to be done."

☪

PALOMA INSISTED I eat first, get my energy up, before we talk. Now a bowl of jasmine rice, barely touched, sat on the table.

She had the answers all right, but I sure as hell didn't like them. She wanted *me* to erase Ivory's memories. I hadn't been bothered by the idea of Charles or Adrian wiping them, but now the whole idea suddenly seemed like stealing—like a complete abandonment of my faith.

Like a mistake I'd made once before and desperately didn't want to repeat.

I shook my head. "It's black magic."

And by that, I meant the *bad* kind. Not the kind most Wiccans knew as the yin to the yang of White Magic. This kind of magic wouldn't bring balance. No, this kind of magic was the kind sometimes referred to as *Hostile* Magic.

"There's no other way," Paloma said. "Only a spirit elemental can extract memories from the Cruor. Your gift will help you. Think this over if you must, but this *is* what needs to be done. If you don't erase her memories of you, she may seek out you or Charles again. I'm sorry."

She stroked her hand up and down my back before leaving me alone in the room.

I rested my head in my hands, staring unseeingly at the wooden floor beneath my feet. I'd expected Charles to do the dirty work. My heart sank at the thought: I'd been treating him like his humanity was less valuable than my own. What did that say about me?

Should I follow my faith or my heart? My intentions were pure, which counted for something, right? Killing Ivory would be far worse than stealing her memories, and the only other option wasn't an option at all—we couldn't walk away. If I didn't do as Paloma suggested, Ivory would find us and attack again. There'd be no hiding from someone who knew me so well.

The sound of a chair dragging against the kitchen's linoleum floor ripped me from my introspection. Charles entered the room and sat beside me on the couch. He was silent at first. Then: "Do you need anything?"

"You wouldn't like it."

He swiveled his head toward me, his gaze blank and the whites of his eyes road-mapped with red. "This isn't about me."

"My shoulder is killing me. Wouldn't your blood . . . ?"

His mouth sagged, more of a slacking of his features than a frown, but he gave a resolute nod. When Adrian had given me his blood all those months ago, it'd only been because neither Charles nor Ivory had been ready to tell me about their own true natures. If I was going to have a bond with anyone, though, I wanted that person to be Charles. Waiting for Adrian to arrive and assist us was simply not an option, and I sensed the side effect of experiencing someone's memories would feel somehow less invasive with Charles than it had with Adrian.

Charles swept hair from my face and grazed my forehead with his lips. He pulled away and tore into his wrist to make a fresh wound from which blood flowed freely. He held his wrist to my mouth, and my stomach churned as the first drops rolled onto my tongue, but I sucked from the wound anyway, drinking until my stomach settled. Charles' blood wasn't cold like Adrian's, but it was just as thick and metallic and sweet.

His emotions rushed through me—anger, devotion, fear, concern. Soon, distinguishing his feelings from my own was nearly impossible. Perhaps my experience with Charles would be different. Would I be burdened with his emotional turmoil, instead of the images of his past? I peered up at him, still drinking, but his expression was blank.

When the high of drinking the blood kicked in, I released his arm. The pain slowly subsided, replaced with a faint, healing tingle. I removed the gauze wrap and bandage, grimacing as the wound healed.

I lifted my gaze to him, wiping my mouth with the sleeve of my sweater. "Are you okay?"

The look of concern in his eyes challenged his smile. "You stopped before it hurt. What about you?"

"I still need time to think."

Paloma joined us in the living room, setting a book in my lap: *Ignisvisum.* The literal translation in Latin would have been 'Fire Vision', but the subtitle read *Scrying with Fire*. Paloma had already told me the details, but reading the pages solidified this living nightmare.

How was I supposed to concentrate long enough to write my own ritual? The ignisvisum itself wasn't wrong, but using it as a method to steal memories was.

The text swam around the pages. I wrote things down, crossed them out, and started over. On my tenth or eleventh attempt, something clicked. The words flew to the page.

Paloma stared out the window, looking over her shoulder every few minutes. Charles stood and took a meaningless trip outside. He wanted to clear his head, too. I dropped my connection with his thoughts and tried to focus on my own.

The decision wasn't impossible. What choice did I have? Performing black magic was our only hope. Even then, I wasn't sure the technique would work.

Charles returned as I was finishing my notes. I closed my notebook and stood.

"I have to do this." The steely edge of my voice felt strange on my tongue.

He sighed, shutting the front door quietly. "I didn't want to pressure you."

Paloma turned to me, took both my hands, and gave them a gentle squeeze. A sad smile crossed her face.

Night had fallen. Charles placed a call to Adrian, telling him everything and asking him to come over as soon as possible. We would need him to relocate Ivory after the ritual, back to where she lived before she came to Colorado. Maybe if she was back in Boston, without any memories of me, she would have no reason to return. But wouldn't she be confused? Would she think she'd gone crazy? I pushed aside the creeping guilt and centered my attention on my only option.

Paloma set up a small altar in the basement while I stood staring at Ivory, my arms crossed. She sat on the floor, chained to the wall and leaning back. Her gaze never left the ground, never rose to mine, but blood streaked down her cheeks from her eyes.

"How could you?" I barely choked the words past the thickness in my throat.

"You don't understand," Ivory whispered.

"Then explain it to me."

Ivory opened her mouth, but then it fell shut, and she shook her head. "I—I can't."

I shook my head and turned away. She tried to use her influence— the warm push she sent out was weak and frenzied—and I blocked her attempt.

"No one can protect you like I can," she said.

"Don't try that crap with me."

"I'm sorry, Sophia. I never meant for—"

"Sorry? You're fucking *sorry*?" I spun back, blinking away my tears, then stormed across the room, grabbed a roll of duct tape from the supply cabinet, and returned to bind her mouth shut.

Paloma rose and placed a hand on my arm. I was shaking.

"You need to stay calm," she said.

I pressed my lips together and stared out the thin slit of a basement window, trying to find an inner calm. All I found was cobwebs hanging between the windowpane and crank and paint peeling away from rusted metal casing. Dead flies littered the sill. Outside was a wash of gray—the bark of cedars, the crumbling stone of the birdbath, the leaden sky.

Charles sat in one of the painted wooden chairs and held a closed fist against his lips.

Paloma nodded at him and then took my hand. "Come sit at the altar."

Tears filmed my eyes, but I managed to detach. I hardened my heart and pushed back as Ivory continued her efforts to influence. None of her thoughts made sense now anyway; they were all panicked, muddled fragments.

I needed her asleep. Paloma handed over a stone mortar bowl filled with skullcap and henbane. My hands numb from adrenaline, I nearly dropped the dish. Shakily, I ground the herbs with the pestle. The mixture in tea could knock a person out, but no way would Ivory willingly drink anything we prepared.

"I'm sorry," I said, before blowing the powder from my palm into her eyes. It would sting, then seep into her retinas and blood stream.

I leaned away as she fought against the chains. Fresh areas of her skin smoked as the chains shook on her wrists. The bloody flesh pussed, and Ivory's fangs descended, tearing through the duct tape. Her cheeks puffed out and saliva escaped her mouth as she spat the tape to the floor.

Her movements became weaker, and before she could say anything, her eyelids drooped, then closed. Her body slumped listless in the chains.

I looked back to Charles. "She could have broken the chains?"

He shook his head. "They're silver."

That would explain why they burned her flesh. Initially, I'd thought those wounds had been from something else, but now that I understood her true nature, the cause was clear.

My gaze panned the room, anxiety mounting. Bright, cheery decor, with chains attached to the wall. A dark-haired girl's limp body sagging against restraints, silver eating away at flesh, searing third-degree burns into her wrists.

No, the room wasn't living up to my intentions. Perhaps I'd put the negative energy here myself.

Paloma handed me a paste made from elderberries to smear over Ivory's eyes, urging me to move forward with the ritual. This was new territory for me. What if the *ignisvisum* didn't work? We had no backup plan.

My confidence ebbed. "Everyone will ask where she went."

"I doubt anyone will be surprised," Charles said, "considering the way she's been acting."

"Stay with me?" I asked, my voice barely a whisper.

He nodded.

Paloma joined me in the opening rites to cast the circle and assisted me with a protection spell. A globe of electricity surrounded us as we knelt in front of the altar. Paloma filled the scrying bowl with chips of driftwood.

"Only you will see the images," Paloma said, "and only you will be able hear her thoughts."

I swallowed and nodded, then threw a lit match in my scrying bowl, the wood catching fire and heating my nose and cheeks. I added a cinnamon stick to aid in psychic vision and, using a small cloth, wiped acacia oil across my forehead to strengthen the effect.

Until that moment, reality could have been denied. Now I had to accept what I set out to accomplish.

"Blazing fire as you dance, give me now the secret glance. Call upon my second sight, make me psychic with your light."

In a quiet murmur, I repeated the words like a mantra, my eyelids growing heavy as I gazed into the fire.

Images from Ivory's mind displayed like a mirage on the rippling air above the embers, and my clairaudience soaked in all her thoughts and every memory and sense of emotion she'd once experienced.

My heart tightened as the air around our circle filled with black smog and the spirits of the deceased, alive during the imprinting of Ivory's memories, struggled to break through our protective barrier. How many of them were we pulling from the afterlife? How many were Morts—spirits of elementals that had never passed on?

I focused on my chant, tuning out the crackle of fire and the moans of spirits, watching the flicker of images in the scrying bowl. A dull pain swelled in my chest as millions of words, stretched over hundreds of years, spilled from her thoughts.

There she was. Ivory—though she thought of herself as Sarah. This wasn't Colorado. This wasn't the world I'd grown up in. Ivory was searching for dry wood and kindling—anything that might catch fire and warm her small home.

A few feet into the woods, a woman sat leaning against a tree. Long, blonde tendrils of hair hid her face, her white bonnet crumpled and dirty.

This was Ivory's life *before* she was turned, *not* just her memories of me. This wasn't what I'd called for with my spell, but backing out might mean losing my only chance for answers.

I waited another moment, willing the memories to fast forward, willing the *ignisvisum* to skip past these moments and arrive at her memories of me—the memories I needed to see.

Despite my efforts, the images continued to scroll. The woman leaning against the tree turned, the moon shining off the tears that soaked her cheeks. She and I could have passed for sisters. I nearly pulled back, determined not to steal memories that had nothing to do with me, but I couldn't tear my gaze away from this woman. In my heart, I knew who she was before Ivory even spoke her name.

"Elizabeth?" Ivory asked.

I should have looked away, but this was possibly my only chance at discovering what happened to Elizabeth's body . . . my only chance of gaining complete control over my clairaudience, of finding a way to protect myself and those I loved from the darkness in the elemental world.

It's often said experiences make a person who they are. But as I stared into the *ignisvisum* bowl and sent my clairaudience out to Ivory, I soon realized it was the memories of another that would forever reshape who I was to become.

{twenty-one}
IVORY'S MEMORIES

Salem, Massachusetts Colony, 1692

THE SKY DARKENED from indigo and ochre into a deep shade of amethyst. The remaining flecks of sun lent a golden warmth to the sepia-washed clearing. Ivory stumbled to a halt, then stepped closer, but Elizabeth remained seated in front of the tree.

She dropped her face into her hands. "Please go along."

Ivory placed the maple wood she'd gathered on the forest floor and hurried to Elizabeth. "What troubles you?"

"Go." Her voice dropped to a whisper. "Something evil has come."

The sadness in Elizabeth's eyes—a beautiful sadness that touched Ivory's heart—created a flutter in her stomach. Ivory held the betraying emotion at bay.

"Don't let the town's talk frighten you," she said. "They're just stories."

Elizabeth rocked slightly. "I can hear things. They will see, and they will kill me."

Ivory glanced back toward the village. "We won't let that happen, now will we? Tell me—"

An energy coursed through her veins. She shot to her feet and looked in every direction for a source, the sky and forest whirring around her. A whispering voice echoed between the trees, as though spoken from many discordant voices: "The heart of the spirit."

Ivory dropped to her knees in front of Elizabeth and placed a hand on either shoulder. "Did you—"

Elizabeth closed her eyes. "I heard."

Ivory gripped Elizabeth's shoulders until her short nails dug against the long sleeves of Elizabeth's dress. "We'll leave—travel somewhere safe and make sense of all this."

"I can't." Elizabeth's voice cracked. "My baby, I can't leave him."

"Nonsense. You must."

Elizabeth stood, shaking dirt loose from her skirts. "I won't."

"I'm sorry," Ivory said, gentling her voice. Unlike Elizabeth, she didn't have a husband or child. She still lived with her mother, father, and sister. How easy it would be to forget the ties that bound most women to the village. "Then we shall carry on until he has grown."

The pair soon learned the Universe had chosen them to restore balance to the earth, an idea their minds would have rejected if their hearts were not so touched by the purity of the Universe's voice.

And so, on some evenings to follow, they stole away into the forest, performing rituals guided by the Universe to conjure peace. Their gifts strengthened over time, and the Universe promised their true purpose would soon be revealed. Elizabeth and Ivory had no common ground otherwise: Elizabeth was married to a tailor, and Ivory was unwed, nearly too old to attract a suitor.

One afternoon, however, Elizabeth told Ivory of a deeper confliction, of the curse of *many* unknown voices, and not only the voice of the Universe.

They were sitting side-by-side near a dried riverbed, and the fabric of Ivory's dress rustled against the fabric of Elizabeth's. Ivory swallowed to steady her own quick, shallow breathing.

"I'm sure sense will come of it in time," Ivory offered.

Elizabeth turned to her. "Such are these times, Sarah, that I think you are the only soul in the world who understands."

Ivory searched Elizabeth's eyes. Her heart leapt forward, and, before she could control her impulse, she pressed her lips against Elizabeth's. Ivory quickly sat back, heat burning her cheeks and ears, but when she dared steal a glance, she noticed a blush creeping from the neckline of Elizabeth's dress and the small contented smile that touched Elizabeth's lips.

In nearby settlements, women were burned alive for such things. But Ivory wasn't willing to sacrifice the hope she found in Elizabeth's company.

Early one evening, while most of the townsfolk were still at work, Ivory opened her window and helped Elizabeth climb into her room. They huddled close under blankets, dressed only in their undergarments, facing each other on a small cot.

Ivory tucked one of Elizabeth's curls behind her ear. "We will leave this place," she whispered, "I promise you. When your child is grown, the time will be kind for our departure."

The floorboards creaked, and Elizabeth's body went rigid in Ivory's arms. Ivory clutched the blanket over their bodies. Her mother walked in and gasped, then spun away and shielded her eyes as Elizabeth quickly dressed and fled the house in tears.

"You are no child of mine!" Ivory's mother said in a voice drenched with disgust. Her hooded grey eyes narrowed, her fists balled on her hips. "They will be talking your death to know what you've done. Wipe her from your mind. Hear me, child, for you will find the end of a noose if you continue this path. May God send his mercy upon you and cleanse the blackness in your soul."

Ivory's sister, Anne, appeared in the doorway, but just as quickly turned and darted from the house, her fiery hair trailing behind and bleeding against the red, setting sun. Ivory refastened the bodice of her dress and chased after. If Anne said anything about what she'd seen . . .

Ivory couldn't let that happen. She rushed out to the courtyard and stood to block Elizabeth from Anne's glare.

A woman across the court dropped her water pail, and a man pulled the reins of a horse to bring his cart to a halt. Even the hammering of a nearby blacksmith stopped, leaving only the scent of fire and hot metal in the sudden silence.

More onlookers gathered by the second, as though drawn by the sudden commotion. Ivory's gaze swept across the villagers, some standing with mouths agape while others whispered amongst themselves. She looked at her own disheveled appearance, and then over to Elizabeth, who had dressed in such haste that her bonnet was crooked and her apron loose.

Ivory and Elizabeth stood without movement, a stunned tableau in the center of town. Anne tilted up her nose, smirking. Dirt scraped beneath her square-toed shoe as she turned toward the gathering of townsfolk.

"Witch!" She pointed at Elizabeth. "She has stricken my sister! She bids the devil's work!"

Ivory searched the faces of the crowd, looking for even one kind expression—*there must be at least one who doubts this accusation*?

But as her gaze landed on one unforgiving face after the other, her hope withered.

☪

AT DAWN the next morning, Ivory fell upon the courthouse, carried by a sea of excited townsfolk. She paused outside the low brick wall surrounding the establishment, but her mother pushed her through, whispering in her ear that seeing this would be a good life lesson.

Once inside and seated, Ivory glared at Elizabeth's husband, who sat on the worn pew at the front of the courtroom. Beside him, Elizabeth's fourteen-month-old sat with his arms hugged around his stomach.

Magistrate John Thornhart entered the room, his long gray hair stiff and thinning, his narrow, aquiline nose pointing toward his dimpled chin. The crowd quieted, nothing remaining but the creak of the wooden pews and the rustle of papers.

"Bring forth the accused!" His powerful voice sent shivers down Ivory's spine.

Two men brought Elizabeth into the courtroom and pushed her into a chair. Ivory's gaze followed the length of her lover's body from untamed hair to bare, dirtied feet, anger bubbling in her chest at the way she'd been mistreated.

Thornhart crossed the room, his shiny black buckled shoes clicking evenly on the wood floors. He faced Elizabeth, his hands clasped behind his back.

"Elizabeth, what evil spirits have you familiarity with?"

"None," she replied.

Thornhart raised one eyebrow and paced away. He looked back over his shoulder to her. "Have you made no contract with the devil?"

"No," Elizabeth said, her voice harder and more direct.

Thornhart pointed at Ivory, his gaze still leveled at Elizabeth. "Why do you curse this woman?"

Ivory shot to her feet. "I have no grievance! She does not harm me!"

Thornhart jerked his head toward her. "Speak not out of turn, I warn you, Sarah, lest you are attempting to curse us as well."

As all the eyes in the courtroom shifted to Ivory, her skin prickled with heat. She lowered herself to her seat.

"Elizabeth, what say you?" Thornhart asked.

"I do not curse her." Elizabeth's voice remained strong. Still, her eyes pleaded to the court, and Ivory's heart dropped to her stomach.

"Who, then, do you employ has cursed her?"

"No creature, for I am falsely accused!"

There was an edge of anger in Elizabeth's voice, and the crowd murmured.

"You bid the work of the devil when you make this woman lay with you as a heathen."

Was the town so sick with desire for a witch-hunt that they would accuse Elizabeth of witchcraft before considering both women guilty of expressing their love to one another?

"Anne, you identified her as the one who torments your sister." Thornhart paused briefly from his pacing. "What have you to say in evidence?"

Anne fingered a small pendant on a chain at her neck. "My sister behaves strangely only when in Elizabeth's presence. The witch is an enemy to all good!"

Ivory kept her arms crossed, hoping her expression was stoic and cold instead of as rigid and fearful as she felt. Already she tasted the tears in the back of her throat.

"See now what you have done, Elizabeth? Redeem yourself and speak the truth, for you have cursed this woman."

Elizabeth's hands curled into tight fists. "I do not curse her!"

"Tell us, Elizabeth. How do you curse her?"

Before Elizabeth could declare her innocence once more, her husband stood. His expression was weighted, and he swallowed. When he spoke, his voice was so quiet Ivory had to strain to hear.

"She tells me of voices that speak to her," he said. "She has been accursed for some time now." He lifted his apologetic gaze to Elizabeth. "I'm so sorry. Please, let them help you."

Ivory nearly choked on the air. Elizabeth had told him? The revelation was a sharp knife in Ivory's heart. How could Elizabeth have been so foolish?

Thornhart's eyebrows rose. "Tell us of this curse, Elizabeth. Confess of it and the evil things you've done as its vessel. It is the only path to redemption."

Elizabeth shook her head slowly. "There is no evil in me," she said. "I have harmed none."

Two girls started screeching and writhing on the ground. One's body went limp.

Thornhart spoke over the crowd's loud chattering. "Order!"

"She has afflicted me, too," one girl cried. "Look at these punctures on my arm. They are the bite marks of her specter!"

Ivory shot the girl a dirty look. The marks on her arm were caused by nothing other than the dig of her own fingernails.

Thornhart whipped his gaze back to Elizabeth. "Why do you torment these children? Why will you not confess, when we can see you clearly for what you are?"

All of the village joined in: "Confess! Confess!"

Though the shrieking of the girls bounced off the room's wooden walls, Elizabeth would not confess. Thornhart asked the jury of their verdict, and they returned a true bill.

'I'm sorry,' Ivory mouthed to her lover, the tears hot on her cheeks. Her nose stuffed up, causing a pressure in her head that throbbed with each fearful thought.

Ivory had been a fool to believe there was any hope. Elizabeth's guilt had been determined by the very fact she'd been accused.

Thornhart declared Elizabeth's execution to be carried out immediately. "Let the first witch hanged be an example."

Anne grabbed Ivory by the arm. "I did this for you, Sarah. It could have been you both meeting an end, had I not accused her."

Ivory didn't believe one word. Her sister had always been jealous of Elizabeth, ever since Elizabeth's family forced her to marry the man Anne loved.

Disgusted, Ivory clenched her fists and pulled away from her sister. "You will burn in hell, Anne, and no prayer will save you."

Two men escorted Elizabeth to the gallows. The sun beat against the planks of the platform where the crowd huddled near. Some of the townspeople cupped hands by their mouths to holler and condemn her. Others held baskets of rotten vegetables, the scent overpowered only by the pine of the newly constructed gallows and the draft of horse manure from the wagon awaiting her corpse.

The rope binding Elizabeth's frail wrists pinched and reddened her flesh. One of the men shoved her toward the platform's steps, but the only sign of fear was the tension along her temples and the slight tremble of her lip.

Elizabeth's gaze found Ivory's, eyes soft and forgiving. A man looped the noose around Elizabeth's neck, and Thornhart's shoes thudded across the planks, somehow louder than the excited murmurs of the crowd.

Children climbed on barrels and the shoulders of their parents for a better view. Townsfolk spat at Elizabeth and tossed their rotten produce. A man to Ivory's side lifted a stone from the ground, but as he cocked his arm back, Ivory jabbed her elbow hard into his ribs and ducked away as he keeled over.

"Confess," Thornhard said, "should you save yourself from the rope."

Elizabeth defiantly stuck out her chin, but her gaze was already dimming. "I have nothing to confess. I meet my fate with a pure heart."

The crowd grew eerily silent. Tears lined Ivory's eyes, but she rigidly held them back. She watched until just moments before they dropped the floor, then turned quickly to leave. She heard the snap of Elizabeth's neck, the tug and creak of taut rope, the shuffle of fabric. An eruption of cheers followed.

Ivory wove through the crowd, trying to hold it together. Guilt dug like sharp nails into her heart. She should have done something more to save Elizabeth. But what? What could she have done, other than get herself killed, too?

Perhaps that is what a real lover would have done. Died alongside a loved one. Never again did Ivory want to hear her name spoken aloud. Sarah was the woman who would have saved Elizabeth from this town, and she had failed.

Ivory turned back, stealing one last glance at Elizabeth's empty gaze. Thornhart signaled to the hangman, who sawed through the rope with a large hunting knife. The body thumped into the wagon below.

Ivory broke out of the crowd and stormed off to a quiet spot they'd kept in the woods.

"Speak to me now!" she cried out to the Universe. "Tell me what you want!"

Garnering no response, she fell to her knees and cried. Her fierce sobbing emptied her stomach of what little she'd managed to eat that morning. When her tears subsided, it was dark, but she knew what must be done. The town would kill Ivory if they caught her, but she refused to send Elizabeth from the world this way.

Elizabeth's body still remained in the open wagon near the platform, crumpled over the loose hay of the wagon's bed, her hazel eyes as empty as buttons that had lost their luster. Thornhart had left her there, a reminder to the townsfolk of what would become of anyone who dared perform witchcraft.

Ivory shook her head, vomit rising from her stomach in disgust at the people of her town. One day, Ivory hoped to see them suffer.

All the houses in the village were dark and the roads bare. Arms looped under Elizabeth's shoulders, Ivory dragged her lover's body into the woods behind a nearby store. She sagged beneath the weight in the same way the weathered roofs of the town drooped from the weight of snow in the winter. Elizabeth's body was stiff and cold to the touch—not how Ivory wanted to remember her.

Ivory's resolve, paired with the overwhelming feeling of loss, pushed her, lending her strength as she pulled her lover farther down the path to a barren clearing that offered little more than a rotted apple core festering in maggots.

She piled dead leaves, branches, and debris near a decaying tree stump and laid Elizabeth's body over the compost. Ivory breathed deeply and spoke to the Universe once more.

"You have made her this way—brought her to this end! Now I return her to you. Take her ashes, so that her spirit may live on."

She burned the body. The skin melted against bones, and blood bubbled until little remained. Smoking charcoal and sulfur accosted her nostrils.

When the fire exhausted and the remains cooled, Ivory wiped the tears from her cheeks and whispered, "Live on, my love."

She covered the evidence with dirt and hiked away from town.

What Anne had witnessed was love, not witchcraft. She had been unknowingly correct when she accused Elizabeth of being a witch, but she hadn't known what being a witch meant. Ivory and Elizabeth had harmed none.

Though more deaths followed, the court's approach shifted by the next hanging. Thornhart was perhaps spooked by the disappearance of Elizabeth's body but clearly not enough to put an end to the horror. Ivory returned to town only long enough to steal Elizabeth's court documents—documents detailing the trial of the only true witch killed during the Salem witch trials—and to murder her sister.

☪

IVORY'S FIRST THOUGHTS upon waking were, as always, of Elizabeth. A sharp pang pierced through her, and she tried to lift her hand to wipe grit from her lips, but instead she found her movement restricted. Her wrists and ankles seared with pain. She could do little more than raise her head and shoulders from the ground. After blinking several times, her eyes adjusted to the dim lighting.

Chains staked into the ground bound her wrists and ankles, the metal burning against her flesh as though heated over a fire before securing her. She glanced around, a stillness where her heart would've normally sped.

Dirty sheets of canvas billowed on every side, and, straight ahead, two flaps opened to a wooded area and a small campfire. The air carried the scent of smoke, cold, and earth.

This was someone else's tent—not her own. A small cot with rumpled sheets and a thin woolen blanket sat to one side of the tent, and to the other side was a wash basin filled with water.

No, not water, she thought. *It's too dark to be water.*

There was a brushing sound outside the tent. Boots scuffing over leaves, she realized as a pair of legs came into view. A man bent to stir the fire.

"You have awakened," he said without looking back.

Ivory tried to speak, but her throat felt cracked and burning. He strode into the tent and crouched beside her.

"There is not much life in these parts. I drained you first"—he pointed to the washbasin—"so that we may eat."

He doesn't mean . . . that is my blood?

"Why?" she whispered hoarsely.

"Please see it as a gift. I could have killed you."

The man turned to face her, his skin an unnatural pallor in the moonlight. His hair was dark, even his eyebrows the darkest she had ever seen, and his nose hooked a little toward the end, dimpled on one side. He sat back and kicked his feet in front of him.

He dribbled something into her mouth—a fluid that soothed her throat. "Drink," he said. "You will feel better."

Each suggestion he made reflected in Ivory's own thoughts. Their minds were as one.

"I must keep you restrained," he said, "until your urges pass. The silver with which I have bound you will sap your strength, but you will see soon enough the great power you now possess."

Without a need for words, the man's knowledge became one with hers. He was her sire—the one who had turned her. She would live eternally. She would never pass to the afterlife where Elizabeth surely awaited her arrival, not unless her life was taken from her, and Ivory already knew she was too much of a coward to allow that, let alone carry out the deed herself.

She would never forgive him for this.

"You have abandoned your former name," the man said, a trace of amusement in his voice. "I will call you *Lenore*."

Dropping her head back, Ivory closed her eyes against a lifetime of memories she wished to forget.

"Do not fear," her sire soothed. "Your wounds will quickly heal."

Ivory bristled at his sentiment. He was wrong. There were wounds in her that would never heal.

• • •

Province of Georgia, 1732

THE HUMAN WORLD moved on without Ivory, and she vowed never to allow something so horrible to happen to any of Elizabeth's descendants. She watched her lover's son from a distance until he grew to have children of his own: the first, a boy, born in 1709, and two years later, a girl. They called her Mary.

Ivory split her nights between playing silent guard and surviving her new life as a young Cruor, at first needing to hunt weekly but soon able to sustain herself on monthly meals.

Over the decades, however, Ivory worried her ways would forever distance her from the Parsons family. She'd need to show some thread of what she had once been, not just some empty shell with a thirst for blood.

It was with this in mind that Ivory stalked the wildlife in the brambles outside the Parsons' home, hesitant to strike. The animals seemed more innocent than the lustful men she usually preyed on. The musk of skunk and the woodsy smell of fox caused her stomach to lurch. As she crept around pinecones and beetles that clung to toadstool stems, she picked up on the spoor of a nearby deer.

When the deer paused to sniff a fallen twig of red berries, Ivory pounced. Her fangs sank quickly into the felted flesh, and her mouth filled with a sour fluid—not the sweet essence of a human. Ivory gagged but forced herself to continue. She craved blood to sate her hunger and needed the hope of regaining a semblance of humanity.

That idea shattered when a soughing wind groaned through the tree branches, and the Parsons' back door swung open. Ivory, frozen in place, rested back on her heels, briars prickling against her calves.

Mary, now close to twenty years and very nearly a replica of Elizabeth, opened the door, sending the smoky scent of their wood-burning stove into the chill night air. She stepped outside and scanned the forest, her hand lingering on the doorknob. After a long moment, she dipped back inside. The click of the door's lock echoed in Ivory's ears.

The deer's blood cooled on Ivory's chin. Her eyes dropped to her blood-drenched hands. What had she become? Even this—the feeding from live animals—wouldn't garner the trust of the Parsons family. If there was any hope of entering the lives of her lover's family, it was in finding a way to walk amongst them while living out her darkness in secret.

And so Ivory continued on, always with the blood of another human on her tongue, neither her nor her sire caring for the Maltorim's order to stop hunting humans.

On some days, Ivory stayed watching over the Parsons' just a little longer than she should, the first rays of light scorching her face and arms before she retreated to the underground. This in itself was a rarity, as there were no other known Cruor at the time who could withstand time in the sun. Perhaps this was a gift Ivory had only because of her first calling—the calling bestowed on her by the Universe that she had abandoned for a life of revenge on mankind.

In 1732, Mary, now with three children of her own, moved to the Province of Georgia, away from the revival fires of Massachusetts. Ivory followed, convinced this young woman needed her protection more than the men born into the Parsons' lineage.

Though Ivory's sire appeased her desire to relocate, he cautioned her against her obsessions. Ivory, however, resented him. He controlled too much of her time and prevented her too often from watching Elizabeth's family.

Late one night during the following spring season, Ivory crept upon Mary's house and stopped behind a tree several yards from the open window of Mary's sleeping quarters.

Mary sat on a small bench in front of a wooden music stand, dressed in a dark blue, tightly-laced linen dress. Her skirts bunched in elegant tiers behind her, and her hair was pinned up with only a few short, curling wisps escaping near the nape of her neck and at the front of her hairline. In front of her, poised on a small stand, was an unfinished sheet of music.

A shaky breath escaped Mary as she rested a violin between her petite chin and bony shoulder and drew the bow across the strings in a slur. She stopped to adjust a few pegs before beginning again, always following the rule of the down-bow on the first beat of every measure.

Ivory had seen musicians perform this way at the orchestra, one of her sire's favorite places to scour for humans. He'd taught Ivory all about music . . . but where had Mary learned? Ivory, stung that she was missing Mary's life, swallowed her hurt and listened to the melody.

The song was slow, sweet, and a little sad. Mary's body and breathing were steady, only the tears streaming her cheeks a sign of whatever pain she harbored. Ivory could not run to her—could not cradle Mary in her arms, could not allow Mary to collapse there and purge her heartache.

The intensity of the piece increased, and Ivory used the back of her hand to scrub the tears away from her own eyes, the sticky blood smearing over her cheeks and along her jaw.

Though Ivory was on the outside looking in, she and Mary were together in this song. They were listening to the same notes carried on the same night breeze. Every few measures, Mary stopped. She dipped a quill into an inkpot resting on a worn blue table before adding fresh marks to her sheets.

Smooth legatos and high notes empowered the piece, with Mary's fingers working the strings furthest from the pegs and occasionally moving down the neck to deepen the sound.

After some time, Mary set her violin aside and sat quietly with her tears.

"Lord, please relieve me of this curse," she prayed. "These voices, these thoughts—they do not belong to me. Even my husband has abandoned me in knowledge of them."

Ivory covered her gasp. Her fingers went numb, and her breath, cold in her chest, rushed from her lungs. For a moment, she thought even her heart had begun beating again, but it was only a memory of a feeling she'd once known.

Ivory considered going to Mary and telling her everything, telling her all about her grandmother and helping her where she had once failed Elizabeth. But Ivory couldn't risk exposing her darker nature, so instead she slinked back to the shadows.

• • •

Savannah, Georgia, 1854

BETWEEN 1732 AND 1854, Ivory's tolerance to the sun grew, though she was still unable to walk outdoors when the sun was at its highest and brightest. A small bronze amulet on a leather cord around her neck—a depiction of Sól, the sun goddess, riding on her chariot— wrapped her in a protective barrier from the sun.

The charm and its magic had been given to her by one of the Ankou in exchange for her turning a young woman—Ophelia—so that she might find a place with the Maltorim.

Though Mary's husband had soiled the souls of Mary's children with his surname, the Parsons' lineage hadn't ended at Mary's death. Ivory sought out Mary's brothers instead.

Ivory's sire implored her to stop returning to Parsons' homes. They needed to keep moving; staying in one place for too long would risk their exposure as Cruor. As though she cared. Of course he wouldn't understand.

181

But as he'd never been one to make demands of Ivory, she stubbornly kept watch, his suggestions of moving on little more than an annoyance. Soon, she hoped, another Parsons woman would be born. Perhaps she might be like her ancestors, Mary and Elizabeth, and Ivory might finally have her chance at redemption.

In 1834, after three generations of boys, Rachel was born into the Parsons lineage. Now an adult, she was burdened with shopping at the market. One day, on Rachel's way home, as the setting sun began to purple the sky, she stopped at a bookstore. Ivory followed, watching Rachel through the shop's window as she traipsed between shelves that sagged beneath the weight of books. Rachel squatted to read titles on a lower shelf but kept sliding book after book back into place.

Rachel reached on her toes and tugged down a book from a higher shelf. The cover read: *The Rebellion of the Beasts*, by Leigh Hunt. Ivory stared from across the road as Rachel turned one crisp page after another.

Rachel got carried away with her reading until the shop owner cleared her throat—a sound all too audible to Ivory's supernatural hearing. When Rachel looked up, the shop owner crossed her arms and raised her brows.

"Of course," Rachel said, tapping a fingernail against the book's cover. "This really is excellent."

She dug through a small pouch and placed her coins in the woman's waiting palm.

When finally Rachel departed, the book sticking out from her basket of goods, there was little light to travel by. A shadowy figure skirted the deadened light of the oil lamps, following Rachel with a knife flashing in his hand.

Ivory rushed up behind him, snapped his neck before so much as a breath could leave him, and whipped him into an alley. She peeked around the corner just as Rachel was taking a final, nervous glance around, her cloak clasped tightly over her trembling body.

Three mornings later, Ivory rested near an embankment a short way into the forest where a stream whispered between the trees. She stared beyond blades of grass, seeded with red poppies that yielded beneath the breeze, waiting for Rachel to take leave from her home. The early morning sun glowed between the oaks with a sweet-tempered light, and shadows fell with an almost kindness to cool Ivory's skin. Even dawn felt hotter to her than it would to a human, but at least the sun's rays no longer burned her flesh.

She plucked a spider crawling across the fruit of a gooseberry plant to feed to a nearby praying mantis but dropped it when Rachel stepped outside. Ivory trailed her to the market, where Rachel perused the courtyard as she picked nuts off a muffin top. Not at all on accident, Ivory bumped into her and sent a loaf of bread tumbling from Rachel's basket to the ground.

"How clumsy of me," Ivory said. "Please, allow me to buy you a fresh loaf."

Rachel's eyes narrowed ever so slightly. Finally, she said, "If you're certain it won't be any inconvenience?"

Ivory, with sallow skin and trapped in the frame of a young woman from the 17th century, must have looked as though she couldn't afford to replace Rachel's bread.

She smiled. "My pleasure, Miss. Wait here."

Ivory returned with a loaf wrapped in a new cloth and a small block of cheese.

Rachel released a breath. "Would you care to join me for lunch? I fear I've bought too much food for one day."

Ivory had been counting on such a kindness. "I've had about all I can eat for one day, but I'd enjoy the company."

Over the years, the two became close friends. Rachel shared her darkest secrets, but there was one Ivory knew she did not share. Perhaps Rachel's family had warned her not to speak of the voices—warned her of the hurt and betrayal that comes with divulging such an affliction.

Years passed without Ivory aging, and though Rachel never mentioned it, Ivory feared what others might think. For this reason, Ivory only ever visited Rachel in secret. Shortly after Rachel's forty-fifth year, she fell ill. Ivory did not need to sneak to meet with her then, for no one wanted to expose themselves to her ailments.

Late one afternoon, when the sun had lowered in the sky to a more forgiving light, Ivory stopped by for another visit.

"You shouldn't have come," Rachel scolded as always, her voice too weak to carry any authority.

She held a cloth to her mouth and coughed, a spray of blood spattering on the small bit of fabric. Ivory kneeled at her side and tried to soothe her until the coughing fit subsided.

Rachel set her rag down and waved toward her bedroom door. "Back away before you become ill."

"You have kept a long life," Ivory said. "But you see me. I have not aged."

Rachel closed her eyes, and Ivory swept loose tendrils of hair away from a face that had once belonged to Elizabeth. Rachel's feverish, sweat-soaked skin burned beneath Ivory's cool hands, but her graying hair was still soft.

"Come with me," Ivory said, trying to use her influence. "I've known your family for centuries, and you can know them with me."

Rachel's mind pushed back against Ivory's influence, shutting down the attempt completely. "Please now, go away. Your words confuse me."

Ivory softened her voice and tried a second time to influence Rachel. "Please, listen—"

Grasping her moth-eaten quilt between her hands, Rachel shook her head. Ivory was running out of time. Her heart ached more with each glance at Rachel's withering body, and she clenched her hands at her sides.

"I can give you eternity," Ivory said. "Give *us* eternity."

Rachel whispered, "Let me die quietly, Lenore. It's—" Her hands softened, releasing the blanket.

"Please don't leave." Ivory repeated the silent prayer over and again as she ran to lock the door.

Quickly, she returned to the bedside, extended her fangs, and sank them into Rachel's neck, releasing the poison that would revive her.

The life returned to Rachel's eyes. She sputtered another cough and grasped Ivory's wrists. "No," she rasped. "Lenore—don't."

Rachel's heart stopped. Her body went lifeless on the cot. Ivory's efforts had been too late to sustain the change.

At that moment, Ivory came to hate the name her sire had given her. *Lenore.* This name was the name of her darkness, the name that put a world between her and her lover's family. The name should have died on Rachel's lips, but would instead follow Ivory forever.

Ivory stormed out of the house. In the cold night air, she cursed the Universe. She tore chunks of soil from the earth and pounded her fists on the ground and cried blood tears against the dirt and grass until she could cry no more.

• • •

Keota, Colorado, 1942

THIS WAS THE HUNT OF MAN. A useless man, more precisely, because the only men of any use to Ivory were the Parsons men, for they were the only ones who might bring forth a Parsons woman and rekindle Ivory's hope for redemption.

But Theodore Anderson was not a Parsons man.

No, Theodore Anderson was a man who had married a woman Ivory had never met but felt she had known for hundreds of years: Abigail Parsons.

After Rachel's death, Ivory had sought out Rachel's brothers and waited several generations for another girl to be born into the Parsons' lineage. The year had been 1920. The current generation of Parsons men died in the war, one of them leaving his son to be cared for by his Aunt Abigail, now Abigail Anderson.

Ivory feared the little boy, Abigail's nephew, might be the last to carry the Parsons' name. People were beginning to have fewer children, sometimes none at all. And, if that were the case, Abigail might be Ivory's last chance.

Theodore Anderson could not be allowed to stand in her way.

Spying him from where she crouched in a nearby ditch, Ivory knew her only hope lay in him not returning home. If she killed him now, he'd be an assumed victim of war. Waiting until after the war was not an option; these days, one could not kill a man so easily without drawing attention.

After the murder, Ivory raced back to Keota, needing to reach town before word of Theodore's death. She made it, much to the misfortune of one of the Army's messengers, whose body now slumped against the crumbling stone of an old well behind her.

Ivory stood in the prairie and stared out over the town. A coyote stalked behind her and growled.

"Oh, come on, you're all right with me." She turned to him, smiling at the eerie glow in his cloudy, pale-blue eyes. "You're one of them? Poor, filthy thing."

The coyote stepped tentatively forward, a light breeze carrying his honeysuckle aroma ever quicker to Ivory. Only the Strigoi smelled and tasted as sweet as humans.

"Come 'ere, boy," she said, drawing him closer with her gentle lilt. He sidled beside her thigh, and she hummed to him. "That a'boy."

She stroked his dusty grey and white fur. The pollen coating his fur left a chalk-like residue on her hand, and she wiped the grit on her skirts and looked to the Methodist church across the way.

"She'll be out soon and heading home."

Ivory grabbed the coyote's snout and gave it a playful shake. The coyote tensed and growled again.

"I am not your enemy." She let out a wistful sigh and turned her gaze back toward the town. "I will return tonight with food and clothes. Yours surely ripped while shifting. But you tell others like you to stay away, understand?"

After a long stare, the coyote took off across the dips and patches of the prairie. Tonight, Ivory would feed.

Hand wrapped around that of a small boy's, Abigail left the church, and Ivory timed enough distance to follow their scent without being seen.

Things had changed over the last couple of centuries. Dirt roads had given way to pavement. The automobile had grown in popularity.

Straight past the cemetery Ivory strode, past women in black dresses, past the general store and post office, and nearer to the heavy shadow of a water tower. She continued until she reached a lonesome house on a large lot of land. Abigail's scent stopped here.

For nearly an hour, Ivory paced down the road from the house, trying to gather the nerve to approach. Finally, she headed up the walkway and knocked on the flimsy wooden door. When no one answered, she knocked again, louder this time, the door giving way under each distinct tap.

A few moments later, the door opened a crack, and a pair of honey-colored eyes peered through.

"Mrs. Anderson?" Ivory asked, already preparing to use her influence. Keeping Abigail calm would be a necessity.

Abigail opened the door the rest of the way and wiped her hands on her apron. "Yes?"

Straightening her skirts, Ivory felt suddenly outdated at the sight of Abigail in slacks. "My name is Lenore Kinsbury. I've brought news from overseas."

"News?" A crease formed between Abigail's eyes, and Ivory got lost in the lines of Abigail's features—features that so closely mirrored the way Ivory remembered Elizabeth. It took her a moment to return to the conversation.

"Your husband," Ivory replied.

"That can't be," Abigail said. "They would send an official."

Ivory retrieved a document from her purse. "I know this is unusual, but these are unusual times, are they not?" She handed the letter to Abigail, who slowly scanned the page.

Abigail's trembling hand covered her mouth, and she stepped back. "No," she whispered. "No, no, no."

Ivory entered the house and gently clicked the door shut. "My deepest sympathies for your loss."

She helped Abigail to the couch. Abigail didn't say anything. She only sat on the very edge of her seat, grief rolling off her like a thick fog. Ivory's stomach twisted, ill over the pain Abigail was suffering, though not at all regretful for Theodore's death.

"Let me put on some tea," Ivory said. "Don't worry about the child. I'll tend to him when he wakes from his nap."

"The child?"

"I . . . saw the baby shoes. By the door."

Abigail sniffed and wiped her eyes. "Of course. The shoes." She took a deep breath. "He's my nephew. My brother passed away."

"My condolences," Ivory said softly. She sensed Abigail on the verge of breakdown. "Tea, then?"

Without waiting for a response, Ivory continued into the kitchen. She wasn't yet used to the smells of a human house. The aroma of recently sautéed onions and the char of an extinguished candle made her stomach lurch.

"Do you have any other family?" Ivory asked, using her influence to send waves of comfort toward Abigail.

"I had only my brother and husband."

"I see," Ivory said.

Steam piped from the kettle on the stove; Abigail must have already been preparing tea. Ivory poured and sweetened the tea, the spoon clinking in the ceramic cups as she stirred, then brought the tea into the living room.

"Perhaps you ought to hire some help."

Abigail chewed at her lip. "I'd never be able to afford it without Theodore. I don't know what I'll do with him gone."

Maintaining Abigail's calm took much of Ivory's mental energy, but she kept the influence flowing as she spoke.

"Well"—Ivory handed her the tea, choosing her words cautiously— "I could use a place to stay. I would be of help. That is, if you wouldn't mind?"

Abigail nodded slowly and sipped her tea. Ivory smiled that her effort to influence Abigail had gone even smoother than she'd hoped. Abigail didn't have the same block Rachel had exhibited.

Abigail swept her arm to indicate Ivory should sit, but in the same instant, a vase on the mantel across the room tipped and shattered on the ground.

"Oh," Abigail said, jumping to her feet. "You best leave. Please, go now."

Ivory froze.

"Go!" Picture frames fell from the walls and the front door rattled fiercely.

Ivory ran to Abigail, placed her hands on her shoulders, and used her influence to send her peace of mind. "It's okay, Mrs. Anderson. It's okay."

They sank down into the couch and Ivory held her as she cried.

"I won't tell a soul," Ivory promised.

☾

WITH IVORY'S HELP, Abigail learned to harness her energy. Unlike her ancestors before her, Abigail experienced only noise in place of the whispering voices.

As the years passed, Abigail and her nephew aged, their family still without answers. Ivory waited for just the right moment to reveal the source of Abigail's gift, while Abigail's nephew tried to find a cure.

That moment never came.

One day, as they were sitting down for dinner, Abigail spoke the words Ivory had always dreaded she might hear.

"There is something wrong with you. You haven't aged."

"Strange, I suppose," was Ivory's reply, her posture straight and her hands tucked into her lap as she watched Abigail eat.

Abigail paused, lowering a bite of food back to her plate. "And I don't believe I've seen you eat a single morsel of food in all the time I've known you."

Ivory couldn't tell her the truth, not with how Abigail felt about her own curse. "You know how I like to bring meals on my hikes."

"Eat with us tonight," Abigail said firmly. She pushed her own dish across the table, her gaze cutting toward Ivory. "I'll make myself another plate."

"Really," Ivory said. "I couldn't. Perhaps another time."

Abigail rubbed her temples. Ivory reached toward her, but dropped her hand back to her lap when Abigail flinched.

From then on, Abigail looked at Ivory only from lowered lids and with wary sighs. Abigail believed herself to be insane. Ivory longed to free her of her false suspicions, but her explanations would not be accepted and, without them, Ivory wouldn't be welcome to stay.

Not even a fortnight passed before Ivory packed her things and returned to confront her sire. She confessed to him of where she'd been spending her time over the years.

"I want to turn Abigail," Ivory told him. "I want to separate from you and go out on my own."

"Lenore," he began gently.

"Don't bother trying to talk me out of it. I've tried once before, and if it hadn't been too late, I'd have succeeded. This may be my last chance, and you will not stand in my way."

"Why would you want this? Isn't the life I've provided you enough?"

"Abigail is so like Elizabeth," Ivory said fiercely. She thought of their same delicate wrists, the way they swept their hair away from their neck in the same fashion, and the way they both stepped lightly, while still giving a sense of being grounded. Ivory stared into the fire, watching the flames steal away the bark of the wood. "I think they are connected—Elizabeth and her female descendants."

"You believe Abigail is a forever girl?" he asked, leaning back and raising his thick, dark eyebrows.

"A forever girl?"

"Reincarnation," he said. "That is what you are asking?"

"Such a thing is possible, then?" Ivory breathed, her eyes widening and her chest filling with hope.

"They say the spirit elementals—oft thought to be women—would be reincarnated if their life was taken prematurely. They were to contain the unfiltered magic of the elements. They were the only ones who would never die an ultimate death, so long as their efforts in life remained pure and their lineage continued."

"Do you mean that Abigail might *be* Elizabeth? That Mary and Rachel were as well?"

"No," he said solemnly. "This was all hearsay. Myths. Fantasies created by those who grieved the losses of their not-quite-human loved ones." His eyes, dark as gray coals that had burned out long ago, fell on hers. "It was all *hope*. Nothing more."

But Ivory's sire had confirmed what her heart already knew. These women were Elizabeth.

Ivory stopped by one last time to see Abigail. Watched her through the window of her home. Elizabeth was there. It was in Abigail's eyes, in the tears she cried, in the smallest nuances of expression that could belong only to one person. That her sire could say otherwise made him unworthy of life.

Three nights later, Ivory decapitated her sire in his slumber, for he refused to release her. For the first time in as long as she could remember, Ivory felt free.

In the years to come, she integrated with the general population. She introduced herself as Ivory, glad to be rid of her sire's name for her just as she'd been glad to purge herself of the name Sarah. She would start fresh. No more Sarah. No more Lenore.

Next time, she would not fail her lover. She would find her young, bind her in friendship, and convince her life would be safer if she didn't carry the vulnerabilities of a human.

Ivory kept vigil for two more generations—watched the nephew, the last Parsons boy, as he grew to have sons of his own, and his sons grew to have sons as well, until, one day, another girl was born into the lineage.

Sophia.

But, to Ivory's heart and eyes, the girl was still Elizabeth.

Elizabeth was . . . me.

{twenty-two}

I'D COMPLETELY MISREAD every moment I'd ever spent with my once-friend. That day Ivory had dropped me off back at home, after I'd been attacked at Club Flesh—she hadn't been angry with me. She'd been *torn*.

When she'd told me she knew someone who'd heard voices, the hate in her expression hadn't been a hatred she felt toward me. It'd been her hatred of herself, of her situation, and of the people who had killed my ancestor. Killed me. She couldn't tell me, though. Not like that.

She'd sped off down the road not because she wanted to get away from me, but because she wanted to escape the hurt she felt sitting beside me, unable to tell me that I was my ancestor—unable to tell me that I had once been her lover and that she'd followed me all these years. She needed me to want to be turned first—to become a Cruor as well—but it was at that moment she realized her plan for this lifetime had failed.

I hated the very thing she wanted me to become.

When the images bled into the darkness, the air grew still. The fire had borrowed Ivory's memories and, since I did not return them, they died along with the fire's embers, lost forever. I wished for someone to steal them from me next.

I dissolved the magic of my circle and dropped my face into my hands and wept. Now I understood why I'd been afraid to open up to Charles about the whispering voices. Now I understood there were deeper parts of me—pieces of my soul—trying to protect me from the possibility of betrayal or death. But through Ivory, I'd still found a way to invite those things into my life. It'd been my soul that resisted Charles but my heart that led me to trust him.

Charles rushed to my side, and I pressed my face to his chest, my tears wetting his shirt. Paloma smoothed my hair. My physical and emotional energy were spent.

Once I wasn't feeling quite so shaky, we headed upstairs to the kitchen where Paloma and Charles listened intently as I conveyed what the *ignisvisum* had revealed.

The final set of images had been familiar. They were of me—the real me. The me not altered by a New England 17th century diet or a husband dead in the war. Not Elizabeth or Mary or Rachel or Abigail—though we were all the same—but me, the person I remembered being. Sophia.

After three centuries, Ivory walked among the living like any other human. Ivory watched through the window of our small home in Keota as Mother held me shortly after my birth in 1987.

She watched me on the playground at school. Killed my father when I was six.

He'd recognized her from when he was a boy. She'd been a friend of his great aunt Abigail. But now he was an adult, thirty years older while Ivory hadn't aged a day. He was unnerved to see her every day—she could tell from the way he looked at her, always shielding his daughter from her gaze—and Ivory knew she'd have no hope of friendship with me if she didn't get rid of him first.

When we moved to Belle Meadow, Ivory followed. She'd been at the movies on my first date, and our meeting in college hadn't been an accident.

Ivory had killed Mr. Petrenko to save me from being arrested for stealing. It'd been her thoughts tumbling through my mind at the time of the murder. She needed to ensure I'd go off to college, where she planned for us to meet. That couldn't happen if I was in jail.

She'd planted Elizabeth Parsons' court document in with my father's belongings. Everything had been a lie. Even her Boston accent had been faked, the voice of her thoughts and memories old fashioned, archaic . . . nothing like the modern voice in which she spoke to me. No wonder I'd never recognized her thoughts before.

And Marcus' interest in me had never extended beyond Ivory asking him to arrange a staged attack. She'd forged the note from him, hoping to spook me, hoping I would turn to her so desperate to protect myself that I'd be willing to become a Cruor myself.

She hadn't counted on my turning to Charles instead. When Ivory's plan at Club Flesh backfired, she'd risked that Charles might tell me her secret, maybe even hoped he would, to save her the trouble, so I might come to her with acceptance and understanding.

When she realized I'd moved in with Charles, she'd ransacked my house out of anger. And the more time Charles and I spent together, the more anxious she'd become, until eventually she saw him as nothing more than a threat. That was when she tried to kill him—when she accidentally attacked me instead.

Now everything made sense, but I felt more lost than I ever had before. At least I really had only taken memories of myself. The *ignisvisum* had only shown the times Ivory spent with Elizabeth's spirit or thinking of her. I struggled to wrap my head around the idea—that Elizabeth's spirit was mine, too.

It was nearly seven at night by the time I conveyed everything to Paloma and Charles. They tried to comfort me, but I shrugged them off. I was all cried out and too mentally exhausted to languish any longer in the heartache Ivory's memories had stabbed through every inch of my soul.

"I'm sorry," Charles said. From the thoughts floating through his mind, he didn't know what else to say.

Gripping my hand, Paloma offered all the support I needed with the expression on her face.

I managed a smile. "These 'forever girls'—have you heard of them?"

Paloma stole a glance at Charles. "As far as the Maltorim is concerned, they never existed."

"And as far as you're concerned?"

"There is too much evidence to deny their existence. After today, after seeing you obtain the memories of your ancestor—of your own spirit—I can say there is no doubt in my mind that they exist, and that you are one of them. It's the only thing that would make sense of everything I've seen in you."

"So what does all this mean?"

"Your previous lives are a part of you, even if you don't remember them. Any abilities you possessed then should be accessible now that you have knowledge of them."

I let her words sink in, but my mind was still on my once-friend. "I don't understand why Ivory thought killing Charles would bring her and me together."

Paloma rose and started another pot of tea. "She was a hurting woman, Sophia. Sometimes people have unhealthy ways of expressing their love. It's not always easy for someone to be turned while grieving. It can affect them indefinitely."

I stared as wax dripped down a candle in the center of the table. Visions stolen from Ivory's memories flashed through my thoughts: flesh wasting away in a fire after Elizabeth's—after *my*—hanging. *Take her ashes, so that her spirit may live on,* Ivory had said.

I blinked, refocusing on Charles. "This is just . . . hard to accept."

He'd tried several times over the last hour to approach me—to comfort me—but each time, I'd pushed him away. I needed space, and he'd finally resigned. Now he merely listened, nodding whenever I spoke. Thanks to our blood bond, his emotions were pressing hard against my own, and part of me wanted to surrender to the anger there, as though his anger would be somehow easier to bear than my own weighted hurt.

The new revelations made me feel safe enough to expose my other secrets. I turned to Paloma. "The blood bonds I've experienced with Adrian and Charles . . . ."

"Yes?" Paloma asked, nodding for me to continue.

"I saw some of Adrian's memories . . . and I've felt Charles' emotions." I looked at him apologetically. As if it weren't intrusive enough to have me in his thoughts, how might he feel about me sensing his emotions as well? He offered a weak-but-understanding smile, and I focused back on Paloma. "Is this because I'm a forever girl?"

"I'm not sure, Sophia." Her eyebrows pulled together. "Not everything in life can be explained."

Paloma dropped a tea bag into a cream-colored ceramic mug and poured steaming water from the kettle over the top. She set the tea in front of me. The water darkened at the bottom as the steam rose to warm my chin and nose.

Just as I was about to take a sip, Adrian walked in. He set his laptop on the counter and turned to Paloma.

"Relocate Ivory. Charles, Sophia—we must talk."

My mind froze at his abrupt tone, then slugged forward. Paloma take Ivory? Adrian was supposed to take her.

Paloma seemed calm in response to what was an exceptionally rude way for Adrian to couch his request. She gave one of her soft smiles. "That shouldn't be a problem."

"I've already secured her in your car."

I hadn't even heard him come in, and already he'd moved Ivory to Paloma's car?

Paloma looked over at me as she gathered her coat. "Please call if you need anything."

"Thank you," I said. "For everything."

She paused in the doorway, giving me one last gentle smile before leaving.

Once the front door closed, I fixed my glare on Adrian. "What the hell is going on?"

"My apologies for rushing at you with this. Please, let us discuss." Adrian paced across the linoleum floor, from a tile near the window to a dented one near the kitchen door. Back and forth, from sienna to mustard, each tile separated by dark grout and imprinted with *fleur de lis*. "I need you both to pay careful attention and stay calm."

Charles' eyebrows drew together. "What's going on?"

"Your parents," Adrian said, directing his gaze toward Charles. He continued in a sunken tone. "I'm deeply sorry to tell you."

A sense of dread clenched my stomach.

Charles' eyes hardened. "Tell me what?"

"They have been apprehended." Adrian wrung his hands together and began pacing again.

Charles stood, fingertips pressed firmly against the table in front of him. "You're mistaken."

"I'm afraid not," Adrian said, stopping to place a hand on Charles' shoulder.

The low lighting reflected off the unshed tears in Charles eyes.

My gaze darted between them. "They who? Thalia's coterie?"

Charles shook his head. "He means the Maltorim."

I barely registered the words. How did they learn of Charles' parents? Now, after hundreds of years?

Adrian leveled his gaze at Charles. An intensity saturated his voice and a sheen of purpose glazed his eyes. "We'll get them back."

How did Adrian know all this? The emotions rolling off Charles revealed complete trust as an undercurrent to his fear and concern. Maybe he could read Adrian's aura and saw him as someone trustworthy. But Charles had failed in his judgments of others before, and while I hated to be skeptical of a friend, I focused on Adrian's thoughts, letting the rest of the noise float into the background.

His subconscious replayed the moment he'd learned the news. After Charles had called, Adrian went to Club Flesh to collect information about Ivory. Instead, he overheard the bar owner speaking with someone in the office. Someone who was looking for Charles and who said his parents were already in the Maltorim's custody.

Charles sagged into the seat across from me. "Us against the Maltorim? Thalia's thugs are one thing, but that place is too heavily guarded."

"We don't have a choice," Adrian said. "Thalia's coterie turned your parents in. They caught them as they were leaving town. Now they are after you, too."

"Do they know where I am?" Charles asked.

Adrian shook his head. "They haven't yet discovered your exact location. Last week they tried to track Sophia but lost her scent a few miles from here."

"I'll help," I said. As much as Ivory's memories weakened my ability to trust, they strengthened my confidence in myself. Somewhere inside of me, a power lurked, waiting to be tapped into.

"No." Charles said in a tense, clipped voice that forbade any questions. "You won't."

Fortunately, I didn't care much what his tone forbade. "None of us may be strong enough alone, but together we might have a shot."

Charles ran his hands over his face. "You don't know the Maltorim."

"Let her assist," Adrian said. "We cannot do this alone."

Charles pressed the heels of his hands into his eyes and leaned back in his seat. He could think things over if he liked, but it wouldn't change anything. I was going to help.

I pulled Adrian into the hallway, and, for once, he didn't seem like he was about to self-combust while standing near me. There wasn't enough time to recap everything, but I gave him the run down on the important details.

"One more thing," I said. "During one of my earlier lives, I exhibited another power, beyond my clairaudience. Telekinesis, I think. Could I channel that somehow?"

Adrian gave a solemn nod and walked to the library room. He indicated the wooden chair at the small desk, and I seated myself and ran my fingers over the scarring of the desktop while he retrieved several books I hadn't read from a shelf.

He sat beside me and pushed over a large tome. "These are transcripts from times of Olde."

I raised a brow and opened to the first page. "Should we get Charles?"

"He will join us when he's ready."

I scanned the content. A few pages were rough and stuck together, and light-brown water stains smudged some of the writing. The book consisted mostly of odd photographs—creatures, almost human if not for their shark-like teeth; close ups of unraveled rope, screw threads, sawdust; stamps from the Cayman Islands, circa 1904; and black lady bugs eating holes through stalks of browning rhubarb.

"What is this?"

"Someone's journal," he said. "I don't know whose."

The photographs served only to intensify the growing pit in my stomach. I flipped through, searching for any relevant text. Between a photograph of the cracked, dried mud of a riverbed and a copy of a veined map outlining Europe, I found some potentially useful information.

I pulled the pencil I'd been chewing on, now perforated with bite marks, away from my mouth. "This is it."

CHARLES JOINED US half an hour later. Our plan hinged on a theory no books had proven: if the power traveled with my spirit, I could tap into five lifetimes of magic, as Paloma had said. This book detailed exactly how achieving this might be *possible*.

I needed a marker from each life: the court document from Elizabeth's trial in Salem would work. For markers to represent my other lives, I selected a violin, Leigh Hunt's *The Rebellion of the Beasts*, and a pair of baby's shoes.

Within a couple of hours, Adrian helped me round up the items: the baby shoes and violin were an easy find, but he'd had to exhaust some of his connections to locate a copy of Leigh Hunt's novel on such short notice. With the items in my possession, I could now channel my previous lives with more ease.

"I'm supposed to do this," I said, confidence settling over every nerve in my body.

Adrian placed a hand on Charles' shoulder. "Do not fear, my friend. She would only be helping."

"We'll see," Charles said.

I sensed his uncertainty. Even without dipping into his thoughts— and it was definitely still more natural for me to avoid using my clairaudience—I was pretty sure he knew I wasn't going to budge on the issue.

Charles pinched the bridge of his nose. "If we're doing this, we'll need to leave for Damascus immediately."

Adrian logged onto his laptop. Charles and I sat alongside him as his fingers clacked over the keyboard at an inhuman speed. I studied the computer screen. The format was foreign to me; Adrian was viewing an impossible IP address.

D-connect—that little Internet card thingy he'd brought over to my house all those months ago. The supernatural Internet suddenly seemed more valuable than the first time I'd encountered it.

"This fellow"—Adrian jabbed a finger toward the text on the screen, the name 'Rhett' written in plain block letters—"has an exceptional reputation. He'll fly us out there, no questions asked."

Adrian scribbled some numbers on a sheet of paper and then furiously crossed them out. "Math is not my strong point. Perhaps one of you might lend a hand? We need to determine the appropriate departure time."

I lifted the page. "I can figure this out."

I factored in time differences and Damascus' hours of darkness for this time of year as well as the plane's travel speed of up to two thousand kilometers per second—about ten times faster than a normal airway plane, and maybe a bit faster than what the US Air Force used. Because supernatural technology was beyond that of humans, we'd avoid detection.

"If we leave at sunrise tomorrow, we can arrive tomorrow evening. We'll need a flight time under twelve hours, but that's nothing his plane can't handle."

Adrian booked the flight using something called ICAO codes instead of the KAPA or OSDI codes normally used by airports.

Charles and Adrian discussed the details of travel, while I worked on developing whatever power I might contain. I sank back to the visions I'd stolen from Ivory along with some strange moments I'd had growing up.

In third grade, an eraser I hadn't even touched had flown off my desk and across the room. I'd gotten detention for that. Another time, when I was sixteen, a door I hadn't even touched slammed in Mother's face, almost as if it had a mind of its own. Or, at least, almost like it shared a mind with me.

Even the dishes that had fallen over during my positive energy ritual might have been a result of my gift. At the time, I thought it'd only been the wind. How many of these moments were signs of my powers breaking through?

The only thing those moments had in common was how hurt or angry or frustrated I'd been at the time. How could my powers be good if they came from negative emotions?

It's all about your intentions, I told myself.

With that in mind, I tried to summon all my hurt and anger, which wasn't too hard. I'd been suppressing those emotions for hours. Years, if you count the rest of my life leading up to this point.

I focused all that conjured energy on trying to move a pencil from the table. When that didn't work, I took a break for a cup of apple-vanilla tea and lit a few candles before trying again. Another thirty minutes passed with no success. I lost count of how many times I tried, but I wasn't giving up. I closed my eyes and centered all my energy inward, trying to build up a store of power, then opened my eyes to try again.

The pencil budged—a small bubble of excitement tickled in my chest—but then the leaden utensil shot across the table and smacked against the wall. The splintered wood and snapped lead crashed to the floor.

I sighed. I had no control over this 'gift' and not much time to gain any. I sat on the edge of the bed with the violin Adrian had run out to pick up earlier. I lifted it and tried to imagine what it would've been like to be Mary. To be *me*.

Taking a deep breath, I pulled the bow across the strings. The air in my lungs felt suddenly strange, and my heart fluttered. It didn't sound as bad as I would've thought. It only sounded uncertain. But the more I gave myself to it, the smoother the melody carried. The same melody Mary had played. It was alive in me.

Once I finished, I felt refreshed. Energized. Charles and Adrian were staring.

"What was that?" Charles asked.

"I—I don't know."

Adrian nodded his approval. "Perhaps that song had been your calling. Many humans called to become elementals have one. Though I must say it's strange yours would be the violin."

"Why?"

Adrian frowned and shook his head. "Let's not concern ourselves with this right now. It would make no difference to what lies ahead."

Something felt off about his tone, but I knew trying to push more information from Adrian would be a waste. I shrugged it off. I didn't know what the song was. I'd never played before—not in this lifetime—but a new passion ignited within me. Now all I needed to do was control the energy.

Thinking it would probably be best to work with something sturdier than a pencil, I grabbed a pen from the kitchen junk drawer and, this time, focused with a destination in mind: moving the pen from the ground to the table. The pen hovered for a moment before falling.

It was Ivory's words to Abigail that finally helped: *Believe in this.* With new determination, I tried again. This time the pen floated up from the floor and over to the table, my energy bleeding out as I lowered it to the table's surface. It dropped the last inch, rolled a tiny bit, and came to a stop.

Excitement drummed inside me. *I* can *do this.* It was totally unreal, thrilling, and terrifying all at the same time. I wished I could bask in my amazement, but reality crept back in—the *why* of my learning to use this skill. The knowing I'd only come to access this power because I'd stolen memories from a friend who tried to kill my boyfriend and that I had to use it because I needed to save my boyfriend's family from being murdered.

For the next hour, I worked until I was too drained to try any more. It was already ten, the last three hours like a small eternity of their own.

I needed a break. And a chance to say goodbye to Lauren, before it was too late.

{twenty-three}

WHEN I ARRIVED AT LAUREN'S, she was sitting on her front porch beneath the overhang, the porch light revealing her thick black hair tied back in a silken ponytail. We'd sat together on each other's front porches many times before, but, right now, we might as well have been strangers. There was no place for me in her world, not anymore.

I plopped down beside her, staring at the small apartment complex across the street. Clouds hovered low in the sky above, heavy with unspent rain. Moisture thickened the air, and the pressure weighed on my bones.

Lauren nudged her shoulder into mine. "Everything okay?"

A painful sensation knotted in the back of my throat. "Isn't it funny how cardinals don't fly south? Colorado gets pretty cold, and they're so small."

"Oh, Sophia," she said. "I'm sorry. I know you two were friends."

"Who?"

"Ivory," she said. "She told me last night she was moving. Isn't that why you're here?"

"Last night?" Ivory couldn't have told her last night.

Lauren opened her hands and splayed her fingers. "She left a letter in my mailbox. I just assumed she'd told you."

Ah. Paloma was covering her bases. "I haven't checked my mail today. That must be why I didn't know."

Way to sound upset, Sophia.

"Things won't be the same without her," I added, trying to sound sincere. Unfortunately, the inflection didn't reach my tone. "Did she say why she left?"

Lauren shrugged. "Said she had a job offer in Boston and that she hated to leave like this, but she had to catch the first plane out and didn't want to wake me. I'm surprised she even bothered to tell me. She hasn't been much of a friend."

I fidgeted with my charm bracelet, focusing on the small violin charm. "Neither have I."

Lauren smiled. "Of course you have."

"No," I said. "I haven't."

My voice sounded shakier than I would have liked. How would she react to the news? She didn't care Ivory had left, but that was only because they'd never gotten along.

The lines in Lauren's forehead deepened. "What's wrong?"

"The thing is—" I watched her expression carefully. "—we're moving."

Lauren shook her head. "You can't."

"We're helping Charles' family with renovations."

Lauren didn't look at me—just pressed her hands hard against the whitewashed planks of her porch steps. "I thought they lived in Japan?"

"You can visit anytime," I said, as though a Band-Aid would be enough. "We'll cover the airfare. Maybe visit your relatives while you're there?"

"Sounds great," Lauren said, but her voice said it wasn't. Then, after a long moment, she lifted her gaze to mine, giving me a dark, silent glare. "To be honest, Sophia, this sucks."

You have no idea.

Maybe I was imagining the sudden silence. The abrupt cessation of night birds singing, wind rustling in the trees, and small animals scampering about.

Lauren tucked up one knee and started peeling the aglet off one of her shoelaces. "When are you leaving?"

I lowered my voice, as if she might not hear me and we could somehow skip this part of the conversation. "Tomorrow morning."

"Tomorrow? Damn it, Sophia. This is almost as bad as what Ivory did." She sighed heavily, flicking away the torn piece of aglet from her shoe. "What's wrong with Charles' parents again?"

"They're putting a new addition on their house. Charles offered to help." Not the best lie, but I needed to tell her something. "Earthquake damage, or something, I think."

"So you'll only be gone for a little while."

"It's a big addition."

"You aren't telling me something."

I frowned, thinking she might believe me if I looked hurt by her assumption. It was low, but I didn't know what else to do. I *couldn't* tell her the truth. "Why would I keep anything from you?"

"It's fine. Go. Have a good time."

"Lauren?"

Her eyes were getting puffy, and she dabbed them with the inside wrist of her shirtsleeve. It only made her eyes redder.

"I'm going to visit," she said. "I'm just upset, okay?"

She smiled through her tears, and that was what killed me: It was her usual smile, one I'd always thought of as real, and now I wondered how much hurt might have always been hiding beneath it.

Lauren insisted on coming back to Charles' house to help clear out the things we couldn't bring with us or leave behind. She even agreed to watch after Red.

Around eleven o'clock, we said our goodbyes. I took a mental snapshot of her standing beneath the porch light outside my front door: Lauren in a tweed, knee-length coat. Lauren in dark blue jeans. Lauren in black rain boots with white polka dots, her skin splotchy and her make-up running.

She turned, cage in hand, and walked away.

☪

ADRIAN WAS ALREADY GONE, probably out tying up his own loose ends. Charles looked up at me from the couch.

"Are you all right?" he asked softly.

"No." I hung my scarf and jacket on the coat rack, kicked my boots in the corner by the door, and stalked into our room.

Charles followed. I could hear him standing behind me in the doorway, feel the sympathy radiating from his body. I stared out the window. The first drops of rain splattered against the windowpanes and beaded together to trail like small veins over the glass.

Charles walked over and placed his hand on my shoulder. Immediately, I caved, turning toward him, and he folded me into his arms.

I buried my face against his chest. I'd lost a lot of people in my life, but this was my first time saying goodbye. My emotions crashed through me. I'd never gotten to say goodbye to my mom, to my dad.

Charles breathed into my hair, and I sighed heavily. I needed to let go of my past. *Really* let go.

"I'm terrified of what's going to happen tomorrow."

Charles nodded. "You don't have to do this."

Didn't I, though? I needed to set aside my need for acceptance from others and worry about accepting myself, my damned 'gift' included. And the only way to do that was to use my abilities for something meaningful. Like standing up to the Maltorim and their prejudices against dual-breeds.

I looked up into Charles' piercing gaze. "I do have to do this," I said. "I absolutely do."

I stepped away from him, determined to focus on something else. I still needed to work on my gift. The stronger I was, the better our chances of rescuing his parents. I sat on the edge of the bed, peeled off my socks, and grounded my feet on the carpet. I centered my energy on a small book resting on the birdcage table near the bedroom door. It thudded immediately to the floor, creating a tent of crushed pages.

I growled under my breath. How was I supposed to be strong enough in time to face the Maltorim if I couldn't move a stupid book?

Rubbing my hand over my face, I crouched down, but Charles beat me to it, his gaze burning into mine. He set the book on the table, the intensity of his gaze dissolving my barriers.

I walked over to the bedroom window and looked out to the yard. Empty.

Moments later, Charles walked up behind me and wrapped one arm around my waist. He swept the hair from my neck and pressed a kiss against my pulse.

"Take a break. You have all night." He punctuated his words with a soft nibble.

I tried to tamp down the arousal his lips created as they tickled against the fine hairs on my neck. Useless effort, that.

"I don't have all night," I said, my words shielding my desires. "I need to sleep."

"Sleep on the plane."

I turned toward him, closing my eyes as his hands massaged my neck, his grip slowly loosening as he moved down the planes of my back. My concerns ebbed at his gentle touch, and I sighed, tilting my face toward his. I wanted his lips pressed against mine—wanted to connect with something other than the pain and fear gripping my heart.

"I'm always here for you," he whispered, each word relaxing another nerve in my body.

"I want to be there for you, too."

I kissed his shoulder, and when I lifted my gaze, his lips captured mine. I couldn't refuse myself this one good feeling—this one escape, these last quiet moments we would spend together.

All this time, I'd battled over whether I should or shouldn't let myself fall in love with him. As though that were something I could control. I'd worried whether it was 'smart' to be in a relationship with

203

an immortal man, knowing we likely had no future together.

Charles, on the other hand, had none of these concerns. For him, it'd always been about my safety. He'd held back in fear of breaking my heart, or perhaps allowing me to break my own. Now I knew we *were* strong enough to overcome the immortality issue. How, I wasn't sure, but I would no longer allow that to stand in the way.

Charles' hands skimmed up my back, dragging my shirt over my head and breaking our kiss. I watched intently as he pulled off his own shirt, revealing his hard, smooth chest. He stepped closer, pressing my back against the wall, the warmth of his chest against mine intoxicating, my want for him flowing through my veins like a drug.

His fingertips traced along my collarbone, his lips trailing behind as he slipped his finger beneath my bra strap and slid it off my shoulder, the heat between my thighs intensifying with each brush of his lips. Slowly, my worries melted away. He dropped my bra to the floor, and I pushed it aside with my toes.

As I unfastened his jeans, one button at a time, a strong mix of love and lust radiated from him, and I eased away from the wall, stepping closer. He was staring at me with an intensity that was new even for him, his gaze sweeping over my bare skin—skin that felt flushed with desire.

He brushed a strand of hair from my cheek. "We'll make it through this."

"I hope you're right."

I kissed his chest once, then leaned my head there, my breasts pressed against his warm stomach. A sigh escaped with his breath and the evidence of his passion grew harder, pressing against my body, just above my hip.

My skirt pooled with the clothes on the floor, and he eased me onto the bed, tracing his fingers along my hairline and down the side of my face, his eyes filled with a familiar, steady heat. Warmth swirled in my stomach and spread through my body. I tilted my chin closer to his face, the distance between our lips shrinking to nothing more than a breath. His hand seared a path down my abdomen, onto my thigh, and his gentle massage sent fiery currents through my body.

"Are you sure?" he asked.

We'd never taken things this far. I'd always been sure I wanted to give myself to him, but my stomach still twisted with nerves.

"Sophia?"

"Yes," I whispered.

His lips explored my breasts, the swell of my hips, the insides of my thighs. His tongue traced the edge of the fabric of my underwear, nudging it aside to kiss me there. I curled my fingers in his hair as his hands fanned across my belly and pressed into the dip, then lowered my underwear from my hips.

"I love you, Sophia." His words mingled with kisses over my body as he slowly returned to capture my lips with his. The taste of his breath, like mint and vanilla, sent new shivers through my body. "And I want you. Forever, always. Whatever it takes."

Caressing the strong lines of his neck and shoulders, I drew him closer. "I love you, too."

His body hovered over mine, leaving me eager for connection. Somewhere along the way, his clothing had joined mine on the floor, and as he lowered himself to kiss me again, his bare thighs rubbed against mine, and anticipation robbed me of my breath.

"This is okay?" he asked, his mouth pressed to my ear.

I nodded, my throat too tight to offer a verbal response. I couldn't deny the throbbing between my thighs, that I wanted him where he was, his body deliciously warm. His breath warmed my neck as he nudged against me, entering slowly, and his gentle kisses on my shoulder relaxed my nerves as he eased in deeper, slowing again at any small gasps that escaped my lips.

His heart thudded against my own as he pressed closer, his body rocked forward, and a soft moan rode my sigh as he moved his mouth to mine and deepened the kiss. The pressure of him inside of me created another kind a pressure—a building need for release. His fangs slowly extended and grazed my lip.

The importance of everything beforehand and everything ahead dissolved. I pushed my bottom lip against one of his fangs and winced as it pricked my flesh. My blood slipped between his lips and slid between our tongues as we kissed.

Charles pulled back, searching my eyes. We both knew even a small amount of my blood would strengthen him. He hadn't had human blood in years, but he needed this.

"It's okay," I whispered, and he kissed me again, sucking gently on my lip.

The kiss tangled me in a web of arousal; my mind became lost, free, uninhibited. Our shallow breaths unified, our bodies bound together, the pressure building, stronger, more intense. Sinful. And yet, in that moment, all my guilt was stripped away.

I'd expect my first time to be awkward. Painful. With Charles, it was anything but. My body surrendered and waves of ecstasy stole away my conscious thoughts. All that remained was blissful nothingness—a sense of oneness with the man I loved and peace over all that lay ahead.

Charles propped on one elbow at my side, his hand drifting over my curves, and I studied his face unhurriedly, feature-by-feature, as if I hadn't already memorized the lines of his face, his strong jaw line, the greenish hue of his chin stubble. As if I hadn't already memorized the way his eyelashes crinkled together and the way his chest felt hard but still warm and welcoming beneath my hand.

He stroked the damp curls away from my face and kissed my brow, and I buried my head in the hollow between his neck and shoulders. We fit perfectly together.

I drifted between wisps of sleep for what felt like hours, though the clock indicated only minutes had passed. My heart sank. Time to leave these stolen moments behind. Our intimacy had resolved many of my unwanted emotions, but one still lingered: fear. Fear of losing Charles, of losing the one person I could be myself with completely. I breathed a sigh of resignation and stared up at him.

"Forever, Sophia," he promised. "We'll find a way."

We showered and slipped into some fresh clothes, then dedicated the next few hours to working on my gift. Object manipulation became easier; items floated from one place in the room to another, some with little more than a quiet thought. A pillow. A chair. A table. Some of the larger items required more concentration, however, and the weight, shape, and size of the objects were definitely a factor.

The ultimate test was lifting a human body. Charles lay on the bed, and I focused on his form. Looking at him rekindled the passion inside me, strengthening me enough to lift him a foot from the mattress.

Perhaps my Wiccan training held truth after all: love was strong enough to ignite my powers.

{twenty-four}

CHARLES AND I ARRIVED at the airport—a little gray slip of a building—at four in the morning. The circles under Charles' eyes were almost purple-black, his eyes bloodshot, his hair unruly. He wore the same clothes as the night before, rumpled and unwashed.

As we passed the two check-in booths, my black dress and heavy makeup garnered a few odd stares. Adrian had suggested darkness would cloak me better outside the Maltorim's asylum if I dressed in black. Only my full-length Gothic dress I'd worn as part of a Halloween costume several years ago had fit the bill. I'd also straightened my hair and smeared some heavy black make-up over my eyelids to disguise my appearance.

I still looked like me, but the changes might be enough to deter those who had only seen me a handful of times.

Or so I foolishly believed.

We followed a nearby hallway to a blue-framed window. Adrian had instructed us to tap once, wait, and tap again three more times. So I did.

A door opened further down the hall, and an older man with ruddy cheeks and a graying mountain-man beard waved us over. Once we entered the room, he eased the door shut.

"You the ones booking for Damascus?" He threw a narrow glance over his shoulder then turned to shuffle a mess of papers on his desk. "Thought there'd be three of ya."

"Our friend will be here soon," Charles said. "He needed to eat before the flight."

The man huffed. "He ain't no bloodsucker, is he? Cuz I don't fly no bloodsuckers, that's for damn sure."

"I don't blame you," I said.

Maybe if I agreed with him, he'd be more open to hearing what we had to say. Normally I wouldn't say one word more than I needed, but we didn't have time to beat around the bush.

"It was Cruor who kidnapped his parents"—I jabbed my thumb toward Charles—"and that is where we are heading now. To save them."

"That right?" The man sat in his chair and swiveled toward us. He swept his hand to a few spare seats, and we sat.

So much for Adrian's claim of 'no questions asked'.

Without any other route to Damascus, our best bet was to gain whatever little compassion this man might have, so I risked laying everything on the table, from the news of the Liettes to our plan to rescue them.

"We wouldn't have known if our friend hadn't told us," I said in closing. "He's not like other Cruor."

The man leaned forward. His breath, heavy on my face, reeked of coffee and cigarette smoke. "Listen here, Miss. Clearly you didn't hear me the first time. I said: I. Don't. Fly. No. *Fucking*. Bloodsuckers."

"Why the hell not?" I demanded.

"I'm a blocker, and ain't many of us left." The man's gaze locked on Charles, one forearm leaning on his knee. "Last thing I need to do is get mixed up with the likes of them."

A blocker? What did that mean?

"Well," Charles said. "I'm Strigoi *and* Cruor. So now you're mixed up with us. We aren't all the enemy."

"I see," the man said, his expression softer now.

I couldn't read his thoughts. Whether that was because he was human or because he was a blocker, I didn't know.

He scratched his beard. "Fine," he said. "Guess I can't in good conscious stand back while the dual-natured are targeted. I'll help, but don't say nothing about it. Name's Rhett."

Just as Charles and I were introducing ourselves, the door creaked on the other side of the room. Adrian let himself in, smiled, and put out his hand.

"I'm Adrian."

"I know who you are," Rhett said, ignoring the offer for a handshake. "No funny business. Let's go."

Rhett led us outside to a dark-blue plane on the tarmac. I'd never taken a flight before. I'd never even left Colorado. At least I wouldn't have to see the world outside whipping past the windows—but that's only because there were no windows, aside from the front windshield.

Funny, since Rhett had acted as though he didn't fly Cruor.

The passenger area consisted of four navy leather seats with a small table between. Once we settled in, the stairs closed back against the plane.

"This thing safe?" I asked.

Rhett grumbled something unintelligible, followed by, "Course it's safe. Safer than any of those other planes you been flying in, and faster, too. My plane is better, you'll see. I'll have you there in three hours."

The fabric of Adrian's seat creaked as he sat forward. "About that . . ."

Rhett turned back around. "What now, kid?"

I smiled, drawing his attention. "Could you decrease your speed by half? We need to arrive at night."

He frowned. "See, this shit right here is why I don't fly you bloodsucker types. I do this, and you don't ask me for nothing else the rest of this trip. We'll touch down around eight p.m., their time. Good? Now shut up and let me fly this thing."

I mouthed the words 'thank you' at the back of his head and sunk deeper into my seat as Rhett closed himself into the pilot's cabin. The plane's engine sputtered to life and continued in a steady, muffled roar.

Charles switched on an overhead light. The plane rattled down the runway, picking up speed. I gripped the armrests and glanced from Adrian to Charles. Both men relaxed back in their seats. I took this to mean the plane's shaking was normal.

Now that we were actually on the plane, everything was catching up to me. My friends, my family, the whole situation.

"Do you think we'll ever come back?" I asked quietly.

"I don't know." Charles' voice deadpanned, his mouth twisting into a grim line. "Thalia's coterie will be looking for us now that the Maltorim is after us. It wouldn't be wise to return."

We were disappearing forever. Just like Ivory. Her name created a pang in my heart. I couldn't help but miss her, even after what she'd done, and I couldn't shake my guilt over stealing her memories. When she woke in her Boston summer home with gaps in her memory, would she at least remember she was an earth elemental?

I took a deep breath. I hadn't stolen *all* of her memories—she couldn't have been thinking of 'me' during every moment spent with her sire.

Charles' chest puffed out and his glassy stare settled on my hands. I was picking at my fingernails and my cuticles had started to bleed.

"You're still upset about Ivory," he said.

I didn't reply. Now wasn't the time. My stomach queasy, my palms sticky with sweat, reality hit me at the core: Charles' parents were in real danger, and we were flying toward a trap. I needed to get ready for the horrors that lay ahead.

"Why is the Maltorim in Damascus?" I asked in a whisper, hoping the sound of Charles' voice would soothe my tattered nerves.

Charles allowed the change in subject.

"Damascus is the oldest city," he said, gently taking my hand. "The Cruor have inhabited the outskirts since about 4000 BC. During the Tel Ramad excavations, the Maltorim was almost discovered. No one has returned to dig at the location since, but the Maltorim have made modifications to accommodate for such an event."

I leaned against him and inhaled, taking in the hint of sandalwood on his shirt. Already my tension was relaxing away.

"Could you keep talking," I asked, "even if I fall asleep?"

I knew the request was weird—maybe even rude on the surface— but Charles smiled, his thoughts confirming he understood, and he continued with his stories about the history of his world.

☪

THE FLIGHT LANDED six hours later, shortly after eight p.m., Eastern European Summer Time. We hurried through the airport, and Adrian hailed a cab.

As the driver whisked toward the city, cobblestone roads and Gothic revival buildings blotted out my fear. I stared with wonder at the angles and arches, pondering how daylight might illuminate this new world.

Charles squeezed my hand, looking to Adrian. "Sophia and I should stop for food while you pick up supplies."

Adrian nodded. The pair seemed resigned to the plan, but I was fighting off surges of hot and cold and a fluttering nausea.

The driver dropped us off in the heart of the old city, close to the Umayyad mosque. The ferocity of the whispers in my mind confirmed the presence of a large elemental community, but my mind kept going back to the same thought: how did Adrian know so much about the inner workings of the Maltorim? I had tried several times to listen to his thoughts but heard nothing he hadn't already spoken aloud.

Once Adrian went his way, Charles and I headed to the shops. Hints of jasmine, saffron, cumin, and nutmeg infused the air, each scent lingering on my taste buds and igniting my hunger.

I slowed, taking in the columned architecture and polished marble courtyard of the nearby mosque. People inside chatted amongst themselves—Muslims, Christians, and Jews, all worshipping together on this night, a subdued sense of piety emanating from the courtyard.

Around the mosque's outer walls lay a marketplace—a series of broken cobblestone paths crisscrossing in what appeared to be no particular order. We passed vendors garbed in red and black threads, some of them packing their spices, nuts, and dried fruits into horse-driven carts.

One booth caught my eye. A young woman with dark hair and a Marilyn Monroe mole was turning tarot cards onto a table.

First, the Fool, inverted—a bad decision. I knew this from when Ivory had done readings at a party in college. She'd taught me all about them, asked me if I wanted to do a reading to channel my past lives. I told her no, that I just wanted to make it through this one.

Now I knew why she'd asked.

When the lady turned the next card, my neck hairs prickled, and a shiver flashed down my spine, causing a small tremble in one of my hands.

Death.

But the death card was not literal.

Not always.

The reader stared right at me, tsking and shaking her head. I quickly looked away. The spread wasn't for me. She'd been sitting with a customer. Still, I had to stop myself from speculating what the next card would have been.

Charles spoke in Arabic with a man a few tables down while I admired a display of Persian rugs, Russian teapots, and age-blackened Greek tableware. Then he pulled me away by my elbow, telling me the man said there was a small shop around the corner that sold falafel wraps and freshly-squeezed mulberry juice for fifty American cents.

The shop owner—a darkly tanned, older man with friendly eyes—sat in a woven lawn chair, a Bengal cat in his lap, his back to a simple wooden door. He invited us in and offered a sample of the food: hummus, tahini, and pita with a hint of lemon, and a tangy mulberry juice reminiscent of grapefruit. We ordered several falafels and a carton of the juice with some Styrofoam cups.

Aside from the interactions with the vendors, Charles hadn't said anything, and I didn't press him for conversation. We arrived back at the main square to meet Adrian, who arrived moments later with a large bag in hand.

"What's your sign?" Adrian asked.

"Sign?"

"Zodiac. You're a Sagittarius, right?"

"I am, why?"

"Come with me." Adrian led us around the corner and into a narrow alley. He crouched down, and Charles and I sat across from him. "You said lifting things was draining, correct?"

"Right."

"I'm presuming you need fire to fully tap into your gifts. You'll certainly need to maintain your energy if you're going to do this."

"Great. What am I supposed to do, set myself ablaze?"

Adrian reached into the bag and set a copper bowl, similar to the scrying bowl I had at home, on the ground. From his pocket, he pulled a crumbled piece of paper and tossed it inside before striking a match to light a small fire.

"Move the flames," he said.

I focused intently on lifting them until they hovered over the bowl, then I lowered them back into place.

"No energy drain," I said. "But we don't have time for me to practice."

Adrian packed everything away and sat back. "Trust, Sophia."

Trust wouldn't cut it. I had no idea what to expect. Going into things without a solid plan—admittedly, that had me on the verge of panic.

"I sense your uncertainty," Adrian said.

I shook my head. "It's silly, really."

"Best you tell us now."

Charles dipped his face closer to mine. "Sophia, if something is bothering you, please speak up."

My shoulders sank, and I gazed at Adrian. "It's just kind of weird how you know all this stuff. The books you have, knowing where this place is, the passages . . . " I stared at my wrist, spinning the coils on the bracelet Charles had given me and twisting the beads. "I'm sorry. I don't mean to sound like I'm accusing you of anything."

Adrian's expression was unreadable. "It's fine." He pulled a wallet from his jacket, slipped out a picture, and handed it to me. "My parents."

The photograph was of a middle-aged couple with the same dark skin and kind eyes as Adrian. By the way they clung to one another, each resting a hand on a young boy's shoulder, it was clear their family was built on love.

I pointed to the boy. "This is you?"

"Before I was turned."

"How did you get this? Photography wasn't invented until—"

"Our world has *always* been far ahead of your own, Sophia."

I shook my head, my gaze returning to the photograph. "So what happened to them?"

"They were human informants for the Maltorim. I was born inside those walls . . . raised there."

I returned the photo and slumped back against the alley wall. "I didn't know."

"They told me my parents died during the elemental war, back in the 1600s. After that, they took me in and raised me to take my father's place." Adrian's jaw tensed for such a brief moment that I wasn't sure I'd seen any movement at all. "They decided to turn me."

His gaze shifted from me to Charles then back again. "I was sent to fight in the war, killing the dual-breeds. I worked alongside Charles, though we weren't friends at the time. When I noticed he always held back from making a kill, I confronted him, and another Cruor overheard. They thought I was the one allowing the dual-natured to go free, and they tried to kill me. In Charles' anger, he shifted and killed those men to save me. It was then I realized he himself was dual-natured.

"Since then," he continued, "I've left the Maltorim, though I'm certain they have never truly let me go. Thalia's clan seems to always be near. When Charles arrived in the area with Blake and Adonis, he joined her clan to try to gain inside information on my behalf, though nothing much came of it."

I closed my eyes. In my heart, I'd always trusted Adrian. It was my mind I remained in constant battle with. When I opened my eyes, Adrian tilted his head, his expression curious.

"What?" I asked.

"You could have taken that from my thoughts, no?"

"I try not to do that to my friends."

Adrian cleared his throat.

"You never thought of it while I was listening," I amended.

"The truth comes out." Adrian grinned and turned toward Charles. "Are you ready?"

Charles was staring out toward the main road, but at the sound of Adrian's voice, he glanced at his watch. "It's time."

{twenty-five}

ADRIAN LED US through a labyrinth of alleyways where stray dogs scratched at soiled potato peels spilling from overturned garbage bins and nearby shop owners scared them away by banging their alley doors with metal spoons. Though cars, trucks, and taxis clogged the roadways, we trudged by on foot, not wanting to bring anyone else closer to the horrors of the Maltorim.

As we reached the outskirts of the city, I held my breath against the stench of exhaust fumes and sewage and fly-infested fish that must have fallen from a truck earlier in the day. The buzzing of insects was a cruel reminder of my curse, a sound I couldn't shut out. Whenever I was too stressed to concentrate, there it was—the buzzing in my mind, overwhelming my ability to focus on the voices.

"I don't think I can do this," I said.

Charles swiveled toward me. "Then don't. I never asked you to."

I didn't say anything—didn't let his sharp tone affect my response. I understood his anxieties colored his tone.

He tensed his jaw and swallowed. "That's not how I meant it," he said quietly. "I don't want you to. You know that."

"I know. But I didn't mean that I don't *want* to. I'm just afraid I won't be *able*." I sucked in a deep breath, trying to push away the hissing in my head, but the noise wouldn't budge. "I don't know if I can tap into my gift. The noise won't stop. I can't focus on any voices."

Charles wrapped an arm around me and pulled me against his chest. His breath warmed my scalp as he rested his chin there. "Let's turn back. We'll find you a place to stay tonight while Adrian and I go."

I pulled away, cutting my gaze toward him. "No. I need to at least try."

"It's not something you can *try*, Sophia. If your gift fails now, you'll have no way to protect yourself."

Adrian put a hand on Charles' shoulder and looked to me. "You've only recently learned how to tap into your gift. It's natural the stress of this situation would cause regression. But if you want to get through this, you have to push your worries away. Where we are going, there is no room for hesitation."

"You think I can do this?"

"Yes."

"And you?" I asked, turning to Charles.

"I don't want you to," he said.

I pressed my teeth together. "Do you think I *can*?"

He gazed solemnly into my eyes. "I know it."

With a resolute nod, I started up our path again. I could do this. Adrian believed it, Charles believed it, and now I just needed to believe it, too.

I tucked my head against Charles' shoulder, the old buildings of the inner city hanging back as we pressed forward. A few abandoned hovels perforated the desolate streets and, beneath the moonlight, patches of grass fought for life among the dusty knolls scattering the fields. Barbed wire fences stretched along the horizon and birds soared overhead, gliding with their saw-edged wings cutting through the air.

Our dirt trail, dry as sawdust, wound toward a cemetery surrounded by towering, decrepit stone walls. A rusty lock grasped the latch of a wrought-iron gate.

We walked past the neglected gate and followed the cemetery wall around the corner. A ways down, Adrian stopped and pointed at one of the stones.

"Here," he said. "My parents made this entrance before they died. No one else should know of it. If we climb over the walls, we'll set off the sensors."

"This place doesn't look like it would have sensors," I said.

Adrian gave me a quieting glare, then turned back to study the stones. Several had symbols, and, after tracing one in particular, he dug a large foreign coin from his pocket and lined it up with a small, encircled half moon.

The wall opened like a sliding door, the top still securely in place. The narrow entrance opened enough for us to squeeze through sideways, then Adrian closed the passage behind us, the walls crushing small pieces of debris as the stones settled back into place.

Light pollution from the distant city reflected off the sky, creating a pale luminescence over the burial grounds. Though my eyes had adjusted on the walk over, Adrian and Charles wove through the gravestones in a pattern I found hard to emulate.

Thousands of headstones cluttered in the dirt, their crumbling limestone spreading as far as the horizon. I tried not to breathe through my nose, but I could still taste the rotting, septic odor filling my lungs.

Charles stopped beside me. His eyes were darker than usual, opaque as the ocean's murkiest waters. "Are you ready?"

There was no being 'ready'. There was only doing what needed to be done. "We need to get your family back," I said.

"*Our* family," he said. His eyes searched mine. "No matter what, do not come after us. It's too dangerous."

I offered a noncommittal, "Mmhmm."

"I mean it, Sophia."

"I know." Something chalky coated my fingers and palm, and I realized I'd leaned on a gravestone. I snapped my hand away and wiped the dust on my pants.

Adrian cleared his throat. "Follow me."

He ushered us toward a cavernous ossuary. The musk of animals stuck in my nose. Human skeletons surrounded a support column and slumped against the walls near age-bleached skulls stacked on piles of ribs and femurs.

These were the remains of spirits who had not been left to rest— those who had been buried in temporary graves and then excavated, their bones crammed in a hollow room due to a lack of burial plots.

This was no place for performing rituals.

Adrian looked from me to the ossuary and back again. "I know," he said, "but it's the only shelter nearby. You can't sit in the middle of the graveyard."

"What if they find me?"

Apprehension rolled from Charles and Adrian in waves. Or maybe it was my own apprehension, rising like the tides and threatening to pull me away in the undercurrents. How could anyone cope with this—this vast, open, unknowingness?

I let their thoughts roll into mine, but they were blocking me out. Adrian was mentally reciting *Reluctance* by Robert Frost, and Charles was thinking about some techie plug-in thing.

"You're both worried. What's going on?"

Adrian opened his mouth, but Charles looked at him and shook his head. "Sophia, of course we're worried," Charles said, "but we didn't want to add to your distress."

"Tell me."

"We're not hopeful."

"Not hopeful of what?"

"I can't live knowing I didn't try to save my parents," Charles said, "but you don't need to be doing this. You *must* stay outside."

Adrian nodded. "We are faster and stronger and far more obligated than you. If anything goes wrong, leave immediately. You'll be able to escape before they discover your presence."

"So this—" I waved my hand around the ossuary. "—this is all hopeless."

Charles shushed me, rubbing his hands gently down my arms. It only made me angrier. "Hopeless, no, but safer. This is the best way for you to help. Trust me."

"And if I never see you again?" I wiped my cheeks with the inside of my wrist. The anger was turning inward now. Anger at my selfishness. "You want me to live with the guilt you can't?"

Charles wrapped me in his arms and kissed my hairline and held me close until I calmed. He pulled back and studied my face. "You all right?"

"You better come back."

"Forever, Sophia. Remember? After this, I promise you, I will seek out the Ankou to become a pure Strigoi and grow old with you." Charles forced a smile, but his thoughts reflected his worries. "I'll be fine."

I would make sure of that, even if I had to go in there and drag him out myself.

"If they do find you," he said, his expression sinking. "Running or hiding would be pointless by then. You only have one hope: Fight. Whatever you do, *fight*."

He dropped the bag of supplies and pulled me hard against him, pressing his lips to mine. My mind held desperately to this moment, wishing he would never let me go, that we could stay suspended in this instant forever, stay here with his hands grasping the dark tiers of my dress, kissing me with a passion that filled me with a sense of life and hope.

All too soon, he let go and stepped back.

"I love you," he whispered.

My hand moved slowly to my lips, my fingertips tracing over them as though I could feel some lingering imprint of Charles' lips. *I might never see him again.* My throat constricted, but I blinked back the tears. The time for panic had passed.

After Charles and Adrian geared up with the earpieces Adrian had bought earlier, they trudged off toward the mausoleum, moving so quickly that they were like mere blurs of color on the air.

As I stepped into the ossuary, the floor creaked. Wood panels peeked out from shifted dirt. Some boards had been broken and tossed aside. I sank to my knees and set the supply bag on a discarded piece of wood.

The *ignisvisum* would allow me to view the events, and my clairaudience would allow me to hear the thoughts of the elemental beings inside. Of course, in this case, I would immediately return the memories so that the fire would not steal them and leave them lost forever.

Everything the *ignisvisum* revealed I would then filter to Charles and Adrian through the remote headset. It was a plan that promised nothing.

I ran through my opening rites until a protective barrier was visibly in place. Spirits floated near, some cupping their hands over the bubble of whitish membrane to stare and howl. Their coal-black eyes made my skin crawl, but they were the least of my worries.

I took the tin bowl from my bag and filled it with cedar chips. I fumbled to strike a match. On my fourth attempt, the tip ignited, and I set fire to the wood. I relaxed my stare on the haze above the embers, mouthing the words to conjure the images. The charred cedar, burning beneath the translucent screen, broke up the vision a few times. I waited until I gained my focus to put on the headset.

"I see you," I said into my mouthpiece.

What I actually saw was Adrian's vision of Charles and Charles' vision of Adrian displayed split screen on the *ignisvisum* projection. Trying to follow both would have drained my energy too quickly, so I focused on Adrian's vision, hoping to keep my sights on Charles as much as possible.

We're going in now, Charles thought toward me.

They entered a mausoleum's austere double doors and squeezed around a makeshift table made of cement blocks and boards of unfinished wood. Partially-melted candles and puddles of stiff wax scattered the workspace.

Charles and Adrian hurried to the back of the darkened room, where Adrian tilted a large plank to the side and stepped through into a small, dirt-packed tunnel supported by wooden beams.

The narrow passage led to another door, but Adrian didn't try to open this one. He lowered onto one knee and swept away the soil with his hand to reveal a wooden trap door. This particular entrance was never locked as only Maltorim members knew of it. I found it odd the place wasn't under camera surveillance, but I guess when you're as powerful as the Maltorim, no one dares break into your premises.

Adrian opened the trap door, placed one hand on either side, and eased down. Charles followed. Stone walls surrounded them, a dark slate floor with water stains beneath their feet as they crept through the underground maze. I could almost feel the dank moisture of the corridors.

The creak and jangle of the cemetery's front gate, racketed by the surrounding spirits, threatened to distract me from my clairaudience, but I focused until the sounds of the real world muted from my ears.

I opened my mind to all nearby elemental activity. I released the thoughts closest to me—the spirits swirling in the darkness outside my protective barrier. One by one, I zeroed out other connections, using Charles and Adrian as markers to determine the placements of the minds I invaded.

It took some effort, but I targeted the thoughts registering closest to Charles and Adrian. The farther they lurked into the dark passages of the mausoleum, the more the new connections grew in clarity.

About three-quarters of the way down the hall, Charles and Adrian paused, half-crouched, looking at each other. Their lips weren't moving, but their wordless communication was amazingly accurate. They pressed against opposite walls and slinked to the opening at the end of the hall.

Two guards awaited out of view. Only another Cruor could sneak up on their kind undetected.

"Left guard is half asleep," I said. "Right guard is preoccupied."

Charles and Adrian whipped around the corner and snapped the necks of both guards. The crack of vertebrae echoed in my mind, and my stomach churned.

How could they kill as though it was nothing? Had there been no better alternative?

My emotions interfered with my signal, and the image rippled, my instincts wanting to block what I'd seen. Pushing aside my fears, I stared at the large hallway the *ignisvisum* displayed.

Charles and Adrian reached a set of arched wooden fortress doors, and I located the thought waves of the people on the other side. Based on the thoughts contained there, I imagined the occupants were engaged in light, candid chatter.

"Five inside," I said.

Adrian and Charles crept past the door, heading down the final corridor that would lead to the Liettes.

I released the people in the other room from my clairaudience and sent my mind out to pick up fresh connections.

Immediately, another presence materialized.

This was the last connection I'd expected to make. This was the last person any of us expected to see here. I tried to find my voice, but

Charles and Adrian spun around before I could succeed.

{twenty-six}

THE *IGNISVISUM* SHARPENED to the point I wasn't sure if the visions were still in my bowl or playing right in my mind.

I shook my head, but Thalia remained in the vision, her hands poised on her hips, her charcoal sweater contrasting with her glowing violet eyes. My stomach felt pinched—stuck between the gears of a turning clock. If Thalia was here, Circe wasn't far. But I couldn't place her, and I couldn't risk dropping any connections to seek her out. I only hoped she wasn't on her way to find me.

My connection to Adrian intensified, my own thoughts seeping into the background as Thalia strutted toward them.

She clicked her teeth. "Hello, *Charlie.*"

The clarity of her spoken words stunned me. It was as though I were there—as though I'd reached beyond my clairaudience. Bitter saliva pooled on my tongue, tasting as I imagined the dank air of the stone passages must.

Thalia's gaze flicked to Adrian, but he only received her passing attention. She already had her sights back on Charles.

Charles' jaw clenched. "What are *you* doing here?"

"You're smart enough to figure that out, no? You fooled me for so long. Thought you were so clever. So tell me—what do you *think* I'm doing here?"

"Nothing good." Rage tightened in his chest, the rasp of a beast rattling inside and waiting to break free. All these things were alive in me, too, because of our blood bond and the mental connection we now shared.

Thalia took him in with a smile. "Tsk, tsk, Charlie. I've broken no laws. You, on the other hand . . . "

His gaze panned the dimly lit halls. They'd been empty—a route for escape—but now other Cruor lurked in the shadows where only the edges of light from the wall sconces gave away their movement.

With a snap of Thalia's fingers, four guards approached, dressed as Continental Artillery: dark blue jackets faced with scarlet, tan trousers tucked into white socks, and black-buckled, square-toed shoes. But their build was much too large for the late 17th century. Thalia mused at their being dressed in these replica uniforms, all to appease the Maltorim's Queen—Callista.

At the lapse in Thalia's attention, Charles lunged for her. Two guards yanked him back, restraining him before he made contact. The other two secured Adrian, who resigned immediately, though Charles tried to pull away. The tallest guard kicked him behind the knee, the force dropping him to the ground.

Thalia, seemingly unaffected, waved her hand, and the guards lifted Charles back to his feet.

He lowered his chin to his chest. *Leave, Sophia.*

Thalia's face hovered right beside his, and she flicked her tongue against his cheek. "You *do* taste funny."

I wiped away the moisture above my lip, but my body was still damp, sweat trickling down my back like tiny bugs fleeing from Thalia's scathing tone.

Charles recoiled from her touch. "What they are doing here is wrong. Why would you get involved?"

"Wrong, Charlie?" She laughed, snatching the earpiece from his and Adrian's ears. She plunked them into the open hand of one of the guards. "Little hypocrite. All these years with your 'We can't hunt humans, it's the law' bullshit. Now here I am, abiding these precious laws, and you condemn me?" She arched an eyebrow, her face frozen as if stapled into place.

Charles gritted his teeth. "The law against dual-breeds is centuries old."

"Boo hoo. The laws are not there for your *convenience*, Charlie. You don't get to pick and choose." Thalia snapped her gaze toward Adrian. "And you, foolish child—you risk your life for this? He is nothing!"

Adrian's fangs crunched down and his face contorted with a snarl. "You're no more than a deadbeat tracker who didn't meet the mark to join the Maltorim."

Thalia's eerie smile slipped for a fraction of a second as she cracked Adrian across the jaw. My own face stung slightly from the phantom impact, and I lifted a hand to my cheek.

"We'll see who makes the Maltorim."

She spun on her heel and began to walk away. After a few steps, she stopped and called over her shoulder to the guards. "

Take them to holding. I'm off to have a little chat with the Queen."

She threw her hand up in dismissal, not bothering to so much as glance back as she strode down the corridor. Her thoughts raced too quickly for me to make sense of them.

I used Adrian as a marker and catalyst into her visions. The *ignisvisum* scratched her sights through Adrian's. I tried splitting the views, but without success.

I had to choose.

☪

THALIA'S HEELS CLICKED down the corridor. The dying torchlight flickered, tossing odd shadows along the floor. The passage reminded me of the entrance to Club Flesh, but the water leaking through the stone walls gave the asylum a more ominous vibe.

Murmurs bled through the archaic doors as Thalia dolefully smoothed her slacks. She knocked. As she lifted her hand to knock again, the door creaked opened and the shadow of a small woman appeared in the doorway.

"Queen Callista," Thalia said with a small bow.

The Queen stepped forward, and Thalia worked through her discomfort to hold eye contact. Sure, Callista could kill her for any small infraction, but she needed to be regarded as an equal—as one worthy of the Maltorim.

Callista's bone-thin figure jutted from the dark room, and she hummed a quiet, offbeat tune under her breath. My heart, affected by her eerie lullaby, stuttered. She tilted her head up, her nose a delicate slope, her robes clinging to her small breasts, her alabaster skin glinting beneath the hall light.

She was only a girl, stuck somewhere between youth and womanhood. Fifteen, perhaps, but an ageless fifteen, and with eyes that seemed much older. Eyes that haunted me, staring so intently into Thalia's that I felt as though she were looking right through her to me.

"Thalia." The name dripped from the Queen's tongue like venom from a serpent's fang.

Black opium incense burned Thalia's nostrils, and she struggled not to wrinkle her nose. "I've apprehended Charles Liette and his companion . . . *Adrian.*"

"I am aware." Callista swept her almost-white hair in front of her shoulder and began loosely braiding. She stared at the ends of her braid, fanning the hair out. When she looked back up to see Thalia still standing there, she released a bored sigh and folded her arms across her chest. "Well?"

Thalia expected an invitation into the room. A long moment passed, Thalia's smile faltering under Callista's glare. "I had come to inform you of their arrival and capture, my Queen."

Callista tapped her foot, and she huffed. "Did you believe we were unaware of their presence?"

"Not at all. I mean . . . " Thalia's weight shifted from one foot to the other. Of course the Queen had been unaware. If she'd been aware, she would have sent out her guards to capture Adrian and Charles. "I only meant—they were alone. In the hall near the holding cells. I tracked them."

"I would hardly call what you do tracking. Now, if you please"—Callista began to shut the door—"I must return to more pressing matters."

Thalia shot out a hand to stop the door from closing. Her cheeks and forehead cooled, a stony mask of dignity freezing her face. Callista was going to listen.

"There is someone else, too," Thalia said. "A spirit elemental."

My heartbeat roared in my ears. How could Thalia possibly know? I inhaled slowly through my nose, trying to slow my vitals as to not drown out the thoughts I invaded. I needed to hear their plan if I was to take action wisely.

Callista stepped aside, sweeping her arm in invitation. "Fine," she said in a measured tone. "Come in."

The lights brightened, and Thalia's eyes widened at the polished marble flooring. Golden light reflected off the floors and highlighted the papered walls: sanguine panels with gold-leaf designs. A grandiose crystal chandelier hung from the ceiling. Parlor chairs with scrolled legs and deep-buttoned chaise lounges upholstered with deep red and royal blue velvet adorned the room, barely clad men and women sprawled on their cushions.

Thalia made a contrived effort to conceal her amazement—oh, how she coveted each item, how she envied the very air the Queen breathed. She returned her gaze to Callista, but the Queen quickly turned and glided over to four young men who stood at attention.

They were the elders of the Maltorim, each in their early teens, some appearing even younger than the Queen. All shared the same pallid skin and coal black eyes and dressed in the same draping black robes with wide sleeves. Callista indicated a parlor chair, but Thalia remained standing.

"Tell me," Callista said, still facing the other Maltorim members. Her body stilled, not even a twitch of a muscle or a sway of her stance. "How do you know this witch you speak of?"

"She found my coterie. She's been with Charles since at least October."

"Here it is March," Callista chided, "and you hadn't alerted us sooner?"

Thalia rummaged for an excuse—something to cover her selfish ploy to gain a place on the Maltorim, an excuse that would cover how she'd wasted time trying to find a way to personally deliver us to the Queen.

"We didn't learn until recently," she finally offered.

Callista growled and spun toward Thalia. "You just told me they have been together since autumn! Why had you not told me when I visited the States?"

Thalia bowed slightly in effort to soothe Callista. "My Queen, we only recently learned of their true natures. When you visited—in September—we weren't aware of her then. Once we were, it would have taken too long to wait for one of your trackers to be sent." The first statement was said in truth, but Thalia was uncertain of her final remark. She hoped to draw attention to herself as a suitable tracker for the Maltorim.

Callista sneered. "So it is then. Where is this girl now?"

"Here, I believe."

"You *believe*, or you *know*? Can you not track her, Thalia?"

"She doesn't have a real scent, she—"

"*What?*"

"She has a scent. What I mean is, it's weak."

"Everyone's scent is weak to you," Callista replied, rolling her eyes.

"No," Thalia said sharply. "Hers is *distinct.* Just mild."

"Distinct?" Callista's eyebrow rose pointedly.

Thalia steeled herself against the Queen's words. "Yes, distinct. You know, the way the forever girls are said to smell. Not human, and yet, not immortal, either."

Had she really been able to tell that much that night in the alley? That would mean she'd known before Charles or me. No wonder she'd said I would be valuable.

"You cannot just toss that around, Thalia. A forever girl." Callista scoffed. She stared into the distance a moment, then her eyebrows pulled together and she lifted her gaze. "Truly?"

"I am certain," Thalia said. "I will bring her to you to see for yourself."

"See that you do not return without her." She started to pace away, but turned around once more. "Alive, mind you," she said with a sickly-sweet smile. "I want to meet this . . . *witch*."

Thalia bowed briefly. "One more thing, my Queen . . . ."

"Say it."

"If I bring you this girl, Charles' fate is mine to decide."

Callista narrowed her eyes. "Fine. Though you must wait until we have extracted the information necessary to unlock the key."

Using my clairaudience, I picked up that 'key' had meant a person . . . or people. But a fog hung over Callista's thoughts, and all I could discern were general ideas and fragments of thoughts. Something protected her mind.

Thalia slipped out of the room and closed the door. Her vision panned across the passageways.

Where are you? she thought, and she started down the hall.

{twenty-seven}

I TUCKED THE MATCHBOX in my pocket. My leg muscles stiffened as I ran, the weight of my legs reminding me of my childhood nightmares. I didn't slow until I reached the mausoleum and crept through the entrance Charles and Adrian had taken earlier.

There was no plan—there was only knowing I couldn't turn away, that I had to go in.

The passages were colder, bigger, and darker than I expected. I'd seen them through Adrian's eyes before, his night vision far superior to my own.

Each step grated in my ears, surely as loud as thunder to the Cruor. My breath came short, my pulse hammered in my throat. Would they sense my approach? Thalia was searching for me, and here I was, padding deeper into the asylum, closer to my capture.

The corridors stretched in every direction, the doors sometimes erratic and far apart and other times evenly spaced and cramped together, all of them eroded at the bottom, revealing rust beneath gray paint.

Charles' voice rang in my head. *Go home, Sophia. Please.*

The deeper into the passages I traveled, the stronger the voice of his thoughts became. A few feet later, I was too close to determine whether I was moving closer or farther away.

I strode through the stone corridors, holding my breath against the damp air and stench of mold as I followed the path Charles and Adrian had begun. Where had they planned to go from here?

The thoughts of three guards rushed into my mind. My adrenaline throttled and power surged through me, boiling beneath my skin. Reaching in the deep pockets of my black tiered dress, I wrapped my fingers around the matchbox. I stood still, my breathing fast and shallow as I scanned the area for a place to hide.

It was too late. They were marching toward me. Cool breath prickled the flesh on the back of my neck, and I spun around. The speed of my movement surprised not only me but also the Cruor who had crept up behind me.

His eyebrows pulled together, first in confusion, then the lines

227

deepening into fury. Another Cruor approached from the other direction. Placing the distance of each elemental was becoming easier.

I lit a match, and the first Cruor laughed.

A match? he thought. *How pathetic.* "What's that for?"

"This?" My heart was thumping in my stomach, but now was not the time to show fear. "This is for you."

I tossed the match and reached out with my hand to hold the flame in the air. No depletion of energy, but the Cruor had me outnumbered.

"What . . . " His eyes widened.

The match distracted him, but the other Cruor rushed toward me. I stepped aside and spread my hands apart. The fire grew, creating a web between them, catching them both on fire. They screamed, but the crackle of fire soon overtook their cries. Smoke burned my nostrils, and, with surprising speed, their bodies reduced to ashes.

I'd killed two men.

I'd killed them, and I didn't feel bad. I didn't feel *anything*. No gut reaction, no moment of guilt. I was responsible for these deaths, and all I could do was stand there, frozen for a moment, hoping I wasn't such an empty shell of a person that my actions meant nothing.

The third Cruor wasn't dressed like the others. His hair was slicked back and he wore a plain black suit with a black dress shirt underneath. He clapped his hands slowly as he circled the scene.

"Quite a show," he said. *Clap. Clap. Clap.* "I especially love the costume. This dark look works well for you. Have you considered Broadway?"

I pushed into his thoughts. Nothing. My breaths burst in and out.

"Yes, that's a neat trick, too." His face was an unreadable mask—blank, empty, callous. He took another step closer and crossed his arms. "Now that I know your gifts, they will be of no use to you."

I recognized him then. He'd sent the Cruor after me at Club Flesh; he'd been the one Ivory had asked to stage my attack. Marcus. I hadn't seen him up close before, but I was certain. And, clearly, he recognized me as well. My new hairstyle and dark make-up had been enough to disguise me in a crowd, but perhaps it'd been too much to expect it would help me here.

"What *are* you?" I asked. Being able to prevent me from using my powers went beyond the abilities of the Cruor.

Marcus tilted his head back and scoffed. "Your question—it offends me. Let us skip the formalities, shall we?"

In an instant, he was standing a hair's breadth away. He glared over my shoulder. "Seems you've killed my brothers." His gaze lowered, burning into my eyes. I went to strike another match, but he knocked my arm away and gritted his teeth. "Enough games."

He grabbed my arm just as Thalia strode around the corner. I couldn't read her at all now.

Her heels clicked along the slate floor as she approached. "Oh, how wonderful, Marcus. Goody me. You've found her."

Marcus turned his glare to her. "She found us." He ended his sentence with a sound of disgust and thrust me toward Thalia. "Just take her."

He turned and headed down the hall, a ring of keys jangling at his side.

"Confiscate her matches," he called behind him as he disappeared into the shadows.

Thalia grabbed hold of my elbow, and I yanked fruitlessly against her grasp.

"I see you've met our disabler," she said. Her hair smelled like lemons and soil. My stomach lurched. She tightened her grip, laughing, and reached in my pocket to retrieve the box of matches. "Guess you don't need these."

As she pushed me forward, I leaned back, refusing to walk the direction she urged. Another Cruor approached. Something pricked my neck.

Everything blurred.

No.

I fought to hold onto consciousness, but my muscles weakened. I sank to the floor, Thalia's elbows hooked under my armpits.

Her voice was there, somewhere, woolen and dreamlike.

"*Take her.*"

☪

I BLINKED MY EYES OPEN. No iron bars. A steel door. A caged light flickered overhead. Mildew spores branched across the bottom of the walls like varicose veins. I heard a distant coughing—a Strigoi being held prisoner. Not Charles. I tried to rub my forehead, but my hands wouldn't move. Someone had roped me to a chair.

The doorknob rattled, then stilled.

An unfamiliar voice echoed through the door. "Turning her would be of use."

"You don't know her." This time, the voice was Thalia's.

"I'll send Marcus."

The door opened. As Thalia entered, her black robes brushed the floor. Her hair was tamer than usual, her expression colder and her violet eyes brighter.

"I would just as soon have you killed," she said, "but I suppose it will still happen. Only more painfully."

This was all she said before leaving.

☪

MY CLAIRAUDIENCE came and went in waves. Marcus was disabling me, though perhaps sometimes he was too far away to do so effectively.

When I had a new surge, I sent my clairaudience out to the Maltorim's main room. Thoughts echoed inside my head—Thalia and Callista I recognized, but no one else. They had with them a human girl, one who would not make it through the night. I pushed my fear for her aside. I couldn't help, only listen.

"If any of you object, you are free to leave," Callista said. Her words were a lie. No one was free to go anywhere if they didn't agree with her, and they knew as much.

"You have my utter and complete loyalty," Thalia replied.

"Give it a rest, Thalia. I knew of Charles long before you came to me."

"Oh?" Thalia sounded hurt to the ears of a quiet Cruor whose mind I had tapped into. "How is that?"

"You know my source."

"Ivory?"

"She contacted me a month back and told me of his nature. Along with the location of the Liettes."

Thalia didn't believe her but dared not accuse the Queen of lying. "She's gone now," she said instead, barely-suppressed anger coloring her voice. "I'm here. And I am the one who told you of the girl. Ivory was keeping her from you."

"It's of no consequence," Callista retorted. "We have but one goal. Ultimately, we protect ourselves and therefore the human race as a whole."

I couldn't believe Ivory had involved the Maltorim. I was only thankful she hadn't told them where Charles lived, but that was likely only because she didn't want them to find *me*.

As Callista spoke, conflicting thoughts echoed from those around her. Most were completely loyal while others knew her for the hypocrite she was. Save the humans—but kill them when she wanted to feed on their blood? Over the years, Callista had done her part to ensure a Maltorim comprised entirely of Cruor. Her loyalties lay with protecting her own kind, and she believed the longer they waited, the faster the dual-breeds would grow in number.

"We have the upper hand now," Callista continued, "and we must extinguish the remaining dual-breeds at once if we want to send a message of zero tolerance. They will only replenish in number, and I don't think I need to tell you all the dangers that would pose."

Almost everyone in the room agreed with her final sentiment.

I allowed more thoughts to filter in. One member carefully watched everyone's actions, and I included her thoughts in my focus. She thought differently—mostly in patterns and pictures—but her mind seemed blank of emotion or reaction. She was mentally filing every spoken word and every Cruor's move.

Callista's very own stenographer.

I closed my eyes, and the stenographer's vision played on the insides of my eyelids.

"I hate to be contrary, my Queen," a young male Cruor said, "but the Universe—"

"Oh, please. Surely you jest?"

"It's only that—"

"It's nothing! The Universe is nothing—they have failed time and again. This is our chance."

No one dared interrupt.

"The Universe has no answers. *I* have the answers. Cloning has brought forth new opportunities, and we are decades further in our advancements than even the top scientists in the world. We will come forth with our cures for disease, and the humans will welcome us with open arms. No longer will we need to live in the shadows. Humans will sacrifice their blood to us in thanks."

"But the witches—"

Callista whipped around. In one movement, she broke a leg off a chair and dove across the room, plunging the wood into the young Cruor's heart. To me, her movements were all a blur, pausing at the final result: her body hovering over his as his veins turned visibly black, his body crumbling to dust, a broken chair toppling behind her. Callista's eyes held a murderous glint, and her mouth twisted in a cruel smile. But all that quickly melted away, a resolute calm reclaiming her features.

She stood, the stake in her hand hanging limply at her side. Blood dripped in small splatters to the floor, turning to ash like a flicked cigarette. "Does anyone else object?"

Everyone looked away except the stenographer.

"As for these *witches*—do not doubt me. We will find them and they will join us," Callista said. "Starting with Sophia. We will guide her into fully realizing her gifts and using them to protect our kind." She gave each Cruor in the room a long stare. None of them made eye contact, though most were devoted to the cause. "She will come around."

I shook my head. In the human world, genocide wasn't acceptable. In the world I knew, people at least felt bad for hurting others or feared repercussions.

But not here.

☪

SOMEONE LAUGHED outside my cell door, and I shuddered. Marcus. I'd spent the last few hours sinking into the recesses of my mind. Already dead. With him near, the elemental thoughts quieted, no longer accessible. *Damn disabler.* There had to be some way around his gift-thwarting ability.

He unlocked the chamber and strolled in. "I sensed something about you that night at Club Flesh," he said casually. "Not quite human . . . and yet, not quite one of us."

I flinched one shoulder in a defensive shrug.

"Now I know what it is. Your soul doesn't belong to you. You've merely *inherited* it. How easy then to sacrifice it for something more." He paused a moment, then added in awe, "A forever girl. Yes, the Queen has told us all about you. I'm always telling her what a shame it is we don't keep more Strigoi with us, if for nothing other than reading auras on our behalf. We would have invited you here sooner, had we known."

When I didn't respond, he pulled from his pocket the matchbox Thalia had taken from me earlier. "You like fire?"

I pressed my lips together.

"That's okay. I don't mind doing the talking." He flipped my box of matches in his hand. "Did you know, in some parts of the world, they used to burn witches?"

He looked at me, as if expecting a response. Or maybe my silence was all he expected.

"Yep, burned them." He drew his eyebrows together, glanced up, and tapped his index finger against his cheek. The gesture looked rehearsed, as though all this was a game to him. My stomach churned.

"Canada. That's it," he said, nodding. "They definitely burned witches in Canada."

"Idiot," I rasped.

Suddenly, he was crouched at my side, lifting a cup of water to my mouth and helping me take a sip. "There she is." He patted my cheek a couple times before standing up again. "Denmark."

I swallowed. Why was he telling me all this?

"I was there," he said, his interest returning to the matches in hand. "In Denmark, I mean. I was there when they burned the witches. Have you ever smelled the burning flesh of a human?" He laughed. "They thought they were burning witches, anyway. Thought they were burning the Strigoi and Cruor and all other elemental beings. But here we are. It was only the innocent who died. This is why we need our wars. This is why Callista needs you. You wouldn't want any more innocents to die, would you?"

"Innocents *are* dying." Did he really not get this? "Your Maltorim is the one killing them."

He set the box of matches on the floor. I didn't need to read his mind to know he was mocking me.

"See you soon, Sophia," he sang as he left the room.

☪

MARCUS RETURNED what might have been days later. The ropes were digging valleys into my chest, arms, wrists, shins, and ankles. I gritted my teeth against the dull, never-ending ache around the edges of the rope where my skin had swelled. My dried tears stiffened on my face, and snot ran down to my lips. I hated how pathetic I must have looked.

He pulled a table and chair into the room and sat with a plate of food. He cut a piece of steak and bit it off the fork.

"You like steak?" he asked, chewing.

I didn't reply.

He spit out the steak and jumped to his feet, toppling the table over. The plate shattered by my feet, startling me. "Do. You. Like. Steak?"

My heart rate ratcheted up, and I couldn't stop shaking.

Immediately, he calmed. "Forget it. I used to like steak." He clasped his hands behind his back and paced the room. Then he was kneeling in front of me again, shards of the broken plate cutting into his knees. "Life as a Cruor is not so bad." He grinned. "Kind of fun."

I tried to appear unaffected but likely failed to grand proportions. "These killings won't help your cause."

"Won't it, though? Tell me: would you give up America?"

"I don't see what—"

233

"Do you know *nothing* of history?" He was up, pacing again. "Your kind killed the Indians so you could have your country. Your freedom. We kill the dual-natured so we can have our lives. You are asking us to give up our very existence." He stopped, snapping his glare toward me. "You think we haven't tried another way? What do you suggest?"

He didn't wait for me to respond—just resumed pacing. "Do you not realize that many of the humans killed over the years were killed *because of* the dual-breeds? Should we allow them to expose our kind—destroy the perfect balance and risk the lives of humans and Earth itself?"

"This has nothing to do with *Earth*," I said.

These people were all brainwashed. Humans hadn't been killed because of the dual-breeds. How could the Maltorim know so much about science, and still be blind to basic scientific truths? Had no one told them correlation doesn't equal causation? Had they not been able to figure that out for themselves?

"You may not see now," Marcus said, "but this is an absolute truth. It's everywhere, all the time. Your ability to understand is irrelevant."

"Steven Robiner," I whispered. I was fairly certain this wasn't what Mr. Robiner had in mind when he was discussing his philosophy.

"So you are familiar?"

"Hardly with your understanding."

Marcus smirked. "Given your *situation*, we will have to agree to disagree." He turned to stare at the wall.

Desperately, I pushed for access to his mind, but he'd completely disabled my ability.

"I was trying to . . . what's the word? Relate?" He walked up beside me and caressed my cheek with the crook of his finger, his skin cold and abrasive. From someone else, the gesture might have been soothing, but from him it was repulsive. "Callista wants to turn you. This will be much easier if you agree."

"No."

"I figured you'd say that. I might be able to help you, though." He lit a match and grasped my wrist. "If you want to be turned, I can give you some anesthetics for this part."

This couldn't be happening.

"Since you'll no longer age, it helps to remove fingerprints first." Still holding the match between his forefinger and thumb, he fanned three of his fingers—no prints. "See? Smooth as silk. Humans cannot track us."

Maybe I could distract him. "Oh?" My voice cracked. "I didn't know that."

He smiled. "Stumbled on the idea by accident. Two birds, one stone."

"Why don't you tell me more about it?"

"Sure."

I breathed out a slow, heavy breath as the match burned down to his fingers. He tossed it to the ground. Sulfur rose from the concrete in a meandering stream of smoke.

He lit another. "I'll tell you while we finish up here."

His words sucked away my hope, and I gasped, the air in the room sharp at the bottom of my lungs. The fire seared my fingertips, and I screamed. I screamed and I heard myself screaming, but there was only blinding pain. I tried to summon my power, tried to focus my energy on reversing the fire, to use it against him. But I had nothing left.

{twenty-eight}

MY BURNT FINGERTIPS still seared with pain, but I had no tears left to cry. A chalky, sour film coated my lips and tongue, and vomit drenched the front of my shirt. Marcus had set the rope on fire earlier, letting it burn my flesh before dousing and retying me, but now I needed to summon my strength.

Maybe if I accepted their offer—if I joined them—I would be close enough to show them another way, show them they didn't need these genocides.

How many of my thoughts were born from logic and how many from fear? Where did my beliefs lay? Was I just as bad as the Maltorim—just as bad as everything I'd ever hated?

Whatever you do, fight.

How I hated that sentiment right now. I didn't feel like fighting, but I didn't feel like dying, either.

With a deep breath to steel myself against the pain, I fought against the rope. I whimpered through my teeth as I wriggled one of my hands free.

Marcus would be returning to burn an answer out of me. Quickly I worked to free my other hand, certain I couldn't take any more. I had to at least fight back, at least try to stop him.

As the rope fell away, I eased to my feet. Clothing, seared straight through in parts and stuck to the pus of my wounds in others, pulled away from my skin as I moved. I gritted my teeth to keep silent, but a pained hiss still escaped.

Damn it.

I tried the door first, not that I was expecting it to fly right open for me. And it didn't. I turned around and surveyed the room. The word 'disgusting' summed up the cell pretty well. I began feeling around the walls for some kind of special stone like what Ivory had used at Club Flesh or what Adrian had used outside the Maltorim's walls. No luck there.

I leaned against the back wall, pulling in some slow breaths as I attempted to slow my heart rate and clear my mind. That didn't work out so great either.

As I pushed away from the wall, something shifted, and I nearly lost my balance. I looked back at the wall only to see a small crack between the stones. It'd slid open.

I pushed again, but it budged only enough to show some kind of latch holding the passageway shut. I didn't have time for this. I grabbed the chair I'd been bound to only moments before and jammed one of the legs in the opening, then thrust the chair sideways. The sliding door budged a little more. The latch had ripped out of the crumbling concrete, but the top portion still held fast.

When I rammed the chair again, the latch broke off completely and the door slid open enough for me to squeeze my way out. I had limped halfway down the hall when a hand clasped over my mouth. My eyes went wide.

"Quiet, now," said a female voice. Though her voice was soft and warm, I remained guarded and unsure. "We don't have time for your efforts. Ye must get out of 'ere immediately, and I'll see to it. But please, *keep quiet.*"

Everything about this woman was petite except for her large, ice-blue eyes. Black hair swept down to the middle of her back, and she smelled of rain and strawberries. She looked no older than sixteen, freckles spotted over the bridge of her nose and fronts of her cheekbones. But her voice sounded older, matured, and from another time and place entirely.

"We've little time. Can ye walk?"

"I . . . think so." The words scraped my throat.

The young woman draped my arm over her shoulder and led me to a dark closet down the hall. She bit into her wrist and held it to my mouth.

"Drink."

The warmth of her blood surprised me. She didn't seem to be in any pain as I fed from her, but she must have been a Cruor, because my pain quickly ebbed. There was some kind of marking on her neck, peeking out from the collar of her dress top. A tattoo?

"We've been waiting for ye," she said. She handed me clothes. "Change quickly."

I peeled the old clothes off the rapidly healing burn wounds and hurriedly dressed. "Why are you helping me?"

"The children will explain," she said, already pushing me back into the hall. "Now, please, 'urry."

The children?

Blood and mucus seeped from the thick, rope-shaped valleys on my arms, chest, and shins, sticking against the otherwise soothing clean clothes. With each step, the wounds contracted.

237

"What about—"

"Shhh. Listen carefully. My name is Ophelia. Things are not as they seem; I am not truly aligned with the Maltorim. I was sent 'ere for ye, many, many years ago. Things are amiss. Ye will fix that, but not today. For now, we must get ye away."

Ophelia? Hadn't that been the name of the young woman Ivory had turned in exchange for the Ankou magic that would protect her from the sun?

"You know Ivory?" I asked, though I was almost certain.

Her brow furrowed. "Who?"

"Lenore—her name was Lenore when you knew her," I said, thinking to the memories I'd stolen from my once-friend.

Ophelia nodded. "Now, please, we must move along."

She stopped short and slid open another section of wall, revealing Charles and Adrian. My heart fell, and I started to run toward Charles, but Ophelia grasped my shoulder, holding me back until the men stepped into the hallway.

"You're alive," Charles said, his voice barely a whisper.

Adrian closed the cell's back entrance. When Ophelia released me, I ran to Charles and hugged him, sinking into his arms.

"You shouldn't have come," he murmured against my hair. "Are you all right?"

I nodded, but I didn't know if or when I'd be right again. I just wanted to go home.

He held me at arm's length, his dark eyes brimming with regret. "We need to leave."

I followed his gaze to the end of the passage, where Ophelia stood between two children, waving for us to follow.

The children were almost identical, save for their opposing genders. Both were no older than six or seven, with the same black hair—the girl's long, and the boy's short—and the same pale skin. Their black button eyes fixated on me. I tried not to stare as we hurried to the Liettes' cell.

"Go without us," Charles' mom said when we arrived. "Protect the children."

Charles shook his head. "We didn't go through all this to leave you two behind."

Henry dipped his head forward to look past his wife. "Son, listen to your mother. We'll never make it—not now."

Charles stormed into the room and lifted Valeria. She looked even younger tonight, a tiny slip of a woman draped over her son's arms. He glared at Adrian. "Are you going to help, or not?"

Henry waved his hand, as if to ward off any help, and wobbled to his feet.

Valeria's darkly-tanned skin had paled, and her auburn hair had lost all its bounce and luster. Henry's skin had turned sallow. Almost translucent.

We wove through the passage until we reached a stairway leading up to a set of double doors.

"I can guide ye no further," Ophelia said. "There'll be a car waiting outside the cemetery walls."

"Thank you," I whispered.

Her ice-blue eyes locked on mine, a hopeful but uncertain smile touching her lips. "Your battle will not end 'ere. Now, go on. Up the stairs wit' ye."

She disappeared down another passage. Adrian and Henry opened the doors and Charles started up the stairs, his mom still in his arms.

Each child took one of my hands. "It's okay, Sophia," they said.

I wanted to shrink back at the sound of their voices, at the way they spoke *together*. How did they know my name? I couldn't hear their thoughts—were they human? What were they doing here?

Shoving my questions aside, I followed Charles up the stairs. No one knew which way to go once we stepped through those doors. Light from the passages faded behind us. The open doors at the top of the steps were an aperture for moonlight, and we stepped outside. Every direction looked the same, the cemetery's borders nowhere in sight.

Adrian turned to the group. "Follow me and be prepared. If Marcus shows, take him out first. He'll disable Sophia otherwise."

Charles set Valeria down. Dead leaves crunched underfoot, the sound unrealistically loud in my ears. Thoughts from different members of the Maltorim mingled with my own. They were close. Watching us. Marcus must have been too far away to overpower my abilities.

I scanned the area for a weapon—something to use other than my mind. A thick branch rested against a headstone a few feet away. Lifting my arm, I visualized the branch floating toward me. It flew from the ground into my grasp.

Circe stepped from the shadows with another young, lanky Cruor at her side. I could just make him out in the limited light: Charles' friend, Adonis. We'd met on Samhain. He and Circe stood at the forefront of the rest of their group.

My adrenaline kicked into high gear, and the branch shook in my grasp. Charles, his back to mine, reached behind himself and touched my wrist, stilling my trembles. The Liettes took a protective stance in front of the children, and Adrian stood to the side.

Circe laughed. "A stick?"

As she spoke, her mind pushed on mine, sending the usual tingle, but I was already in her thoughts, blocking her effort. I picked up on enough to know we wouldn't get far if we ran. Circe and her cronies weren't the only Cruor after us. We had to face them.

Charles eyed Adonis warily. "You're part of this?"

Charles' mind sped through thoughts so quickly I couldn't keep up. I severed the connection and focused on Adonis.

What if they're wrong? Charles can't be a . . . I can't kill him. What do I do? The girl—his gaze snapped to me—*this is all her fault.*

"You don't have to do this," I said to him.

Adonis growled. "Don't talk to me."

"Charles saved you, didn't he?" I asked. "Your maker left you—he turned you and left you with no idea what to do. Charles took you in."

"Shut up!"

Circe stepped forward. "Enough! Adonis, the Maltorim will kill us if we don't return them. That is all you need to know." She softened her expression and locked her eyes on me. Realizing her efforts to influence me had no effect, she grinned. "And you—special, special. They promised you to me."

More Cruor swarmed near. My grip tightened around the branch. They didn't want to kill us—we were worth more alive—but they would if they had to. As far as they were concerned, we were better off dead than out in the world.

Adonis remained a few steps back. "I'm sorry, Charles. This is law."

I snapped the branch in half. The ends were jagged and the branch strong enough to impale the undead. Though I never took my eyes off Circe, I turned my head to Charles and whispered, "*You need to shift.*"

"Be careful, Sophia." He took half of the broken branch from my hand. His body trembled, and I bolted to Adrian's side. The ground shook. Circe and Adonis paused, unable to pull their gazes from the transformation. Charles' skin grayed and his form grew.

Circe lunged forward, casting me a hot, fevered stare. Hatred emanated from her mind and sent a jolt of anger through me, singeing the corners of my control.

"Back off!" I threw my arms out, sending Adonis and Circe stumbling back.

She tumbled to the ground, but before I could repeat my defense, she was standing again. An unnatural grin stretched her face. "Nice try."

Charles' tremors turned into loud pops, his transformation nearly complete. I struggled to hold Adonis back by pushing with my mind but only succeeded in slowing his pace.

Circe's fangs snapped down, and I staked the branch through her heart. It sunk into her chest cavity as though I had plunged into loose clay. I tugged the branch out, and she staggered back. She coughed up thick, black blood. Black veins branched across her skin.

She bit her own wrist and frantically smeared her blood over the wound to no avail. Circe crumbled to the ground, gasping for breath and digging her nails into the soil, until finally her breath sputtered and she fell forward. Her body slowly decomposed. No burst of ash. She'd been a newborn—less than a century old. No wonder she'd been Thalia's pet.

Through the spaces in the crowd, I made out Thalia and Callista as they emerged from the steps leading out from beneath the mausoleum. They prowled away from the building, closer to the action. Thalia, wanting to appear strong to the Queen, suppressed the hurt of losing one of her own. Callista pointed and yelled to other Cruor, commanding them to assist the attack.

The sudden chaos threw Adonis off. He strode forward, radiating anguish.

"Away! Away!" I said, holding my hands toward him. Nothing happened. My body trembled and a wave of nausea washed over me. Marcus was near. He was disabling my abilities.

Adrian blocked Adonis' path. Before Adonis could reach us, something slammed into him. The force of the impact jolted his body forward, his neck snapping instantly. A wooden horn impaled his heart, the tip protruding from his chest and shoving his ribs apart.

I wobbled back, staring at Adonis' dangling boots. Charles had taken the form of a rhinoceros. He'd infused with the branch when he was shifting. Was that another skill the dual-breeds possessed, or were all Strigoi capable of such things?

He lowered the body to the ground and pressed his hoof on Adonis' leg, crushing the kid into place while he pulled his horn free. Adonis' torso ripped in half and his body rapidly decayed.

Taking in deep gulps of air, I looked up to see Charles: a powerful rhinoceros with a wooden horn, emerald green eyes, and silver-brown, leather-like skin covered in blood. Instinctively, I leaned back, but guilt dug at my heart when I saw the hurt in Charles' eyes.

"Silly, silly girl." Thalia stepped out from the pack, her pale skin glowing in the moonlight. Behind her stood two men, nearly seven foot tall each, their skin hinting at sheens of gold in the moonlight and large, translucent, veined wings stretching out behind them, almost as tall as the men themselves.

The Ankou, I presumed, though somehow I hadn't expected them to appear as abnormally large fae. I'd only seen them blur by when they killed the Morts outside Charles' house. They were unnaturally beautiful.

Callista strode past Thalia, leaving her behind like an afterthought. "This has gone far enough," she said, her face unreadable. "Join us or die. We are done playing games."

No sooner had she spoke then the Ankou were at my side, towering over me, seeming as though they would need no supernatural ability at all to squash me. Their size alone would suffice. Yet I was too stunned by their perfection to see them as a real threat. Instead, my fear remained with what Callista might do next.

Swallowing hard, I lifted my chin and boldly met her gaze, gathering as much energy as possible from the electric current that ran beneath the earth's surface. "I'd have to be dead to join you, idiot."

"Guess she'd rather be dinner," Thalia said, her voice emotionless and chilling.

I ducked away from the Ankou as Adrian and Henry sprung forward, tackling Thalia. I motioned for Valeria to run with the children, but she calmly stood her ground. Chills burrowed into my pores, prickling each hair follicle on my arms and the fine hairs of my neck and back.

Deep lines creased Callista's forehead, distorting her expression into something nearly inhuman. Animalistic.

The transformation, a fleeting glimpse of cat-like features that half-deformed her face, faded as quickly as it occurred. Could it be . . . was she one of the cloaked figures I'd seen outside my window after my positive energy ritual?

I shook the thought away and said nothing. Her comrades would not believe any accusation that their leader was a dual-breed, nor would it be right to encourage the execution of anyone based on those merits. Not even Callista.

Callista's hatred thrummed through her—hatred for the dual-breeds, herself included, and hatred for me that I'd given them my acceptance. An acceptance her father hadn't shown when his wife's true nature was revealed through her pregnancy with Callista. He never would have knowingly procreated with a dual-breed, especially not one who was part Strigoi.

My twinge of sadness passed as more Cruor encircled us, Marcus at their lead. He was trying to disable me—I could sense it—but my blood was rushing through my veins, washing his efforts away. Had I somehow overcome his gift, or was he too preoccupied to focus on me?

Charles, in his animal form, barreled at him. In the same instant,

Callista knocked me to the ground. Wind rushed from my lungs, and I gasped for air.

I drove my knee hard into Callista's stomach, surprising us both with my strength. Callista howled and yanked my hair, struggling to get her face close enough to bite me. She didn't have any intention of turning me—as a dual-breed, she'd never be able to turn me herself. She merely hoped to drain me to my death.

With one foot, I rammed at her chest. I gained the advantage long enough to kick her several times in the face. Pain shot through my ankle, but I kept kicking. Black blood oozed from her nose, and she tripped backward.

I stared in disbelief. Was this part of being an elemental? Were even the mortal elementals capable of advanced strength and speed?

I scrambled across the cemetery ground, my body heavy with exhaustion. I stumbled, and my jaw crashed into the soil. Dirt pressed against my lips, gritty on my tongue and teeth. I spat and lifted a wrist to wipe my mouth.

It wasn't long before I saw why the Ankou were present. They weren't concerned with me. They were her for the aftermath. As each body fell to an ultimate demise, so there were the Ankou to collect the spirits, digging long, pointed fingernails into their skulls until the entities exploded into black particles.

Or, perhaps, the Ankou were intended as a distraction. As I spaced out, wondering how the Ankou could be so flawless, one of the Cruor grabbed me. I clung to a gravestone, trying to kick him away, all the while making a mental note not to look at the Ankou ever again.

Charles, now in human form and dressed only in someone else's pants, appeared behind my captor. Though bleeding at the shoulder, he drove a stake through my attacker's back, into the heart. The body of the ancient Cruor fell on top of me before shattering into a pile of dust. Vomit lurched up my esophagus, burning and bitter.

Charles tossed me the stake. He didn't say anything, just gave me an empty look. As another Cruor charged at him, he spun around to engage in combat.

I stood and glanced around, nearly dizzy with confusion over where to look first. Behind me probably would have been my best bet. Something pushed against the back of my skull. A chill pressed into my neck, my back, my thighs, and my stomach lurched. I tried to turn, but my mind and body were shutting down. My vision went black.

My heart went cold next. Another consciousness pressed against mine, but this was not the same as the voices I'd experienced before. These thoughts that weren't my own wanted to drown my own.

A sudden snap shook me at my core, and I tumbled forward. I

243

spun around, and reality crashed into my core when I realized what had just been happening.

Standing there was a Mort. A Mort that had been trying to take over my body—and had been making good progress until an Ankou had come along. This elemental grim reaper had his long fingernails so deep into what would've been the skull of the Mort that they were cutting through the Morts ghostly eyelids.

The two forms blurred, vibrating unnaturally fast as the Ankou fought to bring a final end to the spirit's life. I didn't get to see the result, because a sudden kick cracked into my ribs.

Callista.

As I lay sprawled across the ground, a second blow struck my cheek, and the side of my face numbed on impact. Something wet trickled past my temple. Pain crippled me momentarily, but before Callista could kick again, a sudden energy burst from me, sending her flying over several graves and crashing into a large headstone. She rose to her feet and shook it off, shock siphoning the color from her face.

Marcus' head flew past me, exploding into a small cloud of ashes. He wasn't disabling me anymore.

He wasn't doing *anything* anymore.

The cemetery filled with cries of agony, anguish, and defeat. The movement of those in battle was a blur, but the images streamed clearly in my mind. An electric field domed around me, and I lay there, unmoving.

No one approached.

The world bled away and sound evaporated. Each cry of pain and effort became a dying gasp, as though muffled beneath a pillow. I tilted my head to the side. Charles and Adrian battled three Cruor. The earth elementals seemed to materialize from nowhere. Thalia fought the Liettes, and the children watched, everyone at war around them as if they weren't even there.

Pain came to my body in sharp stabs, and the electric dome around me quivered and then disappeared. A Cruor to my right started to pull her way across the soil. Blood dampened her pale blonde hair. Half of her left leg was missing. She crawled over to me, a mindless minion to the very end, and I staked her though her back, into her heart. The dome flickered on again, but just as quickly, it was gone, and I couldn't recreate it. My powers were on autopilot, and I still had no idea how to control them.

As Callista stalked toward me again, my vision funneled onto her. The power I emitted slowed her, but my energy was fading. I hefted myself up on a nearby gravestone, pain shuddering through my left ankle. My swollen eye threw off my depth perception.

I limped toward a heap of sooty clothes I'd seen Marcus wearing earlier. The scent of burnt Cruor flesh hit my nose, and I gagged as I sifted through the items with trembling hands. The matches had to be in one of his pockets.

Ice spread in my stomach. Something was wrong.

Thalia approached. Blood soaked her face and streaked her hair. Ashes clung to her clothing and dusted her cheeks and chest. Her eyes sparkled in a way that sent chills up my spine. Behind her, beside Henry's remains, lay Valeria's dead body. Her neck was severed three-quarters through.

A scream roared in my mind. Rage engulfed me, filling me with an unfamiliar darkness. I couldn't allow the pain to surface, couldn't accept what I'd seen.

Fumbling through another one of Marcus' pockets, I found the box of matches.

Callista closed in, but my intentions remained fastened on Thalia. I struck a match, tossed it toward her, and held the fire suspended in the air between us. Thalia's lips curled into a smile as she continued her approach. I encouraged the fire's growth, the oxygen around us feeding the flame like gasoline to create a fiery sheet.

A strange sensation gripped me, as though I was an echo of myself, trapped in a tunnel of mirrors, reflecting my image back and forth for eternity. On my command, the sheet of fire swept forward, leaving piles of ash in its wake.

My strength gathered, and I tossed my hands upward. The flames extinguished into a mist.

When I turned to scour for more Cruor, Thalia and Callista were headed toward the mausoleum.

Shit. I'd missed.

Thalia tossed back a cursory glance, a shadow of alarm on her face.

Our location had shifted throughout the course of the fight, and a cemetery wall had come into view. The pressure of battle suppressed my ability to orient myself.

Get away. That was the only thing that mattered. No one from the Maltorim would risk exposure by following us to the city. Not now. Not like this.

I spotted Charles and bolted toward him. "We need to go."

Hurt etched his features—not a wincing pain, but the weighted expression of loss.

"I'm sorry," I barely managed to whisper, so quiet I wasn't sure I'd really said anything at all. My heart longed to console him, but there was no time.

245

I grabbed the hands of the children and ran. Charles hastened after, helping Adrian limp away, their injuries slowing them to a human pace. We reached the cemetery's wall with a new team of Cruor not far behind.

"Go, Sophia," Charles implored.

Blood flowed from a wound on his shoulder, beaded on his chest hair, and dripped down his stomach. More blood drenched his pants. So much blood—it couldn't all be his. *Please don't let all this blood be his.*

"I'm not going without you," I said. No way was he going to underestimate how stubborn I was right now.

"I can't—" He leaned against the wall and slid to the ground, pressing his hand over the gash on his shoulder. "Go!"

I dropped to my knees beside him. He and Adrian were slipping. I scanned the ground. *Something sharp, something sharp. Anything.* A broken bottle someone must have tossed over the cemetery wall in passing caught my eye, and I used it to cut my forearms. As much as I wanted to save Adrian, I wasn't about to let him bite me and turn me into a Cruor. Having him feed this way would be safer for both of us.

Positioning myself between them, I held the wounds to their mouths. "Drink."

Blood trickled onto their lips, but they made no movement.

"Drink, damn it!"

Thin red rivers trickled down my arms and dripped from my elbows.

The Cruor behind us were closing in, trapping us against the stone wall.

The children placed their hands on my shoulders and began chanting. "*Lumen Solis Invicti. Lumen Solis Invicti. Lumen Solis . . .* "

I looked over my shoulder. As they chanted, a light grew in front of them. No, not in front of them. The light emitted from their bodies. The Cruor started to retreat. Charles, Adrian, and I remained wrapped in shadows as the front of the children's bodies grew brighter with each spoken word.

I knew those words. Not in my mind, not from this life—but in my spirit, I knew them.

"*Lumen Solis Invicti,*" they continued.

Light of the unconquered sun.

Their efforts were not enough. They needed me, needed whatever power I stored within me to put their magic into full effect. I knew this in the same way I knew to breathe. It was just a part of me.

I closed my eyes, focusing all my energy into their small bodies, and joined their chant. The light became blinding. I turned away, shielding my face with the crook of my arm, but Charles, Adrian, and I were wrapped in the children's shadow, untouched by their implacable light. A few moments later, the air went cold. Darkness reclaimed the cemetery.

Only the tombstones had survived. The newly silent air—now empty of the cries of battle—filled with shuddering breaths and the winces and moans of Charles and Adrian.

The children turned to me, their skin bright red. I shrieked at their unexpected appearance and swayed back against Charles.

"It's okay, Sophia," they said, reaching toward me.

Their skin lightened more by the moment, returning to their previous pallor. I reached out to touch them, but my hand twitched. What *were* they?

As their hands touched mine, palm-to-palm, they effused a relaxing stream of electricity that entered through my fingertips. They knelt in front of Charles and Adrian.

"What was that?" Charles asked.

"We'll explain later," the girl said, her voice oddly mature. "We must relocate immediately."

The girl touched Adrian's and Charles' wounds, her fingertips glowing red. The touch cauterized the skin, stopping the flow of blood. The boy placed his palm to each man's forehead, and a soft hum carried on the night's chill wind. Both Charles and Adrian's countenances improved.

"Now, Sophia," the boy said.

I couldn't read his thoughts, but there was a knowing. The men still needed my blood. This time they had the strength to feed. They drank just enough to gain the strength to get away, then we scaled the cemetery walls to our escape.

As I heaved myself over, I saw Ophelia standing at a nearby grave, watching. A small smile touched her lips, then she disappeared into the shadows.

{twenty-nine}

THE CAR OPHELIA HAD WAITING for us was old, the gray seats upholstered with perforated leather, each tiny hole an inch apart. The heating vents blew around a mothball odor that reminded me of Mother's coat and vacuum closet back in Keota. My clothes, wet with blood and dusted in ash, squished against the seat, and my stomach sent acrid bile into the back of my mouth.

At first, I half-expected Cruor to chase us down the road, but the further we distanced ourselves from the cemetery, and the faster the night sky lightened, the safer I felt. But we still needed to get Adrian indoors before sunrise.

I wished for the nausea and shaking to subside. A headache settled in. I was neither able to block nor focus on the elemental noise. All that remained was the pulsing hum of whispered thoughts.

A fog lifted from my mind as we pulled away. Not a fog caused by magic or Cruor influence, but the fog of what had happened. Reality crashed into my chest, arresting my lungs and heart with the realization of what I'd done.

As Adrian drove, the children, sitting on either side of me, tended to my wounds with their magic, but because I was mortal, the scars would remain—the thin pink rivers on my arms as well as the burn scars on my shoulders, chest, stomach, and shins that Ophelia had healed. Charles and Adrian had already fully regenerated. No visible evidence of the war marked their bodies.

With my immediate wounds cared for, the children turned and stared out the windows. I leaned between the front seats to check on Charles, who was sleeping in the passenger seat. His chest rose and fell in slow breaths. I touched his cheek with the back of my hand. His skin was feverish and damp.

"Is he going to be okay?" I asked Adrian.

"Quite." He reached to turn on the car radio, hand trembling. "A big shift, is all."

I rubbed my temples to alleviate the pressure. In the rear-view mirror, I saw the creases in Adrian's forehead deepen. Where did we go from here—where would we be safe?

"They could've killed me," I said, more to myself than anyone else.

Adrian heaved a sigh. "I cannot thank you enough."

"Thank me?"

"We'd all be dead if it weren't for you."

I wasn't so sure. Perhaps they wouldn't have escaped without me, but I wouldn't have escaped without them, either. Or Ophelia for that matter.

We passed barren fields as Adrian placed a call to Rhett, his voice a backdrop to my thoughts. "Fifteen minutes . . . immediate departure . . ."

As we turned the car onto the private runway, Charles woke. Rhett had the plane running. We rushed over, his gaze scrutinizing us more harshly the closer we came.

"No, no, no. Not getting in my plane like that, dirty as field rats and smelling of rot." He shook his head. "No way. Ain't gonna happen."

I glared at him. "We paid you."

"Fine," he said, huffing through his nose. "Fine! I don't get paid enough, tell you that. Grab the towels in the back. Don't touch nothing, don't get nothing dirty, or you pay for that, too."

"Go on," I said to the children, shooing them to follow Rhett onto the plane. I turned to Charles and Adrian. "What are we going to do with them?"

A muscle twitched in Charles' jaw. "I couldn't care less."

I frowned. "Are you okay?"

"My parents are dead. What do you think?"

I stared at him with searching gravity. The pain of losing his parents was one we shared, but I wasn't ready to deal with those emotions right now, and there was nothing I could say to make him feel better.

Once we boarded, Charles told Rhett to take us to a location in the Japanese mountains. The Liettes' home, I guessed. Rhett's only reply was a flippant quip that we should do nothing and let him take care of everything, since that's what we were doing anyway.

Adrian lay on a small bunk in the back cabin. I should've been exhausted, but my mind stirred with too many unanswered questions. I grabbed the ragged brown towels from the compartment near the bathroom and tossed them over all the seats. Charles and I sat opposite the children, a small dish on the table between us, empty except for some dusty peanut residue.

"Sorry," I said to the children, "I haven't even caught your names."

The boy introduced himself as Aspen and the girl as his sister, Autumn. "Valeria took us in several years ago—" the boy began.

"Bullshit," Charles said.

The boy blinked. "Did Valeria not tell you of us?"

"My mother," Charles said, turning to me, "would never take in one of the Chibold."

So they were fire elementals? I covered his hand with my own. "Please, let them talk."

Charles was suspicious, and, admittedly, I didn't like the way they kept staring, unblinking, an inky blackness to their eyes. But if what they said was true, they were family.

As I delved more deeply into Charles' thoughts, I read he was only remotely thankful the twins had saved me; mostly, he blamed them that I'd been in danger in the first place. The children clearly had the power to rescue his parents but had allowed them to die and nearly gotten us killed in the process. Why hadn't they acted sooner?

"Tonight's events had to happen this way," Aspen said.

The usual blue vibrancy of Charles' eyes faded to a stony gray, and he clenched his fist over the armrest of his seat. I placed my hand on his arm, hoping to soothe him. We all dealt with grief in our own way. Detachment was the only way I knew. For Charles, grief was handled through anger and a need to place blame.

He slumped in his chair, pressing his lips together.

I asked the children—these *Chibold*—about their capture, about how they had survived so long. The Maltorim had been waiting for us, but not entirely for the reason we had thought. They didn't know how to destroy these children, and the Liettes provided no answer. They'd hoped Charles would help them solve the riddle, that somehow bringing the family together would be the key to solving this small mystery.

"Though our kind are nearly extinct due to the lack of host families, some of us have found a way to survive by helping dual-breeds in exchange for their hosting," Aspen said. "The Maltorim does not take kindly to this, but there is not much they can do. Their only option is to kill our host families, but we protect them. Even once they've ended the lives of the host family, we'd still live for centuries more. The Liettes being alive was the only thing that kept us in holding, and the Maltorim was aware of that. We could have left at any time. They thought Charles might be able to reveal more—reveal another way to end our lives."

"You were trying to help the Liettes, then?" I asked.

"They wanted us to escort Charles once he was ready to approach the Ankou and purge his Cruor side. We were to be introduced to him at that time."

"So what happened?" I asked.

Aspen settled his gaze on me. "*You* were involved."

"Of course I was involved."

"No, you don't understand. Not you, the woman Charles wanted to grow old with. *You*—as in the very reason we were originally sent here."

What the hell was he talking about? "Who sent you here? Why?"

Autumn smiled warmly. "Sophia—this has been hundreds of years in the making. The first attempt had been in the late 1600s, but unexpected events derailed the Universe's plans. As things changed, they had to take additional measures to prepare. Even Ophelia's life has been devoted to awaiting your arrival.

"They brought you back time and again, but the path was not an easy one to resume, to line up as had originally been intended."

She spoke as if the details carried no weight. Perhaps they didn't. Perhaps the night's events rendered everything meaningless.

The Chibold, Charles thought toward me. *My parents would not get tangled up with such tricksters. Don't believe anything they say.*

I disregarded his thoughts. Much as I loved him, he was a horrible judge of character. His perceptions of Thalia and her coterie had been way off. Then again, perhaps I was no better. I'd trusted Ivory for years.

"You could have prevented the deaths of your host family," I said. "I hope you can see why we're hesitant."

Charles crossed his arms, his mouth dipping into an even deeper frown. The shadows under his eyes deepened with each passing moment.

"The Liettes were like parents to us," Autumn said, her voice lullaby-sweet, "but we are here to save something bigger. We needed to meet you, Sophia."

Charles scoffed. "You could have saved my parents and found her later. Or joined them on their visit to the States."

"Brother," Aspen said, his voice darker than his sister's, "we couldn't come forward until now—we simply were not *able*. Sophia had to act first."

The idea was hard to accept, but I'd gone years without even *knowing* about my gifts. Perhaps things were the same for them.

"We would not willingly sacrifice our host family," Aspen pressed. "That would mean risking our own lives. Host families are hard to find these days, and even centuries might not be enough to find one to hide our true identities. Surely you understand that?"

"Why is this happening *now*?" I asked.

"Because you willed it," Autumn said in her musical voice. "Your ritual set these events into motion."

My ritual? My ritual hadn't willed *this* to happen. I'd never want the Liettes sacrificed because of me.

"That ritual was months and months ago," I said. "Couldn't you have come to me sooner?"

Aspen shook his head. "The ritual was only the first step. The herbs you used welcomed not only your purpose but your gifts as well. But you still had to learn, on your own, who you were. To accept yourself for who you were—who you *are*—and prove your strength and loyalty as you did tonight."

Autumn leaned back in her chair, resting her hands in her lap. "By not caving in to the Maltorim's request, you triggered our powers and allowed us to progress on our path. Just as in your first life, you did not cave—you remained true to yourself until the end. That was the moment the Universe was waiting for."

The tension did not leave Charles' neck or shoulders, but some of the anger dissipated from his expression. "What business are we of yours, then?"

"We are your messengers," Autumn said.

"Messengers?" I said, disbelieving. "You're *children*."

"We are, in that we carry a child's appearance. However, we have greater knowledge—one bestowed upon us by the Universe that we are to share with you. We are your guides. The Maltorim remains strong and their plans for the future nefarious. You will need our help."

Guides? Messengers?

Nefarious?

The concept muddied my thoughts, and Charles was still skeptical. I stared blankly at the children.

"At one time, the Universe thrived alone," Aspen elaborated, "but in time it became weak. It spawned humans to recycle the energy. The Universe fed from the positive energy of people at night, pulling them into sleep. The energy allows the Universe to create and put new life into the earth. If the humans die, the Universe dies . . . and vice versa."

"Negative energy poisons the Universe," Autumn continued in place of her brother. "The original immortals were here to clean up the mortal world, but some veered from the path the Universe had set for them. Though the source of the original evil is unknown, we imagine that sometimes the Universe accidentally feeds from the energy of corrupt human life and, in creating elementals, some of that dark energy is unintentionally imprinted."

"What does that have to do with me?"

"This will never be a perfect world," Aspen said, "but it could be better. You will play a role in making that happen. The evil will continue to propagate."

"You could have ended it today," Charles said sharply.

Autumn lowered her lashes, her gaze dipping to her hands. "You cannot comprehend the extent of the Maltorim's progress. Callista has sanctioned others. Damascus is no longer the only home of the Maltorim. Tonight's events were bad enough, but had a dual-breed been responsible for the death of the Queen, the retaliation would've been far worse than what we expect now."

I sighed, defeat sinking further into my core. Did I want to help the Universe? Its track record was shoddy, at best. "What do you need *me* for?"

"To gather others like you, one for each remaining element." Autumn breathed in deeply, fixing her gaze heavily on my own. "Then, you will fight in the Great War. If you do not, the Maltorim will spiral out of control. First, only the dual-breeds will be killed, but soon the humans will be freely hunted as well. The Maltorim claims to want to save the humans, but when the New World begins, the Maltorim will shift to darker means. Their actions could lead to the ultimate demise of our planet. Of our entire Universe."

I shook my head. What did they expect me to do about that? "I— I'm sorry. There's no way. I couldn't stop them."

Autumn's soothing voice was a relief from Aspen's chilling echo. "You will be ready when the time comes, and you will not be alone."

In an awkward moment, she unfolded her hands from her lap and reached to place one over my own. The gesture was something Valeria would do, a movement Autumn was merely parroting from her host mother—staged but unrehearsed.

Charles didn't say a word. His once fiery gaze had extinguished, the irises now dull and clouded. This was the oldest I'd ever seen him look.

"I still don't understand the purpose of you being sent as children," I said. "Won't that make it harder for you to help us?"

"Quite the contrary," Autumn said with a small smile. "To your world, children are the property of their guardians. We are lesser beings, seen as weak, less intelligent, and less deserving of respect. Who would treat us as equals but those who are pure of heart? Through us," she said, "you will make the right allies."

{thirty}

EVEN MONTHS LATER, the misery of that night still haunted me. We mourned . . . Charles, the kids, and I. Even the Liettes' cabin seemed to mourn—the windows sad, rain sliding down the glass like tears some nights, the scarred wooden floor icy as death in winter. The cherry blossoms had at least brought hope in the spring, unfurling their flowers along the peaks of Mount Rishiri.

Plums, so purple they were almost black, sat in the dish between us. Valeria's dish. Months had passed, summer now returned, but the ache of losing loved ones doesn't go away or numb quickly. All the family Charles had ever known were gone now, leaving two orphaned children in their place.

I plucked one of the plums from the bowl and sank my teeth past the tart peel, eyes fixed on Charles. He looked tired, but not as sad. I walked around the table to sit in his lap. He kissed my jaw, my wrist, my fingertips.

"We have each other," he said, and he buried his head against my neck, his light chin stubble tickling my shoulder.

My heart raced as it always did when he was near. A smile softened my lips, and I kissed the top of his head. "We do."

For a long time we just sat there, with the hazy, Japanese summer breeze drifting through the open kitchen window. It was all we needed.

I traced my finger along the scar inside his arm. We both had them—scars the world could see, and also our private scars. Those were the scars we shared.

☪

THE MALTORIM never discovered the Liettes' cabin, and so the location remained a safe refuge for Charles and me to stay with the kids. Adrian found a place in Kutsugata and visited often, bringing us food and supplies. Living more than a few miles away from the common trails did have its benefits, though. It was quiet here. Even the elemental noise was minimal.

I leaned back in our porch swing with a cup of iced raspberry tea and a newspaper I couldn't read. Sometimes the kids would read it to me, try to teach me the language, but today they were sleeping in late. Sometimes they went into hibernation for days at a time, storing energy to channel messages from the Universe.

Charles emerged from the house. "Adrian stopped by last night while you were sleeping. Said Paloma checked on Ivory, and she is doing well. Doesn't seem to remember anything more than necessary."

My heart sped at the mention of Ivory, and my breath caught in my throat. Her name had been lingering around the edges of my mind for months, but I hadn't heard it spoken aloud since I learned she was the one who had informed the Maltorim of Charles' true nature.

"You all right?" he asked.

I smiled, setting the paper aside. "I still worry about the future."

"Most people do." He cleared his throat, and when I looked up, his gaze was steady on mine. "I haven't forgotten."

Before I could ask him to confirm what my heart already knew he meant, I picked up the thoughts from his mind. He was ready to become a pure Strigoi.

Though we had come to trust the children over the months—especially once Charles had found a letter from his mother that explained everything—we hadn't spoken of our plans to turn him to a pure Strigoi. The kids would be able to guide us through the process, but I'd feared bringing it up would rekindle Charles' pain. I'd never wanted this choice to be decided for him.

"When you're ready," I said.

A small grin tugged at his lips. "All those months you pestered me, and now you say when I'm ready?" He extended his hand, and I accepted, allowing him to pull me into his arms. "You really drive me crazy sometimes."

"Only sometimes?"

I smiled against his chest, then peeked up into his deep teal eyes. He opened the screen door behind him and backed into the cabin, tugging me after. The closeness of his body sent a warmth into my stomach, and I pressed up on my toes and kissed him, nearly knocking him the rest of the way into the house. The screen door flapped shut and a picture frame on a table near the door tipped over.

"I need a shower," I said, feeling a little sticky from the heat. "Want to come with?"

Charles' grin broadened. His hands slipped down to my hips as we headed down the hall to the bathroom.

I peeled off my sweat-soaked jean capris and white eyelet halter-top, and we hopped into the shower together, enjoying these moments where we could simply be ourselves. Simply be *together*.

After our shower, I changed into a bikini and some lightweight denim shorts and pulled a wide-tooth comb through my hair. Charles headed out to meet Adrian while I flopped down on our bed to read for a bit. When the front door creaked open, I doggy-eared the page I was on and set the book aside.

"Hello?"

No answer.

"Charles?" I asked aloud.

I could pick up on Charles' presence, but not Adrian's.

I threw my legs over the side of the bed and headed into the living room. Lauren was standing just inside the threshold of the cabin, suitcase at her feet and birdcage in hand. Rhett must have flown her over if she was able to bring Red. Something told me he much preferred flying humans.

I rushed the last few steps into the main room. "No one told me you were coming!"

She grinned. "That's because it was a surprise."

"A surprise?" I looked at Charles. It must have taken a great deal of concentration for him to plan this without me finding out. I'd totally fallen for the whole Adrian thing.

"You've been trapped up here too long," Lauren said. "You do remember what a surprise is, don't you?"

I hugged her tight, probably squeezing the life right out of her, and she held the birdcage away. Charles took it from her to set on the coffee table, and Lauren and I sat down, jumping right into conversation as though we'd never been apart.

"How about that hike?" I asked.

"Charles carried my suitcase and the birdcage," she said with a wink. "You're lucky you have Superman on hand if you insist on living up here. How do you guys do it?"

"Eh," I said. "We manage."

Lauren still didn't know the real reason we were here, and she never would. We'd told her a partial truth several months back: that Charles' parents had died in a car accident and that we'd adopted their kids to raise as they would have wanted them raised—here, in the Japanese mountains. She didn't question it.

"I'm going to visit my family while I'm here," she said. "I can't tell you how much this trip means to me. To finally go see them for myself, to let them see me for who I am. And to get to see *you*. Belle Meadow isn't the same with you gone."

"Oh?"

Lauren frowned, and she cast her gaze toward the room where the children were sleeping. "Are you sure you're ready for such a huge responsibility?"

"No," I said, "but I have to go with it. I have to do what needs to be done, or nothing else matters."

All at once, I wished she could know the full weight of that statement while at the same time I wished she'd never have to understand it.

Lauren pushed herself up from the couch. "I'd better unpack."

"And I'd better help Charles finish getting dinner ready, or we'll never get you fed."

I met Charles in the kitchen and sidled up next to him to help wash and dry fruit for a cobbler. He popped a slice of peach into my mouth and gave me a kiss equally as sweet.

The last traces of the sun disappeared behind the mountains, but tonight there were no shadows across my heart.

When dinner was ready, Lauren carried some wooden bowls and spoons outside to the small picnic table while I brought the freshly-baked bread. Charles followed behind to set a spicy vegetable stew on the table.

Aspen and Autumn joined us, carrying Red out in his cage, which they set on a large, flat stone beside the table. The children sent their thoughts to me—the only way I could read their thoughts at all—and told me the bird was safe to be released. They had used their magic to ensure Red's presence wouldn't harm the natural wildlife of Japan.

I opened the cage door, and Red peeked out. I realized then why I'd always been so drawn to him. Grandpa Parsons had once kept a pet cardinal, one who would sit on his armchair when we visited in my childhood years. Grandpa Parsons would tell me all the ancient myths and legends that his family had once shared with him.

Over dinner, I shared one of his stories—the German legend of the Holy Family.

"There was a time when the world was left in a natural state. It was Autumn, the time of the harvest. The trees were viewed as living beings, not cast down to clear way for modern buildings as they are in our time. Even in those times, there was a hierarchy of importance in life. So it was with a sense of greater value that the Holy Family traipsed the forest trail. The soil shifted beneath their feet, the flowers swayed as they breezed by, and the trees bowed, but there was one family of trees that did not yield in reverence. The Aspens. The Holy Family cursed the trees, and their leaves began to tremble. And that is how the Aspens became known as 'the shivering trees'."

I probably missed the moral when my grandfather told me the story as a small child. Even now, it held a different meaning to me than to most, though it was only natural that everything would be interpreted differently in the context of my new life.

Aspen and Autumn—they were with me now.

As I finished my story, Red strutted out from his cage. After a final chirp, he ruffled his feathers and took flight, soaring aimlessly over the yard before settling on the branch of a nearby cherry blossom tree.

We were home.

ABOUT THE AUTHOR

Rebecca Hamilton writes Paranormal Fantasy, Horror, and Literary Fiction. She lives in Florida with her husband and three kids, along with multiple writing personalities that range from morbid to literary. Having a child diagnosed with autism has inspired her to illuminate the world through the eyes of characters who see things differently. Rebecca Hamilton is represented by Rossano Trentin of TZLA.

To learn more about Autism Spectrum Disorder, please visit: http://www.autisticadvocacy.org

Visit her website at: http://www.beccahamiltonbooks.com

ACKNOWLEDGMENTS

COVER ART PHOTOGRAPHY:

Mike Thomassen

COVER ART MODEL:

Maria Amanda Schuab
http://mariaamanda.deviantart.com/

FONT CREDITS:

Quicksand Book, Trajan Pro, Wicked Grit by http://ajpaglia.com/ and Chicago House font by 'theoriginal19'

FORMATTING:

R.P. Kraul

EDITING CREDITS:

Sol Stein and *Toby Stein* for their early guidance in honing my style and voice, *Leslie Holman-Anderson* for her amazing critical eye, *Angela Zoltners* and *Lynnette Labelle* for their comprehensive support, and *Stewart Kirby* for his fantastic copy-editing service. Thank you also to everyone else who contributed, most specifically *R.P. Kraul, Jennifer Sosniak, Joan Ford, Christi Goddard, Noelle Pierce,* and *S.M. Boyce.*

Made in the USA
Lexington, KY
16 March 2013